Also by Lucy Clarke

Swimming at Night

A Single Breath

Lucy Clarke

A Touchstone Book

Published by Simon & Schuster

New York   London   Toronto   Sydney   New Delhi

Touchstone
A Division of Simon & Schuster, Inc.
1230 Avenue of the Americas
New York, NY 10020

This book is a work of fiction. Any references to historical events, real people, or real places are used fictitiously. Other names, characters, places, and events are products of the author's imagination, and any resemblance to actual events or places or persons, living or dead, is entirely coincidental.

This Touchstone export edition July 2014

TOUCHSTONE and colophon are registered trademarks of Simon & Schuster, Inc.

For information about special discounts for bulk purchases, please contact Simon & Schuster Special Sales at 1-800-268-3216 or CustomerService@simonandschuster.ca.

Interior design by Claudia Martinez

Manufactured in the United States of America

1   3   5   7   9   10   8   6   4   2

ISBN 978-1-4767-5044-6
ISBN 978-1-4767-5045-3 (ebook)

For James

Prologue

Pulling his hat down over his ears, Jackson glances at Eva, who is curled in bed, the duvet tucked under her chin. Her eyes stay closed as she murmurs a sleepy noise that means, *Don't go*.

But he has to. He can't lie next to her feeling the way he does. He's been awake for hours staring into the empty darkness, thinking, thinking, rolling back through his decisions and their consequences. He needs to get out of this house, feel the sting of winter wind on his face.

He lifts a corner of the duvet, just enough to expose Eva's bare shoulder where he places his lips. He breathes in the smell of her sleep-warmed skin. Then he smoothes the duvet back down, picks up his fishing gear, and leaves.

The beach is wild and empty in the gloom. It's one of those English mornings he's still getting used to when dawn never fully breaks and the lamps stay on indoors all day. He paces into the wind, jigging his shoulders to keep warm.

Reaching an outcrop of rocks that stretches right into the sea, Jackson pauses. He watches the waves come plunging and rolling toward the rocks, breaking in an explosion of white water. He waits for a lull between sets and, when it comes, he climbs onto the rocks and hurries across them, making his way toward the very end of the outcrop. That's where the fish will be biting as the current runs the hardest. He's nimble-footed from a childhood spent running barefoot on the rocks and cliffs of Tasmania. He used to launch himself from them into the sea, bellowing and whooping before the water swallowed him.

He makes it to the end before the next set hits, the rocks behind him disappearing beneath a surge of foam. Strong gusts whip the spray off the backs of the waves and the air is alive with moisture. He turns from the wind, crouches down and opens his tackle box. *Christ,* he wishes he'd worn gloves. It's freezing out here. Spray hits him in the back of the neck and it's icy. His numb fingers make him clumsy and he drops a lure and has to scrabble between the rocks to get it. Second time around he manages to thread it with more success.

Eventually he casts out. The motion, once familiar and soothing, gives him no relief this morning. His thoughts too closely match the desolate seascape that broils beneath an angry sky. Standing on the rocks—his body starting to chill—he has the looming sensation that everything is starting to unravel. It is as if he's shedding his skin layer by layer until the sharp bones of who he really is will be visible to everyone.

The vibration of his cell phone startles him. He holds the fishing rod with one hand while he grapples in his coat pocket with the other. It will be Eva. He pushes away the lethal, dark thoughts, letting his brow soften as he imagines the timbre of her sleep-clouded voice saying, *Come back to bed . . .*

Already he's thinking that he will—that he'll forget all this. If he jogs he'll be there in ten minutes. He can slip back into the warmth of their bed, press his body against the curve of hers, and remind himself that it's real.

But when he presses answer, it's not Eva's voice at all.

1

As she leaves the shelter of the headland, the full force of the wind hits Eva. Her hair whips back from her face and she hugs the flask of coffee tight to her chest. Clouds of sand gust along the shoreline, sending a tangled knot of fishing line pinwheeling along the beach.

A woman passes in the other direction, her purple coat flattened to her back by the wind. The fur-trimmed hood is pulled tight to her face, making Eva wish she'd thought to wear a hat. She'd forgotten how raw the weather is on the coast; in London it is muted by buildings and watched from behind windows.

She and Jackson had driven to Dorset last night for her mother's birthday. It was a rush to get out of the city; Eva had been delayed at the hospital trying to turn a breeched baby, but still managed to wrap her mother's present and clear the sink of their breakfast things before Jackson barreled in late and exhausted from a meeting that had run over. The whole week had been like that: grabbing meals at different times, tension from work stalking them home, falling into bed too late and too shattered to talk. She's pleased to have this weekend just to slow down.

Ahead, the rocks where Jackson will be fishing come into focus. Huge somber boulders stretch right out into the sea. She wonders if he's caught anything yet. It wasn't long past dawn when she'd felt the give of the bed as Jackson slipped out from under the covers. She'd heard him stepping into his jeans, pulling on a sweater, and zipping up his coat. He'd leaned over the bed and pressed a kiss on her bare shoulder. Her eyes had opened just enough to see him disappear through the doorway, a red woolen hat pulled down over his ears.

Just beyond the rocks she sees a flash of a boat. It disappears momentarily into a trough and she thinks the conditions are too rough to be out on the water today. She squints against the wind and sees it rise again on the crest of a wave: an orange lifeboat. She wonders whether there's been an accident, and as soon as she has this thought, a slow trickle of unease seeps through her body.

In her childhood summers when her father was still alive, they would come to this beach every morning to swim together, her father making lunging rotations with his long, bony arms in a backstroke. She had loved those swims when the water was calm and the early sun glanced off the surface. But today the sea is something darker, forbidding.

She scans the rocks for Jackson, eyes watering in the wind. He must be here; it's the spot he always fishes when they're visiting her mother. But now all that breaks the gray wash of sea and sky is the lifeboat. Even as she tells herself that the lifeboat could be on a training mission, her knees are bending, carrying her forward into a run.

The flask bounces against her hip and her boots flick up sand. Her breath comes in warm, quick clouds and she feels restricted by the layers of her clothes—her jeans unyielding against her knees, her coat buttons tight against her breastbone.

When she reaches the base of the rocky outcrop, she finds a dozen or so people gathered there. Her gaze moves over them and then travels up the length of the rocks, where waves charge, tossing white water high into the bruised sky. The air is heavy with the smell of salt.

She can't see Jackson.

Eva hurries toward a man zipped into a waxed jacket, his steel-gray eyebrows ruffled by the wind. "Why's the lifeboat out?" she asks, trying to keep the panic from her voice.

"Someone was swept off the rocks."

Her heart lurches. "Who?"

"A fisherman, they think."

For a moment she has a feeling of relief because she knows her husband is not a fisherman: he's a thirty-year-old brand marketer for a drinks company. But then the man is saying, "Young, apparently. But maybe he'll stand more of a chance against the cold."

Eva feels all the air leave her lungs as if someone has grabbed her hard around the ribs. She drops the flask and yanks her cell from her pocket, ripping off her gloves to dial. Her fingers are clumsy with the cold but she turns her back to the wind and keys in Jackson's number.

Pressing the phone to her ear, she paces on the spot waiting for him to pick up.

"Hi, this is Jackson," his voicemail says, and her heart stalls.

Dropping the phone into her pocket, she stumbles toward the rocks. A wide red sign reads DANGER, KEEP OFF. Her scarf flies behind her as she clambers over the wet boulders, the cry of wind filling her ears. Her breath is ragged, and spiked thoughts pierce at her, making her mind whirl. She tells herself to focus only on where she is putting each foot, placing one carefully in front of the other.

Ahead something colorful catches her attention. She picks her way over barnacle-lined rocks until she is close enough to see it.

A green plastic tackle box lies open, wedged between two rocks. She recognizes it instantly: she'd bought it for Jackson last Christmas to house the lures and weights that were gradually filling up his bedside drawer. Now salt water fills the trays, so that two bright blue lures float inside like dead fish.

There is a loud, shattering boom as a wave smashes into the jetty. Icy spray slashes the side of Eva's face and she drops to her knees, clinging to the rock with numbed fingers.

"Hey!" someone shouts. "Get back!"

But she cannot move, cannot turn. She is frozen, fear leaden in her stomach. Her face smarts with the cold and the back of her head is wet. A slow trickle of water seeps beneath her scarf.

Seconds later, she feels the pressure of a hand on her shoulder. A policeman is standing over her, taking her by the arm, encouraging her to her feet. "It's not safe," he shouts above the wind.

She shakes him off. "My husband!" she cries, her words coming out in gusts. "He was fishing! Right here!"

The policeman stares down at her. There is a patch of dark stubble on his jawline, no larger than a thumbprint, which he must have missed when shaving this morning. Something like fear pricks his features as he says, "Okay. Okay. Let's get onto the beach."

He grips her arm, helping her stand. Her legs tremble as they move slowly over the wet rocks, him glancing over his shoulder watching for waves.

When they reach the sand, he turns to her. "Your husband was fishing here this morning?"

She nods. "His tackle box—it's on the rocks."

The policeman looks at her for a long moment without blinking. "We had a report earlier that a man fishing was swept in."

Her voice is small: "Was it him?"

"We can't be sure yet." He pauses. "But it sounds like it's possible, yes."

Saliva fills her mouth and she twists away. The gray-green sea swills with current as she searches it for Jackson. She swallows. "How long ago?"

"About twenty minutes. A couple reported it."

She turns, following his gaze toward a middle-aged man and woman in dark blue parkas, a golden retriever at their feet. "Was it them? Did they see him?"

The moment he nods, Eva staggers past him.

The dog's tail wags frantically as she approaches. "You saw my husband! He was fishing!"

"Your husband?" the woman says, distress clouding her narrow face. "We saw him, yes. I'm sorry——"

"What happened?"

The woman twists her scarf between her fingers as she says, "We'd seen him fishing when we walked past earlier." She glances at her husband. "You said it looked dangerous with those waves, didn't you?"

He nods. "When we turned to walk back, we saw he'd been swept in. He was in the water."

"We called the coast guard," the woman adds. "We tried to keep sight of him till they arrived . . . but . . . but we lost him."

They must be mistaken, Eva thinks. It couldn't be Jackson. "The man you saw—what was he wearing?"

"Wearing?" the woman repeats. "Dark clothes, I think. And a hat," she says, touching the back of her head. "A red hat."

SOMETIME LATER, EVA'S MOTHER arrives. She drapes a blanket over Eva's shoulders and teases a fleecy hat over her short hair while asking questions in a low voice: *How long has he been in the water? What has the coast guard said?*

Eva watches the lifeboat making a search pattern, as if drawing a square in the water and then working outward so the square gets larger and larger until at some point the lifeboat is so far away she wonders if it is even possible Jackson could have swum that far.

She wants to focus on anything but the freezing grip of the sea, so she cushions herself with the warmer memory of Jackson surprising her last month when he'd turned up at the hospital after one of her late shifts holding a bag containing her favorite dress and a pair of gold heels. He'd told her to get changed because he was taking her out.

She'd slipped into the locker room, her heart skipping with excitement, and swapped her uniform for the black silk dress he'd chosen. She'd dabbed on some lipstick and smoothed back her dark hair, and the other midwives whistled and cooed as she came out, giving a little twirl.

Jackson had taken her to a blues bar in north London where the room was lit by candles and the rhythm of the double bass rocked through her chest. She'd leaned her head against Jackson's shoulder, feeling the atmosphere soak through her, washing away the strains of the day. They drank cocktails they couldn't afford, and she danced in high heels that gave her blisters, but she hadn't minded: she loved Jackson for his knack of taking a normal day and carving something beautiful from it.

The loud drone of the coast guard helicopter cuts through Eva's thoughts. The sea beneath quivers and trembles. The white and red colors look bright, optimistic almost, against the darkening clouds, and a ripple of anticipation spreads through the growing crowd.

The policeman stands alone rubbing his palms together to keep warm. Sometimes his radio crackles and he lifts it to his mouth. Eva glances over occasionally, studying him, watching for a sign to tell her how this day will end.

Mostly they wait in silence, listening to the waves crashing at sea, frothing white water bowling into the rocks. Her mother keeps hold of her hand and every now and then she says beneath her breath, "Come on, Jackson. Come on."

WHEN THE LAST BIT of daylight is fading, Eva hears crackling from the policeman's radio. She turns and watches as he lifts it toward his mouth and speaks into it. He looks out over the water and nods once, solemnly. Then the radio is lowered.

He begins moving toward Eva. She shakes her head, thinking, *Do not say it!*

"I'm afraid the coast guard's calling off the search."

Her gloved fingers clutch her scarf. "They can't!"

"The boat's almost out of fuel and the helicopter's lost the light. I'm sorry."

"He's still out there!"

"The coast guard has made the decision."

"But he won't survive the night."

The policeman's gaze leaves her and settles on the sand at their feet.

She feels her mother's hand around her waist, holding onto her, squeezing so tightly it's as if she's trying to absorb Eva's pain.

"He's out there," Eva says finally. She pulls away and staggers down the beach, where the faint lights of the quay glow in the distance. She hears her mother calling after her, but she will not look back. She knows exactly where she needs to go.

Jackson is her husband and she will not give up on him.

THE FISHERMAN IS JUST stepping onto the quay when Eva approaches him. "Is this your boat?"

"Yeah," he says suspiciously.

She snatches a breath. "I need you to take me out in it. I'll pay."

"Lady, this boat isn't going anywhere—"

"My husband was swept from the rocks this morning," she says.

"Your husband? Christ! I heard about it over the radio."

She moves right past him, climbing into the boat as if she's about to commandeer it.

"Hey, listen—"

"You understand currents? Tides?" she says, trying to keep her voice level and focus only on the practical details.

"Sure, but I can't—"

"Please," she says, swinging around to face him, her composure cracking. "You have to help me!"

Once they reach the open water, the boat pitches and rolls with the waves. Eva grips the side, her fingers aching from the cold. She won't let herself think about this because if she admits that her feet are numb and that the temperature has dropped so low that she can't stop shivering, then she'll also have to admit that Jackson could not survive this.

The rocky outcrop looms like low-hanging fog. When they near it, the fisherman cuts the engine. He shouts above the wind, "We'll drift with the current now."

He moves toward her holding a yellow oilskin. "Here. Wear this over the life jacket."

The material is rough and cold, the long sleeves scratching the chapped skin on the undersides of her wrists where her gloves end. She glances down and sees a thick smear of blood across the breast of the jacket.

"Just fish blood," he says, following her gaze.

Eva glances around the boat deck, where lobster pots and dark heavy nets laced with seaweed are stacked. There are lights on the boat, but they're not nearly bright enough. "Have you got a flashlight?"

"Sure." He lifts the lid of the wooden bench and pulls out a flashlight with a glass face as big as a dinner plate.

He passes it to Eva, who holds it in both hands to support the weight. She flicks the switch and points it at the black water. The beam is dazzling and she blinks several times until her eyes become accustomed to it.

He fetches a second, smaller flashlight and begins searching the water beside her as they drift. Dark waves swim in and out of the beam like bodies rearing up, and then recede again.

"Your husband fish a lot?"

Husband. The word still sounded fresh and sweet. They had been married for just under ten months and the sight of his wedding band still made her catch her breath with happiness. "We live in London—so he doesn't fish as much as he'd like. He used to as a boy. He's from Tasmania."

"Where's that?"

She forgets that some people know little about Tasmania. "It's an island off southeast Australia. Almost opposite Melbourne. It's an Australian state."

As she looks down at the inky sea, Eva's thoughts drift back through the day. She pictures Jackson trudging up the beach with his fishing gear. Would his head have been fuzzy from drinking the night before? Did he walk along the shore and think of her still snug in bed, or remember their lovemaking last night? Was there any point when he'd considered turning around and stealing back into the warmth next to her beneath the duvet?

She imagines him on the rocks threading fishing lures onto the line with numb fingers, then setting out the catch bucket.

She imagines that first cast, the smooth flick of the rod. *The surf's good for the fish, livens them up,* he'd told her before.

He knew his fish. His father had run a cray boat for a decade, and Jackson studied marine biology. Living in London as they did, there wasn't much call for marine biologists, but he said he got his fix of the coast whenever they visited her mother. In Tasmania, he owned an old sea kayak and would paddle through empty bays and inlets with a fishing rod hooked at the back of the kayak. She loved his stories of cruising beneath mountains and alongside wild coastline, catching fish to cook up on an open fire.

There is a loud splash by the boat's side and Eva gasps.

The flashlight has slipped from her fingers, an eerie yellow glow falling through the dark water. "No! No . . ."

She wants to reach down, scoop her hands through the sea and save it, but the light flickers as it sinks, and then goes out.

"I'm sorry! I thought I had it," she says, grasping the sides of the boat, leaning right over. "I've lost it. I can't see anything now. I'm sorry . . . I . . ."

"No matter," the fisherman says gently.

She hugs her arms tight to her chest. Her lips sting with the wind chill as she stares out into the endless darkness. "How cold is it?" she asks quietly. "The sea?"

He sucks in his breath. "I'd say it's about eight or nine degrees at the moment."

"How long could someone survive in it for?"

"Hard to say." He pauses. "But I'd think a couple of hours at best."

There's silence save for the creak of the boat and the slap of waves against the hull.

He's dead, she thinks. *My husband is dead.*

We only had two years together, Eva. It wasn't long enough.

There were still things I was only just beginning to discover about you; that your toes wriggle when you're nervous; that your standards for cleanliness are bordering on slovenly; that smell is your strongest sense and you sniff everything you buy—books, a new dress, the cellophane wrap of a DVD.

I only recently found the ticklish spot behind your knees that makes you crumple to the ground with gulps of laughter. And I love that my friends think you're so levelheaded and pragmatic—yet you cannot get ready for an evening out without hurtling around the apartment performing a circus routine of cleaning your teeth while having a wee, or putting on your makeup in between mouthfuls of dinner.

When we met for the first time and you focused your wide, hazel eyes on me, I felt like I did as a boy—light, hopeful, free.

Like I said, Eva, two years with you wasn't long enough.

But it was two years more than I deserved.

2

Eva sits on the edge of the bed gazing numbly at the phone in her hand. She's still in her pajamas, yet she has the feeling it is nearing evening again. Her mother keeps popping upstairs to encourage her to do things: *Take a shower. Get some fresh air. Call Callie.* But everything feels so utterly pointless that Eva doesn't even answer. Instead, she stays in her room waiting for Jackson to walk back in, kiss her on the mouth, and say in his beautiful, lilting accent, *Don't worry, darl. I'm here now.*

It's been four days. The coast guard tells them it is possible his body will wash up farther down the coast, toward Lyme Regis or Plymouth, because of the strong northeasterlies. But she's not ready to think about a body, her husband's body . . .

The red woolen hat Jackson had been wearing was recovered. An apologetic policewoman brought it around sealed within a clear plastic bag. Eva had stared at the condensation forming against the polyethylene, thinking it looked as if the hat were breathing.

Downstairs she hears the low voices of her mother greeting someone. Her name is spoken and then Jackson's. She catches the word *tragic*.

The house has been awash with visitors and Eva finds it odd

how similar death can be to birth: the cards propped on window-sills, the bunches of flowers perfuming each room, the food in plastic containers stacked in the fridge. Then the hushed voices, broken sleeps, and the knowledge that life will never be the same again.

She blinks, her focus returning to the phone. She must speak to Dirk, Jackson's father. She feels guilty that it was the police, rather than she herself, who informed him of what happened. But Eva couldn't. She just couldn't find the words.

She glances at the long number written in pen across the back of her hand, then dials. Pressing the phone to her ear, she listens to the foreign ring tone, thinking about the physical distance between them. They are on opposite sides of the earth; there it is morning, here evening; there it is summer, here winter.

She has only spoken to Dirk once and that was before she and Jackson were married. They kept in light contact by writing and she took pleasure in composing those letters on quiet evenings curled up on the sofa. She loved receiving Dirk's replies, which were written in a spidery hand on airmail stationery and gave her a glimpse of Jackson's life in Tasmania.

"Yeah?" a gruff voice answers.

"Dirk?" She clears her throat. "It's Eva. Jackson's wife."

There is silence at the other end.

She waits, wondering if it's a bad connection. She runs her tongue over her teeth. Her mouth feels dry and somehow swollen.

"Right," he says eventually.

"I . . . I've been wanting to call . . . but, well." She pushes a hand through her matted hair, rubbing her scalp. "I know the police have spoken to you."

"He drowned. That's what they told me." His voice wavers as he says, "Drowned while fishing."

"He was swept in by a wave." She pauses. "The water here—it's cold. Freezing. A lifeboat came. And a helicopter, too. They searched all day . . ."

"Have they found his body?"

"No. No, not yet. I'm sorry."

There is silence.

"They found the hat he was wearing," she offers, although she knows this isn't enough. Nothing—other than Jackson—can be enough.

"I see," he says slowly.

"I'm sorry. I should've called you sooner, not let the police do it, but . . . I just . . . I can't seem to get my head straight." She feels tears blocking up her throat. She takes a breath. "None of it feels . . . real."

Dirk says nothing.

She swallows back her tears and takes a moment to gather herself. Then she says, "There'll need to be a funeral . . . or memorial." These are words her mother keeps on saying to her. "I don't know when it'll be yet . . . after Christmas, I suppose. Maybe you'd like to come over for it?"

"Right." She hears a chair being scraped across a floor, then a clink of glass. She waits a moment.

When Dirk doesn't say anything, she finds herself filling the silence. "I know you don't like to fly, but if you did want to come you'd be welcome. You could stay at our place . . . my place," she corrects herself. She squeezes the roots of her hair, feeling herself coming undone. Everything she has wanted to say seems to have been tipped out of her brain. "Jackson's brother is welcome. I know things between them were . . ." She fumbles for a word, but only comes up with "strained."

"No, no. I don't think so. I don't think it'd work."

Her throat thickens. She wants Dirk to say he'll come. She may not know her father-in-law, but they are connected by their shared love of Jackson, their shared loss. "Please," she says. "Think about it."

SOMEHOW, TIME CONTINUES TO crawl forward. The days pass for Eva in a thick fog of grief. She'll only remember brief moments from this period: a tray of food untouched outside her door; a dawn walk to the rocks, from which she returns soaked and shivering; a bunch of lilies that drop orange pollen onto her mother's glass table, which Eva smears with a fingertip.

Now, a month later, she stands in her dressing gown in front of the full-length mirror. In half an hour a car is arriving to take her to her husband's memorial. She is twenty-nine and a widow.

"Widow," she says to the mirror, trying out the word. "I'm a widow."

Leaning close to her reflection, she sees how drawn she's become. The skin around her nose and the corners of her mouth is pink and cracked. She notices the new crease between her eyebrows and presses her fingertips against it, trying to smooth away the frown that seems to have settled there.

Footsteps sound up the wooden stairway, accompanied by the jangle of a bracelet sliding along the banister. Then there is a bright knock at the door and Callie, her best friend, sweeps in, filling the room with her smile.

She lays a dress on the bed, and then she crosses the room to Eva and wraps her arms around her from behind. A head taller, Callie rests her chin on Eva's shoulder, so both their faces are visible in the mirror.

In a low voice she says, "This is going to be a hard day. But you will get through it. And you will get through the other hard days that follow. And then there will be some days when it's not so hard. Okay?"

Eva nods.

Callie fetches the dress and holds it up for Eva. "I got it from that shop you like near Spitalfields. What do you think? If it's not right, I've got two backups in the car."

Eva undoes her dressing gown and steps into the heavy black material, which tapers in at her waist. She pulls the zip up her side and then faces herself in the mirror. The dress fits as if it's been made for her.

Callie smiles. "You know what Jackson would've said, don't you?"

Eva nods. *Look at you, darl. Just look at you!* She closes her eyes, briefly losing herself to the memory of his voice and the image of him taking her hand and turning her once on the spot, making a low whistle as she spun.

Callie glances at her silver wristwatch and says, "The car will be arriving in twenty minutes. When we get to the church, you're just going to walk straight in with your mother. I spoke to the priest about the music. That was fine to change tracks."

"Thank you."

Callie squeezes her hand. "You okay?"

Eva tries for a smile but it doesn't come. Her head throbs at the temples and she feels raw inside. "It feels . . . too soon."

"What do you mean?" Callie asks softly.

Eva bites down on her bottom lip. "Four weeks. Is it long enough to wait?"

"Wait for what?"

She swallows. On the morning of your husband's memorial

service you do not say, *I am still waiting for him to come back.* So instead she says, "It's just . . . I can't picture it, Cal. I can't imagine my life without Jackson in it."

IN TASMANIA, SAUL UNCLIPS his seat belt and leans forward, his thick hands locked together on the steering wheel of his truck. He gazes through the windshield at the view from the top of Mount Wellington. On a clear day it feels as if you can see the whole of Tasmania from up here, but this afternoon the vista is obscured by the gathering clouds.

Beside him, his father shifts in the passenger seat as he slips a silver flask from his suit pocket. His hands tremble as he unscrews the lid. Whiskey fumes seep into the truck. "One for courage," Dirk says.

Saul looks away, watching instead as the mourners arrive in their dark suits. Some of them are friends of Jackson's that Saul hasn't seen in years—from school, or the boatyard—but most are people Saul's never even met.

Dirk tucks the flask back in his pocket. He sniffs hard, then says, "Ready?"

Saul slips the key from the ignition and climbs out of the truck. Sharp mountain air fills his lungs, and his borrowed suit jacket flaps in the breeze. He does up his top button, then bends to look in the dust-covered sideview mirror as he straightens his tie.

When he's done, they walk reluctantly toward the group of mourners. Beside him, Dirk says, "No father should have to outlive his son." He gives a terse shake of his head, adding, "England! He should never've bloody gone there!"

"Will there be a service or anything over there?"

"Yeah. They're having a memorial, too."

"Who's arranged it?"

"His wife—"

Saul stops. He turns to look at his father, who has frozen on the spot, his mouth hanging open. "What did you just say?"

Dirk screws up his eyes, then rubs a thick hand across his face.

"Dad?"

Dirk exhales hard. When he opens his eyes, he looks directly at Saul. "You and me, son, we're gonna need to have a talk."

3

Eva slots the key into the door lock, then hesitates. She hasn't been back to their apartment since Jackson's death. She's been staying with her mother, as she wanted to get through Christmas and then the memorial before she could even think of returning. Perhaps it was a mistake to refuse her mother's offer of coming to the apartment with her. She'd insisted on doing it alone, but now the idea of going inside fills her with dread.

She takes a deep breath, then pushes open the door, putting the weight of her shoulder behind it to force it over the mound of mail on top of the doormat. With her foot, she moves aside junk mail, Christmas cards, and bills, and squeezes into the hallway. The air smells musty and stale, and there's an undertone of leather from Jackson's coat that hangs on a hook behind the door.

She puts down her bag and moves silently along the hall, peering into each room. She has the strangest sensation that if she moves slowly enough, she may catch Jackson lounging on the sofa with his feet on the coffee table, or see his long back in the shower as water streams down his body.

But, of course, the apartment is empty. A deep wave of loneliness storms her. It is so intense and so absolute that it steals the breath from her lungs and the floor seems to lurch beneath her. She leans against the wall for balance, breathing deeply till the sensation passes. She must hold it together. Jackson has gone and she is alone. These are the facts and she needs to get used to them.

After a moment or two, she swallows, lifts her chin, then propels herself toward the kitchen. In a rush of movement, she throws the windows wide open, hearing traffic, voices, the scuffling of a pigeon on the roof. Then she flicks on the central heating and hurries through the apartment switching on lamps, radios, and the TV. Noise and light and fresh air swirl through the rooms.

Eva keeps her coat on and returns to the kitchen. She will make tea, and then unpack. Kettle. Fill it with water, she tells herself. She curls her fingers around the handle, glancing away from her reflection, which is distorted in the curve of aluminum. She carries it over to the sink—and then freezes.

A used tea bag lies there, bloated and dried out, the basin stained rust brown around it. It's Jackson's. He had the infuriating habit of dropping his tea bags in the sink, not the garbage can. Seeing it is such a tiny, inconsequential detail of his life, but somehow the mundaneness of it is what chokes her.

She stands there staring with the kettle poised in her hand, thinking that right now she would give anything to watch Jackson walk into this kitchen, make a cup of tea, and drop the tea bag into the sink with a wet thud.

Eva puts the kettle back and drifts into the bedroom, where the radio is blasting out a tinny pop tune. The electronic beat is like an itch in her head and she snaps it off. She stares at their unmade double bed, biting on her lip as memories filled with warmth and comfort float toward her. Before she can stop herself, she climbs into the bed in her coat and pulls the covers up to her chin.

Grief is physical, she thinks. It feels like something corrosive is burning through her insides, dissolving layers of herself, leaving her raw. She buries her face in Jackson's pillow, breathing in the faint musk of his skin through her sobs.

EVA MUST HAVE FALLEN asleep because, when she opens her eyes, the room is in darkness. Her head throbs and her skin feels clammy and hot. She shakes herself free of her coat and sits up, switching on Jackson's bedside lamp.

His drawer beneath it is ajar and she pulls it wider, her gaze wandering over bundles of receipts, a pair of broken binoculars, a pack of cards, condoms, a book about Henry VIII that he'd never finished reading, two AA batteries, and some loose change.

She slips out a photo of them that had been taken in Paris, where they're standing overlooking the Arc de Triomphe. Just after this photo was taken, the rain had come down and they'd run into a café, the floor soaked from dripping coats and shaken umbrellas. They'd dried off eating pastries and drinking coffee, and by the time they'd left, the sun was glaring off rain-slick sidewalks.

As she leafs through the rest of the items in the drawer, she sees an envelope addressed in her handwriting. She tugs it free and finds it is a letter to Dirk. It was her most recent one about a surprise trip to Wales that Jackson had arranged. She'd thought they were going to see her mother, but he managed to distract her so completely that it was half an hour into the journey before she realized they weren't heading to Dorset at all. He'd booked them into a cozy B&B in the Brecon Beacons and they'd spent the weekend strolling through damp bracken-lined mountains and making love by the open fire in their room.

At the bottom of the letter she sees that Jackson had added

his own message asking if his dad had seen many Wallabies games. Jackson always liked to include a personal note and he sent the letters from the mail room at work, but he must've forgotten this one.

As she returns it to the drawer her fingers meet a second letter, which she slips out. It is another one of hers to Dirk, the date showing the end of August. She scans the contents, which are innocuous: an account of a summer picnic on Clapham Common; a trip to see *A Midsummer Night's Dream;* a photo of them at a gig.

She smoothes both letters out on her lap, an uneasy sensation stirring in her stomach as she wonders why neither was sent. She checks through the drawer again but doesn't find any more. Logic tells her it must have been a simple oversight, yet she can't help wondering if there was another reason why Jackson hadn't sent them.

A WEEK LATER, EVA is sitting in a bar with Callie, a bottle of white wine in an ice bucket between them. Callie pours generously and slides a glass across the wooden table to Eva. "Drink."

Eva obeys, taking a large gulp. She had called Callie in tears after her first shift back at the hospital.

"What happened?"

"I . . . I just couldn't handle it. I left. Ran out."

"It was your first day."

"I thought I was ready. I delivered the baby and everything was fine—I was focused. I barely thought about Jackson. But, afterward . . ." She shakes her head.

Eva had lifted the baby from the birthing pool and handed it carefully to its mother, a Polish woman called Anka, who looked spent. The new father had gazed at his son in wonderment, placing the backs of his fingers gently to the boy's cheek. Then his eyes lifted to meet his wife's. There was a moment when the room went still. He had said something in a choked voice, the words floating to his wife, whose lower lip trembled as she smiled.

Eva hadn't needed to speak Polish to understand what he was saying. He was telling his wife that she was incredible, that he was so proud of her, that he loved her deeply. It was this look, the intensely intimate moment between husband and wife that followed the strain and exhaustion of labor, that had always made Eva love what she did.

But today, she had felt paralyzed by it. She had stared at the couple—who were only a year or two older than her and Jackson—as she realized with silent horror that she would never know what it would be to hold Jackson's baby in her arms, or to have him look at her in that way, to be loved like this man loved the mother of his child.

Because her husband was dead.

The thought had slammed into her, and suddenly she was backing away and asking the support worker to call another midwife. Then she was sprinting down the corridor, bursting into the nurses' toilets, and leaning over the sink just in time for bile and tears to be caught in the ceramic basin.

"I couldn't stand it," she tells Callie. "I literally could not stand seeing the husband and wife together. In love. I envied them so much I couldn't breathe."

"That's how I feel at weddings."

Eva manages a laugh.

"I was starting to forget what your laugh sounded like."

Eva tilts her head to one side. "You're dressed up. You were out, weren't you?"

"Only with David," Callie replies, waving her fingers through the air.

"I'm so sorry! He was taking you for dinner. You were going

to talk about the Melbourne contract. You told me yesterday. My head's all over the place."

"You did me a favor. He'd booked a table at Vernadors," she says, rolling her eyes. "I ate there before Christmas and was in bed for two days. Never touch their mussels."

"I remember."

"Course—Jackson was there too that night! I bumped into him having a business dinner. God, hardly the way to hook a new client. Give them food poisoning."

"He was fine."

"Well, yes, but he did grow up eating stuff he'd scraped off rocks." Callie takes a drink, then tops up both their glasses. "So, tell me exactly where you're at."

"It was a rough day, that's all."

"Cut the crap. This is me. I want to know everything, all the gory, grisly details of how catastrophically bad your life is right now. Spill."

Eva takes a deep breath. "I . . . I just . . . I don't even know where to start." She lifts her hands to her head, squeezing her hair at the roots. "I can't bear it. I literally can't bear it. I miss him so much. I think of him constantly. I mean *constantly*. I have full-blown conversations with him in my head. Some days it hurts so much, I don't think I can do it. I feel like I'm just dragging myself forward, when all I want is to close my eyes and sleep. I want to wake up sometime in the future when it is easier, less painful than this."

Eva swallows and continues. "And Mum . . . she's calling me continually to ask if I'm okay, telling me I can move back home." She shakes her head sharply. "And I'm not okay. Of course I'm not! But moving in with her isn't what I want. I'll suffocate there. I can't go back." She bites down on her bottom lip and then says, "I thought we'd have our whole lives together. And now . . . he's dead. I'll never get to see him again, or hold him, or hear his laugh . . . or do any of the things we'd planned. And it feels so . . . unfair. Why Jackson? Why did it have to be him? We were married for less than a year. We had everything ahead of us—and he died!" She slams her palm down on the table, making their wineglasses tremble. "I'm furious with him for being so fucking stupid, for being out there on those rocks in the middle of winter, fishing! And I'm furious with Mum for asking us to come and stay that weekend. But mostly . . . mostly I'm furious with myself—because if I'd gotten out of bed a few minutes earlier, or not bothered making a thermos—then I'd have been there in time. I'd have told him to get off the rocks. And then . . . he'd still be here."

Tears roll down Eva's cheeks and Callie reaches across the table and squeezes both her hands.

"I hate this, Cal. I hate feeling like this. I'm so lonely without him. The apartment . . . it's awful. It's so quiet. It's like the life has been sucked out. I'm living in a vacuum." Eva slides one of her hands free from Callie's and wipes her face. "At night it's just me in there and our bedroom . . . it feels so empty . . . so silent. I sleep with the fucking radio on and a hot-water bottle wrapped in Jackson's clothes! It's pathetic!"

Eva reaches for her wine and takes a long gulp, draining half of it. "I wanted—needed—to go back to work, to keep myself busy, help me stay sane. But today, God, it was awful. That poor couple." She shakes her head again. "I'm not sure I'm ready to be back."

The lights in the bar are dimmed and the music is turned up as the bartender sets the ambience for the evening ahead. "You're an incredible midwife," Callie says, leaning in closer to be heard. "You could open a florist's with all the bouquets new mothers send. But maybe it is too soon. Give yourself some time."

"What would I do with it? I feel so . . . separated from him. I know that sounds ridiculous—because *of course* I feel separated: he's dead! It's just, there's no one I can share this with. I'm so grateful to have you to talk to, but what I mean is, there's no one here that knew him, *really* knew Jackson like I did. His friends are great and adored him, and Mum liked Jackson, but she's grieving for me, not him. I feel like I need to be around people that really loved him, like I did."

"You mean his family?"

She nods. "His dad still hasn't called back. I keep trying him—but he never picks up."

"Maybe it's too hard for him right now."

Eva finishes her wine. "I've been thinking," she says, running a finger over the stem of her glass, "what if I went out there?"

"Tasmania?"

She nods. "I want to meet Dirk. Meet Jackson's old friends. See where he grew up. We were planning to go together in the autumn. And it's not far from Melbourne . . ."

"So you could come and visit me!" Callie finishes, a smile spreading over her face.

Callie was due to start a six-month contract there in February but kept on saying that she would cancel it if Eva wanted her to stay in London.

"I could even meet you in Tasmania," Callie says, "and then we could fly on to Melbourne together. The company's paying for my apartment. It's a two-bed place, so you would have your own room."

"What about David?"

"He doesn't do long haul. Tells me it plays havoc with his sleep patterns. That's what happens when you screw a forty-five-year-old."

Eva tries for a smile, but feels the sadness that lingers around her mouth and in the dark hollows beneath her eyes.

"Seriously, Eva, why not take a sabbatical? Give yourself some time."

She nods. "I've been thinking about it."

"Have you spoken to your mum about this?"

Eva shakes her head. "She won't like it." Her mother's life had been punctured by sadness; she'd lost her second daughter at birth and then, twelve years later, lost her husband to a stroke. All her love—and all her fears—were poured into Eva.

"You've got to do what feels right for you, not what your mum wants." Callie pauses. "What would Jackson have said?"

Without hesitating Eva says, "Go. He'd have told me to go."

We talked about taking a trip out to Tasmania. You wanted to meet my family, go for drinks with my friends you'd heard stories about, see the shack on Wattleboon where I'd spent my summers.

People often think of Tassie as Australia's poorer brother because the climate is cooler, the cities are smaller and less sophisticated, its brutal history as Van Diemen's Land is never forgotten. Yet I've always loved it for exactly those reasons: it's wild and rugged, with a shadowy past, and enough raw wilderness to lose yourself in.

I'd love to have hiked with you in the eerie beauty of Cradle Mountain, where moss drips from the trees, or shown you the wombats that amble on the tracks around Wineglass Bay. We could have been tourists together and taken a boat out along the east coast to see the whales cruising by, or eaten soggy fries and gravy from Buggy's Takeout in Hobart.

You used to ask me so many questions about Tasmania, as if by trying to understand the place you could piece me together. But there was a lot I didn't tell you about my life there; whole chunks of time that I left out, people's names I never mentioned, things I wanted to forget.

I'd've liked to have shown you every edge of Tasmania because I know you'd have fallen in love with that little island in the sea. But the truth is, Eva, I never planned on taking you there. How could I?

4

There is a bus ride to Gatwick, a long wait in the overcrowded fug of the departures lounge, a plane seat with a dusty headrest, a bleary-eyed refueling stop in Dubai, a further twelve hours in the same cramped seat, a frantic run to the domestic terminal in Melbourne, and then a smaller plane heading finally for Tasmania.

As they descend through broken white clouds, Eva peers through the scratched window of the plane. The Southern Ocean meets the winding Tasmanian coastline that unfurls in a mass of inlets, bays, and wind-ridged channels. She sees farmland, forest, tree-lined hills, and only a scattering of houses. What strikes her is the space. Almost a quarter of Tasmania is classified as a national park, an isolated island wilderness, dropped off the coast of mainland Australia.

She feels the symmetry of her journey, which is unfolding in reverse of the flight Jackson made to the UK two years earlier. That's how they'd met: on the plane, with Eva boarding in Dubai after spending a week there with Callie, who was working on a shoot.

She had a pounding hangover made worse by the depressing thought of returning to Dorset, where she was still living at her mother's while she tried to save for a place of her own. She barely registered the man in the seat next to hers as she sank down and took out her book. It was only when he introduced himself that she'd turned and looked at him properly. He had pale blue eyes that were clear and cool against his tanned face, and he smiled as he shook her hand, showing a row of strong white teeth.

"I should warn you," he'd said, the drawn-out vowels of his accent warm in her ear. "I've a low boredom threshold—and I got on this plane in Australia. If you want to request a seat change, now's your chance."

She'd felt herself smile then, and when she glanced down, she saw he was still shaking her hand.

Like any traveler, he didn't want to talk about where he was from, but where he was going. He asked question after question about England and so she'd told him about the hectic pace of the capital and how it sprawls out for miles and miles. She told him that Big Ben isn't actually the name of the clock tower, but the bell within it, and that parts of the Tower of London are over nine hundred years old. She told him what she loved about England: the culture, the history, the mixture of cities and agriculture. And what she hated: the pigeons, the weather, the political correctness gone mad.

In return he told her that he was a marine biologist and she was captivated by his stories about working off a dive boat on the Great Barrier Reef, where he led tourists in coral restoration projects, or the three months he spent teaching teenagers to dive at an outdoor experience camp on the east coast of Tasmania.

After the drink cart passed, he poured her a glass of red wine from a miniature bottle, then leaned back in his seat and said, "So tell me, Eva, what is it you love about being a midwife?"

She liked the question and the way he listened closely as she answered. "Everyone assumes it's the babies—that all midwives love newborns. But for me it's working with the women. I get to share one of the most intimate and important experiences of their lives. It's a privilege."

Jackson had studied her for a long moment and then his gaze trailed to her mouth.

She had felt heat rise in her cheeks. "What about you? Why marine biology?"

He'd not answered right away, just sat there, thinking. Then he smiled as he told her, "It was a book that made me want to study it."

Eva had tilted her head, intrigued.

"Most Saturday afternoons me and my brother would go to a secondhand store looking for good finds. Sometimes we'd pick up old reels or bike wheels. This one Saturday, I bought an old khaki backpack for a dollar. When I got it home, I found there was a book stuffed inside. It was called *The Sea Around Us* by Rachel Carson, an American marine biologist. It might sound stupid now, but at the time—I was thirteen—it felt like that book was meant to find me, as if it had stowed itself away. I wrote my name in it and read it cover to cover. I swear I looked at the sea differently after that." He paused. "It seemed like a mystery waiting to be explored."

It was then, that moment sitting beside him in the narrow space of their plane seats, that Eva felt something sway and tip inside of her.

When they got off the plane in London, they were still talking. They went through passport control in different lines, but met again after customs. Eva was staying the night in Callie's empty apartment, so they shared a taxi through London and he stared out of the rain-smeared window, not hiding his wonderment at the grandeur of the city. Before she got out, he asked for her phone number.

He called her the following morning and they spent the next three days in bed together, only leaving to buy croissants and fresh milk. When she finally returned home to Dorset, it was to pack up her things and move to the city with a man she barely knew.

Falling in love took her by surprise with both its strength and its suddenness, so unlike the steady relationships she'd ambled through previously. It was as if she'd slipped into a parallel world, one where only she and Jackson existed. In those first few months they mapped each other's bodies, created a dialogue punctuated with their own private jokes, filled a past they hadn't shared with the sheer and vivid pleasure of the present.

Now Eva feels the bump and jar of the plane as the wheels touch tarmac, wind roaring against the wing flaps.

"Welcome to Tasmania," the captain says, and Eva feels her heart clench.

IT IS ONLY MIDMORNING when Eva arrives at her hotel, so she dumps her luggage, peels off her winter clothes, and steps into a cotton dress. Her legs look pale and dry as she slips on a pair of leather sandals, then leaves to get her bearings in Jackson's city.

Hobart, Tasmania's capital, is set on the banks of the Derwent River, with the foreboding presence of Mount Wellington towering behind it. She heads out along the marina, the warmth in the air easing the tension in her muscles. Expensive yachts and tourist boats are moored beside battered fishing vessels, and shadows of fish circle in small shoals, breaking the surface to pick at sodden crusts of bread.

It's a Saturday, but there's still none of the rush or frenetic pace of a city. Everyone seems to be milling around in cafés, men wearing sneakers or hiking boots, and women casual in flip-flops and shorts. After London, Hobart feels like a village—small, informal, laid-back.

She drifts on toward Salamanca, where a market fills the street. The air swirls with scents of fruit and sugared doughnuts—the faint whiff of the marina hovering in the background. She barely registers the stalls selling olives, vintage handbags, beaded jewelry, antique books, or the shoppers with colorful bags swinging from their hands. All she feels is the empty space at her shoulder where Jackson should be.

She imagines the warmth of his hand around hers as if they were walking together. She'd have persuaded him to pause at the antique jewelry stall so she could sift through old brooches and beautiful pocket watches, and he'd have wanted to buy her the prettiest one with money neither of them had. As they walked together he would've whispered a private joke about the man with the handlebar mustache selling cider, and then tugged her forward to introduce her to a friend he'd caught sight of, proudly saying, "This is my *wife*."

When Eva looks down, she finds the fingers of her left hand are unfurled at her side as if reaching for him. She quickly stuffs her hand in her pocket and hurries from beneath the canopies and out into the open air.

She lets her legs carry her forward, moving through the modest city shopping center onto tree-lined residential streets, and eventually into a well-maintained park where groups of young people loll on the grass talking and listening to music, cigarette smoke drifting into the air. Two women in tie-dyed skirts stand beside a table stacked with books, where a hand-painted sign reads: FREE BOOKS ☺.

Feeling the wooziness of jet lag suddenly overtaking her, Eva finds a bench in the shade of a large gum tree and takes a moment to rest. Eating nothing but plane food for the last thirty-two hours has left her nauseous, and she thinks she'll buy some fresh fruit and then return to the hotel and give in to sleep.

First, though, she takes out her cell phone and tries Dirk. She wasn't able to get a hold of him before she left England, and as the phone rings and rings, she pictures a man standing with his hands in his pockets, a slight stoop to his posture, watching her number flashing up, but not answering. With a stab of frustration she ends the call, deciding she will go to his house instead.

She is slipping the phone back into her pocket when it suddenly rings.

"Yes?" she answers, expectant.

"You've landed?"

"Oh. Mum," Eva says, pushing a hand back through her short hair. "Yeah, a couple of hours ago."

"How was the journey?"

"Long. But fine, really."

"Are you at the hotel?" her mother asks, a slight shrillness to her tone.

"No, I'm sitting in a park. I went for a walk." She glances at her watch and realizes that if it's midday here, then it must be midnight in England. "Mum," she says, suddenly wary. "What is it?"

There's a pause. She hears her mother draw a breath. "Oh, sweetheart," she begins. "They've found a body."

EVA RUNS A DEEP bath, pouring in a miniature bottle of the hotel's bath oil. Steam swirls in lemon-scented clouds as she peels off her clothes and steps in, hot water creeping over her ankles and shins. She lowers herself down, leans back against the tub and groans.

A body.

It washed up two hundred miles along the coast, just beyond Plymouth. It was on the late news this evening, her mother told her. They're doing tests to confirm the identity and should know the outcome in a few days.

Eva had wanted this news.

But also not wanted it.

She bends her knees and slides under the surface of the bath water. Her short hair fans and swirls around her face. Warm water fills the pockets of air in her nose and ears, popping and tickling, pressing against her eyes and the seal of her lips. Underwater she's aware of her pulse amplified in her ears.

She makes herself open her mouth. Water spills over her tongue, the insides of her cheeks, the roof of her mouth, the back of her throat. She wants to sit up, cough, open her eyes—but she holds herself still.

Her lungs begin to ache and she feels the weight of water holding her down. Her body fires out panic signals, sparks of pain shooting into her nerve endings.

She thinks of Jackson beneath the cold, brutal waves, his large hands flailing for purchase, the weight of his clothes and boots dragging him down. She pictures his eyes bulging in terror, salt burning them as he fights to live.

Then she imagines that moment when there are no more sips of oxygen to absorb, and he inhales—freezing salt water sucked deep into his lungs.

She bursts from the bath, water sloshing over the tiled floor, her mouth wide open, gasping.

This is how it felt, Eva, when I went under. The icy shock of that sea was immense. My whole body contracted: my heart squeezed tight, my muscles clenched, my tendons constricted. With that first smack of water, all thought was flushed out.

The sea was bitter and relentless——shifting, pulsing, whirling, gripping me, yanking me under. An attack from all directions. My clothes became a fishing net, tangling me further. I kicked and thrashed, my breath ragged, limbs turning hopelessly. It was like no sea I'd ever known.

I don't know whether it was minutes——or even just seconds——before the water started to numb me to the bone. My body convulsed with shivers, the fear of death ballooning in my brain.

I fought for as long as I could, your image bright in my mind. But gradually all the pain and struggle seemed to slide away with the heat of my body, the fight in my muscles——and I gave up.

That's all I can tell you, Eva: eventually I gave up.

5

Eva parks the rental car on the opposite side of the street to Dirk's house but doesn't get out. Her palms are damp from where she's been gripping the steering wheel and she wipes them against her jeans.

She studies Dirk's house, which looks tired in the afternoon sunshine. Red flakes of paint peel away from the blistered siding revealing a white undercoat. The front garden is overgrown and two plant pots lie broken on their sides. The curtains are open, which she hopes is a sign that he is in.

Feeling queasy with nerves and expectation, she climbs from the car, crosses the street, and walks the short length of the pathway to his front door. There is no bell, so she knocks, then stands back with her arms at her sides. She hopes Dirk will be in; she's eager to hear his voice, to see Jackson in his face.

She wonders what they'll talk about, whether there will be any common ground beyond Jackson. She tries to remember the walks Dirk mentioned in his letters, or the name of the book he was enjoying when he last wrote, but her mind feels permeable, facts and information draining away. She'd like to establish a connection, something enduring so that they can have a reason to keep in touch.

She hears movement from inside, as if a chair is being scraped across a floor. A moment later the door is opened by a man wearing a flannel shirt tucked into belted jeans. He has no shoes on and his gray socks are thinning at the toes.

Her breath catches as she sees clues of Jackson locked within the angle of the man's nose, the line of his brow, the shade of his eyes. "Dirk?"

"Yeah?"

"I'm Eva Bowe. Jackson's wife."

His brow furrows into rows of deep creases. He rubs a large hand across his forehead, as if he's trying to release a memory of this arrangement. The skin on his cheeks is bright red, broken capillaries spreading like a map over his face. "What . . . what're you doin' here?"

"I tried calling."

He looks past her as if he expects to see more people. "You've come from England?"

She nods. Her toes squirm in her sandals as she tells him, "I flew in three days ago. I . . . I wanted to come to Tasmania. See where Jackson was from. See where he grew up. Meet you." She is babbling and stops herself.

Dirk stares. "It's a long way."

"Yes," she says.

He steps back from the doorway. "You'd better come in."

He leads her into a small living room where a timeworn green sofa faces the window. A whiskey bottle and glass stand on a side table and a television plays on silent, some daytime game show with an overdressed host. A pile of videos is stacked at the bottom of the unit, and somehow the sight of these relaxes her: Dirk is a man who still hasn't made the switch from VHS to DVD, despite having had more than a decade to do so.

"Sit yourself down," Dirk says, pointing toward the sofa.

"Thank you."

He switches off the television and stands in front of it, wiping a hand over the sides of his thinning steel hair. He rolls his shoulders back and stretches his chin away from his neck. He's a big man, tall and broad. She imagines that once he'd have had a muscular build, but now it seems as if all the muscles have sighed, slumping comfortably into old age.

"So. You're Eva."

"Yes."

He digs his hands into his pockets. "Wanna drink?"

"Water would be great."

He trudges out of the living room and she lets out the breath she'd been holding. From the kitchen she hears a cupboard being opened, the clink of glass, the whir of a tap.

While she's alone, she takes in the room. There are no paintings on the off-white walls, and the carpet is thin underfoot. A brass barometer stands on the windowsill next to a model boat with a broken mast. On the dust-filmed coffee table a bunch of dead lilies stand in an empty glass, and she wonders whether they've been there since Jackson's death.

Dirk brings in two glasses of water on a tray. He sets them down beside the flowers and his hands shake as he passes Eva her glass. He looks older than she'd imagined, more weatherworn and tired around the eyes.

He remains standing, saying, "Bit of a shock, this."

"Yes, sorry. I did call, but there was never any answer. I couldn't even leave a message. I thought about writing . . . but I wasn't sure a letter would reach you in time."

"You'd be better off sending a pigeon," he mocks. "What is it you're doin' here?"

"I . . ." She falters, the abruptness of the question throwing her off her stride. She moves her thumb back and forth across the cool curve of the glass. "Jackson and I had planned to come out here together in the autumn, so I thought . . . well, I thought I'd come anyway . . ."

Eva shifts on the sofa, unsure what else to say. Her eyes dart around the room and fall on a photo that's tacked to the wall. "Jackson," she says, her head swimming with the pleasure of seeing his image here.

Dirk turns to look at the photo. "Australia Day that was taken. Nineteen he was."

In the photo Jackson looks fresh-faced and tanned, free of the creases that were beginning to branch out from the corners of his eyes and mouth. He is half smiling, his lips turned up toward the left. He's standing on a sun-scorched lawn wearing a blue vest that swamps him. His hair is chin length, longer than she's ever seen.

Eva leans closer, noticing something else. In his right hand he's holding a half-smoked cigarette, his easy grip suggesting a comfortableness that comes from habit. She had no idea he used to smoke. She feels oddly exposed by this lack of knowledge. She wants to ask Dirk how long Jackson smoked for, yet knows there would be something humiliating in the question.

She pulls her gaze away from the cigarette and focuses on Dirk, who is saying, "I miss him like hell." He carefully lowers himself into the chair opposite her, asking, "What happened that day? Can you tell me about it?"

"Yes. Of course." Eva puts down her water and locks her hands together in her lap. "We were visiting my mother for the weekend. She lives on the south coast, in Dorset. Jackson had got up early to go fishing."

"For what?"

"Bass or pollock," she answers, pleased by the question. Dirk was a fisherman once. "He was casting off some rocks—but it was a rough day. Strong winds, big swell. He got knocked in by a wave." She twists her wedding ring around her finger. "A lifeboat came out and the coast guard helicopter. They searched all day . . ."

"He was always a strong swimmer."

"The water temperature—it was only about eight or nine degrees. He was in winter clothes. It would've been hard for anyone to swim."

Dirk shakes his head, saying, "After all these years running boats, I never lost anyone. And then Jackson"—he sighs heavily—"he's just line-fishing and goes down."

"His body," Eva begins, then hesitates. She is still waiting for confirmation that the body washed up in Plymouth has been positively identified as Jackson. In a matter of days she will know. Finally know. And then what? If it is him, will she fly home—have some sort of funeral service so the body, or its remains, can be buried? She realizes there's no point telling Dirk about it yet, not until she has the facts. "I'm still hoping his body will be recovered."

"Don't matter to me," he says with a shrug. "The ocean's a good place. I'd rather him be in it, not buried in some bloody awful coffin stuffed in the ground for the maggots to get."

Eva thinks about this for a moment and wonders if maybe he's right. Perhaps Jackson would've preferred that. She finishes her water and says, "The memorial service for Jackson was beautiful. A lot of people came."

Dirk nods.

"There was a guest book. I haven't brought it with me—but if you'd like to read it, I could send it to you?"

"Nice of ya to suggest it." He reaches for the whiskey bottle and pours himself a glass. She can smell the pungent vapor as he lifts it to his mouth. "We had a memorial here."

"Did you?" she says, surprised. "Where?"

"Top of Mount Wellington. Just a few of us." He takes another drink, emptying the glass.

She's hurt that she didn't know about this, wasn't invited. She would like to know who came to mourn him, what was said, whether there was a burial of any personal items, but Dirk is up on his feet, saying, "I think we should have a drink to Jackson."

He leaves the room and returns a moment later with a spare tumbler. He grabs the whiskey bottle and Eva tries to tell him that she's driving, but already he's splashed whiskey into her glass and is refilling his own. "To Jackson!" he toasts.

Eva takes a small sip. She's always hated whiskey and the taste turns her stomach. She breathes steadily through her nose until the nauseous sensation passes, then discreetly slips the glass aside.

As they continue to talk, Eva watches the alcohol working through Dirk. He becomes more expansive, sip by sip. "I remember Jackson diving for his first abalone," Dirk says, resting the whiskey glass on his knee. "He can't have been more than eight or nine, and he dived right down to this shallow ledge. There they were—all the abs just lined up—so he found himself a sharp stone and he prized the biggest one of them all right off the rocks. Came up grinning, holding it in the air like a trophy. He was too excited to stop diving, so he slipped it in the pocket of his swimming trunks and kept on going."

Dirk asks, "You ever seen an abalone?"

She shakes her head.

"They're as big as your hand, shell on one side, and a dark tough mollusk on the other. When Jackson was done, he ran up the beach to show Saul and me, trying to pull this ab from his pocket. But it had suckered onto his thigh so hard that he had no chance of getting the thing off. I yanked his chain for a while, telling him that it'd take a month of being out of salt water for the ab to loosen its grip. Should've seen his little face! Course, in the end it came off. But it left a big old bruise that lasted the summer. We used to tease him that it was a love bite," he says, his face creasing into a smile.

As Dirk continues to talk and drink, his eyes become glassy and she catches the beginnings of a slur to his words, but still she listens closely. Even when the whiskey causes him to muddle his son's names and he tells her Saul was always the traveler, Jackson the Tassie boy, she doesn't interrupt. Eva will do nothing to stop his flow, because she is just grateful to hear the words of somebody who loved Jackson as deeply as she did.

"Did Saul and Jackson used to be close?" Eva asks.

"Tight as a mussel. Did everything together. They were an enterprising little duo. Used to get up early and snorkel off the jetty down at Wattleboon, looking for lost squid jigs to sell to the tourists and make a bit of extra pocket money."

"But they haven't been close for a while?"

He shakes his head sharply.

"Is Saul still living in Tasmania?"

"Yeah. Works over at the university in Hobart. Doing some big project on cephalopods. That's squid to you and me." He takes a glug of whiskey and she sees him wince, placing a hand over his stomach.

"Hobart. Is that where he lives?"

"No, no. Moved to Wattleboon Island. Built himself a place out in Shoal Bay."

Eva's head tilts. "That's where you used to have a shack, isn't it?"

"Yeah, beautiful place." Under his breath he adds, "But too many bad memories for me."

"I'd like to meet Saul."

Dirk's expression turns wary. "Why?"

"He was Jackson's brother."

"Nah, don't think he'd be too keen."

"It's important to me."

He looks at her closely. "Sorry, Eva, but I think you'd best forget about the idea." He lifts his glass and downs the whiskey.

JACKSON HAD TOLD HER that his father liked a drink, but he'd never explicitly said Dirk was an alcoholic. But he is; she can see it in the high color of his skin, the broken veins across his cheeks, and the way his fingers cling to the glass. It hurts knowing Jackson left out this information, as if he didn't trust her enough to show her the darker corners of his family life.

She wonders how Jackson would feel now if he could see his father getting steadily more drunk after Eva has traveled thousands of miles to meet him. A quiet anger simmers inside as she thinks about her countless calls that went unanswered, and the invite to the memorial she'd extended to him—but that wasn't returned.

It feels like a personal affront to Jackson, and before she can check herself, she is saying, "You didn't come to our wedding."

Dirk shrugs. "England's a long way. A lot of money." He pours himself another whiskey, the neck of the bottle clattering against the glass. He swirls it around and then takes a slug. Is that his third or fourth since she's been here?

"Weren't you interested in seeing who your son was going to marry?" she presses Dirk, wanting to understand his absence.

"Y'know what?" he says, and there's something in his tone she doesn't like, a loosening, as if whatever he's been holding back is beginning to spill out, dragging with it the sharp edges of his thoughts. "I wasn't interested. Because I didn't want him to marry you."

Her eyes widen.

"I thought he was bloody mad! And I told him." He shakes his head. "You two should never've gotten married."

She feels as though she's had the breath kicked out of her. "What?"

Dirk runs a thick hand down the length of his face, exhaling loudly. Then he gets to his feet and crosses the room unsteadily. He sets his hands square on the windowsill and looks out onto the street.

"Dirk?" She shakes her head back and forth. "Why are you saying this?"

He shrugs. "I'd never have seen him again. He wouldn't have come home when he was married. That's all."

Tears burn the back of her throat.

When Dirk turns, his expression has softened and she thinks he's going to apologize. But then he says, "Listen, Eva, I can see you loved Jackson. And I'm sorry for what you're going through. I am. But my boy's dead. You being out here isn't going to make that any better. So I reckon it might be best if you go now, don't you?"

6

A knot of anger is wedged into the pit of Eva's stomach as she replays Dirk's words: *You two should never've gotten married.* She keeps reminding herself it was the whiskey talking, or perhaps the lash of his grief, but the remark has left her unsettled.

She is even more determined now to try to find Saul. As she leans her elbows on the ferry railing, watching Wattleboon Island come into focus, she wonders how Jackson would have felt about her coming here to meet the brother he hadn't spoken to in over four years. The few times Jackson mentioned Saul's name, his expression darkened, as if Saul's betrayal still had the power to wound him.

The island reveals itself by degrees; first the forested sea cliffs rising up in the distance, then the green curve of the hills. Jackson had talked about his summers spent here with a sense of nostalgia, as if the island were both treasured yet also lost to him—a place he could never get back to.

From her pocket she takes out the free visitors' map she'd picked up at the ferry building and unfolds it, the edges flitting in the breeze. The map shows one road running the fifty-kilometer length of the island, and stemming from it are veins of unsealed tracks and four-wheel-drive routes leading to secluded inlets and bays. Looking at the key, she sees there is a pub, two cafés, a doctor's office, a general store, and a community hall. Most of the symbols denote boat launches, surf spots, camping areas, and hiking trails.

She locates Shoal Bay in the southeast corner of the island. While she doesn't know Saul's address, with a population of only five hundred permanent residents, someone must know which house is his.

The crossing only takes twenty-five minutes, but by the time the ferry docks, Eva feels as if she's arriving at the edge of the world. The small throng of passengers return to their cars. Engines are started and cars nose forward as the boat ramp is lowered.

Just beyond the dock a hand-painted sign reads: PLEASE REMOVE WATCHES AND MOBILE PHONE BATTERIES. YOU'RE ON WATTLEBOON NOW!

The road is quiet—just the occasional motor home or truck passes in the other direction, surfboards and bikes strapped to roofs. She drives with the windows down, absorbing the smell of sun-warmed grass and the salt breeze drifting in. She sees two hikers standing before a shallow lagoon with binoculars hanging around their necks, a flock of black swans drifting beyond them.

When she gets to the general store, Eva pulls in. It's a simple building with a cork bulletin board tacked to an exterior wall, which is filled with handwritten signs about boat trailers for sale, holiday cottages to rent, and two kelpie pups that need a home.

The door is propped open by a faded ice-cream sign, and inside a stocky woman with a wedge of yellow hair plants her hands on the counter and smiles. "G'day. How's it goin'?"

"I was wondering if you could help. I'm looking for Saul Bowe's place on Shoal Bay."

"Well, that's easy," she says, smiling. "It's the only house in the bay. You keep on this road heading south for about five minutes. You'll pass a berry farm on your right and you wanna take the track straight after that. Leads you right down to the bay."

"That's great—"

"But he won't be there now. Saw him launching the boat 'bout couple of hours ago." The woman comes around from behind the counter and crosses to the open shop door, from which she peers out. "His truck's still there," she says, nodding toward a group of vehicles parked beside a long wooden jetty. "Might wanna wait for him there. Tide's just turned, so he'll be in soon." The woman glances sideways at Eva. "Known Saul long, have ya?"

Eva guesses that this is a store where gossip is traded along with the groceries. "I knew his brother."

"Brother?" the woman repeats, eyebrows lifting. "Well, I'll be damned. Never even knew Saul had one."

THE JETTY IS BUILT on thick wooden stilts, and a few fishing boats are moored to its side. She sits in the car for several minutes, but even with the windows down, it's too hot to stay in for long.

Climbing out, she crosses the parking lot onto a white sand beach that is peppered with dried shreds of seaweed. The afternoon is clear and still, the smell of fish hanging in the warm air. She slips off her flip-flops and wades into the water. It's deliciously cool around her ankles and she stays there, lolling in the shallows for some time.

Looking down at the sea around her feet, she tries not to think about the body washed up in Plymouth that is now lying in an autopsy lab waiting to be identified.

Now and then boats drift up to the jetty and people get out to unload their catch, but none of the men seem young enough to be Saul.

She remembers lying beside Jackson one morning, tracing the weave of his chest hair with a fingertip as she'd asked, "Tell me about your brother."

She'd caught the change in rhythm of Jackson's breathing as he'd answered, "Nothing to tell."

His eyes had darkened and he rolled away from her, climbing from the bed.

"Jackson?"

He'd paused, his posture rigid. When he spoke there was a grave edge to his tone. "You can't trust him. He's a liar. That's all you need to know."

There were other conversations about Saul, including one where she finally managed to get him to tell her why they'd not spoken a word in four years. But after a time, she stopped mentioning Saul's name, hating to see the way Jackson's face clouded with hurt.

Feeling light-headed from either the heat or the lingering residue of jet lag, Eva pads through the warm sand in search of shade. Her phone rings in her pocket and she slips it out, squinting at the screen in the sunlight. Seeing her mother's name, Eva freezes. She'll be calling with news of Jackson's body.

She stands there, blinking at the phone, heart racing. Eva's not sure that she wants this news, wants to live with the absolute finality of it.

Finally she answers, pressing the phone close to her ear. "Is it him?"

She hears her mother draw a breath. "Sorry, sweetheart. It wasn't Jackson. It's not his body."

She blinks.

Her mother says something about the results coming in last night and that she only just saw the light flashing on the answering machine when she woke.

Eva remains silent, trying to absorb what she's being told.

"I'm sorry. I shouldn't have said anything before we knew for sure. I just didn't want you hearing about it on the news, or something dreadful like that."

"Whose was it?"

"What?"

"The body. Whose was it?"

"Oh. Yes. It was a man from Worthing. A forty-five-year-old. Married. He jumped from a bridge six weeks ago."

Eva swallows. She wonders how his wife must feel right now. Would there be some sense of closure now that there was a body to bury? Perhaps that's how she herself might have felt. Or maybe what Dirk had said was right: Jackson's body is better left in the ocean.

"Eva? Are you still there?"

The sun beats down on her head and she feels exhausted, buffeted by her emotions. Her mouth is dry and she can't remember drinking anything today. She moistens her lips, tries to swallow.

"Sweetheart? Talk to me, please."

"I'm here," she says weakly, a feeling of nausea rising up through her stomach. She lifts her gaze to try and focus on something. A blue boat is drifting toward the jetty.

She stares at it unblinking. Then a strangled sound escapes her lips.

There is a man on board who looks so much like Jackson that, for a moment, Eva lets herself believe it is him.

"EVA? EVA?" HER MOTHER repeats with rising panic.

But Eva isn't listening. She is stepping forward, narrowing her gaze.

The way he stands, one hand slung in his pocket, his shoulders loose, is exactly like Jackson. Dark hair curls down over his ears and he wears a gray T-shirt with shorts, and sunglasses that hide his eyes.

Saul, she thinks. *It must be.*

There is a second man on the boat, bare-chested and wiry, who leaps onto the jetty and jogs along it toward the parked vehicles. He jumps into a truck and reverses the attached boat trailer down the ramp.

"Eva? Are you still there?" her mother is saying. "Please, Evie, you're scaring me."

"I've got to go. I'll call you later."

Once the boat is dragged from the water, Eva watches Saul push his sunglasses onto his head and shake hands with the other man. Then he hauls a large icebox from the boat and walks down the beach in her direction. He stops at the fish-gutting station and sets down the box. He can only be twenty feet from her.

She doesn't move; her legs feel weak and she tries to steady her breathing, which is coming too fast.

From the icebox he grabs two silver fish by their tails and lays them on the bench. He takes a knife from his pocket and slices through their pale bellies, then scoops out their guts with his fingers. He works through three more fish and a couple of squid. Eva is used to the sight of blood, yet the dispassionate movement of his hands through the guts makes her uncomfortable.

She goes to turn away, but as she does, Saul looks up.

Eva's lips part in surprise. His eyes are nothing like Jackson's. They are dark and intense, not the pale blue of Jackson's irises, which she'd always loved.

"You're Saul," she finds herself saying. She steps forward. "I'm Eva, Jackson's wife."

He stares, his dark gaze pinned to her face. She reads no warmth in his expression. Then he bends down and scoops another fish from the cool box, slaps it on the bench, and continues gutting.

"You've been fishing?" she asks ludicrously.

"Yeah."

"Catch much?"

"Enough."

She can feel herself sweating beneath her dress. She takes a deep breath. "I hoped we could talk."

"Oh, yeah?"

"About Jackson."

He glances at her through the corners of his eyes. Doesn't say anything.

"I've come a long way."

He sighs, putting down the knife. "Look, I don't wanna be rude, but Jackson and I hadn't spoken in a while."

"I know that," she says, failing to hide the anger in her voice. "I just wanted to meet you. You're his brother."

He looks directly at her, but doesn't speak.

"I thought you might want to hear about his life in England. Know what he's been doing since you last saw him."

"Then you thought wrong."

She shakes her head, astounded. The heat of the sun pounds down and her entire body feels too hot. She should leave now, return to the car, and blast out the a/c. But she's too angry to stop herself from saying, "He was your brother. And he's dead. Is this conversation all he's worth to you?"

She wants him to have to witness the horror of Jackson's drowning, make him stand on that wind-stormed shoreline as she had, watching the lifeboat turn empty circles in the water, see the helicopter slicing the freezing sky.

When Saul says nothing, tears begin to sting beneath her eyelids. She will not cry in front of this man, so she turns and begins striding away. Her heart is racing and she finds herself struggling to catch her breath. Clouds seem to gather at the corners of her vision and her legs feel unsteady.

She hears a voice and it is so like Jackson's that she wants to turn and see him on the beach calling to her. But the voice is so far away, and as she swivels to follow it, she finds her body is suddenly light and loose, but she isn't turning, she's fainting.

SAUL SITS WITH HIS hands spread over his bare knees. Smears of fish blood stain his fingers, and the undersides of his nails are dark with squid ink. He taps the heel of his boot against the linoleum floor as he waits.

The medical center is sterile and white, and he feels conspicuous in his outdoor gear. He is sure the smell of fish clings to him. He takes his sunglasses from his head, cleans the salt from the lenses with the corner of his T-shirt, and then holds them on his lap, worrying the arms open and shut.

There is a poster on the wall ahead about alcoholism with a picture of a liver made to look like a ticking bomb. He shifts in the plastic seat, angling himself to face the clock.

Eva's been in with the doctor for twenty-five minutes. He thinks about the fish he's left on the gutting station in the early-evening sun. Gulls would've had them by now. There's more in the icebox and he can't remember if he left the lid off. If he has, it won't be long till they're ruined. He hates to waste fish. He wishes the doctor would hurry the hell up.

He tries to hold onto his anger at the interruption to his day, but his thoughts keep getting back to Eva: the way she lifted her chin when she spoke to him, the clipped English accent, the flare of her nostrils before she strode away with her arms swinging at her sides. And then she had faltered. He saw her hand lifting as if searching for something to grab onto.

He had just stood there, watching as she fainted.

He feels bad about that. Bad for upsetting her. But what else could he say? He doesn't want her here. Doesn't want to be involved. Saul is barely holding himself together. Now she's here wearing her heartbreak on her sleeve and he doesn't know what to do with it.

The door opens and suddenly Eva is walking out. She looks so small, a fleck of a woman with her pixie-short hair and wide hazel eyes. She goes straight to the desk and pays.

He follows her outside. In her silence he asks, "So, what did the doc say?"

Immediately he regrets the casualness of the question.

Eva's face is pale and her arms hang loose at her sides. She looks shell-shocked.

Her voice is a whisper. "I'm pregnant."

7

She is ten weeks pregnant. Ten weeks a widow.

Her mind spins back through all the clues she had missed: the nausea she'd thought was a reaction to grief; the exhaustion she'd attributed to jet lag; the missed periods she hadn't even registered in the blur of her loss. She thinks of the evening before Jackson's death, when he'd turned to her in the narrow bed of her childhood room. He'd pressed his body against the curve of hers and they'd made love with a quiet intensity.

Eva feels the divots and juts of the road jarring through her spine as Saul drives her back to her car. Neither of them speaks. She grips the sides of the truck seat, careful not to put her hands anywhere near her stomach.

Saul cuts the engine.

She looks up, surprised to see they are back at the jetty already. The sun is sinking toward the sea, the heat fallen from the day.

"I'm a midwife," she says quietly. "I didn't even know I was pregnant and I'm a midwife."

Saul doesn't say anything.

Her hand moves to her forehead as she says, "I . . . I just can't believe it."

"It'll all work out," Saul says, and she hears the uncertainty in his voice.

They do not know each other, yet he is the only person apart from the doctor who knows she is pregnant.

After a moment, Saul asks, "Where are you staying?"

"I'll find a hotel."

"On Wattleboon? There aren't any."

"Then I'll go back to the mainland."

He glances at the clock on the dash and sighs. "Last boat ran quarter of an hour ago."

She's unable to think about this problem; the one inside her is absorbing all her thought.

He grabs his cell phone from the dash and climbs out of the truck, swinging the door shut. She watches through the windshield as he calls someone, pacing up and down as he speaks into the phone.

Eva doesn't move. She's remembering the night she and Jackson spent at a B&B in Wales. They'd been showering, steam curling from their wet bodies. Jackson had run the bar of soap over Eva's middle, telling her how much he wanted to have children with her. *Two,* he'd said. *Two girls.*

There is a strange, incredible irony that, as Jackson was being dragged down toward his death by freezing waves, a new life was being made inside her.

She muses on this idea until the truck door opens and Saul says, "You've got a place to stay. There's a shack down my way you can have tonight. The owner's outta town. We'll get your car in the morning."

"Right." She doesn't know if this is what she wants, but she doesn't have any other option.

She fetches her bag from the rental car while Saul strides down the beach to collect the icebox he'd left out.

The truck shifts as he clanks it in the back. Then he climbs in and guns the engine.

SAUL KNOCKS THE TRUCK into a lower gear as he turns onto the track leading to the bay. He sees Eva grab hold of the handhold as they bounce along, evening sun slanting through the thick branches of the gums. He's supposed to be up at Dune-back Point meeting a couple of friends for a barbecue. Saul was bringing the fish. He'll have to call them, tell them he's not going to make it.

"This is it," he says, yanking up the hand brake at the track's end. He climbs out and leads the way through a clearing in the trees onto the beach.

The shack is nestled into the sand, a stone's throw from the water. It's been here since he was a boy and he tries not to think about who used to live here. The current owner, Joe, did a bit of work on it a couple of years back after a big winter gale half buried the place in sand. Joe dug it out, replaced the windows, and made a deck at the front that's perfect for sinking a few beers on a summer's evening.

He climbs onto the deck and hooks the key out from under a cluster of pebbles. He unlocks the place and walks in, the smell of mildew and damp salt hitting him. He pulls up the blinds and cranks open both windows to let the breeze in. He hopes Eva isn't too prissy as the shack isn't in the sharpest condition. But when he glances around, he sees she's just standing on the deck, staring out to sea.

He pulls out some of the junk cluttering the living area: canvas chairs, a grill, a fraying windbreak, and puts it all on the deck to make some space. "It's basic," he tells her, "but there's a bed in the back room and the sofa folds into a bed, too. There's a shower—an outdoor one—but the water runs hot. I'm just gonna check the gas is on."

He goes around the back to the gas locker and is pleased to find it is all connected. He checks the shower, too, and finds a big huntsman spider sitting in the shower tray along with a collection of leaves and sand. "Sorry, mate," Saul says as he scoops up the spider and chucks it onto the beach.

Back in the shack, he runs the tap and the water tank seems to be working just fine. He offers to bring some food from his place, but Eva says she'll be okay, and he gets the impression that she just wants to be on her own.

"I'll come back in the morning. Run you to your car."

"Thanks."

"If you need anything, my place is just up there," he says, pointing to the other end of the bay.

He says good-bye and climbs down from the deck, relieved to be on his way. Then he remembers he hasn't checked whether there was any bedding. When he turns back, he sees Eva has already sunk down onto the sofa, her head cradled in her hands.

When Dirk had told Saul what he knew on the bleak afternoon of Jackson's memorial, Saul had slumped back in his seat, stunned. He'd said right then that he didn't want anything to do with it, didn't even want to meet Eva.

Yet here she is.

He sees her shoulders begin to shake as the tears come. He takes a step toward the shack, then hesitates. Something tells him it's cleaner not to get involved. So Saul ducks his head and walks on.

LATER THAT EVENING EVA manages to fall asleep, but she wakes hours later gasping into the pitch-black. Disorientated, she struggles free of the covers, her skin damp with sweat. She flails for a light switch, but her wrist bone connects with something hard and the crash of broken glass fills her ears.

Finally she finds the light. A glass has smashed, water pooling over wooden floorboards. She can't place the room she's in. Her gaze darts around, then halts on a large driftwood mirror at the end of the bed. The image reflected back is of a woman with ghostly white skin, her eyes sunken in shadow, her face gaunt.

Then Eva remembers: she's in Tasmania.

Jackson is dead.

She is carrying his child.

She leans against the bedroom door, feeling the coolness of the wood through her T-shirt. Her head bows into her hands and she closes her eyes, battling against tears.

The quiet in the shack rolls over her, only the low murmuring of the bay audible. Somehow the near silence feels wrong, smothering. Her jaw tightens as she strains to catch some sound. Anything.

Panic spikes over her skin as she realizes what it is she's listening for: Jackson's breathing.

She is expecting to hear the soft draw of air in and out of his lungs, which was the rhythm she fell asleep to every night. The absence of it fills her with a crushing loneliness. She wraps her arms tightly around herself, feeling the rapid thud of her own heartbeat. But there's no comfort in it, so she crosses the room and digs in her suitcase, pulling out a red-checked shirt.

It was Jackson's favorite, the one he'd change into when he got home from work, pushing the sleeves up and leaving the collar wide open. It was a shirt so loved that he didn't mind that it was missing two buttons or that the collar was starting to fray.

She pulls it on now, her fingers drawing the fabric tight to her body, and picks up her phone.

She is contemplating calling her mother. She'd like to hear her familiar voice right now; it'd be midmorning in England and her mother would be home, perhaps ironing with the radio on, or putting something in the slow cooker for dinner. But then Eva pictures herself saying, *I'm pregnant*—and realizes she's not ready to make that call. Not yet.

She fetches a blanket and walks out onto the deck. The air is cool, scented with salt and a faint tang of wood. There are no lights other than the stars, and the darkness is unsettling. Looking toward the edge of the bay where Saul's house stands, she feels a thread of unease snake through her. He is the only one who knows she is here, a man Jackson told her he couldn't trust. She wishes she hadn't left her car at the jetty; she would feel safer knowing that she could leave.

She settles into a canvas chair on the deck, the seat damp with dew. The sound of her cell phone suddenly ringing makes her jump, the screen flashing like a siren in the darkness.

Pressing the phone to her ear, she answers. "Hello?"

There is the sound of a connection at the other end, a distant line. But no voice.

"Hello? Eva speaking."

She waits, hearing only the bay murmuring beyond her.

"Hello?" she repeats. "Sorry, I can't hear anything. Hello?"

Silence.

Then there is a faint noise and she is almost certain that it's the sound of someone drawing a breath.

A moment later, the line goes dead.

Eva stares at the phone in her hand. The display shows that it was an international call, but there's no number. She waits, hoping the caller will ring back. She is desperate to hear a familiar voice from home, someone to remind her that she's not alone.

But the caller doesn't phone again. Eva draws her knees to her chest, and pulls the long sleeves of Jackson's checked shirt down over her hands. She buries her face into the open collar and breathes in deeply, trying to draw his scent from the fabric.

But there is nothing.

HAZY MORNING SUNLIGHT TEASES Eva awake and she opens her eyes to the shimmer of the bay. Her clothes feel damp and her neck aches. She rolls her head from side to side to loosen the muscles in her shoulders. The blanket has slipped to the ground and she sees her hands are resting on her abdomen.

She removes them in a flash and holds onto the sides of the chair. She sits like this for a moment, looking as if she is bracing herself.

Then very slowly she draws her hands back to her stomach, sliding them beneath her shirt. Her fingertips move in a slow circle across the warm skin of her lower belly. It is faint, but it is there: the swell of a baby.

Jackson's baby.

She realizes that a part of Jackson is still here, still living. He has left a piece of himself behind for Eva to nurture. She feels a surge of love for him that enfolds her like an embrace. The corners of her lips lift into a quiet smile as she imagines Jackson watching her as she sits here looking out over the bay, their baby growing in her stomach.

She stays on the deck with her hands on her stomach for some time, letting her thoughts settle around the idea of their child. Eventually she goes into the shack, changes into a pair of shorts and a cardigan, and packs up her bag. She makes a cup of instant coffee and sits on the edge of the deck to drink it, wondering when Saul will come for her. Looking toward the far end of the bay, she can just make out his house. Tall trees clamber up a rocky hill and at the top there is the slant of a roof.

Her gaze sweeps away over the bay, which is glistening beneath a rising sun. There's an outcrop of dark rocks at the edge of the water, and beyond them the contours of Tasmania are mauve shadows in the distance.

At the edge of her vision she notices someone down by the shore. She shades a hand in front of her eyes and sees Saul at the water's edge, slipping on a pair of fins. He moves into the shallows and seems to melt into the water, kicking with powerful strokes.

She watches him swim until he's right out in the middle of the bay. There he stops and floats on the surface, arms outstretched at his sides.

After a minute or two he makes a smooth dive and the sea settles around him as if he had never been there.

Eva waits.

Time passes slowly.

She knows he will come back up, yet she feels her heart quicken.

Twenty seconds, now. Thirty, perhaps?

She becomes aware of her pulse ticking in her throat and the cold Atlantic sea dripping into her thoughts. The flash of an orange lifeboat. The roar of a helicopter in the sky.

Her mouth turns dry as she waits, her gaze pinned to the point at which he dived down. He has to come up. She knows he must. Yet her heart is drilling against the cage of her ribs.

Without thinking, she is suddenly jumping from the deck and jogging toward the water. With each step, she is back on that Dorset beach in December, gusts of sand sheeting along the beach, the wild, gray seascape empty of Jackson.

Eva stops at the shoreline, panting. The sun glances off the water, making her squint as she scans the bay for Saul. But it is mirror flat; there is not a ripple.

Sweat prickles underarm. Could she swim out far enough to reach him? Would it be better to call for help? Would anyone even hear?

More images flood through her mind: a policeman speaking into a radio; a crowd of people huddled together, waiting; a lifeboat making a search pattern in the raging sea.

Then suddenly there's movement out in the middle of the bay. Saul breaks through the surface. She imagines the water pouring from his face as he gasps for air.

She steps back, the tension in her muscles sending tremors through her body and making her knees shake. She waits for the tide of relief to fill her, but it never comes. Because all Eva is thinking is: *It's not Jackson.*

WHEN SAUL WADES IN, he finds Eva standing on the shore, her expression taut. He puts down his mask and fins and wipes the salt water from his face. "Everything okay?"

She nods quickly. She takes a breath, then asks, "Good dive?"

"Like glass out there."

She glances over the length of the bay. "It's quiet here."

"Yeah, every so often you get the odd fishing boat or kayaker passing. That's about it."

Silence follows. A gull soars above, white wings struck with sunlight. They both watch as it glides beyond them, dipping low to the water.

Saul shifts on the spot. "The shack all right for you?"

"Yes. Very comfortable," she answers banally.

"Good."

"Thanks for organizing it."

"No problem."

Small talk sets like a cast around the delicate bones of what they're both afraid to talk about: Jackson.

"I can run you to your car in a bit?"

She nods. "Thank you."

"Where'll you go next?"

"Hobart, I suppose. Maybe I'll try and get in touch with some of Jackson's old friends. I'll figure it out," she says with a brave smile that doesn't quite reach her eyes.

Saul thinks about her drifting around Hobart, asking questions about Jackson—and he knows that's not a good idea. All the tension that his dive had eased now begins to creep back into his body, tightening in his temples and the base of his jaw.

He looks toward the shack, turning an idea through his head. Out here on Wattleboon barely anyone will remember Jackson, as he hasn't been on the island since he was fifteen. But in Hobart there are people who know.

After a moment Saul says, "The shack's free for a while. You're welcome to stay on, if you want?"

You asked me once why Saul and I fell out, so I told you.

But it was only half of the truth.

I was shaving at the time, and carefully smoothed foam over my jaw as I contemplated my answer. I needed to get it right.

"It was my birthday," I began, feeling my heart start to pound. "I had a barbecue down on the bluff near where I was living. I didn't organize many things like that, but I wanted to that year because there was . . . this girl. Someone I thought was special. I wanted to introduce her to my friends."

I drew the razor over my cheek, pulling my lips to the side to keep the skin taut as I told you, "Saul turned up late—and drunk—but I was just pleased he'd come. I slung an arm over his shoulder and walked him to the barbecue, where my girlfriend stood. Before he'd even said a word, I knew he was gonna make a play for her. I could see just by the way he was looking at her."

"Did he?" you asked carefully, watching my reflection in the mirror.

I laughed, a dark sound. "Couldn't help himself. He always had to get the girl. I saw him with her later that night. Right in front of me—like he didn't even care. Like he wanted me to see."

"I'm sorry."

I shrugged, tried to brighten my voice. "Maybe it worked out for the best. Saul kept on seeing her, so I ended up getting out of Tas for a few months."

"That's when you went to South America?"

"Yeah. Traveled up through Chile and Peru, then across to Brazil. I surfed, hiked, got some work building trail paths, bought a motorbike in Brazil. It was a good time—a good thing for me to do."

"What about when you came back?"

"She and Saul were livin' together up north. I stayed down south. We didn't see each other."

"They're still together?"

"No. Not now."

"And you can't forgive him?"

I put the razor down and clenched the edge of the sink, lowered my head. "He's a liar. I can't trust him."

You crossed the bathroom and placed the flat of your hand in the space between my shoulder blades and ran it in smooth strokes. It was like you were reaching inside me, soothing somewhere that I didn't know still hurt.

I looked up and our gazes locked in the mirror. "Do you think people can change, Eva? Do you think it's possible?"

I think the intensity of my voice startled you because you dropped your hand and said, "Yes. People can change."

But here's the thing that terrified me: What if they can't?

8

Eva drifts through the shack as her mother continues talking. She catches the words *scan, due date, trimester*—words she associates with work, not her own pregnancy.

She pauses by a photo of her and Jackson she'd brought with her from England. It was taken last summer at a 1920s-themed jazz festival in London. In the picture Eva is wearing a drop-waisted flapper-girl dress and a beaded headband, and Jackson has one hand around her waist, and with his other he's touching the brow of his black hat, laughing. There's sun flare behind them and they both look tanned and happy, in love.

Tucking the phone under her ear, Eva takes down the picture. It's housed in a thin glass frame, and she uses the hem of her dress to clean her fingerprints from it. She moves the fabric in slow circles until the glass is polished clear, and then she sets it back on the shelf.

"So you'll be coming home?" her mother is saying.

"Home?" Eva repeats, tuning back in. "No. Not yet."

"What?" The pitch of her mother's voice rises.

"It hasn't changed my plans out here."

"What about your scan?"

"They do have hospitals in Australia," she says, rolling her eyes. "Anyway, Callie will be out here in a few days."

Eva doesn't need her mother to worry about all the details; she just needs to hear someone tell her, *This is fantastic news! You're going to be a wonderful mother, Eva.*

"You'll worry me to death traveling around out there on your own, pregnant." Her mother's emotional fragility has always meant any problem instantly becomes hers. The pregnancy would become about *her* anxieties, *her* involvement, *her* fears. "What about if you have your old room back and I make the spare into a nursery—"

"Mum," she cuts in firmly as she pushes away from the wall and steps out onto the deck. The beach is empty and sunlight shimmers tantalizingly over the bay. She's been on Wattleboon for three days now and already feels a strangely intimate tie to this island, knowing that Jackson spent his summers here as a boy. He would've played on many of these beaches, surfed and dived in the waves, fished from the jetty and from his father's boat. And now, all these years later, Eva and the baby she carries inside her are also here—walking the same shorelines, seeing the same vistas. It's as if she can feel Jackson's footprints still warm under the sand.

She tells her mother, "Right now this is where I want to be."

THAT EVENING, EVA GRABS the bottle of wine she'd bought earlier and sets out along the shore toward Saul's house. He hasn't visited her at the shack and has only cast a cursory wave in her direction when he's been going out diving in the bay. It feels as if he's purposely keeping his distance.

The smell of seaweed is ripe in the air and crabs scuttle between the tide line and their holes as she passes. At the end of the bay, stone steps cut into a rocky, tree-lined hill. She follows them up into Saul's garden. Set back in the gum trees is a modest wooden house built on stilts. A wide deck runs along the front and the whole place blends so seamlessly into the surroundings that it could almost pass as a tree house.

She finds Saul gutting fish on an old wooden workbench, beside which is a faded blue kayak. He has his back to her and is wearing a dark T-shirt with canvas shorts, his feet bare. She watches him for a moment, her gaze lingering on the broadness of his neck— the shape so like Jackson's. Her fingertips twitch as she imagines touching the soft dark hairs at the nape of her husband's neck, then running them beneath the starched cotton of his shirt collar, where the smell of aftershave always lingered on his skin.

Without realizing, Eva sighs and suddenly Saul's head snaps up. His hair is mussed around his face, the dark brown sun-lightened in streaks. "Eva."

"Hi," she says, uncertainly. "I . . . I brought this." Saul stares at her, then at the bottle of wine in her hands.

"It's for you. To say thanks—for the shack."

"You didn't need to," he says almost tersely.

Realizing he can't take the wine because his hands are bloodied from gutting, she draws it awkwardly to her side.

"Dinner?" she casts into his silence, nodding toward the fish.

"Yeah." There's a pause, then, "Did you wanna . . . ?"

She hadn't meant the question as a self-invite and feels her cheeks reddening. Yet at the same time she realizes that she would like to stay—to have a chance to talk. Eventually she says, "That'd be great."

Three lime-green birds burst from a tree behind them. Eva turns, watching their brilliant wings beat at the sky.

"Swift parrots," he says, following her gaze. "Arrive every

spring. Come over the Bass Strait from the mainland. I think they're nesting in one of the tree hollows behind the house."

The birds make a high-pitched piping noise as they disappear into the canopy of another tree at the far side of the garden.

Eva takes in the rest of the surroundings. "Lovely place you've got out here. This is where you used to come as kids?"

He nods.

"Where's the shack?"

"Used to be right where the house is now."

"Oh." She remembers Jackson pulling her onto his lap and telling her, "Owning a shack is a Tassie thing. They're bolt-holes, a place to disappear to when you're craving some space, some wilderness." He'd spoken of his plan to one day do up their old shack for his father. "Dad loved that place once. Maybe he could love it again." Eva had noticed the sadness clouding Jackson's expression as he'd said that, and realized how deeply he missed his father. She'd threaded her arms around his neck and kissed him on the mouth. "What was that for?" Jackson had asked.

"Just for being you."

Saul says, "I'm gonna run these guts down to the water. Go in and grab a drink."

Inside, the house smells new, like freshly sawn wood. The living-cum-dining room has sliding glass doors that lead out onto the deck. In the corner of the room there's a wood-burning stove and two baskets of kindling and logs. The place is furnished simply with a wide brown sofa, a low coffee table in a grainy wood, and a large bookcase lit by two old fishing lamps.

Photos hang from the walls in glass frames: an underwater shot of sunlight streaming through the sea's surface; sand dunes so vast and perfect they look like a mountain range under fresh snow; a photo of Jackson wearing a heavy backpack as he stands in front of Machu Picchu.

Saul has a good collection of marine books—*The Australian Fisherman, A Biography of Cod, Sea Fishing, A Reflection on Freediving, The Sea Around Us, Knots and Rigs, Shipwrecks of Tasmania*—but also a wide range of fiction spanning the classics to modern literature.

Then she sees a name on a book spine that catches her attention: *Lynn Bowe*. Saul and Jackson's mother.

She sets down the wine bottle and carefully slides the book free.

Jackson had told her that their mother had been a writer. Apparently she loved coming to Wattleboon because the space helped her think. When the boys were little she'd take them up to a clearing on one of the capes and they'd spend the afternoons reading or drawing while she wrote.

On the inside sleeve there is a black-and-white photo of a graceful woman with long hair swept into a simple chignon. She has the same dark eyes as Saul, large and serious.

Turning the page, Eva reads the dedication: *For Dirk. Always.*

She tries to place the man she visited with his thinning socks and whiskey breath as the beau of this beautiful young woman. She knew from Jackson how devastated Dirk had been by Lynn's death. She was the head of their family, the sun around which the men orbited.

"My mother," Saul says.

Eva turns, startled.

Saul stands in the doorway, his dark gaze pinned on her. She feels heat rising in her cheeks. "She was very beautiful."

"Yes," Saul agrees. "She was."

She wants to say something more, but then Saul turns and moves into the kitchen.

HE WASHES HIS HANDS and dries them on a tea towel, then begins roughly chopping red chilies, garlic, and a bunch of coriander.

Eva leans against the kitchen counter and offers to help, twice, and the second time Saul tells her she can make a salad just to give her something to do.

He begins stuffing the fish with the chopped herbs and spices, finding it odd having a woman in his house after so long.

Eva asks, "Did you catch those today?"

"Yeah. Aussie salmon. I got out with the spear gun after work. I was lucky—they were just schooling right out front." He lays each fish on a large square of tinfoil, thinking of the shoal that had curled above him, their silver tails catching in the sunlight. He'd hovered there, just watching. Some days he didn't even pull the trigger, he just liked seeing the way they moved through the water, scales glinting.

"Do you prefer it to line fishing?" she asks, drawing the knife through the tight red skin of a tomato.

"Feels like a fairer fight," he tells her. "You only spear what you can eat, plus there's no bait involved. If you come back with nothing, well, just means the fish were havin' a better day than you."

"You were diving without a spear gun that first morning I was here."

He nods. "Sometimes I just go out for a free-dive. You know, breath-hold diving—no scuba gear."

"I've seen a TV show about that. Isn't it where people are diving down to crazy depths?"

"Some people are. The record for free-diving—and this is without weights or sleds, just literally swimming straight down and then back up on one breath—is one hundred and twenty-one meters."

"No? They must have incredible lungs. Do you measure how deep you go?"

He drizzles chili oil over the fish and squeezes a couple of wedges of lime on top. A nick on his forefinger stings as the lime seeps into it. "No, I'm not interested in that side of it. I suppose I like it because there's no tank involved or gear to mess around with. Plus, you see more. Fish can be put off by the bubbles when you're breathing off the tank."

Eva scoops the tomatoes she's sliced into the salad bowl, then begins chopping the lettuce. "What do you see around here?"

"Wattleboon's cold-water diving, so it's different from the tropics. You get rays, tiny handfish, gummy sharks, sea dragons."

"Sea dragons?"

"They're related to the sea horse family, but the dragons are bigger." Saul rinses and dries his hands, then pulls a sourdough loaf from the bread bin and saws hunks from it. "Wattleboon is one of the few places in the world where you find them. It's a good place to free-dive."

"Jackson said he loved coming out here as a boy."

There he is. Jackson. Cutting straight back into the center of Saul's thoughts like a cool knife.

Saul had been at his father's house when the news from the police came through. Dirk was watching the television, beer in hand, as he reached for the phone. Saul had felt a shift in the air, as if all the windows had suddenly been closed. He turned and saw his father sitting up rigidly. Dirk's mouth opened, but he didn't say a word. He simply held out the phone to Saul, who took it and listened to the distant English voice of a police officer talking about fishing, a wave, an accident. Saul asked where it'd happened, who'd been there, whether a body had been found.

Afterward he realized that he'd asked more questions in those few minutes than he'd asked about his brother's life in years.

"Saul?" Eva is saying.

He is standing stock-still, the bread knife in his hand.

"I'm gonna light the barbecue," he says quickly. He swaps the knife for the tray of fish, then strides from the room with his eyes lowered.

THEY EAT ON THE deck, watching the dusky pink clouds feather away into night. Saul says very little and Eva picks at the fish, a faint feeling of nausea hovering nearby.

When she's eaten as much as she can manage, she sets down her knife and fork, then slides her sweater off the back of her chair and pulls it on.

"We can go inside," Saul says.

"No, it's nice out." She looks up at the emerging stars; there are no clouds tonight and she thinks in another half hour the night sky will be dazzling. Citronella candles burn at either end of the table, and the air swirls with a lemon scent.

In the quiet she hears the stirring of the bay and the chirp of crickets in the bush. "When I met your dad," she says, glancing across at Saul, "he mentioned he doesn't come out to Wattleboon anymore."

He nods slowly.

"Is that . . . because of your mother?"

Saul leans his elbows on the table and looks out toward the bay. "Her ashes were scattered up at the cape. I think he's always felt guilty about not going there since."

"I wish I had Jackson's ashes," Eva says, the admission surprising her.

Saul turns to look at her.

"It's just . . ." she says, "maybe it would help." She draws a candle toward her and runs a fingertip around the warm, supple wax close to the wick. "A few weeks after Jackson drowned, I walked down to the beach where it happened. It was freezing. There was frost on the sand, but the sun was out and the water seemed peaceful. I remember just standing there, staring at the sea, thinking how impossibly serene it was—yet only weeks before . . ." She pauses, swallowing hard. "One minute I was standing on the shore, and the next I found myself wading in."

She feels Saul's gaze move over her face as she continues.

"I know it must sound crazy, but I needed to be in the sea to feel what Jackson would've felt." She'd wanted to feel the water soaking his clothes, the cold turning his muscles to lead, the waves pulling him under.

"You needed it to feel real."

She nods, pressing her fingernail into the candle. "It's hard—there not being a body." She digs out a warm lump of wax that she rolls between her thumb and forefinger until it hardens. "But it's good to be out here, seeing where Jackson grew up. There are so many things I never asked him—so much I want to find out."

Two years. That's all she'd shared of Jackson's thirty years of life. A fragment. Her hand travels to her stomach and she realizes the need to build a connection with his past is even stronger now.

Inside, a phone rings. Saul looks relieved by the distraction and leaves the deck. She hears him answer, saying, "Dad?"

Eva leans back in her chair looking up at the stars, wishing Jackson was with her, wishing she could share the news of their baby with him. Over the past few weeks she's learned a lot about loneliness. It isn't just about remote places or a lack of contact with people—it's a sensation that something has been carved out of you.

When Saul doesn't return, she begins clearing the plates from the table, scraping the fish bones back into the foil and then stacking the plates. She carries them into the house—but pauses when she catches her name.

Saul is talking in another room and Eva hovers, listening. "She came out here like you said . . . Yeah, Thursday."

Saul exhales hard. Then there's the sound of footsteps pacing back and forth. "No. Course I didn't!"

Eva holds her breath, straining to hear.

The footsteps stop. "Just that one time . . . No, haven't heard from her since."

When she hears him finishing up the call, she backs out of the house onto the deck, and returns the plates to the table, pulse racing.

Saul comes outside with his hands dug into his pockets. He shifts his weight as he says, "I've got a bit of work I need to get done for tomorrow."

"Then I suppose I should be going," she says curtly.

"I'll see you down the steps."

Before she can tell him that she's fine on her own, he's taking a slim flashlight from his pocket and leading the way. He shines the light behind him so that she can place her feet in the beam. "Careful," he says. "Some of the steps are a bit loose."

They descend in silence, the air growing cooler. When they reach the beach Saul stops to face her. Away from the candlelight, the darkness suddenly feels consuming. She thinks of the strange lie Saul just told his father and a prickle of uncertainty travels over her skin.

Jackson's voice echoes in her head: *You can't trust him. He's a liar.*

She feels a surge of hurt and confusion over the oddly abrupt ending to the evening. Her teeth clench around the words she wants to say. Yet something pulls her back.

Saul is her—and her child's—only link to Jackson. She feels the fragility of that connection as if it runs between them like a single fine thread. She needs to hold onto it tightly so it doesn't slide out of her grasp.

BACK IN THE SHACK, Eva shuts the door firmly and switches on all the lights. She tugs at the cord of the blinds, disturbing a moth that flies straight toward her, its dusty wings brushing at her cheek.

Eva shivers, turning a circle in the room. *Alone. I am alone.* She tries to keep her breathing level and push away the hollowing sensation of loneliness.

She sucks in a deep breath and crosses the room to the photo of her and Jackson at the jazz festival. She angles it toward the light, longing to be back there with the sun on her skin, hearing the rhythm of the music, feeling Jackson's arm around her waist.

In the light she can see two marks on the glass either side of the photo. They look to be thumbprints, as if someone has just plucked the photo from the shelf to look at. Her brow furrows as she remembers polishing the frame this morning, removing every trace of dirt and grease. *How can there be thumbprints?*

Perhaps she'd made them just now as she'd picked up the picture. Holding the frame, she places her thumbs in the exact spaces where the marks are.

Yet the prints don't fit; hers are almost half the size.

She brings the frame even closer to the light so that she can be sure. She is almost certain that these are not her thumbprints.

She sets down the photo with a sharp shake of her head. She's being absurd; they must be hers. No one else has been in the shack.

9

A week later, Eva is leaning back against the sun-warmed hood of her car, watching the Wattleboon Island Ferry plow toward the shore. Callie is on board. She's flown in from the UK to spend a few nights here before they travel on to Melbourne together.

As Eva waits, she twists her wedding band between her thumb and forefinger. Then she slips it off and angles it toward the sun to read the italicized inscription.

This day and always.

Today should have been their first wedding anniversary. How short *always* turned out to be. She presses the ring to her lips, feeling the smooth warmth of the metal.

Months ago, Jackson had arranged for them to spend their anniversary in the Tower Lighthouse in Dorset. They'd first stayed there on their wedding night, laughing as they'd climbed the spiral staircase up to the glass lantern room, the train of her dress making a low swoosh behind her. They'd drunk champagne and watched stars glinting through the skylights.

But tonight the starlit room at the top of the lighthouse will be empty.

Engines churn as the ferry draws into the dock, the thick smell of diesel swirling in the air. A loud wolf whistle makes Eva look up. Callie stands on the deck in a pair of dark glasses, waving with both hands.

Eva slips her wedding ring back on. Then she takes a deep breath, snaps her heels together, and salutes.

She sees Callie's head tilt back as she laughs.

When the passengers disembark, Eva rushes forward, throwing her arms around her friend.

"It's so wonderful to see you," Callie says, keeping hold of Eva's hands as they step apart.

"I can't believe you're actually here!" Eva says. "How was the flight? You must be shattered."

"I'm fine. Absolutely fine. How are you? I want to hear everything! How's Tasmania?"

Just seeing Callie here—someone so known to her, so constant, so familiar—undoes something in Eva that she's been battling to keep locked away. Without warning, her smile begins to falter as tears fill her eyes.

Callie reaches a hand to Eva's arm. "Darling, what is it?"

"Nothing," she says, blotting at her face with a sleeve. "Sorry! I'm just happy to see you."

"Tears of joy?" Callie pushes her sunglasses onto the top of her head and peers at her.

Eva had planned to tell Callie about the baby after they'd had a chance to catch up. But now Callie is fixing her with her pale stare and Eva knows she's going to have to say it right here as the cars from the ferry crawl past.

She clears her throat, shifting on the spot.

"Oh my God!" Callie's hands fly to her mouth. "You're pregnant, aren't you?"

———————

THEY DON'T RETURN TO the shack right away. Callie insists on a detour. "I think it's this one," she says, pointing to the turnoff.

"Are you going to tell me where I'm actually driving us to?" Eva asks, swinging the rental car onto the unpaved track. A cloud of dust trails behind them as they fly along, sending gravel spraying.

"Nope. It's a surprise. All will be revealed when we get there."

"You've only been here an hour and you're already bossing me around." Eva puts the car into a lower gear as the road ascends, cutting through a forest of gum trees. "How do you even know where this way leads?"

"Research. You know I don't rest. Information is my sleep."

Eva slows the car a little, nodding to Callie's right. "Wallaby."

Poised at the roadside, the wallaby watches them through large brown eyes. Then, in a flash, it springs across the track and disappears into the bush, its heavy tail thumping the ground. Callie smiles. "God, it feels a million miles from life in London."

They drive south for another five or six kilometers before the trees begin to thin. "First glimpse of the sea," Eva says, looking west over wild, scrub-lined hills that roll away into the silver shimmer of the sea below. "I haven't been this far out yet."

Callie says, "We must be almost there." Then she twists in her seat to look at Eva more fully. "I still can't believe it," she says. "You have a person in your stomach. A *person,* Eva. Living in your stomach."

Callie can't have children. She was diagnosed with endometriosis at seventeen, and even following treatment, the gynecologist gave her very low odds of ever becoming pregnant. Callie's always claimed she didn't want children anyway, and Eva understands why she needs to believe this.

But Callie had always been the one, out of all of Eva's friends, who was most interested in her work as a midwife. She asked questions about everything, wanting to know what had happened to the woman who had premature twins, or the pregnant girl who was refusing cancer treatment, or the IVF lady who'd miscarried four times. She loved hearing other people's stories and Eva quietly hoped that one day Callie would have a story of her own to tell.

"Do you feel different?" Callie asks. "You must. Have you had morning sickness? Or weird cravings?"

"No cravings. Just morning sickness that comes in the evenings."

"Do you mind if I feel it?" Callie asks.

"Sure, but there's not much to feel yet."

Callie reaches across and places a hand on Eva's stomach.

Eva keeps her eyes on the track ahead, a sudden surge of emotion rising in her throat.

"Have you felt any kicking?"

She swallows. "Still a bit early."

"It's incredible, isn't it?" Callie says, her voice filled with wonderment.

Eva presses her lips together, nodding. But as she drives, tears begin rolling slowly down her cheeks.

"Eva?"

"I'm sorry." She takes one hand off the wheel and wipes her face. "I just . . . I want him here so much, Cal. He should be here for this."

"I know, darling. I know. Here, let's pull over."

Eva pulls into the side of the track as more tears spill down her face. She presses the heels of her hands against her eyes. "I can't do this without him."

"You can! I know you can."

Sobs roll through her body as she thinks about all that Jackson will miss: being there for the birth; watching the baby's first steps; tiptoeing through the house to leave out a Christmas

stocking; taking him or her to school on their first day. There
will be a thousand important moments and Jackson won't be
there—not for any of them.

"You're not alone, Eva. I'm going to be right there with you,
every step. Okay? And I know it's Jackson that you really want,
and that what happened to him is awful and unfair and such a
terrible, terrible waste—but he's not gone, Eva. Not really. He's
still with you, watching over you." She pauses. "And you know
the best thing of all?"

Eva blinks, looking at her.

Callie places her hands over Eva's stomach. "Jackson's left
you this. It's a gift."

Eva feels the warmth of Callie's hands resting over the tiny
life growing inside her, and she thinks, *Yes, this is a gift.*

She wipes her face with her sleeve, then sits up straighter,
composing herself. She reaches for the key in the ignition, but
Callie says, "Actually, we're already here."

Eva follows the direction Callie is pointing in.

Her breath catches: ahead of them is a brilliant white lighthouse rising proudly out of the cliff top, its western side glowing
a warm gold in the late-afternoon sun.

Callie says, "I know this isn't the Tower Lighthouse and I'm
not a six-foot-two Tasmanian, but I've got a bottle of champagne
in my suitcase. So how about a—*tiny*—drink with me beneath
the lighthouse?"

Eva puts a hand to her mouth. She shakes her head as she
looks at Callie. "You remembered."

"Happy anniversary, darling."

THEY RETURN TO THE shack feeling windblown and tired.
Callie points toward the rocks at the edge of the bay. "Is that him?"

Eva follows her gaze to where Saul stands in the shallows. They haven't spoken since the dinner at his house and she recalls the uncertain feeling that crept over her skin as they stood together on the beach afterward. "Yes. That's Saul."

"The estranged brother," Callie says, wiggling her eyebrows. "What's he like? He's younger, isn't he?"

"Yes, by two and a half years."

"Does he know he's going to be an uncle?"

"Yes, but I don't think he'll be throwing me a baby shower."

"Oh?"

Eva tells her about Saul's oddly reticent manner as they leave the deck and wander along the beach to meet him. "I can't figure him out, Cal. He offered up the shack so I could stay—yet at the same time it's like he doesn't want me here. He never comes by to see me or to ask how I'm feeling about the baby. He's not even interested in Jackson's life in London."

"Do you think it's because of their falling-out?"

Eva lifts her shoulders. "Maybe he feels guilty. Saul never apologized—and now it's too late to put it right."

A few minutes later they reach Saul, who is standing ankle-deep in the shallows, chipping at the rocks with what looks like a palette knife. Seeing Eva and Callie, he stops what he's doing and wades onto the shore.

"All right?" Saul nods at Callie when Eva introduces her. "I'd shake your hand, but . . ." He lifts his damp hands, which are flecked with shards of shell and grime.

"What are you collecting?" Eva asks.

"Oysters."

"To eat?"

He nods, then pulls one from the net bag hooked over his forearm. "Want one?"

Eva looks at Callie, then says, "Sure."

Saul takes a penknife from the pocket of his shorts, releases the blade, and pushes the tip of the knife into the hinge of the shell. Then he twists it to pry the shell open. When the lid comes off, he holds it in his palm and runs the knife under the muscular part to loosen the glistening flesh.

"Isn't there some rule about shellfish and pregnancy?" Callie says to Eva.

"These couldn't be any fresher," Eva says, "so it's perfectly safe."

"Just because you're a midwife, I don't want you cutting corners and being all cavalier."

Eva smiles. She takes the oyster from Saul and tips it back, swallowing it whole. The flavor is light, crisply cool, with a touch of the sea.

Saul pulls out another from the bag and works the knife into it, then hands it to Callie. "So you've just arrived?"

"Yes, a few hours ago," she says, accepting the oyster. "I'm here for four nights, and then we're heading on to Melbourne."

"Callie's going to be working on a show out there," Eva explains.

"A bloody awful show," Callie adds. "We've got a celebrity chef visiting people's homes and seeing what he can do with the ingredients in their cupboards—then eating dinner with the family."

"Melbourne's a good city," Saul says to them both. "Maybe you'll enjoy it."

"Do you know it well?" Callie asks.

"I studied there."

"Oh, like Jackson," Eva says. "I didn't realize you both went to the same university. Did you overlap?"

Saul's brow creases. "Jackson didn't study in Melbourne."

"Excuse me?"

"He lived there awhile," Saul tells her, wiping his hands on the back pockets of his shorts, "but he was working."

A slow heat creeps up her neck and into the base of her cheeks. Has she gotten this wrong? She's certain it was Melbourne. She hates to think that any details of his life are slipping away from her—or that Saul might question how well she really knew him. She turns the empty oyster shell through her fingers, asking as casually as she can, "Where did he get his degree, then?"

A quizzical expression settles over Saul's face. "He didn't. Jackson never went to college."

"Of course he did. He has a marine biology degree." It's one of the first things they'd talked about when they met on the plane. She's no idea why Saul would think otherwise.

She watches the slow shake of Saul's head. "No. He worked in Melbourne for a couple of years, but he never got a degree there—or anywhere."

Eva turns to Callie, wanting her to make sense of this absurd conversation. But Callie is looking at Saul carefully, as if she's contemplating what he's saying.

The heat is now full in her cheeks. How would Saul even know what Jackson was doing? He was happy to cut Jackson out of his life years ago—so what kind of relationship must they've had before that? Her fingers clasp tight around the oyster shell, the jagged edges cutting into her palm. All she knows is that she needs to end this conversation, get away from Saul. She does her best to smile as she says, "We must be getting our wires crossed somehow."

"Yeah," he concedes quickly.

"That was weird," Callie says a few minutes later as she and Eva walk up the beach together. "What did you make of it?"

"I don't know," Eva says, shaking her head.

"Do you think . . . is there any way Saul might be . . . right?"

Eva feels herself stiffen. "What, Jackson doesn't have a degree? He just made it up?"

"No, I'm not saying that! What I mean is, could there have been a misunderstanding?"

"How do you misunderstand whether your husband went to college or not? I know Jackson didn't use his marine biology, but that's only because we didn't live near the coast."

"True." Callie hooks her arm through Eva's. "Saul's probably just made a mistake. You said they weren't close. I wouldn't worry about it."

Eva nods, but as they walk toward the shack, she glances at Callie and she can tell her thoughts are lingering on the conversation with Saul, doubt flickering bright in her mind.

I was never sure what Callie thought of me. I think men are always nervous about the best friend—she had your ear a long time before I stepped into your life.

Knowing how much she meant to you, it was important to me that we got on. For my part, I liked Callie. She was a good friend to you—loyal, supportive, kind—and that's all that mattered. But she never really warmed to me, I could see that.

The evening you and I got engaged, we had friends over to celebrate, didn't we? I was grabbing another bottle of champagne from the fridge, when Callie came in with a tray of empty glasses. I hadn't spoken to her yet that night. She set the tray down, then leaned against the sink, her eyes shining as she said, "You must be over the moon."

I thought it was an odd remark. Not "Congratulations" or "You both must be over the moon." I grinned as I said, "I am. I feel like the luckiest bastard in town."

Callie didn't say anything.

"I guess it must seem quick," I heard myself adding in her

silence, "but it feels right, you know?" When she still didn't speak, I went on. "Eva's amazing. Literally amazing. I don't know what I've done to deserve her." I took a deep breath and told Callie the one thing I wanted to believe more than anything: "I'm going to make Eva happy."

She pinned me with her cool gaze and said, "I really hope you do."

When she left the kitchen, I stood there holding the champagne bottle, my celebratory mood vanishing. I knew then that Callie would always be keeping a watchful eye on me, making sure I didn't hurt you.

The last time I ever saw Callie was in a restaurant in London. But she definitely wasn't watching closely enough that night.

10

The morning is still, as though the island is holding its breath. There's not a ripple of wind on the water and the sky is blue and cloudless. Eva stands at the end of the jetty, the sun hot on her skin. Beside her, Callie is checking e-mails on her phone, a hand shading the screen from the glare.

Eva listens to the faint chatter of two children catching crabs, their nut-brown legs dangling toward the water. A gull stalks up and down, patrolling near the sandwich crusts the children have discarded.

She rubs a hand over her eyes, wishing she'd slept better. Perhaps a few extra hours would've improved her mood. Yesterday she'd felt positive; she and Callie had spent the morning picking blueberries at the berry farm, and the afternoon chatting about baby names over cappuccinos and muffins at the Bakehouse Café. Yet she'd woken feeling overwhelmed by thoughts of Jackson. That's the thing she's learning about grief: there's no traceable pattern—it doesn't get steadily easier in incremental degrees. It shifts and grows and shrinks at will, catching her off guard.

Her hand moves lightly to her stomach as she wonders whether she can really make this work. She needs to be both a mother and a father to this child and she is scared she isn't going to be enough.

She wants to believe that she'll bring her child back here one day. She could show her son or daughter this jetty, sharing the story Dirk told her about Jackson as a boy diving for squid jigs to sell to tourists. She wants to know the minutiae of the memory: how old Jackson was; what swimming trunks he wore; whether he had boyish, gangly legs or baby fat around his middle. She hasn't seen a single childhood photo and has heard only a handful of tales. There's still so much she doesn't know.

"Here he is," Callie says, nodding toward Saul, who is drawing the boat beside the jetty.

He is wearing a sun-faded cap and his T-shirt is a murky shade of blue with a smear of oil on the right sleeve. He looks tanned and relaxed as he loops a rope around a metal post on the jetty.

Callie had persuaded Saul to take them out in his boat to see Wattleboon from the water. With them leaving for Melbourne in two days, this was Callie's way of offering Saul a chance to step up to the mark of being a brother-in-law. But Eva knows a few hours on a boat won't change much. She suspects that Saul's hesitance to talk about Jackson has deeper roots than they can see.

Callie is the first to climb aboard, using Saul's arm to steady herself. The small aluminum boat with a half cabin looks tired in the harsh sunlight. Callie sits at the back, where a beach towel has been spread over the metal seat.

"Ready?" Saul says to Eva, holding out his hand.

She tries to work a smile through the muscles of her face. "Yes."

She takes Saul's hand, feeling the warmth of his fingers closing around hers. It's the first physical contact they've had, and her gaze travels to their joined hands. His fingers are wide and long like Jackson's, but they are also deeply tanned with a scar cutting across his second knuckle.

When she'd held hands with Jackson, they'd developed a private way of communicating where one of them would squeeze the other's hand twice in quick succession, meaning: *I've got you*. She remembers the unspoken reassurance she'd felt when his fingers squeezed hers on the way to a hospital appointment, or when they were sitting in a back pew at the funeral of a colleague, or on the subway in rush hour.

Saul releases her fingers and turns away. She blinks as her empty hand falls to her side.

"Eva," Callie calls. "Sit back here with me."

Eva drifts toward the stern, and as she lowers herself down, Callie whispers, "You okay?"

She tries to swallow the rising tide of emotion as she nods.

Callie's gaze travels to Saul. "He reminds you of Jackson, doesn't he?"

"Sometimes."

Saul unties the boat and the engine growls as he maneuvers them away from the jetty.

Once they leave the bay, they pick up a little speed and Eva hugs her arms to her chest to keep out the breeze. They're on the southeastern side of the island, which is completely uninhabited and designated as a national park so that the old-growth forests and wildlife can flourish.

"This is beautiful," Callie says, sitting forward and pushing her sunglasses onto her head as she watches the landscape unfold from the water. They cruise beneath towering dolomite sea cliffs iced with green woodland, and past secluded coves only accessible by boat.

In Eva's silence, Callie talks to Saul, asking about the history of the island. He's difficult to draw into conversation at first, but after a while Callie seems to wear him down and he tells her about the Aboriginal people who were the first inhabitants, the women diving for shellfish and crays, and the men hunting seals. He talks about the whalers who arrived thousands of years later and built stations on the headland so they could spot and hunt for the southern right whale.

Eva closes her eyes and turns her face to the sun, content just to listen. She arches her back a little, feeling bunched up and cramped in her stomach, and then focuses on the soothing motion of water swelling and ebbing beneath them. Saul's voice washes over her. The timbre of it is so similar to Jackson's that if she concentrates on the gravelly lilt, she can almost fool herself into thinking that it is Jackson, not Saul, who is here with them.

SAUL LEANS HIS HEAD out of the boat cabin, glancing over the water. Last time he was here, a pod of bottlenose dolphins was racing right beside the boat, launching into the air, arching and twisting for the sheer pleasure of it. He'll keep an eye out today. Dolphins might be just the thing.

Eva's quiet this morning and has this faraway expression as if she's someplace else. He realizes that he hasn't heard her laugh yet, not once. He's noticed the light curve of laughter lines bracketing around her mouth and wonders, *Who were you before this?*

He takes the boat around Eagle Cape, where the wind blows right at them. Luckily there's barely any swell. After a few minutes, he comes across the small cove he was heading for. It's sheltered by tall cliffs and the water is almost still. He cuts the engine and the boat slows, skating quietly forward. He leans over the side and sees the sway of sea grass below. "Fancy calamari and fries tonight?"

Callie raises an eyebrow. "Will it involve having to catch it?"

"Might do," he says with a smile. "I've got two rods."

"You'll make some girl very happy, I'm sure."

He smiles. He feels more relaxed out here on the water, knowing they're not gonna bump into anyone who could make things difficult. "Eva, how about you?"

She glances up as if pulled from a daydream.

"D'you want to fish?"

She visibly stiffens.

Then he realizes: Jackson died while fishing. "Sorry, it was a stupid idea."

"No, I'd like to."

He catches the determination in her tone and nods once at her, then sets up both reels, attaching bright orange-and-pink squid jigs to the lines.

They move to the side of the boat and Callie joins them, perching on an upturned bucket with her arms folded. Saul passes Eva a short fishing rod that has masking tape wrapped around its handle. "It might not look like the most professional equipment, but this is my favorite. I don't let just anyone use it—only people who I think are gonna catch me a lot of squid, you understand?"

Eva manages a smile as she nods.

"You see down there? That's a sea grass bed. Now, the squid—hopefully—are just gonna be cruising around, doin' their thing. I want you to let the line right out until you feel it hit the bottom. Then just wind it in a couple of feet. The trick is to catch the squid's attention, make it look like something's in the water that it wants to eat. So just give your line a smooth pull upward every now and then."

She watches the motion he makes with his line, then does the same with hers.

"That's good. You've got it."

"You're a pro," Callie says.

After a few minutes Eva asks him, "Did you and Jackson fish together much?"

"When we were boys," is all he answers. As he reels in the line, his mind wanders back to visiting Wattleboon for the first time. Saul must've been about six, Jackson eight, and their dad had given them a bucket and a net, telling them to go down to the bay and find seven living things from the water.

They caught white bait, two different types of crabs, a sea anemone, and a mussel. They searched for over an hour but were still two short of their goal. Defeated, they trudged back up the bay to where their mother and father stood with their hands clasped. Jackson had plonked down the bucket and shrugged. "That's all there was."

Dirk had crouched down and inspected their finds. Then he beckoned them closer and said, "You've got your seven, right here." He showed them the tiny flecks of plankton moving around and a translucent shrimp that was hiding beneath some seaweed. "The ocean's full of life. You've just gotta keep your eyes open to see it."

"I was thinking," Eva says, working the line up and down, "that I'd like to meet some of Jackson's old friends."

Saul feels the muscles in his shoulders tighten.

"Do you think you could get in touch with any of them before we leave?"

He pushes up his cap and wipes a hand across his brow. "Might be a bit last-minute."

"It's worth a try," Callie adds. "We could go for a drink with them. We've got a couple of days still."

"Don't think I've got any of their numbers."

"What about the people that went to the memorial?" Eva asks. "You must've been in touch with them?"

He feels beads of sweat gathering on his forehead. "Maybe I'll have some of their numbers."

"So you'll call them?" Eva persists.

There is a pause as he struggles to work out how to answer. He doesn't want to lie, but how can he say no? "Sure," he says eventually, hoping his expression is more convincing than his voice.

Suddenly Eva's fishing line pulls taut and she gasps.

"You're on!" Saul says, relieved at the shift in focus.

"What do I do?"

"Start reeling."

Eva braces her legs as the rod bows. She holds tight, keeping it close to her chest.

"That's it, just reel it in nice and slow."

Her hand turns steady rotations as the squid fights the line.

"Keep the line nice and taut so he can't get off."

Callie points to the surface. "There! Squid!"

Rising from the water a southern calamari shimmers as Eva tows it toward the boat.

"Do I keep going?" Eva asks, her expression tight with concentration.

"Yep, all the way."

The squid's body turns an angry red as it's reeled into the air, tentacles writhing. "Lower it down now."

Eva carefully lowers the squid, and as soon as it's on the deck, Saul crouches down and holds its smooth back as he frees the jig from its tentacles.

Callie cranes forward to see.

He feels the squid begin to heave beneath his fingers. "You might wanna stand back."

Eva shuffles away, but Callie stays where she is, stooping down to peer at it.

Suddenly the squid shoots out ink, black and thick, in two rapid bursts. It splatters across the deck, covering Callie's shins.

"Fuck!" she gasps, horrified.

Eva's gaze moves between the streak of black ink covering Callie's legs and the outrage on her face.

And then Eva is bending forward, laughter roaring from her mouth. The sound rolls out in waves, loud and rich. It washes over the boat like a balm, and Saul finds himself grinning.

CALLIE SITS ON THE bottom rung of the boat ladder, her feet dangling in the water as she cleans her shins, still muttering about the squid. Once all traces of the ink are gone, she lowers herself in, gasping at the cold. She kicks away from the boat, calling out, "It's glorious!"

Eva unties her sundress and steps out of it, leaving her in a burnt-orange bikini. Glancing down, she sees the neat curve of her stomach, the skin taut. She'd love to dive off the side of the boat, pointing her fingers and toes and slicing into the sea, but instead she makes herself climb carefully down the ladder and lower herself in.

The sea wraps around Eva's body like cool silk as she swims with smooth, slow strokes, squinting against the sun's fierce reflection. She's been swimming almost every morning in the bay and feels forgotten muscles developing in her arms. She joins Callie, who is floating on her back, arms spread.

"This is bliss," Eva says. She rolls onto her back and lets the water take her weight, her hair swaying around her head. She closes her eyes and listens to the light slapping of water against the hull of the boat. Somewhere above them a bird is calling.

She feels a tweak in her abdomen and her eyes flick open as she thinks, *Was that the first kick?* She waits, barely breathing, for it to come again—and it does, only this time it's a deeper twinge that makes her wince.

"Eva?"

She treads water, working out where the sensation came from. "Just a twinge, I think."

"The baby?"

"Yeah. I might swim back."

"Let's take it slow."

Eva swims in the direction of the boat, the water lapping beneath her chin. She thinks how odd the sensations of pregnancy are; so many new feelings and physical changes. No matter how many women she's been a midwife to, it's different when it's your own body.

On her next stroke, she feels as if something is pulling tight inside her and she gasps, placing a hand over her abdomen as she stops to tread water again.

"Eva?"

She exhales steadily, waiting for the feeling to pass. "I want to get out."

"We're almost there," Callie says. She touches Eva's shoulder lightly, guiding her as they swim.

The pain eases again and Eva reaches the side of the boat and rests there, holding onto the ladder.

"You okay?" Saul asks from the boat.

As she pulls herself up the first rung, the pain hits again. This time it's not just a twinge, but a deep, stomach-wrenching cramp.

Gripping the ladder, she holds herself very still. Her eyes squeeze shut as the pain wrings through her. "No! Please!"

She knows exactly what is happening and why the pain in her stomach is hitting like a clenched fist. She knows why Callie is suddenly gasping; why Saul has dropped his fishing rod and is holding her by both shoulders; why, when she looks down, the insides of her thighs are streaked red.

11

Nudging the door open with her shoulder, Callie moves into the dim room carrying a tray of tea and cookies. The blinds have stayed drawn all day and the air feels heavy and stale. Eva's curled on the bed, the duvet pulled up to her chin. "Darling, I've brought you some tea."

Eva says nothing.

She sets down the tray, then pulls up a chair and sits close to Eva, whose eyes are open but unfocused. Callie reaches out and gently smoothes her hair from her forehead. Her skin is waxy and cool to touch. "And cookies, too. The orange chocolate ones."

Eva blinks but doesn't speak. Since the miscarriage she's barely left her room. Callie was supposed to be in Melbourne two days ago, but managed to delay her flight till tomorrow, pleading with her director to let her arrive late to the shoot.

"Have you spoken to your mum yet?" Callie asks.

Eva shakes her head.

"I really think you should."

There is a long silence before she says, "I can't."

Callie understands why: Eva's mother lost her second daughter at birth. Grief had ripped through her life and manifested itself in a fierce protectiveness of Eva. Callie always remembers how wild

Eva was when she first met her at college, as if someone had just cut her tether and she couldn't stop running. But when Callie went to stay with Eva during the holidays, she was amazed at the change: around her mother Eva was someone quieter, more sensible. It was as if she felt like her mother had suffered enough and she wouldn't give her anything else to worry about.

"Your mum will want to know," Callie says. "She'll want to help."

"I don't need help. I need to be left alone."

Callie forces a smile. "Why don't you come outside? I think there'll be a beautiful sunset tonight."

Eva lifts her head a fraction. She looks Callie straight in the eye as she says, "Go. I want you to go."

CALLIE SITS ON THE deck, chewing the edge of her thumbnail, the faint taste of nail polish bitter on her tongue. It's heartbreaking seeing Eva like this.

"How is she?"

She starts, having not seen Saul approach. Lowering her voice, she tells him, "Not good. She's still in her room." She shakes her head slowly from side to side. "I don't know what to do."

"It's just going to take time."

She nods, knowing that's the simple truth of it. "What's that?" she asks, noticing the dish in his hands.

"Fish pie. Just some leftovers."

Callie stands and takes the heavy ceramic dish that's plump with creamy mash. She can tell it's far more than leftovers. "That's kind," she says, trying not to sound surprised. "Thank you. I'll just put it inside."

When she returns to the deck, Saul asks, "Did you manage to get an appointment?"

"Yes. She's booked for an ultrasound in two days. But I won't be there. I have to leave tomorrow. I couldn't get any more time." She pauses. "I hate thinking of her going to the hospital on her own."

Saul looks toward the shack, but says nothing.

Callie lets the silence stretch out, waiting for him to offer to go in her place.

After a moment Saul digs his hands into his pockets and says, "I better head back."

"Why don't you at least go in and see her?" Saul has visited every day to get an update on Eva, but hasn't gone into the shack to talk to her.

He hesitates, seeming to consider it for a moment. Then he casts another glance toward the shack and says, "Just let her know I said hi."

She watches Saul's long strides as he moves back down the beach. Then suddenly Callie is on her feet, clambering from the deck and hurrying through the sand after him. "Wait!"

He turns, squinting into the sun.

"Please. Go in and see her. I'm leaving tomorrow, Saul. I need to know she's not going to be on her own out here."

He rubs a hand over his jawline. "Maybe she should be going back to Melbourne with you."

Her eyebrows arch. "You don't want her here—is that it?"

He looks down at the sand between his feet, saying nothing.

"She's your sister-in-law and she's going through hell. The only reason she's even on Wattleboon is because she wanted to meet *you*! I don't care why you and Jackson fell out, but don't punish Eva for it."

"Punish?" Saul says, eyes flashing. "I'm protecting her!"

Callie draws her head back. "From what?"

"Nothing," he says quickly.

"What are you talking about?" She takes a step forward. "Protecting Eva from what?"

"Just forget it."

She can see his jaw tightening with the effort of containing his anger. She wonders what exactly happened between Jackson and Saul. "That day you were collecting oysters, you said Jackson never did a degree in Melbourne. Is that true?"

He returns her gaze. "Yes, it's true."

"So why did he lie to Eva?"

His dark stare moves to the shack, then he shakes his head, turns, and stalks down the beach. This time Callie doesn't stop him.

EVA STARES AT THE trail of steam curling from her mug of tea. She feels numb, empty, like a hollow tree: dead but still standing.

She longs for Jackson. She wills him to crawl into this bed, wrap his arms tight around her, tell her, *You'll be okay, darl.* Just an hour, one more hour with him, that's all she's asking for. She would give anything, do anything, for that.

Sometime later the door cracks open. Callie again.

She comes close, bringing with her the fresh scent of the bay. Her cheeks are flushed. "Look, Eva, you're not going to like this, but I've just called your mum. I told her."

Eva feels a bolt of outrage and sits up. "No—I said no!"

"She's going to call you in five minutes. Your phone's here," Callie says, sliding it across the bedside table toward Eva. "You need to talk to her."

She starts to protest, but Callie hasn't finished. "And when you have, I want you to get dressed. Saul's made us fish pie for dinner and you and I are going to eat it together on the deck."

Callie pulls open the blinds and soft evening light fills the room.

Eva blinks, shading her eyes with a hand.

As Callie leaves, she pauses in the doorway, saying, "This will get easier, Eva. I promise you."

Then she is gone and Eva hears her in the kitchen setting out plates and cutlery. She runs a hand through her unwashed hair. Her temples throb and her tongue feels swollen and dry.

Eva glances at her phone. She doesn't want to speak to her mother because she knows she can't be strong. There is no game face when you've lost everything.

She hugs her arms around her middle, feeling the tender ache in her womb. As a midwife, she knows the risks in early pregnancy: one in four pregnancies ends in miscarriage. Still, she has no words to explain the guilt she feels: Jackson had left her with the gift of a new life, a final piece of him—and she'd let it die. All she wants right now is to be pregnant again, to fill this awful void inside her with Jackson's child, to keep him with her. But there won't be another baby. It's so final and so devastating that Eva can barely breathe with the pain of it.

When the phone rings, the whole room seems to vibrate with the shrill sound. She reaches for it and presses it to her ear. Her voice cracks as she says, "Oh, Mum . . ."

TWO DAYS LATER, WHILE Callie is on a plane to Melbourne, Eva lies on an examination table watching the ultrasound monitor carefully. She sees her uterus as a grainy black-and-white image. It is empty. Completely empty.

The sonogram technician seems pleased by this as she rolls the wand over Eva's stomach once more. "You won't need a D and C, which is great news. It looks like all the products have gone."

Products, Eva thinks. Has she ever used that term herself? Yes, she probably has. She knows that clinically a fetus is only referred to as a *baby* when it's capable of maintaining life. But it does not feel like a fetus or products that have been lost. It feels like her baby. Jackson's baby.

"That's what made it so hard," her mother had confided when they'd spoken yesterday. "I carried your sister for nine months. I loved her. But when she died—I felt like it was only your father and I who *knew* her."

They'd never talked so openly about her mother's grief, and Eva felt as if a barrier between them had finally been removed. Eva talked and cried freely and her mother didn't tell her to come home, she just listened—and that was everything.

The sonogram tech wipes the gel from her stomach with a wad of tissues and then Eva slides off the couch and pulls down her top. Her movements feel heavy and slow. She picks up her bag and holds it to her stomach. The tech opens the door and, perhaps seeing Eva's wedding ring, says, "You and your husband may want to wait a month or so before trying again. Just to give your body a chance to settle back down."

Eva stares aghast at this woman. She wants to correct her, but her throat is too choked to speak. She drifts into the waiting area, which is filled with pregnant women, young children, husbands.

At the end of a row of plastic orange chairs, Saul sits with his knees wide apart, his head hanging forward and his large hands clasped.

When he catches sight of Eva, he stands immediately. He must see something in her expression because as soon as she reaches him, he says, "Let's get outta here."

He walks at her side as they move down a long corridor and out through automatic doors. They cross the parking lot toward the truck, and he opens the passenger door for her and she climbs carefully inside.

It's only then that she begins to cry. She covers her face with her hands as tears stream down her cheeks, the sound of her sobs filling the truck. She feels Saul's eyes on her and imagines he wants to get out, step away from her grief.

But then she feels the warmth of his hand around her wrist. He gently draws her hands from her face, forcing her to meet his gaze. He doesn't look embarrassed or awkward. He just tells her, "You're going to be okay."

She hears the firm certainty in his voice, sees the steadiness of his gaze, feels the strength of his grip—and she wants to trust in him.

I like imagining what we'd do if we had just one more night together.

Sometimes I picture the winning-lottery-ticket version of this answer: a tropical beach, fresh lobster, champagne, you in a flowing dress, barefoot. But that's not really what I'd want. If we could be anywhere, I'd choose the bedroom of our rented apartment in London. Yes, darl, our old bedroom with its cracked ceiling, drafty, single-paned window, and the mattress that sagged in the middle. I wouldn't even mind hearing next door's bad Nineties rock music thudding through the walls because it'd remind me of when you stood on our bed playing air guitar at three in the morning when we couldn't sleep.

So I'd spend our final night in that room—in that bed—and we'd laugh together, and make love, and I would memorize every detail of your body: the feel of your hipbones, the taste of your skin, the wisps of finer hair at the edges of your temples, the amber flecks of your eyes.

I know that some people probably thought that we were reckless in our relationship. I'm sure your friends blamed me—thought I moved too quickly, spent money too easily, swept your days up into mine. And they were right. But when I was with you, Eva, I felt the strongest urge to live life for the moment, because I never knew when it was going to end.

12

Time slides by. Eva sees it pass in shadows between day and night, in the dwindling bag of coffee Saul spoons into a mug each morning when he visits, in the thickening layers of salt blurring the shack windows. Callie calls her daily, sometimes hourly, and Eva listens to the words of comfort and encouragement that she whispers from the corner of a set in Melbourne.

This morning she stands on the deck, a hand placed over her stomach. There is no longer the firm, small roundness to it. It has only been ten days and already it has flattened, all physical trace of the pregnancy gone. The bay is glassy, the goose-belly gray sky reflected on its surface. It makes Eva think of the Dorset coast and the early-morning walks she'd taken as a teenager when the sea was still and quiet.

She sees Saul at the far edge of the bay, making his way along the shoreline toward her. He visits each day before work, and on the days she feels she can't get out of bed, he sits at the far side of the room on a wooden chair that looks too feeble for his frame, talking lightly about his plans for the day or bringing her something to read from his collection of ocean books. She is grateful to him, immensely grateful, yet she wishes it were Jackson who was here with her, not Saul.

When he gets closer she sees he is wearing a wetsuit rolled down to his waist. "Going free-diving?"

"Yep." He smiles at her, sunlight falling across his face. "And so are you."

"Sorry?"

"I thought you might want to give it a go."

"No," she says immediately. "I can't."

"But you haven't been in the water since——" He doesn't finish the sentence.

"I know. But I just . . ." *Just what?* she thinks. She was too sore to swim immediately after the miscarriage, but now physically she feels fine. There is nothing stopping her.

"You'll love free-diving." He turns and looks at the bay as he says, "The moment you dive under, everything else slips away. No matter how wound up I am before I get in, all of that disappears underwater."

Eva had wanted to dive from that first morning she saw Saul moving fluidly through the bay. But she's not sure she's ready; she feels heavy, as if her grief is a weight, physically pressing her down.

"I've got a wetsuit for you," he says, opening the bag he's holding. "It was in the lost-and-found box at work. I'm no good on sizes, but it looked about right."

Eva finds something unbearably touching about the idea of Saul searching through wetsuits at work, planning this. Trying, in his own quiet way, to help.

"Will you give it a go?"

She looks at him, then slowly she nods. "Yes. I will."

THE WETSUIT IS A bit long in the arms and loose at the back, but all in all, it's not bad. On the shore, Saul fixes a weight belt around Eva's waist and hands her a mask and a pair of fins.

As they wade into the sea, Saul says, "See that cluster of rocks out there to the left of the bay? You good to swim that far?"

"I'll be fine," Eva says.

Saul spits into his mask and rubs it around with his fingers. Eva does the same and then she pulls on her fins and kicks away from shore.

The wetsuit shrinks against her skin, a cold trickle of water seeping down the gap at her back. She swims slowly, the weight belt feeling heavy at her waist as she finds her stroke. Saul stays at her side, never overtaking her. It's good to be moving again, shaking off the inertia that had settled in her limbs. She has swum in the bay many times, but never with a snorkel mask. The visibility is incredible; she sees the pattern of ridges on the seabed and the glistening clarity of the water ahead.

When they reach the rocks at the far edge of the bay, they tread water and Saul pulls out his snorkel to tell her, "We're going to dive down to the bottom—it's not deep here, maybe fifteen feet. You know how to equalize?"

She nods.

"Good. Keep equalizing as you go so your ears don't hurt. Then I just want you to try and stay on the bottom for as long as your breath will comfortably hold you. Try and do everything slowly. The stiller you can be, the less oxygen you'll burn. And don't force it. When your body tells you it's time to surface, you listen to it."

Eva readjusts her mask, takes a gulp of air, and dives under, holding her nose and blowing out air to stop the pressure building in her ears. She kicks a few times to reach the bottom and then positions herself flat. As soon as she stops kicking, she finds herself popping right back to the surface.

She snatches another breath and goes down again, her body fighting against the water to keep her under. Within a matter of seconds she is back on the surface again, gasping for air. "I can't stay down," she tells Saul, frustrated.

"This time, when you swim down I want you to hold onto a rock. Wrap your hands around it and just hover there. We'll go down together, okay?"

She takes a deep breath and dives under again, Saul with her. Underwater he moves gracefully as he swims to a rock ledge and holds onto it, beckoning her over.

Eva kicks toward the rock and clings onto it as well, but even as she holds it, her legs begin floating up above her head. She fights to keep her body level with Saul's, but already she is out of air and has to let go and pings back to the surface.

She snaps off her mask. "I can't do it," she tells him when he surfaces.

"Listen," he says, swimming over to her side. "Free-diving isn't about how long you can hold your breath for or how deep you can go. It's about understanding yourself and what you're capable of—and then exceeding those limits."

"But I can't even stay under for thirty seconds."

Saul pulls his mask down around his neck as he treads water. She sees a faint red indentation left behind on his forehead. "You were rushing. You've got to learn to get in the right mind-set before going under." He wipes water from his eyes. "Sometimes I just float on the surface, breathing through the snorkel and slowing my heart rate. Then, when I'm relaxed, that's when I dive down."

"Okay," she says. "I'd like to try again."

Eva floats on the surface with her face in the cool water, arms spread at her sides, letting the water bear her weight. She takes steady breaths in and out through the snorkel, watching Saul dive under, his sleek black shape gliding beneath her.

Once her breathing has regulated, she draws in a deeper,

longer breath, then dives down. She doesn't kick hard for the rock, rather angles herself toward it and lets her body descend in a smooth point. She grips it and begins calmly letting out her breath, silver air bubbles shimmering as they rise. Moments feel slower underwater and it seems to her as if her muscles relax, loosen. Something inside Eva falls still.

Eventually she lets go of the rock, and looking up, she gently kicks for the surface. When she breaks through it, she doesn't gasp a panicked breath, but inhales slowly, deeply, filling her lungs with fresh air.

As she waits for Saul to surface, Eva realizes that for the few seconds she was underwater, she wasn't thinking or worrying. Instead she was just in the moment, absorbing her surroundings, and she sees that this is exactly what Saul wanted her to experience.

SAUL SLIPS OFF HIS fins and wades through the shallows behind Eva.

Reaching the beach, Eva pulls off her mask and stands with her hands on her waist, catching her breath.

"What did you think?" he asks.

"I loved it," she says quietly, as if she's surprised by the fact. "That last dive, I came up feeling . . . I don't know how to describe it. Energized . . . but also, peaceful."

He smiles, nodding.

Eva tries to remove her weight belt, her chilled fingers grappling with the safety catch.

"Here," he says, stepping forward. He takes the belt in one hand and attempts to release the catch a couple of times, but the clasp is jammed. He has to slip his hand between the belt and Eva's wetsuit for purchase, and this time, when he pulls it firmly, the catch releases.

Glancing up, he sees Eva's gaze is fixed on his face. "Thanks for taking me," she says.

There is a drop of water just below her left eyebrow, a perfect single sphere. He has a curious urge to put his lips to it and taste it. Surprised by the thought, he hands back the weight belt. "No worries."

"Saul," she says, the seriousness of her voice drawing his gaze back to her face. "I wanted to ask you something."

He shifts, the sand moving beneath his feet.

"I called Callie last night and told her I was thinking of staying in Tasmania a little longer. Just while I get my head together. What would you think if . . . if I stayed here in the shack, just for another week or so? Would that be okay?"

The neck of his wetsuit feels too tight, as if it's constricting his breathing. He wants to unzip it, yank the damn thing off.

Eva must read his hesitation. "It's only that Callie thinks she'll be working crazy hours. I was just worried I might be a bit cooped up in her apartment, that's all."

He knows Eva cannot stay on Wattleboon for much longer— not without everything coming undone. He's already taken too great a risk as it is. "Listen, Eva," he begins.

She tilts her head to one side and the drop of water on her eyebrow runs to the corner of her eye, where it rests like a tear.

Despite every logical thought in his head, he finds himself saying to her, "Stay as long as you need."

13

Most days Eva finds herself eager to free-dive. Now that she's relaxed underwater, she's noticing more: seaweed with the hues of autumn, tiny boxfish that look as if they've swallowed an ice cube, crayfish that lurk in cracks in the rocks. Even on days when the visibility is poor, she enjoys the sensation of the swell moving around her and the clicks and echoes of the sea. It's here that her thoughts fall still.

Now she returns to the shallows and slips off her fins and mask, salt water dripping from the ends of her hair. She grabs a towel from the shack and cranks on the outdoor shower. Under the warm running water she massages shampoo, then conditioner, through her hair. She rinses it, gazing up at the hazy clouds forming in the early-evening sky.

Eva cuts the shower and dries herself, then moves inside, throwing on a big sweater and a pair of jeans. She grabs a glass of water and eats a bowl of cold pasta left over from lunch while leaning against the kitchen side.

Standing there, she rereads a few pages of a book Saul lent her by Jacques Mayol, a prolific free-diver who writes poetically about the union between humans and water. She's already read it cover to cover, fascinated by his theories about dolphins and the aquatic nature of man. She's made pages of notes, something about his writing inspiring a connection between her work with water births and free-diving.

She checks her watch, running a finger beneath the strap where her skin is still damp. It's only seven o'clock. She doesn't fancy another evening alone watching the portable TV that only picks up flickering reception on two channels.

She washes up her dish, then does some halfhearted tidying around the shack, which is already neat. She picks up her book and puts it down again, feeling restless. What she'd like is a beer and some company—and she takes this as a good sign. When Saul stopped by the shack before work, she'd suggested going to the Wattleboon Tavern this evening for a drink—but he couldn't as he'd be working late. Eva had felt an odd sting of disappointment at his answer, as if she somehow knew he'd say no.

Perhaps I'll go anyway, she thinks. Deciding to ride the moment of optimism, she swaps her sweater for a pale gray camisole, grabs her wallet, and then leaves for the pub on foot.

The Wattleboon Tavern is a squat building made from cement blocks that have been painted a sage green. A liquor store is attached to its rear, like a fanny pack strapped to a bad outfit. What it lacks in terms of elegance, it makes up for in location: it faces the Duntree Channel, and as the sun lowers, golden light streams through the wide windows.

Inside, the place hums. People crowd around dark tables drinking and talking, and the air smells of freshly cooked fries and the yeasty flavor of beer. Cricket plays on a flat-screen TV high on the wall, watched by a small audience with necks craned. Opposite the bar a doorway leads into a gaming lounge, where men in work boots and ratty T-shirts stand in front of flashing slot machines.

As Eva waits at the bar, she glances around, surprised to see so many young people. She'd imagined they'd all leave for Hobart or even mainland Australia once they'd reached eighteen, but they're here grouped around tables in their skinny jeans and skate shoes.

Eva orders a beer and takes a seat on a stool at the edge of the bar. It's nice to be away from the shack and see the routines of other people's lives on Wattleboon. She imagines Jackson would have liked bringing her here; he always loved nights out, being sociable. Last summer they'd been at a wedding where the bar staff left at midnight, but there was still a fridge full of alcohol that the newlyweds had paid for. Jackson—with his shirtsleeves pushed up and a tie wrapped around his head like some Eighties rock hero—vaulted over the bar and began serving drinks. He created amazing concoctions from the alcohol and mixers left, and the guests cheered as he raced through their orders, tossing bottles of vodka and rum through the air and catching them backhanded.

Eva had laughed with her head thrown back, amazed by his flamboyance. When the rush had passed, he'd slid a cocktail across the bar and said, "For you, madam. For being the most beautiful woman in the room."

"Except for the bride," she amended with a small smile.

He leaned close to her and whispered, "Including the bride." He'd kissed her on the mouth and she'd felt desire rush through her.

From somewhere within the pub comes a bellow of laughter that makes every nerve ending in Eva's body fire. She knows that laugh: the timbre, the depth, the way it rumbles as it's released.

Suddenly she is rising from her stool, turning on the spot, searching for Jackson among the crowd.

The laughter comes again and Eva follows the sound toward a group of people who are sitting in the corner of the pub. She sees the broad set of a man with his back to her, his shoulders quaking.

Saul.

Her stomach falls with disappointment.

It is a moment before she remembers Saul told her he'd be working late tonight.

Her cheeks redden as she realizes that he used work as an excuse for not going for a drink with her. She'd thought they were becoming friends, but perhaps Saul just felt sorry for her: she'd lost her husband and baby, he could hardly ask her to leave.

Clutching her bag, Eva ducks her head and makes her way through the crowd, keeping her gaze fixed on the exit.

HE SEES A FLASH of dark hair, a slim, tanned arm. He glances up and catches the back of Eva disappearing out of the tavern door.

Shit, he thinks.

Grabbing his phone and truck keys, he makes an excuse to his friends, then jogs across the dusty parking lot and sees Eva striding away down the road.

He has to run to catch up, loose change jangling in his pocket. "Eva!" he calls. "Wait!"

She turns. Her cheeks are flushed.

Saul comes to a stop in front of her. He can feel beer swilling in his stomach. "You were in the tavern?"

Her chest rises and falls as she says, "I decided to go on my own—since you were working late."

"Yeah, sorry," he says, rubbing a hand over the back of his neck. "I finished earlier than I thought . . ." The lie sticks in his throat.

They're standing on the roadside and a truck flies past with a kayak tied to its roof. A loose bungee strap bounces against the wheel arch, then swings high into the air.

"You could've just said no. I do understand you've got your own life here."

Tension throbs in his temples and he runs a hand back and forth across his forehead. He doesn't say anything.

"Do you wish I'd left with Callie—is that it?"

"No . . . I . . ." He doesn't know what to say. Yes, he wishes she'd left. No, he wants her to stay. "I like having you here, I do. But . . ." He trails off again, frustrated. There's no way for him to explain why he lied to her.

"Then what is it, Saul? Why didn't you want me to come to-night? When I asked you this morning about going for a drink, you already knew you'd be here, didn't you?"

He tries to offer a casual no, but the word comes out sounding insolent, defensive.

She shakes her head, eyes narrowing. "Jackson warned me that you were a liar."

The sting of the words cracks in the air like a whip. "What?"

She lifts her chin. He remembers the gesture from the first day he met her when she'd just arrived on Wattleboon. He'd seen a fire in her then, and despite everything she's been through, it still flickers now.

"I know about your fight, Saul. Why the two of you fell out."

He stares at Eva, his heart rate accelerated. "And?"

"So I know about what happened on his birthday four years ago. I know how you turned up at the barbecue, made a deliberate play for his girlfriend. Took her home with you."

A mosquito buzzes close to his ear. He doesn't move to bat it away.

"How could you do that to your own brother?"

When Saul speaks, his voice sounds hollow. "I didn't. She was *my* girlfriend, Eva."

EVA STARES AT SAUL as he says, "Jackson was the one who took her."

She shakes her head, amazed by the audacity of the lie. "Bullshit."

His eyes stay locked on her face. "It's the truth. She was my girlfriend, Eva."

She remembers how Saul had lied on the phone to Dirk; lied about working late tonight; lied to Jackson. "Truth?" She moves past him and strides along the roadside.

She is about fifty feet away when she hears Saul call after her, "Jackson's birthday is on the fifteenth of July."

So? she thinks as she continues.

"That's the middle of winter here. You said he'd had a barbecue for his birthday—but why would anyone have a barbecue on the beach in the middle of winter?"

Eva stops.

"The barbecue was for *my* birthday," he calls. "It's on the seventh of March. Our summer."

She turns now.

"She was my girlfriend."

Her teeth press against her bottom lip as she hears Jackson telling her, *You can't trust him. He's a liar.* Yet she has begun to. She thought they'd become friends.

Saul walks along the roadside, stopping in front of her. "I'm telling you the truth, Eva."

She shakes her head. She won't believe it.

"That's why I left Tas—went to South America for a few months. I needed to get away. I couldn't stand seeing him with her."

She balks. "South America?"

He nods.

"Jackson went there. Not you!"

"Jackson?" His brow furrows. "Until he went to England, Jackson hadn't been outside of Australia."

She breathes out hard, shocked by the madness of what he's saying. She has no idea why Saul is doing this. She opens her mouth to confront him when something Dirk said pushes into her thoughts: *Jackson was the Tassie boy, Saul the traveler.* Dirk had been drinking at the time and she'd assumed he'd gotten his sons' names muddled. *But what if he hadn't?*

She touches her hairline, thinking, thinking.

"Eva," Saul says carefully and levelly, drawing her gaze to his. "Everything I'm telling you is the truth."

That word again, *truth*. It is Jackson she trusts. Her husband. The man she loved and planned to spend her life with. The man she's lost. "Why are you doing this, Saul? Jackson told me all about South America—Chile, the Atacama Desert, Peru, Brazil—I know about his trip."

"He never went to those places."

"And you did?"

"Yes."

A group of drinkers tumbles out into the pub parking lot. She hears an engine being started up, bass booming from the vehicle before the door is slammed. "I flew to Chile first and spent two months traveling up the coast, surfing. Then I drove right through the Atacama Desert and up into Peru. I picked up some work in a nature reserve building trail paths for a few months."

Eva's fingers are clenched at her sides as she listens. The description is an echo of Jackson's travels. She has no idea why Saul is using Jackson's words to try to tear at her memory of her husband.

Saul continues. "In Peru, I headed first for Chincha. I wanted to hike Machu Picchu—that's why I'd gone there in the first place."

No, she thinks. *That's why Jackson went there!*

"Afterward, I flew to Brazil, where I met up with a friend of mine." He tells her about a hostel he worked at in Brazil, but she already knows the story—knows all of the stories—and she can hear Jackson telling her how he'd bought a beat-up old motorbike from the hostel owner and rode it along jungle paths where the foliage was thick and the air dense with moisture.

She wants to tell Saul to stop—stop talking!—but he goes on, her husband's memories spilling from his mouth. His lilting accent is so much like Jackson's that it feels as if his voice is ripping her open.

She lifts her hands to her ears to cover them, but she can still hear him. Suddenly she is drawing her right arm back, then launching it forward at speed. Her palm connects with Saul's face and she hears the slap of her fingers against his cheek.

Finally, there is silence.

14

The palm of Eva's hand smarts as it hangs limply at her side.

Saul doesn't move. His eyes are on her, wide with shock.

"I . . . I . . ." She cannot finish the sentence. Her legs are trembling as she turns, crosses the road, and then begins to jog. Her feet move heavily at first, sandals clacking against the tarmac, but then as her legs find a rhythm, her speed builds.

She runs beside a row of weatherboard houses, the smell of a barbecue swirling in the air. Beads of sweat bloom across her forehead and blood rushes to the surface of her skin. She keeps on going, flying along the roadside in the fading light.

A car passes and she senses the turn of a passenger's head as he or she stares after Eva, but she concentrates only on the motion of moving forward, distance judged in landmarks: an old barn where two mares stand with their heads together; a tractor without wheels in a gateway; a field planted with neat rows of strawberries.

Then she veers from the road onto the gravel track that leads to the bay—and it's only then that she slows to a walk. She places her hands on her hips and blows out hard, her pulse still sprinting.

Gum trees frame the track, their warm smell thickening the

still air. She walks through their shadows, her body shaking from the exertion.

Why had Saul said those things? Why wouldn't he stop? She pictures the earnestness of his expression as he explained about the feud. He looked genuinely shocked when Eva contradicted him. She tries to contemplate the possibility that what he was saying is true—but she can't, not when she can hear the smile in Jackson's voice as he told her how he'd had to fix the motorbike he'd bought in Brazil with only the tools on his penknife, or when she can recall his wistful description of the sun rising through a shroud of mist from the top of Machu Picchu.

Something sharp pushes through her memories, like a shard of broken glass: there is a photo on the wall of Saul's living room of the towering peaks of Machu Picchu. When she'd first glanced at it, she'd assumed it was Jackson standing in the foreground with his backpack on—only that couldn't be right because if the brothers weren't close, why would Saul have a picture of Jackson?

She runs a knuckle over her lips as she tries to picture the photo again. She can see the rich green peaks, the tops of them veiled with mist, but the image of the figure beneath them is indistinct in her mind.

When the track curves off to the right to lead her toward the shack, Eva doesn't take it. She keeps moving forward. Straight to Saul's house.

SAUL'S TRUCK HASN'T PASSED her, so she knows the house will be empty. No one locks their houses on Wattleboon, so she's not surprised when she finds the side door into the kitchen open.

Her heart beats harder as she steps inside. The smell of wood and something peppery tinges the room. It is almost dark now, but she doesn't reach for a light. She lets her eyes adjust to the dimness, making out the shapes of kitchen units, a mug tree on the windowsill, the toaster tucked in a corner.

As she passes the sink, she sees the small round shape of a tea bag that has been tossed there.

The hairs on the back of her neck stand on end as if someone has blown icy breath beneath her collar. She gazes at the tea bag unblinking, losing all sense of her surroundings. It's as if she's back in her apartment in London looking at the rust-colored stain in their sink from where Jackson had left his tea bag. She can almost smell the earthy musk of Jackson in the air, hear the sounds of traffic and sirens from the street below their apartment.

She wants to be back there so much that images of Jackson and Saul, London and Wattleboon, twist and knot together so they are no longer separate, but rather one continuous tangle of thought.

Beyond the open door, a bird calls and she turns. Outside there are no streetlights, no roads, just trees and only a glimmer of the bay. She is in Wattleboon, in Saul's kitchen. It is his tea bag discarded in the sink. Not Jackson's.

A shared habit, that is all.

She forces herself to take several deep breaths, swallowing down the irrational panic.

Then she leaves the kitchen and heads for the living room, not letting her eyes roam beyond her purpose now. She passes the sofa and edges toward the far wall of the living room, where three framed photos are hung.

It is the middle one she stands before, her gaze leveled.

She sees the tall peaks of the mountains and terraces, and the silhouette of a man in the foreground, wearing a backpack. She leans closer to see his face.

She wills it to be Jackson so deeply that his and Saul's features blur in her mind so she no longer can tell who is who. Her thoughts spin with uncertainty and she takes two steps to the left, hitting the light switch with the heel of her hand.

The room glares into life and she stands rigid before the picture, blinking in the clear image: Saul at the summit of Machu Picchu.

Just like he said.

She tells herself that the photo doesn't mean anything. Both brothers could have traveled there, or Saul could've doctored the image somehow.

Behind her she hears movement and Eva becomes aware that someone else is in the house.

Slowly, she turns.

Saul is standing in the doorway. "What are you doing?"

She glances toward the photo on the wall. "It's you. Backpacking. In Machu Picchu."

"Yes."

"Jackson could have gone there, too."

Saul looks at her levelly. "He could have, but he didn't. Jackson never went to South America. I'm sorry, Eva."

Her thoughts spin with confusion. *Why is Saul saying all this?* "Jackson's degree," she says, remembering her conversation with Saul when he was collecting oysters. "You said Jackson never studied marine biology."

"He didn't go to college. He lived in Melbourne for a while, but he was working as a cocktail flairer."

Bile rises in her throat. She pictures Jackson behind the bar at the wedding, tossing bottles high into the air and swinging the liquid into glasses. She had laughed at his showmanship and asked where he'd learned to do it. He'd said, *I had a lot of time on my hands when I was a student.*

Eva has the sensation that she's standing very high up on a ledge. One wrong move and she could fall. She needs to be still, to find balance. Yet she senses that there is more to come—she can feel it twisting around her ankles like a strengthening wind.

She stacks each of the facts like bricks, trying to make something solid from them.

Jackson didn't do a marine biology degree. Saul did.

Jackson didn't have his girlfriend taken from him. Saul did.

Jackson didn't travel around South America. Saul did.

She swallows, pushing down the slick of bile. "Then the things he was telling me . . . they belonged to you." Nothing makes sense. "What else?" she hears herself saying. "What else are you saying were lies?"

"I don't know . . ."

"After college, what did you do?" she asks, her voice stretched thin.

"Eva—"

"Please!" she begs. "Just tell me!"

He looks at her steadily. "I took a dive job on the Great Barrier Reef for a season, working with tourists on coral restoration projects. Then I came back to Tassie for a while. Worked for this outdoor experience company that put on activity camps for kids. I was teaching them how to dive—"

"The camp was on the east coast. You lived in a wood cabin for three months."

A vein in Saul's temple flickers and pulses. "That's right."

"Jackson told me he worked there for a season. Did he?" she says, hearing the desperate edge to her voice. "Did he ever work at a camp like that?"

His head moves from side to side. "No."

Eva grips the neckline of her top, pulling it away from her

flaming skin. Panic sparks through her body. How could it all be lies? "So what was Jackson doing during that time?"

Saul opens his hands in front of him. "He worked in a boat-yard for a few years. Before that he was working in a pub down in Sandy Bay. He put on events for a while—small music festivals, dance nights, that sort of thing."

In London, Jackson had a job with a drinks company. He was knowledgeable and had a good understanding of the trade, and was great with clients. He'd never used his marine biology degree, and Eva had never questioned it. Why would she? They lived in the city, not by the coast.

The idea that Jackson had been lying is unfathomable. She feels dizzy, as if the ground is swaying beneath her. She crosses the room to the window and grips the window frame to hold herself steady. In the fading light outside, she notices the sea kayak tucked against the bench where she'd seen Saul gutting fish. "Is that your kayak in the garden?" she asks, keeping her back to him.

"Yes."

"Did Jackson ever own one?"

"A kayak? No. Not that I know of."

So his beautiful tales of paddling in glassy bays, watching white bait flicker silver in shoals below, were fiction? Is that what she is expected to believe?

"Photos," she says, suddenly turning. "You must have photos from college, from your travels."

"Yes, I've got pictures," he tells her.

"I need to see them."

SAUL GOES INTO HIS room and pulls out the drawer beneath his bed. Inside is a slim file of letters, a bag of photos, and a wooden box with rusted hinges. It's the box that he finds his hands hovering above.

He removes the lid and leans in close, breathing in the smell of salt and the chalkiness of pebbles. Inside are items he'd saved from their family shack: a thick glass bottle they'd found washed up in the bay, which he and Jackson filled with tiny shells; an oily green feather from the plume of a swift parrot; an abalone shell, the outside aged and brittle, the inside still gleaming with the memory of a former beauty; a pack of cards, the seams bound with aging tape.

He picks up a well-thumbed Wolverine comic belonging to Jackson, the edges curled and stained with mildew. He'd found it behind the bunk bed when he threw out the mattresses. Jackson had loved reading comics, losing himself in the fantasy of all those wild adventures and the mythical powers of the superheroes.

Growing up, the real superhero in Saul's life was his brother. Jackson was the guy who could dive down and come up with an abalone in each hand, or do a tailspin on a skateboard before anyone else was even into skating. He was popular, brave, and he made everyone laugh. So it amazes Saul that Jackson wiped out his own history and replaced it with his brother's.

He puts the comic aside, then turns his attention to the photos Eva's asked to see. He empties the bag of pictures onto the bed and begins riffling through them, looking for any of him as a student or when he was traveling. He picks up one of Jackson that was taken when he was living in Melbourne. He's wearing a dark polo shirt, the name of a bar printed in gold on the front. He is grinning as he spins a cocktail shaker; his hands are blurred, too fast for the shutter to catch.

Of course Saul had always known Jackson was capable of lying. He remembers the wildly exaggerated stories he used to tell as a boy, which would make his father laugh and their mother frown a little. But this? It doesn't make any sense to him. He's only just coming to realize how deeply Jackson had deceived Eva, and the knowledge of it makes Saul uncomfortable—complicit by default.

As he flips though more photos, he comes across a picture of Jackson taken almost three years ago that Dirk had given him. Saul looks closely at the image of his brother, wondering whether he should tell Eva everything he knows. His hesitation isn't out of loyalty to Jackson: he's dead, so what does it matter? Nor is it out of loyalty to Dirk, who has asked him to keep quiet.

As he tucks the photo at the back of the drawer and gathers the rest of the pile, he realizes that he's hesitated this long because he cannot bear to see what the truth will do to Eva.

EVA SITS ON THE sofa, her knees hugged to her chest. Her thoughts skitter and slide, as if moving across ice. It seems utterly incredible to her that Jackson could have been lying this whole time. They had loved each other, made marriage vows, spent hours talking about their pasts, their futures.

But a doubt skates forward: she had only known Jackson for two years. She'd fallen in love so swiftly and unexpectedly, had she really paused to take stock? Within a few months he'd already been welcomed into the fold of her friends and was treated by her mother as part of the family. It had given Eva a great feeling of intimacy and security.

Yet she'd not met anyone from Jackson's past, not even his family. She'd been introduced to colleagues and friends he'd made since moving to London, but none of them had known Jackson any longer than she had. With mounting dread she realizes that Jackson could have created any past he'd wanted and nobody would have known.

"I've got these," Saul says, returning to the living room and handing her a slim pile of photos.

The sofa dips as he sits beside her and she catches the smell of the lab still on his clothes.

The first few pictures are of Saul, and her hands tremble as she flips through them: Saul on the back of a motorbike, a surfboard bag hooked over his shoulder; Saul and a friend backpacking through a verdant jungle; Saul on a dive boat in tropical waters; Saul wearing a black gown and mortarboard as he holds a rolled-up certificate against his chest like a sword.

Her breath shortens as she looks through photo after photo, all evidence that Saul did the things Jackson had claimed to have done.

The first photo she sees of Jackson is a shot of him standing in a boatyard. He is wearing faded blue overalls that are rolled down to his waist, and he is sticking an oil-smeared finger up at whoever was behind the camera. In the next photo his hair is cut shorter and he's pointing toward a huge banner that reads TASSIE DEVIL BEER FESTIVAL! There are more photos of Jackson: on nights out with friends, skateboarding in a half pipe, kicking a football on the beach.

She looks through the pile twice more and then lays the photos carefully on the coffee table. They confirm everything Saul told her, yet it still seems impossible. She shakes her head slowly from side to side, saying, "I don't understand how this could be true."

Saul's gaze travels to the dark bay outside. She watches his face, waiting for him to speak.

When he says nothing, Eva asks, "What is it?"

A muscle below his eye flickers. "Nothing."

Eva leans her head against the sofa. Maybe there were signs—things she'd ignored. She is thinking back to a party a few months ago when they'd been talking to a colleague of Jackson's. The man had asked if they'd wanted to come to the Cotswolds the following weekend to celebrate his fortieth birthday. Without a moment's hesitation, Jackson had answered, "Buddy, we'd have loved to, but Eva's mother is in town. It's her birthday, so we're doing the whole dinner-and-a-show thing." It was an outright lie, one that tripped off Jackson's tongue with such ease that Eva had to pause for a moment to think, *Is my mother going to be in town?*

But, was the occasional white lie reason enough to suspect a bigger deception? Her thoughts slide back to the plane journey when she'd first met Jackson. She'd found him cocksure but funny, and he'd interested her with his talk of hiking in South America and stories of working on a dive boat in Australia. But they had been lies—right from the start.

Even if his lies began as a bit of fun, a game, surely there was a point when he must have thought: *I need to tell her the truth.*

The picture Jackson created of himself on that flight was what had drawn her to him. Their conversation had flowed easily; in fact, Jackson had said most first dates last a couple of hours, theirs lasted ten. But what if none of it was real?

She remembers something else he'd told her on that flight, something she needs to be sure of. "What made you want to be a marine biologist?" she asks Saul.

He inclines his head slightly, surprised. "It was a book, actually."

She blinks, waiting.

"I found it when I was a kid. It was tucked inside a backpack I bought from a secondhand store. I read it cover to cover and it made me see how we still have so much to learn about the ocean. I guess it was that—the mystery the book left open—that made me want to be a marine biologist."

Suddenly Eva is up on her feet. She lurches across the living room toward the bookcase. She has seen the book before. She knows she has.

She crouches, running her hand across the spines of books: *The Australian Fisherman, A Biography of Cod, Sea Fishing, A Reflection on Freediving,* and then there it is: *The Sea Around Us,* by Rachel Carson.

Eva slides it free. She feels the cold weight of the book in her hands. Slowly, she opens it.

There, on the inside cover written in fading blue ink, is the owner's name: *Saul Bowe, age 13.*

The book slides from her hands and crashes to the floor, pages splayed.

"Eva?" Saul says, standing.

She hears the concern in his voice, but doesn't answer. Her throat feels too tight. She can barely breathe; she needs air. She staggers past him and out onto the deck, where the floodlight flicks on, dazzling her. She grips the railing feeling the hard edges of the wood beneath her fingers, and she clings to it, gasping.

She desperately wants to believe that the book, the story, belong to her husband—not Saul. But she can't because already the trust between them has lost its strength, like a bridge cracking and splintering beneath her feet.

As she feels everything falling away, what terrifies Eva most is that she's no longer sure whether it was Jackson she fell in love with—or someone else entirely.

You caught me in the act of lying once. It was a stupid lie, too. Unnecessary. We were in a bar and a colleague of mine asked us to the Cotswolds for the weekend. The man bored me with his talk of cars and golf, and all I wanted was to spend the weekend with you eating croissants in bed with the papers, making love, taking a lazy stroll by the river. I knew you wouldn't want to go either, so I told the colleague that your mother was coming up for the weekend.

I didn't think it'd be a big deal—it was just one of those small white lies that couples make all the time.

Only I did it too well.

I glanced over at you and your head was tilted to one side, a quizzical expression making your brow dip, as if you were thinking: Is my mother going to be in town?

When you realized it was a lie, your expression changed as quickly as if I'd slapped you.

That look stayed with me; it felt portentous, a foreshad-

owing of how I might hurt you if I wasn't more careful. I don't think it was the lie itself that you disapproved of, it was that there was a moment where you couldn't tell the truth from the fiction.

Sometimes I couldn't tell the difference myself.

15

Sleep eludes Eva for the third night in a row. She wipes the tears from her face, then gathers up the duvet and trudges into the living room. She sits on the floor with the duvet around her shoulders, and spreads out the photos of Jackson that Saul had given her.

Images from her husband's past stare back at her.

She picks up the nearest photo, one of Jackson standing in a boatyard in a pair of blue overalls. Her heart contracts as she studies the familiar lines of his brow and jaw, his beautiful eyes. Yet nothing else about that photo is familiar to her.

"Why did you lie?" she whispers, the words reverberating in the empty room.

Her fingers tighten at the edge of the photo as she thinks of all the times he'd deceived her. She hears the sound of tearing before she realizes what she's doing. When she looks down, the picture is torn in half. The sensation is so satisfying that she rips it again into quarters, and then again, and again. She holds a fistful of ripped squares in her hand and throws them to the floor. Immediately she picks up the next photo—the one of Jackson cocktail flairing—and shreds it into pieces. She doesn't care that these pictures belong to Saul. She just wants them gone. All of them.

She rips with abandon, her teeth gritted, anger pouring out of her. Eva doesn't stop until every last photo is destroyed. Then she sits back, her breath ragged. Shreds of photos are scattered around her like debris after a storm.

In her lap, a single corner of a photo lies there: Jackson's mouth, his lips upturned in a smile. She picks it up between her fingertips and brings it close to her face.

Jackson's beautiful mouth. A mouth she'd kissed. A mouth he'd pressed against her neck, sending shivers of desire through her. A mouth that had spoken words of love.

Surely, that was all real?

Her anger recedes like a wave drawing back, and in place of betrayal, she feels a bewildering sense of compassion because, what leads somebody to wipe out their history and borrow someone else's?

"Why?" she pleads again. "Why didn't you tell me?"

Something catches in her mind. A rainy evening in London. Jackson returning from a run. The slap of wet clothes on the bathroom floor. The hiss of the shower, then the damp warmth of steam against her skin as she slipped inside the bathroom to say hello. But then she'd caught sight of Jackson through the gap in the shower curtain, and had paused. His arms were locked over his head, his body hunched forward as if bracing for impact. Sobbing.

She had wanted to pull back the shower curtain and reach for him, yet she sensed that it would be the wrong thing to do. Jackson had waited until he was alone to cry. Understanding that it was a private moment he didn't want witnessed, Eva had crept from the bathroom and gone about starting dinner.

Later, when Jackson came into the living room smelling of soap and deodorant, he'd smiled, kissed her brightly on the lips, and told her what a great run he'd had.

If I'd pushed you to talk right then, would you have? she thinks. *Is that all you needed?*

Why hadn't she? What sort of wife lets that go? They'd made love so tenderly that night, but still she didn't ask him what was wrong. Her heart breaks at the thought that he hadn't trusted her with the truth.

Eva hunches forward as sobs rock through her body. She holds her head in her hands as she cries, unable to look at the torn images of her husband.

SAUL FINDS EVA ASLEEP on the shack floor. He doesn't mention the ripped photos, or the chaos of the place. He just tells her that he needs her help. "I've got a day of squid tagging to do out at a test site on the east coast. My lab partner just canceled. Without the results, my project's screwed. I need you to stand in. Would you?"

She protests, saying there must be other people at the university who could help—and she's right. But he insists that no one else is available. He's firm and persistent, knowing he needs to get her out of the shack, get her active.

Finally she agrees and they leave Wattleboon on the next ferry and drive up the east coast in a light drizzle to launch the boat.

Now they're on the water and a stiff breeze streams across the sea stripping away voices, thoughts, breath. Eva holds onto the side of the boat as they plow through the sea, her hair blown back from her face.

When they get out to the test site, Saul throws down the anchor and they begin tagging. It takes them two hours to tag thirty squid, and when he fits the final tag, Eva angles the clipboard toward him saying, "We're done."

Saul empties the two large buckets of tagged squid back into the sea and, for a moment, the water is seething with southern calamari. Last week he'd planted an acoustic receiver in the seabed and now the microchips in the squid will send data to the unit every time they pass within a two-hundred-meter radius of it.

He fills the empty buckets with water and sloshes them over the deck to run off the worst of the squid ink. "Thanks for your help," he says to Eva, who hooked half the squid he's tagged.

"Thanks for making me come." She smiles for the first time that day and the sun spills over her face, lightening her eyes. He feels something stir in his chest. He turns away, setting down the bucket and then tidying a lose rope tangled on the floor.

"Have we time for a free-dive?" she asks.

"Definitely," he says, pleased. "There's a great spot on our way back over a giant kelp forest."

He takes the boat down the coast until he sees the rocky cove where the kelp forest lies. He anchors, sets down the ladder, then pulls out masks and fins from beneath the seats while Eva puts on her wetsuit.

When he straightens, he catches a flash of her tanned, lithe back as she arches, pushing her arms into the sleeves. He watches for a moment, unable to turn away. Her hand reaches for the zip, and as she pulls it, sunlight glances off her wedding band like a wink.

Saul steps back. Seeing that ring and all the promises that it encircles, he feels a stab of fury at Jackson. He'd taken so much that wasn't his to take. Saul can't even begin to understand the reasons behind the decisions he made.

A cautious friendship is growing between him and Eva, and he's come to care about her in a way he didn't expect. That's why he owes her the truth. It was easier to put it off before when he didn't know her and thought she would only be passing through.

He wipes his hands over his shorts, his heart quickening at the thought of what he must say. He exhales a long, low breath, then says, "Eva, I need to talk to you."

She looks around. Her face is lightly tanned, but there are dark shadows beneath her eyes. She leans against the boat's side as she puts on her fins. "What is it?"

His throat tightens around the words he has to say. "It's about Jackson."

She freezes, her foot half in the left fin. "Can we not?"

"Sorry?"

"I don't want to talk about him right now. I can't. I just need to be in the water. Not thinking or going over and over everything."

He looks at her, surprised. She used to want to talk about Jackson all the time, finding ways of weaving him into conversation just so she could say his name aloud. But as he looks at her now, it's as if a shutter has been yanked down.

"I'm sorry, Saul. I'm just exhausted by it all."

He could make her listen, insist that she did. And that's exactly what he should do. But instead he nods and says, "Okay."

EVA DESCENDS THE BOAT ladder, mask on, fins wagging awkwardly on the rungs. She remembers the last time she was holding this ladder, streaks of blood lining her thighs. She can't think about the miscarriage, just as she can't think of Jackson. It's too painful right now. As memories start pushing forward, Eva lets go and drops into the sea.

Underwater, her thoughts disperse. She is weightless. Her eyes adjust to the blue light and the great depth below her. She kicks lightly away from the boat and feels the groundswell as the sea surges beneath her. She likes the sensation: the drag as the swell sucks her toward it, then the feeling of being lifted and rolled gently forward.

She surfaces to adjust her mask, pushing aside a lock of wet hair breaking the seal.

Saul drops from the side of the boat and swims to her. He treads water. "You okay?"

She nods. "The visibility is great."

He explains the dive path they'll take, swimming straight out to the giant kelp forest against the current, then coming back with it along the cliff line and over reef and weed beds, then returning to the boat.

She follows Saul, who swims a few strokes ahead of her, his long fins making only the slightest fizz in the water. Now that Eva is beginning to learn more about free-diving techniques, she can appreciate his skillfulness. With seemingly little effort, he propels himself forward as if gliding.

When they reach the giant kelp forest, Eva dives down to look at the tall branches growing from the seabed. Thick, ribbed fronds sway in hues of chestnut and amber. Where the light catches it, the kelp glistens and Eva runs her fingertips over the glossy surface. It is as if she's swimming in the canopy of a rain forest.

Saul is treading water when she comes up for air. "I'm going to make a deeper dive," he tells her. "You wanna come?"

She nods and prepares her breathing, relaxing for a moment at the surface to slow her heart rate.

Saul dives first and she follows, filling her lungs with air before falling headfirst through the blue silken water. Her hair swirls around her mask and she kicks down with a light flex of her fins. She loves the feeling of the descent, her body and breath working against gravity, taking her deeper into the heart of the sea.

The underwater world opens up to her and she sees a wrasse, brightly colored with a puckered mouth, lazily weave in and out of the kelp. She feels the temperature turning cooler as she descends, swallowing to equalize the pressure in her ears every few feet.

Saul drops through the water ahead of her. He angles himself toward a large stalk of kelp and holds onto it, glancing back at Eva to do the same.

She grips her hands below his and they hang about fifteen feet under the surface, resting there. Her eyes begin to pick out the detail in the kelp, its different patterns as if scalloped by the sea.

Saul makes a circle of his thumb and forefinger, asking if she's okay. She returns the signal and nods, smiling. It's strangely intimate to be suspended beneath the sea together, their heart rates slowing as they drift beside each other. Somehow it is here that she feels safe, calm—as if they're in a cocoon, sealed off from the rest of the world.

Eventually her lungs begin to tighten and she looks up and kicks.

At the surface a smile passes between them. Water drips from Saul's eyebrows and lashes, and glistens in the creases of his smile. Eva feels her heart quicken.

They continue diving through the kelp, then over reef and craggy rock. Later they come to a weed bed that looks stunted and dull after the kelp forest, but she enjoys seeing the brightly colored fish darting through it.

There is a tap on her arm and Saul is pointing toward something in the weed bed. She follows the direction of his hand, straining to see what has caught his attention.

As the seaweed sways, she notices a glimpse of color ahead. She waits a moment for the seaweed to stir again—and then she sees it.

Her body fires with excitement at the otherworldly sight: a sea dragon drifts before them. Its body is a reddish color and looks as if it's been lit from the inside, electric pinpricks of blue and yellow spotting and striping its surface.

It glides with the current, graceful and poised. She is enchanted by its shape, the arched neck and dragonlike head, and the proud curl of its tail. She watches, caught in a moment of intense wonderment. Her lips turn up into a smile around her snorkel and she feels the sea wash against her teeth.

The sea dragon continues its slow dance through the water, drifting right past them. It is only when it disappears behind her that Eva realizes she needs air.

She kicks hard for the surface and she and Saul break through it, grinning.

EVA STRIPS OFF HER wetsuit, then wraps Saul's beach towel around herself. She pushes her hair back, squeezing the water from the ends, feeling so much better for the dive.

Saul has changed into shorts and a pale gray T-shirt, his collar dark from his wet hair. His expression is relaxed as he looks out over the water. Eva realizes how kind he's been these past few weeks, offering her a place to stay and looking after her in the wake of the miscarriage. It's strange to think that when she first met him she'd believed him to be someone completely different.

Saul goes into the cabin and rummages in a plastic bag, asking, "D'you want a sandwich? I've got prawn or bacon."

"Bacon, please." As she crosses the boat, she feels something sharp slice into her foot and cries out.

A hot pain shoots through her heel and she hops, lifting up her foot to look. "Shit!" Embedded in her skin is a fishhook, two of the barbs sunk deep into her heel.

Saul comes to her side, angling his head to see the damage. "Where did that come from?"

"No idea."

He moves a plastic crate toward Eva and says, "Sit. I'll get it out."

He disappears into the cabin and returns with a tattered red first-aid box, which he sets down beside her. Then he leans over the side of the boat and washes his hands. He dries them on the bottom of his T-shirt and she sees a glimpse of his stomach, the skin there paler than the dark tan on his forearms.

He draws an icebox opposite Eva and sits on top of it. "Give me your foot."

Eva knows that she could take the hook out herself, yet she finds herself wanting the reassurance of Saul's hands against her skin.

She raises her foot and Saul places it carefully on his thigh. Her toenails are unpainted and she sees that the seam of her wetsuit has left a red indentation along her calf.

Gently, Saul angles her foot to get a better view of the hook, his brow furrowing as he assesses the damage. "This is going to be a bit rough, but I've got to ease this thing out. You okay with that?"

Eva nods. "Do it."

As he pulls the hook, she grips the sides of the crate, feeling the metal snagging against her skin. The pain in her foot is hot and fierce.

Saul pauses a moment and Eva exhales, catching her breath. "You're doin' good. One barb out. One more to go. Ready?"

She nods and grits her teeth. This time the pain is more intense, like a knife being stabbed in her foot. She squeezes her eyes shut and starts to count. Before she reaches four, it is over.

"Here you go," Saul says, holding up the offending hook.

She angles her head to look at the sharp barbs. As she draws her foot away, Saul says, "You're not finished." He takes out an antiseptic wipe, and cupping Eva's heel in one hand, he carefully smoothes the wipe over the wound.

Eva winces. "Sorry. I'm not brave."

He looks up at her, his gaze steady. "You're incredibly brave, Eva." Then he smoothes the Band-Aid carefully over her heel, pressing down the sticky edges with his thumbs. When he is finished his hands stay lightly clasped around her foot.

Eva does not withdraw her leg. She waits, watching him.

Very slowly, Saul's fingers travel over the sides of her heel, tracing her bare ankle. She is aware of the gentle pressure, the warmth of his touch. Her breath catches.

Saul looks up and she meets his gaze.

He blinks, suddenly removing his hands and standing. "Sorry," he says in a low voice.

As he steps aside, Eva rises, too, and catches his hand instinctively. "Saul . . ."

He freezes, eyes lowered. Then, very slowly, he turns back toward her. Eva's heart drums as his gaze moves from their joined hands, over her body that is wrapped in his towel, and up to her face.

Looking into his eyes, she feels a connection pulsing between them that she is only just starting to understand. She becomes viscerally aware of every detail of his face: the salt caught in the stubble on his jaw; the stray eyebrow hairs that won't grow in a smooth arch; the darkness of his eyes that are fixed on her.

She does not know who moves first. She is simply aware of their bodies drawing together, her hand reaching for him, his palm on her cheek.

The kiss is tender. She tastes warmth and salt, and her eyes flutter closed. She feels their tongues meet, feels his shoulders beneath her hands, feels the press of their hips. They fall into each other, sinking into one another's longing and need.

And then, moments later, they are slowing down, pulling away as her thoughts rush headlong toward Jackson: his hands, his skin, his touch.

She rests her forehead against Saul's shoulder, the taste of him still on her lips, the memory of her husband still in her mind. Saul holds her in his arms and they stand like this, feeling the sea surging beneath them.

16

Saul draws the boat beside the jetty, hearing the rub of fenders against the weathered wood. Eva climbs onto the jetty and he watches her walk the length of it, his truck keys dangling from her fingers, the white Band Aid flashing on her heel.

He runs a hand through his salt-matted hair, thinking about that kiss: the sweet softness of her mouth; the press of her hands on his shoulders; the smooth skin of her throat. He'd wanted to peel away the damp towel she was wrapped in and touch every inch of her, lick the salt from her skin. But they'd stopped. They had no choice.

It was a mistake.

One he knew he wanted to make again.

He shouldn't have even brought her along on the research trip. It was too risky; too many people about. He scans the parking lot, checking for any vehicles he recognizes, but thankfully it's clear.

He watches Eva pulling herself into the driver's seat of his truck, then hears the grunt of the engine as she reverses, lining up the trailer with the boat ramp. She looks tiny sitting upright in his seat, her chin lifted to peer in the rearview mirror.

He calls out for her to stop when the trailer reaches the

water, then he drives the boat forward, feeling the clunk of metal beneath him. On his signal, Eva pulls away, engine straining, and the boat is dragged from the sea.

When the boat is out of the water, Saul jumps down, the gravel sharp on his bare feet. "Great job."

Eva smiles, her lips parting over white teeth, and he feels the strongest urge to lean down and kiss her again. He makes himself turn away and secure the boat to the trailer while Eva heads for the restroom at the edge of the parking lot.

He takes the straps out of the truck and begins looping them around the metal bars of the boat when he hears his name. "Saul! Long time no see, mate!"

He turns and sees Flyer loafing toward him, a squat man with more beard than hair, whom Saul knows from his schooldays.

Shit, he thinks, glancing over his shoulder to check for Eva.

"How are ya?" Flyer asks, pumping Saul's hand.

"Good. All good," he says, knowing he must keep this conversation short.

"Caught your dinner?"

"Not today. Just tagging." The sun is starting to burn through the clouds and Saul feels hot beneath his T-shirt.

"I got a load of flatties. Bloody things were practically jumpin' in the boat. Didn't even pretend to fight."

"Too easy."

"Saw the terns diving out there," Flyer says, rubbing his nose, which is sunburned from a summer on the water. "Reckon the tuna must be schooling."

"Yeah?"

"Wouldn't mind getting out there soon with the big gear."

Saul nods.

"Bumped into Jimmy a while back. Said your place's all done up."

"Finished just before Christmas. Nice to be in. There's still stuff to do."

"Ain't there always? I'd never see a bloody fish if I worked through the list that needs doin' round our place." Flyer continues talking, telling Saul about the solar panels he got halfway through installing, but had to stop because the roof tiles started coming loose. "It was like ridin' a bloody sled up there. The wife cracked the shits over that, I can tell ya."

But Saul isn't paying attention, as he's caught sight of Eva making her way toward them.

Saul turns to Flyer, who is deeply involved in his story by now. Just as he is about to interrupt and tell Flyer he's got to run, Flyer notices Eva. "Who the heck is that?"

Eva stops at Saul's side and smiles lightly, glancing between the men.

Saul has no choice but to introduce her. "Flyer, this is Eva. Eva, Flyer."

"G'day," Flyer says. He wipes his palms on his T-shirt and shakes her hand. He straightens a little and smoothes back what hair he has. In the presence of female company, Flyer is all charm. "You've been out on the water, too?"

"Just helping Saul."

"Where d'you recruit your assistants from, mate?" Flyer says with an easy grin.

"That'd be tellin'."

Flyer is about to say something further, but Saul cuts him off. "We're gonna have to shoot. Get the gear back to the lab."

"Sure thing," Flyer says, but doesn't move to leave. Instead, he is leaning close to Saul. "Hey, mate . . ." His tone is altered and Saul knows exactly what's coming. His heart begins to pound. "I was sorry to hear about Jackson. Keep meaning to call to arrange a beer or somethin'."

Saul feels dull-witted and can't think what to respond with. "That'd be good," he manages eventually.

"Tragic, wasn't it? He was fishing off some rocks, I heard?"

Saul nods slowly. He is acutely aware of Eva standing at his shoulder, her head lifting in interest at the mention of Jackson. "Yeah, fishing in England. It was a shock," he says vaguely.

"I'll bet. My missus heard about it. Tells me Jeanette is havin' a tough time. Distraught, she reckons."

Saul swallows, feeling the blood pumping hard around his body.

He senses Eva's gaze on him, silently asking, *Who is Jeanette?* He cannot look at her.

Flyer continues. "I know things between them hadn't been good for a while, but she was still his wife."

It takes all of Saul's effort to keep his hands at his side, not to ram his fist down Flyer's throat to make him shut the hell up.

"Anyway," Flyer says brightly, as if relieved to have gotten that out of the way. "Best let you get on—but great to see you, mate." He squeezes Saul's shoulder. "Let's do that beer soon, eh?" Then he winks at Eva and says, "See ya, love," before striding back to his car.

Saul doesn't move. His pulse throbs in his neck.

Silence swells between him and Eva. He can feel the burn of her gaze on him.

When she speaks, her voice is deadly quiet. "Jackson had a wife?"

EVA WAITS FOR SAUL'S answer. Waits for him to tell her that Flyer was mistaken.

The harsh glare of the sun exposes every detail of his expression. She sees the sweat on his brow, the vein standing proud at his temple, the squint of his eyes as he looks past her, just beyond her shoulder.

He swallows. "Yes, Jackson was married."

She leans forward as if she's taken a blow to the stomach. Saliva swills around her mouth and she clamps her hands over her lips. *No, no, no!* He can't have been married before. He would've told her. It would mean he'd had a wife. A wedding day. A wedding night. She screws her eyes shut as unbearable images rupture her thoughts.

"Eva . . ."

"Who is she? How long were they married?" Her voice is a thin thread, trembling with questions. "When did they get divorced?"

Saul exhales a long, low breath, pushing out all the air from his lungs. His gaze is pinned to hers and the intensity of it scares her. "They never got divorced."

She blinks. "What?"

"He was still married to her when he . . . married you."

Time becomes suspended, as if everything has been stripped away: the sound of boat engines, the smell of the sea, the feel of the sun on her skin. There is nothing, only the words that Saul has just spoken, which scream and claw through her skull. *He was still married to her when he married you.*

The air is like a wall, solid and unmovable. She can't breathe. Her ears fill with the rushing sound of blood. The ground seems to tilt. She sees Saul's hand reaching for her arm, but all she knows is that she doesn't want him near. She yanks her arm away, stumbling backward.

She presses herself against the truck, air surging into her lungs. Her chest rises and falls. The metal bodywork is hot against her back and she feels a wave of nausea push through her. She breathes deeply, willing herself not to be sick.

"I . . . I don't understand. It wasn't legal? Our marriage wasn't . . . real?"

He is shaking his head, repeating the word, *Sorry*.

"Oh God . . . I . . . I . . ." She breaks off, squeezing her hands to her head. "Then it's *bigamy*," she says, the word sounding so alien on her tongue.

None of it feels real; it's as if she has stepped out of her body and is watching the conversation as a bystander. She can hear her voice, but isn't aware of actually framing the questions she asks: "Who is she?"

"Her name is Jeanette."

"Is she Tasmanian?"

He nods. "Lives up in the north—"

"Does she know about me?"

"No. They were separated a while back—"

"But not divorced?"

"No. Not divorced. But I don't think they were in touch."

Saul says this to try to make it better—but it doesn't. Nothing can make this better.

Her clothes stick to her damp skin. The stones are sharp against her throbbing heel as she paces alongside the truck, her mind loosening. She presses her fingertips to her forehead trying to still her thoughts, but her memory of Jackson is fracturing into sharp, jagged pieces that feel as if they're tearing through her skin.

Then suddenly she stops and turns to look at Saul. "My God," she says, her eyes widening. "You knew. This whole time, you knew."

"No, Eva. Listen," he says, lifting his hands in front of him. "I knew when Jackson married Jeanette. But I had no idea about you. Not until after Jackson's death. I promise you. Dad's the only person Jackson ever told."

She laughs then, a sharp hysterical sound. Dirk knew that his son had two wives! Her visit to him begins to make sense. That's why, after a few whiskeys, he admitted that Jackson should never have married Eva.

"Why didn't you tell me?"

He shifts. "I didn't want to hurt you . . ."

It's a pathetic answer, insulting in its weakness. Her fingers slip into the pocket of her shorts and she fishes out his truck keys. With one quick movement, she slings them as hard as she can into the water. They make a small splash and disappear.

Saul doesn't turn around. His eyes are locked on her. "Eva . . ." he begins.

But already she is turning from him, from Jackson, from both their lies.

She grabs her bag from the truck and begins to run as everything that she believed in splinters around her.

17

Melbourne rears up tall and angular, muscular skyscrapers squaring up next to each other under a darkening sky. The taxi weaves through the city streets and Eva stares blankly through the window watching streetcars slide by, their carriages full.

The driver calls over his shoulder, "You said Borralong Street, right? What building?"

"Parkside," she tells him.

They roar on. Eva's gaze travels to her engagement ring and wedding band. The polish of the platinum has been dulled by salt water and sunscreen, and they stick faintly to her skin as she twists them off.

She turns her wedding band slowly through her fingers, reading the italicized inscription: *This day and always.* She shakes her head at the irony. She will not wear them—not when there is another woman who's already been promised an *always* from Jackson.

She opens the window a crack; fume-tinged air and the rush of traffic flood in. Without pause or ceremony, she lets both rings drop from her fingers. They clink against the taxi's side and then are lost beneath the wheels of other vehicles.

She closes the window and sits back, inspecting the pale band of skin encircling her finger. The flesh beneath looks wasted and shrunken from the pressure of wearing the rings. She rubs at her finger, trying to massage life back into it.

Eventually the taxi pulls up outside a prestigious apartment building with stylish curved balconies and gleaming tinted windows. Callie is sitting on the steps in the fading evening sun, dressed in a pair of tailored trousers and an open-necked cream shirt. She must've come straight from the studio. Eva can't even think what day of the week it is. All she knows is that just a few hours ago she was on a boat catching squid in Tasmania—and now she's in Melbourne.

She pays the taxi driver and climbs out with her bag. Callie steps forward, and Eva falls into her open arms. Callie smells of perfume and mints, and her bracelets jangle as she holds Eva tight to her. After a few moments, she takes Eva by the hand and leads her inside.

They ride up several floors in a mirror-paneled elevator. Eva keeps her gaze lowered, careful not to catch her reflection. Her flip-flops look tatty and worn against the polished floor and there is a faint smear of an ink stain on her shinbone that looks like dirt.

Callie unlocks the door into a bright, spacious apartment and Eva follows her through to the kitchen. Two wineglasses wait on the marble island. Callie takes a bottle of white wine from the fridge and pours them both generous glasses.

Eva's hand trembles slightly as she lifts the wine to her lips. The cool liquid slides down her throat and she leans back against the kitchen table, letting out her breath. She'd called Callie on the way to Hobart airport when the shock was still so fresh that she didn't even believe the words that she was saying. But now the truth is working into her and she feels as if she's splitting open at the seams.

"Tell me exactly what happened," Callie says.

Eva puts down the wine and grips the counter, repeating the conversation between Flyer and Saul.

Callie listens, rubbing her brow as if massaging in the information. "I'm staggered. Staggered," she repeats, shaking her head. "How could he? I just . . . I can't believe he'd do this to you. Jackson? He loved you. Why did he do it?"

Eva squeezes her temples, where a deep pressure feels like it's building. "I've no idea."

THEY TRAMP UP THREE flights of metal stairs to reach the roof terrace. Callie is relieved to find they're the only ones up here tonight. She sets down their wine on a table at the edge of the terrace and they settle into a low double seat, looking out over the city. From a nightclub somewhere, a laser light beams up at the sky.

Eva tucks her feet beneath her and cups her wineglass. With her salt-stiffened hair, flip-flops, and denim shorts, she looks like a castaway washed up in the city. Noticing that Eva's hands are trembling, Callie asks, "Darling, are you warm enough?"

"I'm fine."

"Have you got anything else with you?"

She shakes her head. "I came straight from the boat. Maybe I should've gone back to Wattleboon. I wasn't thinking. I've only got my handbag."

"I can sort you out with everything you need. You don't have to go back, not if you don't want to."

Eva leans her head back and looks up at the sky. She sighs. "Did we rush it, Cal?"

"You and Jackson?"

"I never expected to fall in love. Not so quickly. It just . . .

happened. I know everyone thought we were moving too fast—but it just felt right."

Callie presses her lips together, but doesn't say anything. Music drifts through a window below, and there is a hum of traffic beyond.

"Did you like Jackson? I mean *really* like him? I somehow got the impression that you never warmed to him."

"Did you?" Callie says, surprised. She runs her finger along the base of the wineglass, thinking about the question. "I liked Jackson, I honestly did, it's just . . . I suppose he wasn't who I'd have pictured you with."

She remembers feeling as if Jackson had just barreled into Eva's life with his big personality and big gestures. Within three months they'd rented an apartment together in London and on weekends he would sweep Eva off to Paris, to Wales, to Oxford, to Cornwall. The speed and suddenness of it all was so out of character for Eva, who'd always been careful to retain her independence in previous relationships.

When Eva was visiting her in Dubai the week before she met Jackson, she'd confided in Callie that her life in Dorset had become static and she was thinking of moving to London. Maybe she feared she was slipping back into the too-quiet rhythm of her childhood. And then Jackson turned up, a burst of energy promising to fill her world with color.

"Did you have doubts about us?"

"I never doubted he loved you. Not once," Callie answers truthfully.

"But?" Eva prompts.

"But . . . I don't know . . . it's difficult to explain. Maybe I just wondered if he'd look after you."

"What do you mean?"

She thinks of the ease with which he spent money, never putting anything aside for the future, and the nights out they'd all go on—Jackson pushing to continue on to the next bar, the next club, even when Eva was exhausted from her shifts. "I suppose what I mean is, as much as he loved you, I always felt like he put himself first."

Eva hugs her arms around her chest. And that's when Callie notices: her wedding and engagement rings have already gone.

THEY'VE BEEN ON THE roof terrace for an hour when Eva's cell phone vibrates. She pulls it from her bag and stares at the name flashing on the glowing screen.

"Who is it?" Callie asks when Eva doesn't answer it.

"Saul." Eva turns off the phone and stuffs it back in her bag, which she pushes under the table with a foot. "He had so many chances to tell me about Jackson."

"Maybe he didn't want to hurt you."

Eva's thoughts trip back to the boat ride earlier in the day. Had that really only been this morning? She remembers the way he'd carefully held her foot as he'd smoothed the Band-Aid over her heel, and the exquisite tenderness of his lips against hers. "I kissed Saul," she says quietly.

Callie straightens. "What? When?"

"Today. Before all this . . ."

"Jesus, Eva. What happened?"

"We were on his boat. And . . . I don't know . . . somehow we kissed."

She can see by Callie's expression that she is thinking the exact same thing as Eva: *But he's Jackson's brother.* Eva picks up her wine and takes a long swallow, feeling the dull heat of shame in her cheeks. "I don't know why I did it."

"You've been through such a huge loss—and Saul's your link to Jackson. Maybe he helps you feel closer to Jackson," Callie suggests gently.

Eva presses her lips together as she nods. She cannot deny she found comfort in hearing Saul pronounce the occasional word in the way that Jackson might have, or catching the same vibration in their laughter.

"It was just a kiss, darling. Don't beat yourself up about it."

Eva doesn't say that when she was in Saul's arms, it was the first time in months that she'd felt light. It may have been just a kiss, but in it she'd tasted the first stirrings of possibility.

SAUL SLINGS HIS PHONE on the table, then goes outside onto the deck.

Low clouds veil the stars tonight, making it seem as if the night is pressing down on him. He stands with his hands gripped to the railings, feeling the grain of the wood against his palms.

There are still no lights on over at Eva's shack. She's not coming back here, not tonight. He imagines she's in Hobart somewhere, or perhaps in Melbourne with Callie. He just hopes that wherever she is, she's okay.

Christ, he's been an idiot. He should've told her the truth about Jackson that first day she turned up on Wattleboon.

But he hadn't—and then she'd found out she was pregnant and he couldn't do it after that; she just seemed too fragile.

Or maybe that's bullshit. Maybe sometimes it's just easier to lie.

A bat swoops low overhead, the thrum of its wings making the air vibrate. He sees it dip again and then disappear into the trees.

He runs a hand across his unshaven face. He feels the nicks

on his fingers from wrestling tags into all those squid. He'd loved having Eva on the boat, watching her concentration each time she hooked a squid, her face so serious as she reeled it in. It'd been incredible free-diving together, too; diving deep through the kelp forest and sharing the beauty of watching a sea dragon drift by. And that kiss: that was really something. He doesn't want to even pause on how good that felt, not when he's messed everything up so badly.

He should never have taken her up the east coast. Letting her stay on at the shack was stupid enough, but he'd told himself that it was a better option than Eva wandering around Hobart trying to meet up with Jackson's old friends.

He replays the conversation they had after Flyer left, how her whole face stretched thin with pain. Then she'd bent forward as if he'd punched her in the stomach.

Seeing her like that, hurting so badly, made him feel black inside. He keeps on asking himself over and over, *Why the hell did Jackson do it?*

IT'S AFTER MIDNIGHT WHEN Eva crawls into bed. She is desperately tired, but can't drift off, as her mind is still pawing through the day's events.

When sleep finally claims Eva, her dreams are disturbed and broken. She finds herself walking along a darkened hallway toward the sound of voices—but when she calls out, no one answers and her words echo off the narrow walls.

Reaching the end of the hallway, she sees Jeanette sitting at the kitchen table, her back to Eva.

Jeanette says something and then stands, lifting a plate. As she moves, Eva sees there is someone else at the table.

Jackson is facing her, eating a bowl of cereal drenched with milk. Eva's throat vibrates as she screams.

But Jackson doesn't look up. No one does.

Eva staggers forward into their kitchen. "Jackson? How? I . . . I don't understand. You're dead! You're supposed to be dead!"

She spins around. Jeanette is washing a dish in the sink, and Jackson continues to eat his cereal. "Why are you pretending you can't hear me?" she cries.

Their faces are blank. No one so much as glances up.

And then she realizes: they can't hear her, or see her, because it is Eva who is dead.

She wakes, clawing at the covers.

Her breath is ragged as she twists free of the duvet and sits up. She reaches for the light and blinks as it flickers on. Her body is slick with sweat, her hair pasted to her forehead.

A dream, a dream, she tells herself.

She lurches from the bed and goes to the window, pushing it open. The air is cool against her face and she gulps it in, tasting the heaviness of the city. Tears stream down her cheeks, emotion thickening her throat.

Why has Jackson— the man who promised to love and honor her—done this? Her memories feel uprooted, like trees ripped from the earth in a storm.

She concentrates on trying to regulate and slow her breathing, using the technique she'd learned from free-diving. It takes several minutes, but when she's caught her breath, she dries her face and looks at her watch. It's 3:20 A.M. She cannot go back to sleep, not when her nightmare still keeps the bed warm. She'll get a drink; her throat is dry and she can feel the stirrings of a headache in the base of her skull.

She creeps from the room, picking her way carefully along

the hall and into the kitchen. She had forgotten how in a city, rooms are never truly dark. The lights from the surrounding apartments, offices, and streetlamps cast just enough of a glow for her to locate a glass on the draining board. She fills it with water and drinks it down, the cool liquid soothing her throat.

Then she moves through the living room and pushes open the doors onto the balcony. Somehow she had expected to hear the bay, but instead she hears traffic, voices, a hum of something electric. The oversize T-shirt she's borrowed from Callie stirs lightly around her thighs and goose bumps rise on her skin.

She stands on the balcony, looking south over the city in the direction of the coast. Somewhere beyond there, across the Bass Strait, lies Tasmania. And living on that island is a woman who also calls Jackson her husband. Eva tries picturing her. Is Jeanette beautiful? Young? When did they marry? What was their wedding like? Did Dirk go? Did Saul?

Eva's thoughts trail back to her own wedding. She remembers the butterflies of excitement in her stomach when she heard the first chords of the organ. She'd walked slowly down the short aisle, her arm linked with her mother's, her eyes on Jackson. He'd been standing with his hands clasped together, watching her with a deep, unblinking focus.

When she reached his side, she could see beads of sweat on his brow and feel the heat radiating from his body. She knew he was nervous, but she'd thought: *What groom isn't nervous on his wedding day?*

When her mother passed her hand to Jackson, Jackson's palm felt hot and damp. As the organ played its final bars, his gaze was still pinned to her face. She watched as a bead of sweat trailed down his forehead and got caught in his eyebrow. "You okay?" she'd whispered.

"You make me a better person, Eva," he'd said, a low intensity to his voice. "We're meant to be together. Aren't we?"

"Yes," she'd said, squeezing his hand twice.

Jackson had smiled, his expression softening into something more familiar. Then he'd turned to face the priest, ready to make vows that had no more substance than air.

On the morning of our wedding I got cold feet. Not about you. Never about you, Eva. I promise you that.

Our service was at one o'clock, but at noon I was still sitting at the pub in a pair of jeans and a T-shirt, looking into the bottom of a whiskey glass. I was picturing you and Callie getting ready together in your old bedroom at your mother's house. It would have been chaos—clothes and makeup and shoes strewn around the room. Callie was probably feeding you champagne, your mother constantly poking her head around the door.

I stood up from that pub stool, knowing I couldn't go through with it.

I was walking back to your home, working out what I was going to say—what possible explanation I could have given you for calling off the thing I wanted most in the world— when the wedding car drove past me on its way to collect you. It was an old white VW Beetle, with a huge cream bow tied from the sideview mirrors to the bumper.

When I saw it, all I could think of was how in an hour's

time we could be sitting in the back of that car as husband and wife. I wanted to marry you so much, and at that moment it seemed worth it, whatever the cost.

So I ran back to the hotel, pulled on my suit, shoved my feet into new shoes, and sprinted to the church. I arrived three minutes before you.

When the organ played those first chords, I turned to watch you walk down the aisle. You looked so beautiful. I know all grooms say that—but honestly, Eva, you did. I don't know the right words to describe the cut of the dress or what you'd done with your hair. All I know is that you looked more incredible than I could have imagined.

At the altar you asked me if I was okay, and my reply was a whispered question: "We're meant to be together. Aren't we?" I put our fate in your hands, and of course you answered, "Yes," because you didn't know everything back then.

You still don't.

18

Eva is swept along the rush-hour streets of Melbourne. It's a Friday evening and the buzz of the weekend fills the air. The crowd deepens as she passes the train station, where food stalls sell popcorn and waffles, neat trays of sushi, and onion-drenched burgers. Traffic is backed up in the streets and she hears the ring of cable cars above the thrum of voices and engines.

To the passing crowd, Eva could be just another tourist taking in the city, or an office worker on her way to meet friends for a drink. Nobody knows her—and the anonymity is a comfort.

She catches the low, vibrating tones of a didgeridoo up ahead and is drawn toward the sound. She manages to squeeze through the press of people crowding the wide pavement and sees two young men in low-slung jeans at the center, busking. One blows into the didgeridoo, his hands cupping the mouthpiece, and the other raps clever lyrics with his lips to a microphone as the crowd nods and dips to his beat.

These are the pockets of city life that Eva once loved, where around every corner there is something vibrant to discover. But today she can't feel it—neither the buzz and energy of the performers nor the rhythm of the music in her chest. She feels deadened.

Eva's been in Melbourne two weeks now, and she spends her days walking. She is learning the routes and layout of the city: where the best parks lie; which walls are covered in street art; how to reach the alleys that bustle with quirky shops. She doesn't think she ever walked so much in all the time she lived in London. Her heels are blistered and sore, but she needs to keep going, to do something.

She'd called home earlier and had a disjointed conversation with her mother. She hasn't told her what's happened yet. She can't bear to. Eva needs her mother to keep on believing her marriage to Jackson was real and that they were in love—so that she can keep believing it, too.

As her mother talked, Eva felt removed from the conversation. "I had another card from one of your friends yesterday. This one was from—" She'd paused, reading the name. "Sarah. So lovely that everyone's thinking of you."

Eva couldn't even place the name. It was as though her brain had been shaken so that everything was jumbled, information difficult to reach. As her mother read out the kind message about Eva's loss, all Eva was thinking was: *If only you knew.*

The crowd presses around her and she feels the heat of other bodies, the air thickening. The soulful song of the didgeridoo weaves into her thoughts and she finds herself thinking, *Jackson would've loved this music.*

But then she shakes her head: *Or would he?* She thought that she'd known the intricacies of his tastes: that he loved reggae, rock, and blues, but wouldn't listen to anything with an electronic beat; that he'd eat olives and anchovies by the jar, but wouldn't touch capers; that he was particular about wearing good shoes, yet would wear the same pair of trousers until the knees wore thin. But now, how could she be confident about where the truth ended and the lies began?

The crowd around her grows and tightens. Just as she is turning, thinking, *I want to leave,* across the street she catches sight of someone so familiar that her mind stalls.

She knows it can't be. Knows that it is impossible that he's here . . . yet . . .

She struggles amid the people, twisting around to see him more clearly.

There he is! Walking on the opposite pavement! Her heart rate flares as she sees his long, fluid strides, and his thick dark hair cut close to his head.

"Jackson!" she cries out, but his name is swallowed by music and traffic.

As the crowd continues to move around her, she loses sight of him. She pushes up on her tiptoes, craning her neck to see. But she can't locate him.

"Out of my way!" she cries, fighting her way through. He's here! He's right here. She needs to get to him. Speak to him.

She uses her elbows now, pushing past a tightly packed group of teenagers who scowl at her beneath heavy hair and piercings.

She cannot lose him! She jumps, pushing herself up using other people's arms and shoulders—and catches another sight of him. He's still on the other side of the road, heading north.

Her breathing is ragged now as she moves through the crowd, forcing her way past two men who curse at her. Then suddenly she is free and is rushing forward, crossing the road toward Jackson . . .

There is a deafening screech of tires and the blare of a horn. A taxi roars to a halt just a few feet from her. She freezes, heart hammering against her ribs. The taxi driver holds down the horn again, and Jackson turns at the sound.

Only he is not Jackson. He is just a man of a similar age, with a similar build. Now that she can see him properly, her mistake is clear.

She staggers back onto the sidewalk, where people stand staring at her. The taxi accelerates away, the driver shaking his head as he mouths the word, *Crazy*.

SAUL HOLDS THE LAST nail steady as he bangs the hammer down with quick, hard taps. The wood splinters slightly where it's aged, but the nail eventually goes all the way in. He's losing the light and the mosquitoes are starting to prowl, so he'll have to call it quits for tonight.

He steps back to inspect his work, nodding to himself, pleased. He's been working on this project for most of the summer, just using an hour here or there whenever he's free. Another couple of days and it'll be finished. He could even get it tied up this weekend now that his friends aren't coming to stay. He feels bad for canceling, but he's just not in the mood for company.

Saul knows that what he should be doing this weekend is visiting his dad. It's been ages. But he's still pissed at him. If Dirk hadn't asked him to lie to Eva, maybe she'd still be here.

He puts the tools away, then drags the tarp over the wood, securing it with a few rocks. He adds a couple of extra ones at the corners since the wind is starting to pick up.

He ducks inside to grab a beer, and takes it down to the bay. A southerly is blowing straight in from Antarctica, bringing with it a deep chill. The water is already churned up, so there'll be no chance of a free-dive this weekend. He drove down to Broken Point earlier and the swell was blown out, too. He hates the bloody wind. No good for anything.

He moves along the shore, kicking up the foam that's trembling on the tide line. No footprints other than his own down here tonight. That makes him feel low. He takes a long gulp of beer, barely tasting it, and walks on toward Eva's shack. He visits every night, just to check in case she's decided to come back.

Just as he expected, her stuff is still inside. He sits on the sofa and finishes his beer. At first Saul kept telling himself that she'd return for her belongings, but now two weeks have passed and there's still no word. She doesn't answer any of his calls, and in the back of his mind he's thinking: *Clothes and toiletries, they're replaceable. She doesn't need to come here again.*

He sets the empty beer down and picks up the free-diving book that's open on the table. He'd lent it to her when they'd first started diving together. He loved her enthusiasm for free-diving and the long discussions they had about it. She'd taken to it quickly, as if she was born to be in the water. He spends a few minutes thinking about some of the dives they'd made together, the determined look on her face as she filled her lungs with air before making a neat surface dive toward the ocean bed.

He misses Eva more than he had imagined and doesn't want to think about what this means. She brought the bay to life and now it feels empty without her.

With a sigh, he gets to his feet and leaves the shack.

He'll check again tomorrow.

Saul and I were close once. It seems an age ago now, but we were. I loved being the older brother and getting to do things first, like showing Saul how to gut a squid and take out the quill, or carve a branch into a spear.

One of our favorite things was cliff jumping. It started when we were just kids and we'd dive off the low cliffs and rocks around Wattleboon. Back then, Mum was still alive and she and Dad would take photos with an old film camera and coo over how brave we were. Those early dives were rarely higher than ten meters, so it was all about skill and grace, about seeing who could do a double rotation, or who could keep their swan dive in free fall to the last moment.

After the bush fire, we didn't come back to Wattleboon, so we found new places to cliff-jump. Dad didn't watch anymore—he was still trying to hold onto the business, tell himself that the drinking was just a phase. But Saul and me wanted to get out of that house as much as possible.

The cliff jumps we found got bigger and riskier. Saul would scout them out from the water up, swimming with his mask and fins to check the depth, looking for submerged rocks, finding the right place to climb back up afterward. Me, I used to like standing on the cliff top and looking down, relying on instinct to know if I could make it. I think Saul thought I was brave—but I wasn't. I went for those big, wild jumps without checking the water below because I didn't care about the landing or coming back up. All I wanted was to jump.

19

A weekend vibe swings through the waterfront bar; faces are tanned and the chatter is loud and vibrant.

Eva wants this brightness to flow into her, but instead she feels like a rock jammed into a fast moving river: dark and hard and impenetrable. Conversation and music move fluidly around her, but she is stuck firm.

"Darling?" Callie is saying as they stand beside a tall table they're sharing with another group of women. "Are you okay? We can go somewhere quieter. Go back to the apartment, if you prefer?"

Eva doesn't want to be cooped up in there, and she doesn't want to be feeling like a specter in the crush of this bar. It was Callie's idea to go out and Eva is doing her best to make an effort. At the restaurant she'd had no appetite and washed down her sushi with mouthfuls of wine so that Callie wouldn't worry that she's not eating.

"Are you okay?" Callie repeats. "Really?"

"I . . . I'm just . . ." *What? What should she say? Exhausted? Numb? Quietly splintering?* "I'm just going to get us more cocktails." At the bar she has to shout above the music to order two Long Island iced teas. She does a shot of sambuca while she waits, the hot sweetness burning her throat. She wipes her mouth on the back of her hand, hoping the sambuca will help shake off the deep weariness that clings to her.

She's not sleeping. Every night her dreams are smothered beneath the same disturbing nightmare that Eva is walking along Jeanette's hallway, only to reach the end and find Jackson living there happily. The nightmare is so vivid that Eva wakes twisted in the covers and dripping with sweat, his name on her lips.

Suddenly Eva wants to be in England. She wants to see her mother. She wants time to rewind and for it to be two years earlier, and for her to be moving along the aisle of a plane looking for her seat number, and rather than taking the empty seat beside the tanned stranger with the clear blue eyes, Eva wants to have walked straight past him. She wants Jackson to have never entered her life.

Yet she also wants Jackson here. Right now. She wants to feel his strong arms wrapped tight around her. She wants his baby to still be growing inside her, to feel Jackson's hands on her pregnant belly. She wants to hear him say, *I love you,* with his lips close to her ear. She needs him to tell her: *You've got it all wrong.*

She knows she should hate him for what he's done, but she can't because she still remembers the Jackson who'd lifted her onto the kitchen counter, put a glass of wine in her hand, and then lowered his face to hers, whispering, "I've been waiting for you to get back." And the Jackson who, on the evening they moved into their apartment, asked her to unpack one of the boxes, then watched as she pulled out a bottle of champagne with a note around the neck that read: *We're home.*

That Jackson. That's the one she misses.

There is a hand on her back and she swings around.

"Here, I've got them," Callie says, easing the drinks from Eva, who hadn't realized she was holding them.

Eva follows Callie back to the table, her thoughts spinning. "Why did he marry me?"

"Because he loved you." Callie places the drinks down and then reaches out and takes Eva's hands. "I know everything's a mess right now—but please, darling, just remember that he did love you. Everyone could see how crazy he was about you."

"How do I know, though? What if that was just another lie?"

"It was real."

"Who was he, Cal?" she says, withdrawing her hands. "I don't even know, not really. Everything was lies. His whole past was borrowed from Saul. He had another wife. It makes me question . . . everything."

"What do you mean?"

"I don't know." She shakes her head. "I can't let him go. There was no good-bye. No body. Nothing. When he died, I thought . . . that was it. That was the worst thing—the very worst thing— that could happen. I'd lost the person I'd planned to spend the rest of my life with. But it wasn't," she says, her hands balling into fists. "The worst thing is: now I've lost my past, too."

EVA LOSES COUNT OF the number of cocktails she's had, but by the way she sways onto the dance floor, she guesses it must be a lot.

She and Callie dance within a crowd, colored lights strobing over bodies, illuminating a pair of silver heels, the swing of a loosened tie, the blink of false lashes. The air is warm with the smell of perspiration and beer. Eva spins, feeling a rush of air around her thighs as her dress swirls.

She remembers seeing Jackson dance for the first time and she'd laughed, amazed by how good he was. He moved with confidence and a swagger, as if the music was playing through his body. Her mother had always said, *Be wary of a man who can dance.*

Had her mother been wary of Jackson? She seemed genuinely elated when they'd announced their engagement. But perhaps her fondness for him was only an extension of her love for Eva. Had anyone seen what she hadn't?

Her feet move over the polished black floor. The bass of the track vibrates in her chest, and she shakes her body to the beat. She's distantly aware of Callie saying something to her, but Eva spins away, letting the crowd become a blur around her.

She allows the alcohol to loosen the hard knots of memory and she twists, light and free, as music falls through the air around her.

CALLIE WATCHES AS EVA dances with her head tilted back, as if only loosely attached to her neck. Eva is drunk, too drunk. She's been taking an extra shot every time she goes to the bar.

Two men watch appreciatively as Eva swings her hips. She looks beautiful, but God, she looks sad. It's as if someone has reached inside her and turned out a light.

When the song changes Callie slips over to Eva and leans close to her ear, saying, "Let's go back now."

"Back? No!" Eva weaves beyond her in the direction of the bar.

But Callie knows she needs to get Eva home. She threads her arm through Eva's, saying, "There's a club farther down the street. Fancy taking a look?"

"Sure," Eva says, letting Callie lead her through the crowd and toward the door.

Outside, the air is cool after the clammy heat of the bar. They walk slowly along the pavement, low laughter ebbing from a bench where a crowd of teenagers loiters, holding beer cans.

When Callie sees a taxi, she steps forward, raising her hand. It pulls up next to them. "Let's jump in."

"What about the club?" Eva slurs.

"Oh, we passed it. I don't think it was open."

Eva unlinks her arm from Callie. "You're lying." The headlights of a passing car illuminate them both so that for a moment she can see the anger in Eva's narrowed eyes.

"Listen, Eva—"

"I hate being lied to. I fucking hate it!"

"Okay, okay! There's no club. I just wanted to get you home." Callie glances at the taxi. "Please, Eva. The taxi's waiting."

Eva twists away from her and starts walking unevenly back toward the bar, her heels making hard clicks on the pavement. Then she stops to crouch down and starts pulling things out of her handbag. She yanks out her cell phone, sending coins spinning to the ground.

Callie dashes over to Eva, giving up on the taxi. "What are you doing?"

"Calling Saul."

"What?"

"Everyone's been lying to me. It's bullshit. It's fucking bullshit!"

"Oh, darling," Callie says, seeing the tears filling Eva's eyes. "Don't do this."

"I need to talk to him," she says, clumsily scrolling through her numbers.

Callie presses a hand to her forehead. "Listen, how about you call Saul in the morning? It's late now."

"I'm going back there."

"Where?"

"Tasmania," Eva says, pressing call.

Callie reaches forward and lifts the phone from Eva's hands.

Eva's face twists with outrage. "You're taking my phone away?"

"You can call him in the morning—but not like this."

"Like what?"

"You're drunk. I need to get you home."

"You don't want me to speak to Saul," Eva says, straightening, "because I kissed him—and you think it was a mistake."

Callie knows there's no point trying to talk when Eva's like this, but she feels a nerve firing up inside her. "Of course it was a mistake—he's Jackson's brother!"

"Don't you think I know?" Eva spits through gritted teeth. "Don't judge me. I've never said anything about the men you're with."

"I'm not judging—"

"What about David? The self-proclaimed eternal bachelor. You were only with him because he didn't want to get married, didn't want children."

Callie balks, shocked by the veer of the conversation.

"It was the easy option," Eva continues, "because you're scared of getting too close to someone who'll want more. Who'll want a family."

Callie feels as if she's had the wind knocked out of her. Eva may be drunk, but what she is saying cuts right to the bone. Callie turns from her to catch her breath.

"You're just going to leave?"

Callie is on the verge of tears and feels a wall of exhaustion closing in on her. She doesn't have the energy to deal with this.

"I'm being a bitch! Are you going to let me get away with that? Tell me what a bitch I am! Tell me!"

Callie takes a breath, then turns back to face her.

Eva is standing in the middle of the sidewalk, her arms hanging loose at her sides, her body leaning unstably forward. Her face is wet with tears and a streak of mascara is smudged beneath her left eye. She looks haunted.

Callie moves toward her and takes Eva's damp face in her hands. "You are my best friend and you're going through hell right now. No matter what you say to me, I will not leave you."

Eva's chest rises and falls as she breathes in Callie's reassurance. Then she nods and, in a voice so small it could be a whisper, says, "Thank you."

THE FOLLOWING MORNING, EVA wakes feeling stiff, knotted. It's as if her body has been wrung out, all the moisture squeezed from her so that every joint grinds as she crosses the bedroom. Her eyes burn as she opens the blinds onto midmorning sun.

She hears the apartment door open and the squeak of sneakers along the hall. Callie must have been out jogging. The bathroom door clicks shut and the rush of the shower sounds through the wall.

Eva takes a deep breath, then sets about changing into a T-shirt and a pair of shorts. The dress she'd borrowed from Callie is heaped on the floor and she shakes it out, draping it over the back of a chair.

She leaves the bedroom and goes into the kitchen, opens the fridge, and gets to work.

By the time Callie comes in wearing a crisp cotton dress, her wet hair smelling of shampoo, Eva has made a fresh fruit salad and a pot of strong coffee, and has laid out croissants and jam.

"Looks nice," Callie says.

Eva carries two glasses of apple juice to the table, saying, "It's a peace offering."

"None needed."

They sit opposite each other and Eva pours the coffee. She

splashes in milk and slides a mug to Callie. "I'm so sorry about last night. I was a mess."

"It's fine. Don't worry about it." Callie says this without looking at Eva.

"I feel terrible."

"Honestly, don't even mention it." Callie smiles, but there is something strained in the set of her lips that tells Eva she should drop it.

"So, how was your jog?"

"Nice. It's hot out already. It's going to be a lovely weekend."

"Great."

Eva spoons some fruit salad into a bowl, but the sweet smell of it overpowers her and she covers her mouth with her hand.

"That bad?"

She nods, breathing deeply through her nose. She pushes the bowl aside.

"Go back to bed if you like. I need to go into the studio anyway." She takes a sip of coffee. "Maybe we could do something tomorrow. A trip to the coast?"

"Listen, Cal," Eva says, pushing back her chair. "I'm not sure I'll be here. I've decided to go back to Tasmania."

Callie's mouth opens. "What? When you said that last night, I thought you were . . ."

"Drunk? I was. But I meant it." Eva realizes her mistake too late, the remark implying she meant the things she said about Callie, too.

There is a clink as Callie puts down her spoon. "Why are you doing this?"

"I thought I could walk away from everything, but I can't."

"How will going back help?"

"I'm not sure. All I know is I've got so many questions and I'm not going to find the answers here."

"Questions about what?"

"Everything. I want to know who Jeanette is, how long they were married, why they separated, whether they'd been in touch since. I need to understand." Her thoughts feel flayed, set loose in all directions, scrambling over distant memories, dragging out scraps of history and circling, circling over the word, *Why?*

"But what if there aren't any answers? Jeanette might not want to speak to you. We don't even know if she's still in Tasmania."

"Saul will."

Callie eyes her closely. "Why are you really going back?"

"I've already told you," Eva says tightly.

Callie looks at Eva for a long moment, then she shakes her head. "You shouldn't have gone to Tasmania in the first place. It was my fault for encouraging you. Going back won't make this better."

"So what will?"

"Time. Looking forward. I don't know. I haven't got the magic solution. I just don't think it's a good idea for you to be in Tasmania on your own." She pauses, her finger tracing the edge of her place mat. "Perhaps you should think about . . . speaking to someone about how you're feeling."

Eva stares at her. "You mean a therapist?"

"It might help," Callie says softly.

But Eva doesn't want to talk about what's happened; she wants to know *why* it happened. She needs answers—and a therapist isn't going to have them.

Eva is going to go to the person who just might.

The idea of you finding out the truth terrified me. There were some days when I thought I couldn't keep up the pretense any longer.

Before I came to England, my life was a mess of mistakes scrawled across a white page. When I met you, I thought I could just turn that page over, start again. But I was wrong.

I don't expect sympathy from anyone: I put myself in this position, no one else. But I do want you to understand, Eva, that it was hard for me, too. The life we'd made together was incredible—more than I could have ever dreamed of—but even during our happiest times, I was always waiting for that moment when it would start to come undone. There were times when I actually wanted it to. I wanted to be caught out, confronted, held accountable—just so all the stress and lies would be over.

One evening I went for a run after work—I did that sometimes to try and shake off the anxiety. But I couldn't outpace it that night. It ran alongside me, reminding me of everything I'd done, everything I could lose.

I came home and sobbed in our shower. I didn't hear you come into the bathroom—but I heard you leave. You must have seen me in there crying, but you didn't ask what was wrong. Maybe you thought I'd tell you when I was ready. Or, maybe there was a part of you that was scared to know.

20

Eva stands on the deck of the shack, breathing in the smell so familiar to her now: salt air, eucalyptus, a briny tinge of seaweed. The bay is calm, a gentle breeze quivering over its surface. Large clumps of kelp lie on the shoreline like sleeping seals, and she imagines there must have been some strong winds while she's been away.

She turns from the view and wanders inside, lightly trailing her fingertips across the kitchen counter. Everything is exactly as she left it. The only clues that time has passed are the wrinkled, waxy skins on the apples left in the fruit bowl and the layer of fur in the coffee mug that stands beside the sink.

She moves into the bedroom, pausing in front of the mirror to look at her reflection. Another clue of time, she thinks as she examines the dark hollows beneath her eyes. Sleep has become something elusive, chased away by anxiety. The one question that stalks her through the night: *Why did Jackson marry me?*

There must be plenty of facts to explain *how:* how he forged the paperwork, how he managed to juggle so many lies, how he got away with it. But all Eva is interested in is *why?*

She hopes she's doing the right thing by returning to Wattleboon. Perhaps Callie was right to warn her against it, because simply being here pulls Jackson even deeper into her thoughts.

A wasp flies dozily into the room, causing her to glance up. She watches as it makes a large, haphazard circle of the room, then flies straight for the window, which it hits and falls to the ground, stunned. Swiftly, she grabs an empty water glass and crouches down, trapping the wasp. It buzzes against the ridged glass.

Eva fetches a magazine and slides it under. As she does, her eye catches something on the wooden floorboard beside her. It's a marking, one she's not seen there before. Something has been scratched into its surface. She tilts her head and sees small, angular letters freshly carved into wood.

Her breath catches in her throat as the letters form into a word: *Jackson*.

She sits back sharply, pressing herself to the wall.

The air contracts around her. Her ears fill with a rushing sound as blood races to her head.

She blinks, staring at his name. It is right there in the wood. Slowly, she lowers a hand toward the floorboard and runs a finger over the grooves. She is not imagining it. They are real. She feels each letter in turn, as if she can read something more from them.

Leaning down so that her face is only inches away, she examines the inscription. She notices now the dark film of dust and sand that has worked its way into the letters. They are not freshly carved at all. From the look of the grime filling each groove, the inscription must have been here for years.

Eva sits up, shocked at herself. Grief or misplaced hope had prompted her first thought: *Jackson is here*. She shakes her head. The rational explanation was clear. Jackson had grown up in this bay, had probably been friends with the owners of this shack. Either bored or just young, maybe he had once carved his name into the wood.

Eva knows Jackson is dead. She does. She was there on the beach. She spoke to the witnesses, the police officer, the coast guard. She felt the icy water, saw the waves churning up the sea. But still. She knows that Jackson had deceived her so deeply that the smallest seed of doubt has been planted, enough to make her trawl over every detail of that day, of every day, to see if there was anything that she'd missed.

She squeezes her eyes shut, telling herself: *Keep it together, Eva.* Then she gets to her feet, grabs the glass with the wasp, and carries it out of the shack. As she passes the shelf in the living room, she pauses.

It is empty. The framed picture of her and Jackson at the jazz festival is missing.

She steps closer and stares at the shelf. She knows the photo was there when she left—she looked at it every day. There is absolutely no way she would have misplaced it. Her skin prickles cool as she glares at the empty space where it should be.

Her concentration must slide away from her as she hears the thrum of the wasp as it escapes the glass. It flounders upward, toward Eva's face, and she swipes a hand through the air, batting it away.

Suddenly she feels a vibration of wings caught within her sleeve. She panics, yanking at her cardigan and shrugging it from her shoulders in a rush of movement.

But she is too late. The bite of its sting pierces her forearm like a hot needle.

SOMETIME LATER EVA WALKS over to Saul's place, her arm still throbbing. She finds him bent down, repairing something beneath the deck of his house. On hearing her voice, he turns sharply, clunking his head.

He comes out blinking, rubbing his hair. He's wearing a thick navy sweater, the sleeves of which are starting to fray. His shorts are rolled up, as if he's just waded in from the water, and the skin on his upper thighs is pale where it hasn't seen the sun. "Eva? You're back."

"Yes."

"Where've you been?"

"With Callie."

"I've been calling you. I wasn't sure if you were coming back. You left your stuff, but . . . well, I wasn't sure . . ." His sentence trails off. He shoves his hands in his pockets.

"How did you know I'd left my things? Have you been in the shack?"

"The shack?"

"Did you move the photo?"

His brow creases and he looks at her blankly. "What photo? Eva, what are you talking about?"

"Of Jackson and me. It was on the shelf when I left. Did you move it?"

"No, of course not!"

She looks at him for a long moment, weighing up whether or not she believes him. Perhaps it is possible that she moved it herself. Her head was all over the place in the days before she left.

"Listen, Eva," he says, taking a step toward her. "I'm sorry I didn't tell you Jackson was married. I should've."

"Were you hoping I'd never find out? That I'd just fly back to England and that would be it?"

He holds her eye as he admits, "Maybe at first. Yes."

There's a pause. "And later?"

"And later," he says, his gaze slipping toward her mouth and then returning to her eyes. "I wasn't sure how I felt."

"I trusted you," she says quietly.

Saul moves forward so there are only inches between them. She feels the physical proximity of him and is aware of her heart beating faster. Suddenly she is remembering the day on the boat, the press of his lips against hers and the strength in his arms as he held her. She forces herself to breathe slowly. She cannot allow herself to feel this.

"When you turned up on Wattleboon, I thought you'd be here for a few hours and that'd be it. Dad had begged me not to say anything, so I didn't. But then," he says, pausing, "you stayed."

When he speaks again, his voice is low, intense, as if he is willing her to understand. "I didn't want to lie to you. That's not who I am, Eva. But the idea of telling you—God, I kept goin' over and over it. You'd just found out you were pregnant—I couldn't tell you Jackson had another wife, not then. And afterward . . . after the miscarriage . . . it just felt cruel. I couldn't do it. I'm sorry."

He removes his hands from his pockets, and for a moment, she thinks he's going to reach out and hold her; instead, he places his palms together in front of him as if he's about to pray. "I want to be honest with you now. I want to be honest with you always. There are things we need to talk about—"

"I want to meet her," she interrupts.

He draws back a little, his hands falling to his sides.

"I need to talk to Jeanette. That's why I've come back."

He closes his eyes and swallows.

"What?" she says, a twinge of anxiety beginning to stir. "What is it?"

He opens his eyes and looks at her steadily, his mouth tightening over something he doesn't want to say. "There's a child, Eva. Jackson and Jeanette had a child."

SHE SITS AT THE table opposite Saul. There is a smooth white pebble on top of a pile of mail, and a book spread open about cloud formations. She runs her thumbs along the edge of the table, thinking.

Jackson had a child. A son, Saul tells her, called Kyle. He is three years old. Eva works out that Kyle would have been nine or ten months old when Jackson left for England.

She thinks of the baby she lost and how, even before it had been born, she had already begun to love it. She flattens her hands against the table, the wasp sting just a dull ache now. "How could he leave his own child?"

Saul doesn't answer.

In delivery rooms she'd watched fathers fall in love with their children; she'd seen the way their eyes grew damp as they cradled them for the first time; she'd heard whispered, choked words of welcome and love—and she thinks, *I did not know my husband.*

She tries to recall whether there were any signs that Jackson had been in touch with his son through Jeanette, but she can't think of any; no private phone calls or e-mails, no photo slipped into his belongings. But the idea that he had no contact with Jeanette and therefore, Kyle, is worse than believing that he had.

He'd always talked about wanting a family. *Two girls,* he'd said.

Eva looks at Saul. "You said Jeanette lives in Tasmania still."

"Yeah, in Warrington, in the northeast."

"Did Jackson live there with her?"

He nods. "I never visited them, but I know the area. It's a remote town on the coast—mostly just farmland. Jackson had a job in a pub, Dad said."

She tries to picture Jackson living somewhere isolated and rural and it surprises her given his love for the city. But then, so much has surprised her. "Have you met her? Jeanette."

Saul draws his hands to the edge of the table and looks up at Eva. "She's the one," he says, his gaze darkening. "The woman Jackson and I fell out over."

It takes a moment for this to register. Jeanette was the woman Saul had been in love with, the same woman who had left him for Jackson.

Now it begins to make sense why the brothers never made up. Not only did Jackson take Jeanette, but he married her, too. They had a child. How could Saul bear to watch all that?

She thinks about this faceless woman who was the mother of Jackson's child and a sharp flash of pure jealousy seizes her: Jeanette had a child with Jackson.

Eva's child died.

She keeps her gaze on Saul and asks, "Will you tell me about her?"

THE CHAIR CREAKS AS Saul leans back, wondering where to begin. "We've known each other since we were kids. Her family," he says, pausing, "they owned the shack you're staying in—before Joe bought it."

Eva balks. "Jeanette used to live there?"

"In the summers, yes. I know that must be strange for you," he says, understanding the irony that both of Jackson's wives had spent time in the same shack. "But it was the only place I could think of for you to stay."

"Jackson's name—it's carved into a floorboard in the back bedroom."

"Is it?" he says, not sounding surprised. "Maybe Jackson did it as a kid. Or Jeanette could've—she had a crush on him growing up." He reaches for his glass of water and takes a drink, then sets it back on the table. "Jeanette and I used to hang out a lot when we were younger. We were the same age." He looks out briefly toward the bay. "Then, when we were thirteen, there was a bush fire."

"The fire that killed your mother?"

He nods slowly. "After that, our family stopped comin' out here—it was too hard on Dad. So I didn't see Jeanette for years. We met again by chance almost a decade later at a mutual friend's wedding. We spent the whole night talking, catching up, and I guess things grew from there. We were together for a few months and I thought it was serious . . ."

"But then she met Jackson," Eva says.

He nods, remembering the night of his birthday. Jeanette had worn a white sundress and in the dusk she looked ethereal as she turned to face them. Saul noticed the way Jeanette's gaze locked with Jackson's and how she'd smiled at him, a finger touching her collarbone.

"There was something between them from the start," Saul tells Eva. "Just the way they looked at each other gave it away."

"What happened?"

Saul draws a slow breath in. "Jackson persuaded Jeanette and me to go into town with him after the barbecue. He got us into this club he did some work for and sorted out a load of free drinks. I bumped into a couple of guys I knew and had a quick beer with them."

Saul shifts in his chair. "Afterward I went to find Jeanette. She was sitting with Jackson in the corner of the club. There was this look about them—maybe it was their body language, or the intensity of the conversation they seemed to be having, but I knew something was going on. Then, while I was standing right there, Jackson kissed her."

Saul remembers the fury he felt in that moment. He cared about Jeanette—thought he even loved her. "I was so angry that I knew if I went over we'd end up in a fight. So I left." He had jogged home via the beach, where he stripped off and swam out to a marker buoy, burning off some of his rage in the water.

"Jeanette called me the next day. She didn't ask why I'd left the club, or what I'd seen. She just apologized because she was breaking up with me. She didn't mention Jackson. Neither did I. That's what made it so strange. Jackson never said sorry. I don't know if he felt guilty—or if he just didn't care. There was no argument, no fight." They had simply stopped speaking and drifted out of each other's life, like a tide that was always going to turn.

"So Jackson kept on seeing her," Eva says, "and you went to South America."

He nods. "Dad was the only one who saw them—and I didn't want to hear anything about it. Didn't even want to hear his name. There were a few bits I caught, of course; when they got engaged, when they had the baby. The next thing I heard, they'd separated and Jackson had gone abroad."

"To England," Eva says with a smile so sad that he wants to reach across the table and hold her. "Your friend—Flyer—he said Jeanette was distraught over Jackson's death. Do you think she still loved him? Even after he left?"

"It's difficult to know. But from some things my dad said, I'd guess yes."

Eva muses on this for a moment and then she says again, "I'd like to meet her, Saul. Would you take me?"

21

They fly along the highway in the lashing rain, the truck's wheels kicking up sheets of water. Fishing rods jig and dance on the back shelf, reels clacking together. Eva gazes out through the rain-smeared window at the wide expanse of Great Lake, rain and wind churning its surface.

The drive to Jeanette's home in Warrington is over four hundred kilometers. She thinks that if a map of Tasmania looks like a heart, they are on the course of an arrow shooting diagonally through the center of it.

Eva's seen little of Tasmania beyond the watery edges of Wattleboon Island, but she doesn't make an effort to notice the small townships dotting the lake or the shadows of mountains in the distance. She just wants to get there. Get this over with.

She runs her forefinger over one of the truck's air vents, wiping off a film of dust. Back and forth she trails, revealing the smooth plastic beneath. They'd set off yesterday evening and she and Saul had taken rooms at a motel to break up the journey, but she'd barely slept, the same nightmare about Jackson tearing into her dreams. She'd found herself gazing at the red digits on the clock on the nightstand as they tripped through till dawn.

Saul glances at her. "You okay?"

She blinks and withdraws her hand, wiping it against her jeans. She feels wired, on edge. She shouldn't have had the espresso at the gas station, but she needed something to take the edge off her tiredness. "I'm fine," she says. She rubs her eyes with the heels of her hands and then stretches, her fingertips pressing against the roof of the truck. She twists around in her seat and faces him. "Am I doing the right thing?"

"How d'you mean?"

"Turning up at Jeanette's house. Telling her about Jackson."

He watches the road as he asks, "Why do you want to meet her?"

She presses her fingertips to her temples. The idea has been burning in her thoughts for days and all she knows is that she must do this. "I need to meet *her* to understand why he married *me*."

"Then it's the right thing."

Eva leans her head back against the seat rest. "But is it fair to Jeanette? She's got no idea Jackson married me. And I'm going to be the one to break it to her."

"You're just telling her the truth."

"Should I be?"

"What would you've preferred? To know everything you do now—or to still be in the dark?"

THE LANDSCAPE CHANGES FROM flat plains to craggy mountains as the road climbs through tight switchbacks. Water streams off dark granite mountainsides and the trees drip with moss.

At some point on the drive, Saul's cell phone rings but he leaves it when he sees it is his father. He doesn't want to have to tell him that he's sitting in the truck beside Eva and that they're on the way to meet Jeanette. He knows exactly what his father would have to say about that. He'll call him back later tonight and arrange to pop by in a day or two. Last time Saul visited he'd checked the bins and knew from all the empties that Dirk had been hitting it hard. Saul should be stopping in on him every day, but it depresses the hell out of him to see his dad this way.

An hour later, the road begins to flow over hillsides and green pastures, where cattle huddle together in the rain. Beside him Eva gazes out at the fields flashing by. She looks exhausted, her eyes ringed by dark shadows. He wants to take her hand in his, tell her it's going to be okay. But he can't. The kiss on the boat is just a beat of memory now, unmentioned. He wonders if Eva regrets it, or whether she lets it play over in her mind in quiet moments of the day, the way he does.

Suddenly she is looking at him, her brow furrowed. "Did Jeanette go to the memorial?"

"Jackson's memorial?" he says, taking a moment to place her question. "Yeah, she did."

A flicker of anguish passes over her face, which he understands: Eva had traveled all the way to Tasmania so she could grieve with Jackson's family, yet it must seem as though they'd already shared their grief with Jeanette.

"Did she do a reading? Say anything?"

"No. Only Dad said a few words. We kept it brief. The cloud came down on the mountain. Everyone was cold."

A truck passes in the opposite direction, a rush of air and spray whooshing by. When it's gone the road is empty again. Tin cattle sheds and the occasional farmhouse are all that break the endless stretch of green on either side of them.

"Did she bring Kyle?"

"No. She came alone. Some of us went to the pub for a drink afterward—but Jeanette didn't."

"Why not?"

"Don't know. I guess it was hard for her. Everyone knew she and Jackson had separated. Maybe she didn't feel . . . entitled or something."

"Did she cry?"

Saul glances around, surprised.

"I'm sorry. I just want to understand as much as I can."

He sighs. "Yeah, she cried. Sobbed, actually." He thinks of Jeanette standing apart from the crowd, pressed against the railings at the top of Mount Wellington. She seemed to lose it, burying her face into her balled hands, heavy sobs escaping that sounded so raw they made everyone look at the ground.

"Does your dad get along with her?"

"Not really. I think he resented her for coming between me and Jackson."

"You both fell in love with the same woman," she says so quietly, it's almost as if she's speaking to herself.

After a moment, she looks across at Saul, asking, "Why are you taking me?"

From the way she is looking at him, he can guess what she's thinking. But he's not doing this because he still harbors romantic feelings for Jeanette.

"I'm taking you because you asked," he says simply.

"THIS IS IT," SAUL says sometime later.

They swing into a gravel driveway and pull up beside a white Ford with a muddied license plate. The rain has stopped but puddles tremble on the drive and thick drops slide from leaves. The house is a modest single-story with a small garden. There is a blue plastic slide on the lawn with a broken bottom step.

Saul cuts the engine and unclips his belt. "You ready?"

Eva doesn't move. She stares at the house where Jackson once lived with his wife and son. It seems impossible that those four walls contained such a huge, yet hidden part of his history.

Maybe it'd be better for Jeanette to remain an indistinct image in Eva's mind, not someone real she then has to live with. She tries to ignore the doubt and anxiety that blow through her mind like a hot wind. They've come all this way; she must go through with it.

Yet dread pins her to the seat. "I . . . I can't do this." The words seem impossibly weak, but she realizes they're true.

"Eva?"

Her breath shortens as she says, "Can we go? Sorry. I just want to go."

"But we've just—"

"Please," she begs in a voice so desperate she barely recognizes it as her own.

Saul reaches for the key in the ignition, but something makes him pause.

She follows his gaze and sees he is looking toward the front door, where a woman of Eva's age has just stepped out. Her hair is dark red and she wears a pair of jeans and a large T-shirt that hangs off her slim shoulders. Her feet are bare. She is staring at the truck, arms folded, trying to place it.

The woman's eyes widen with surprise as Saul steps out of the truck. Her arms unfold and she touches her hair. She smiles a little, a small, perplexed look. Eva then sees how beautiful she must have once been.

"Saul?" Jeanette says. "What are you doing here?"

"Sorry for just turning up. I'm here with . . . a friend," he says, glancing over at Eva.

Jeanette's gaze follows his.

Eva knows she must get out of the truck, but her legs don't seem to be working. Her palms are damp and she presses them against her thighs. She can feel the heat of them through her jeans. *This is his wife. The mother of his child.*

Saul takes a step toward the truck. "Eva?"

She has no choice. Taking a deep breath, she clanks open the door and climbs out. She doesn't see the murky puddle in the driveway and her feet sink into it, cold water seeping into her sandals. She steps quickly aside, humiliated.

When she looks up, she reads no warmth in Jeanette's expression. Eva tries to pull her lips into a smile, but her face feels frozen. The two women stare at each other.

It is Saul who eventually breaks the silence. "Jeanette, this is Eva. She's come to talk to you about Jackson."

I used to have nightmares about you and Jeanette meeting. They started in the weeks running up to our wedding. I'd imagine you arriving at the altar in a beautiful white dress, the light from the stained-glass windows catching in your engagement ring. But then when I lifted up your veil, it was Jeanette's face I saw, not yours.

Because of that nightmare, I asked you not to wear a veil on our wedding day. I told you I thought they were a bit old-fashioned— do you remember?

The visions of you and Jeanette meeting weren't only confined to my sleep. I was cooking scrambled eggs one evening when you came in from a late shift. You were full of chatter, like you always were after work, and you told me a new nurse had started: Jeanette.

I stopped stirring. My head felt dizzy and hot, like a fever had erupted. "What does she look like?"

"Look like?" you repeated from behind me, bemused.

I corrected myself immediately. "I mean, is she old or young?"

"She's about my age, I guess."

The eggs were starting to stick to the pan, but there wasn't space in my thoughts to stir them, nor turn off the gas. It took every shred of my concentration to knit the next three words together. "Where's she from?"

You paused for a long time, thinking. Then you said: "Leeds."

I laughed. Actually laughed with relief.

"What?" you asked, coming to my side so you could see my face.

"Sorry," I said, finally snapping off the burner, then turning to you. "It's been a crazy day at work. Just ignore me." I threaded my arms around your waist and kissed the smooth stretch of your neck. "All you need to know is how happy I am to have you home."

As I held you in my arms, I knew then that I would do anything to stop you and Jeanette from meeting.

Anything.

22

The hallway of Jeanette's home is dim and narrow, and the air smells of burned fat. Eva's wet sandals squeak as she walks the length of it, hoping she's not leaving a trail of sopping footprints. She passes a row of little boy's shoes lined up beside a blue stool and she has to force herself to walk on.

They enter a square living room that smells faintly musty, where two tired-looking sofas face a low table. Toy cars are parked on top, several of them missing wheels or doors.

Eva and Saul stand near the window, which overlooks the garden. Outside, an empty clothesline sways in the damp breeze.

Jeanette remains in the doorway, arms hugged to her chest. No drinks are offered. No one is invited to sit. Heavy frown lines have furrowed into her brow, but Eva can see clear hints of beauty in her high cheekbones and pale green eyes. *This is the woman he first loved,* she thinks.

"My son's asleep," Jeanette says, and Eva cannot tell if she means it as a plea or a warning.

Eva takes a step back, anchoring herself between the windowsill and a dark wooden sideboard, on top of which several framed photos are staggered. She wants to turn and look at them, see if Jackson is in any of the pictures, but her gaze snaps up to meet Jeanette's, who says, "Either of you mind telling me what this is about?"

Saul looks to Eva.

She knows that this is her cue—but all she is thinking is that Jackson once lived in this house. Had he ever perched on the sofa, rocking Kyle in his arms? Had he pulled Jeanette close to him to gaze out the window together at a storm rolling in? Had he watched a rugby game on TV, sitting forward with his fists pressed to his mouth, the way he had done in their home in London?

"Eva's come over from the UK," Saul says to fill the silence. "That's where she met Jackson." He nods for Eva to go on.

Her mouth feels dry and her pulse ticks in her throat. "Can I use your bathroom?" she blurts.

Jeanette smiles tightly. "It's at the end of the hall. On the right."

Anxiety spins through Eva as she steps into the hallway. Her recurring nightmare of Jackson rises so vividly into her thoughts that she has to pause, a hand reaching out to the wall to tell herself: *It is only a dream.* Yet exhaustion is blurring her perception of reality so much that it's as if she'll turn a corner and find Jackson here.

She needs to splash water on her face, calm down. She begins moving along the hallway, but when she reaches the end, rather than turning right into the bathroom, she finds herself hovering outside the door opposite.

The name KYLE is spelled out in brightly painted wooden letters and the door has been left slightly ajar. She glances quickly over her shoulder and then steps in.

The drawn curtains lift in the breeze. The room smells sweet, of fresh laundry and wet grass. A young boy sleeps curled on his side, his back to her, his chest rising and falling softly. She desperately wants to see his face, to see Jackson's features.

Her hand trails to her stomach, a cave of emptiness opening inside her. She wants to touch this little boy, hold him in her arms. His dark hair looks blissfully soft, a faint curl at the nape of his neck. She takes a step forward, moving closer to him. A floorboard strains beneath her feet and Kyle mutters, shifting in his bed.

Eva freezes. If she wakes him, she will have to explain to Jeanette and Saul what she was doing in his bedroom. She waits, barely breathing, wondering how many times Jackson had stood where she is now, watching his son drift off to sleep. It seems unthinkable that he could have left this little boy, walked out on his family, and made a new life in England.

When Kyle settles, Eva quietly retreats into the hallway and stands there for a moment, dizzied by the sight of him. Suddenly this all feels too real. In coming here, she's witnessing the proof of Jackson's deception: he was a father; he had a family; he had an entire life she knew nothing about.

She glances up and down the hall and then, inexplicably, finds herself moving toward the room next to Kyle's. Easing the door open, she goes in.

A bedroom, presumably Jeanette's. It is neat, although the double bed is unmade. There is only one bedside table and on it there's an empty glass and a pair of silver earrings in the shape of half-moons. She slides open the drawer beneath it and sees a flashlight, two novels, several hair clips, and a tube of hand cream missing its lid.

Carefully shutting the drawer, she then ducks down and peers beneath the bed. The only items under there are a black suitcase and a balled-up sock. She gets to her feet, blood rushing to her head and pinpricks of light darting across her vision. She needs to get out of here, go back to the living room before they start wondering where she is.

But Eva finds herself crossing to the corner of the bedroom

where a narrow pine wardrobe stands. Her fingers curl around the wooden handle and she pulls it back, heart pounding. Inside is a row of women's clothes, the soft scent of lavender lifting from the fabrics. She trails a hand through cotton dresses, pairs of women's jeans, a thick woolen sweater, a purple coat with a fur-lined hood, an orange-and-tan scarf. She thinks: *Nothing of Jackson's.* Then she closes the wardrobe and slinks from the room.

Other than the bathroom, there's one more doorway off the hall. Eva pushes it open, entering a spare room filled with junk: an exercise bike, boxes of paperwork, a rocking horse with a broken spring. She opens a filing cabinet and trails her fingers through sheafs of papers that are ordered into slim green files.

Beyond the room she hears Jeanette's voice and she freezes, eyes darting to the door. She can't think how long she's been gone. What if Jeanette comes looking for her and finds Eva rifling through her belongings? Her pulse throbs in her neck as she waits, listening.

After a moment, Jeanette's voice continues and Eva realizes that she and Saul must still be in the living room together.

She continues flicking through the papers in the filing cabinet. They are innocuous, just bills and bank statements. Then suddenly her fingers stop over a piece of paper on which she sees Jackson's handwriting.

She pulls it out, drawing it close to her face.

It is only a gas bill, but in Jackson's squat hand he has written the word *paid,* along with the date of three years ago.

It should mean nothing. It's not a love letter or a clue as to Jackson's mind-set, yet it knocks the breath from her body. Before there had just been other people's explanations, but here was proof of a life lived without her. She pictures the same handwriting on the corners of their bills at home. The easy, almost casual duplicity of it enrages her. She grabs the edge of the page and tears his handwriting from it. Screwing it into a ball, she stuffs it in her mouth, working her teeth over the chalky paper, which turns sodden and slippery. Her teeth keep on clenching harder, her jaw muscles straining, her tongue pulling Jackson's words around her mouth.

Then she stops. She is shaking. Her mouth hangs open as she sees the madness of what she is doing. Quickly, she shoves the torn bill back into the filing cabinet and closes it. Then she retreats from the room and hurries into the bathroom, locking the door behind her.

She spits the slimy paper into the toilet bowl and flushes it, watching the fragment whirl downward and finally disappear. She grips the edge of the sink, realizing she has been searching Jeanette's home looking for clues of him. She is coming unhinged.

Eva turns on the cold tap and splashes her face with icy water. Then she pats her skin dry and faces herself in the mirror. Her eyes are wild, glittering. *You are losing it,* she tells herself.

She runs a hand back through her hair as this thought settles, then she waits in the bathroom until her breathing begins to slow.

SAUL SITS WITH HIS hands clasped, thumbs tapping together.

"What's this about?" Jeanette asks from the sofa adjacent to him.

"I'd rather wait for Eva."

"And I'd rather you tell me what's going on. You bring a stranger into my house and tell me she wants to talk about Jackson. Who the hell is she?"

"Please, Jeanette. Can we just wait till Eva's here? It's better she explains."

"Well then," she says, folding her arms, "we'd better dust off the small talk." Jeanette had always had an air of defiance about her, as if she were daring the world to do its worst. But he knows it's all front.

She settles back into the sofa as she asks, "How's that place of yours out in Wattleboon? Heard you'd moved in."

"Yeah. Before Christmas."

"It's a beautiful spot," she says. "Used your inheritance on it, did you?"

He nods. "That and some savings."

"Jackson frittered his. But I knew you'd keep yours aside, do something with it. You always had vision, Saul."

"Thank you," he says, surprised by the generosity of the comment. "What about you? You and Kyle settled up here?"

She shrugs. "For now. We're near Mum, which is something."

Outside, water drips from the gutters in heavy drops that land on the windowsill. "I still can't believe he's gone," Jeanette says quietly.

Saul rubs a hand over his jaw. "I know."

Her fingers move to the delicate gold ring she wears on her wedding finger and she twists it absently as she admits, "I miss him like hell."

When he and Jeanette were a couple, they'd gone up to the Bay of Fires for a few days, and he remembers sitting together on the huge lichen-stained rocks watching the sun go down. She'd opened up, telling him about the difficult years as a teenager living in her stepfather's house. They'd talked about what they both wanted from the future, and he'd been surprised and touched by the modesty of her dreams. There were no great career ambitions or desires for wealth—all she wanted was a small house near the water and a family. Maybe she'd thought she'd found that with Jackson.

There is a long silence only broken by the sound of a door being opened and then the tread of footsteps along the hallway. They both look up to see Eva moving into the room. Her face is pale and she looks wild-eyed.

"Sorry," she says, attempting a smile.

She stands with her back to the window. He hears her intake of breath and then she says, "I should explain why I'm here."

"I MET JACKSON TWO years ago on a flight to England," Eva begins, her gaze on Jeanette. "Our seats were next to each other and we got talking. When we arrived in London, we swapped numbers and started seeing a bit of each other."

Jeanette's expression is completely neutral, unreadable.

Into the silence, Eva pushes forward. "I didn't know anything about you—or Kyle. Jackson told me he was . . . single." She pauses. "I ended up having a relationship with him . . . and a few months later we moved in together." Eva stops again and rubs the back of her neck. "I'm sorry, but there's no easy way to say this: Jackson proposed to me and we got married in February last year."

Jeanette's gaze is locked on Eva's face. Eva can feel the heat behind Jeanette's stare. On the sideboard a wooden clock ticks.

"I had no idea he was already married. I would never have had a relationship with him if I'd known."

Jeanette blinks. "You're telling me that my husband *married* you?"

"I know what a shock this must be. I didn't know you existed, not until very recently. I wasn't sure whether to tell you . . . but I thought you should know the truth." Eva grinds to a halt. She knots her hands in front of her, shifting her weight onto the other leg. She wishes she were sitting down.

Jeanette still doesn't move. "You met on the flight he took to England?"

Eva nods.

"So the same day Jackson left me," Jeanette says slowly, "he met you?"

"I . . ." Eva shakes her head, not sure what to say. *Had it been that quick? Had Jackson literally walked out of one relationship and straight into another?*

Jeanette tells her, "I didn't even know he was in England until he died. I've never been there. It's like a world away."

"I'm so sorry. He lied to us both."

In the corner, Saul shifts. Jeanette turns to him. "Did you know he was going to marry someone else?'"

"I had no idea."

"He must've told someone."

There's a pause. Then Saul says, "Dad."

She laughs, shaking her head. "Your bloody father! He never thought I was good enough for either of his sons." Her lips tighten. "When Jackson left, I called your dad, asked him where Jackson was. But he wouldn't tell me. Said he'd gone traveling— that was all he'd say."

Jeanette's hands ball into fists at her sides—and Eva notices with a lurch the gold wedding band still circling her finger. Her gaze lowers to her own hands, which are bare of the rings Jackson had given her. She wishes she still had them now, as if needing to prove to Jeanette—to herself—that their marriage existed. She slips her hands behind her back.

Jeanette rises to her feet and faces Eva, saying, "We have a son. Kyle. He's three. Jackson walked out on me when Kyle was a baby. Can you imagine what that's like? What sort of man does that?"

"I—"

"And now you come here to tell me that *my* husband, the father of *my* child, fell in love with *you*!"

Eva takes a small step back, pressing herself against the wall. "I didn't know he was married—"

"Get out."

"I just wanted—"

"Get out of my house. Now!"

Stunned, Eva begins to move. As she turns, her gaze falls on the display of photos on the sideboard. At the front is a picture of Jackson. He is standing behind Jeanette, his chin on her shoulder, his palms pressed against the swell of her pregnant stomach.

When Eva looks up, Jeanette is watching her. "We were a family."

23

Eva winds down the truck window to let the harbor breeze wash in. They are parked in line at the ferry terminal, waiting to get the last boat back to Wattleboon. The mud-coated truck in front of them has left its engine running, diesel fumes overlaying the clean salt air. The light is beginning to fade and she thinks it'll be dark by the time they get in.

The drive back from Jeanette's has taken six hours. A road map, bottles of water, and empty potato chip bags lie at her feet. She dusts a few stray crumbs from her lap, desperate now to get out of her creased clothes and into the shower.

She keeps thinking about how earlier she'd crept through Jeanette's home, rifling through her drawers and cupboards—with the hope of finding what? Some clue that Jackson was telling the truth? Some clue that he was lying?

Beside her Saul runs his thumb over the steering wheel as if he's lost in thought. He looks tired; stubble grazes his jaw and his hair sticks up at the back where it's been rubbing against the headrest. The last few weeks have been tough on him, too, she realizes.

"Thank you," she says suddenly. "For taking me to Jeanette's." Saul had given up most of his weekend to drive her across the state and back again. She wonders whether she's been too hard on him, blaming him for Jackson's mistakes when Saul was only trying to protect her from them.

"I'm just sorry it didn't go better," Saul says.

"I don't know what I was expecting. Jeanette and I were never going to be friends." She slides her hands beneath her thighs. "I guess I just hoped we'd talk more—that maybe she'd be able to answer some of my questions. I walked away too easily."

"Maybe when things've settled you could try again?"

She shakes her head. "You saw how she was. She threw me out."

"She must've been in shock."

"It was more than that. Jeanette blames me. She made me feel like I was just Jackson's mistress."

Then she asks, "Was it strange for you seeing Jeanette again?"

He shrugs and she thinks he's going to brush off the question; instead, he leans forward, resting his clasped hands on the steering wheel as he says, "It reminded me how far in the past all that is. Maybe I've spent so long being angry about what happened, I believed there was more between Jeanette and me than there really was."

She's surprised by the feeling of relief that sighs through her body.

"I think you did the right thing going there today," he says.

"Do you?"

He nods. "I should've told you the truth when you first came to Wattleboon." His gaze locks onto hers. "You don't know how much I regret that."

A low heat spreads across her cheeks beneath the intensity of his stare.

"I wish that wasn't how we met, Eva."

She presses her lips together. Nods. "I know."

On the dash, Saul's cell phone rings, but his eyes don't leave Eva's.

She feels her face growing hot. She glances at the phone, saying, "Maybe you should answer it."

After a moment, Saul reaches for it. "Saul Bowe speaking." There is a rise in his tone as he says, "No? When?" He rubs the back of his head, asking, "For how long? Right, right. Okay, I'm on my way."

He drops the phone into his lap and starts the engine.

"Saul?"

He glances ahead, then back over his shoulder at the line of cars parked nose to bumper. "Shit!" he says, smacking a hand on the steering wheel.

"What is it?"

"My dad," he tells her. "He's in the hospital."

AN HOUR AND A half later, Saul stands beside his father's hospital bed, his hands deep in his pockets. His father sleeps. A tube runs into a vein on his arm, sending a measured dose of morphine around his body. His top half is bare and Saul finds something shocking about the gray, wiry hairs that spread across his chest and the prominence of his rib cage, which rises and falls beneath thin, sallow skin.

Saul hasn't seen him bare-chested in years. He remembers his father striding around the deck of the cray boat, his skin glistening with sweat, thick muscles rippling beneath deeply tanned skin. During school holidays, Saul and Jackson crewed on the boat and loved seeing their father at the helm, bellowing instructions and jokes at them and the rest of crew.

The bed sighs as his father stirs, opening his eyes. "Saul."

"How you feelin'?"

He swallows. Licks his lips. Smiles a little. "I'll be fine."

Saul jangles his truck keys in his pocket. "Will you? I spoke to the doctor. It's not acute anymore," he says, referring to the attacks of pancreatitis his father's been having over the past few years. "It's chronic now. Your pancreas is a mess. They're testing you for diabetes, too. He tell you that?" Saul doesn't know why he's being so bullish. He feels out of control here, thrown off balance by the sight of his father like this.

Dirk winces as he struggles to push himself upright. Saul helps him, carefully gripping his upper arms as he shuffles up the bed. The skin on his father's biceps feels loose, the muscles wasted.

"Sorry to cause you this trouble."

Saul returns his hands to his pockets. "I don't want you to be sorry. I just want you to be well."

"I've done this to myself. We both know that."

The booze, the bloody booze, Saul thinks. "How long've you been in pain?"

"Ah, awhile."

"Has it been bad?"

"Some days it's worse than others."

"You're thin as a rake."

"Bulimia. They don't want you on the catwalk if you're a pound over eight stone."

Saul cracks a smile. "Only thing you'll be modeling is a hospital gown if you keep this up."

"I know, I know."

Saul's voice grows quieter. "You should've told me you were ill."

"What would you've done? You've got a busy life, Saul. It's down to me on this. I'll deal with it, eh?"

"You called me earlier."

"Yeah, thought I might need to see the doc."

Saul feels terrible about not answering his father's call. He looks closely at Dirk; the whites of his eyes are yellowish and heavily veined and his skin looks washed out, as if the life in him has been drained. "Chronic pancreatitis—it's serious. It's gonna reduce your life expectancy, that's what the doctor reckons."

"I know."

"So you'll stop the drinking?"

His father sighs. "I want to. I always want to." He doesn't say any more and Saul understands; it's a conversation that they've had too many times before. Wanting to stop and stopping are two different things.

They fall into silence, listening to the electronic beeps of Dirk's monitor.

"You gettin' looked after all right in here?" Saul asks for something to say.

Out in the corridor a male nurse passes by pushing a trolley and calling out a chirpy hello to them both.

"Sponge baths aren't what they used to be," Dirk says.

"The old dog hasn't lost his sense of humor, then."

"Nah, just his dignity."

They talk for a few minutes more and then Saul says, "I've been thinking. What if you come and stay with me once you're out of here? Just till you're back on your feet." The offer may be prompted by his guilt, but Saul knows it's the right thing. Seeing his father in the hospital like this is a stark reminder that the years are creeping up on them. If they're ever going to close the gap that's been steadily widening between them, it's got to be now.

"On Wattleboon?"

Saul nods.

"Nah. Don't reckon that'd work."

"Why not?" Saul asks. He's not going to let his father off so easily.

"Dunno. It's just not for me."

"Used to be."

"Yeah, well. That was a long time ago," Dirk says, his expression darkening.

Saul knows that Dirk hasn't stepped foot on Wattleboon since the bush fire, but that's got to change. It's Saul's home now and he wants his father to be part of his life there. "You haven't even seen the house yet. I think you'll like it."

"It's a nice offer, son. I appreciate it. I do. But I'm just not sure I can."

"Think about it, won't you?"

Dirk nods, his eyes slowly closing.

EVA LEAVES THE CAFETERIA carrying two coffees in plastic cups. Her fingers begin to burn, so she puts them down and pulls her sleeves over her hands before picking them up again.

Wandering back through the maze of corridors, she smells antiseptic, bleach, and the warm fug of overcooked food. She wonders if every hospital smells the same the world over.

When Eva reaches the gastroenterology department, she finds Saul standing in the waiting room, gazing out the window. He looks too large and too tanned against the pale, sterile decor of this room.

"How is he?" she asks, coming to his side. She places their coffees on the windowsill; they breathe two small clouds of condensation onto the glass.

"They've given him some more morphine. He's sleeping."

She nods. "How long do they think he'll be in for?"

"Reckon he's looking at a week. They want to get his weight back up. Make sure he can hold his food before he leaves."

"What have they said about the drinking?"

"If he carries on, he'll kill himself. His pancreas is screwed. Even if it settles this time, there'll be scarring, which'll make other attacks more likely."

"Do you think he'll be able to stop?"

"Maybe. For a while. He's had some sober spells. Made a year once."

"How do you feel about it?"

"What? Him being in the hospital?"

"His drinking."

Saul looks surprised, as if no one's ever asked him that question before. "He's been an alcoholic for more of my life than he hasn't. I don't like it—but I can't change it."

Eva waits; she's learning that Saul is someone who needs to be given the space to talk.

After a moment, he continues. "I've not been good at understanding it. I mean, I understand what triggered it. But I just . . ." He presses his palms against the window. "I just can't understand why he still does it to himself. I know it's an illness, an addiction, or whatever the hell the doctors call it, but still, if he just— stopped."

He shakes his head again, dropping his hands to his sides. "He looks so old," he says quietly.

"He's tough," Eva tells him. "He's going to be okay."

"He called me earlier this morning and I ignored it. I hadn't been to see him in ages. I should've been checking in on him. I know how cut up he is over Jackson. His drinking would have been worse than ever. There's no excuse; I pass his house every time I go in to the lab." He looks over at Eva and says, "He could've died. He's all I've got left, and he could've died."

Eva steps forward and puts her arms around him.

They stand together in the waiting room, voices of nurses and visitors drifting past. She feels his breathing slow in the space of her arms. Gradually the tension slides out of him. Out of her. Pressed together as they are, the rest of the world recedes.

THEY BOOK ROOMS FOR the night in a motel near the hospital. The interior is dull and timeworn but the shower is powerful and Eva lets the water sluice over her, hot and welcome. The tension in her neck and shoulders loosens, and gradually the day begins to leave her.

The bathroom is thick with steam when she steps from the shower, small pools of water following her across the linoleum floor. Wrapping a towel around herself, she wanders into the bedroom, searching the motel's drawers for a hair dryer. Not finding one, she makes the mistake of pausing to sit on the edge of the bed, which is so soft beneath her that she thinks she'll lie back, just for a moment.

She has almost drifted off when she's startled awake by the sound of knocking. Clutching her towel to her, she darts across the room, picking up her clothes from the floor and tugging them on.

Flushed, she answers the door, the towel still in her hand.

Saul stands before her, smiling his easy, welcome smile. "You hungry?"

"Mmm . . . but I'm not sure I can face getting back in the car."

"Want to order in?"

She locates a glossy pamphlet for a pizzeria and they order two pepperoni pizzas, which arrive fifteen minutes later. They sit on the bed picking up hot slices, melted cheese dripping from their fingers.

"Sorry we didn't make it back to Wattleboon," Saul says.

"Well, they don't do pizza delivery to Wattleboon."

"True." He grins.

When they're finished, Saul wipes his hands on a napkin, balls it up, and shoots it into the wastebasket.

Eva fetches them beers from the minibar and they pop open the tops and clink cans. "Cheers."

Leaning against the bed headboard, they talk about ordinary things—books, films, friends—and Eva feels herself relaxing, a pleasant tiredness hovering nearby.

When her phone vibrates, she stretches across to the bedside table to reach for it. Looking at the screen, she sees it is Callie and finds herself hesitating. They've only spoken twice since Eva left Melbourne, and the conversations were stilted, almost formal, as if they were both treading carefully. She knows Callie will be calling to see how the visit to Jeanette's went, but right now Eva doesn't want to think about Jeanette or Jackson—or any of it.

"Everything okay?" Saul asks.

"That was Callie," she says, glancing at her phone. "When I was in Melbourne, we sort of had a . . . fight. She didn't want me to come back to Tasmania." There's a pause. "She thinks I'm making a mistake."

"Are you?"

She meets his gaze. "I don't know."

"Eva," he says, looking at her levelly, "I'm glad you're here."

He is watching her, his gaze so intent that it seems to reach right inside her, as if he can see into her very being. She is aware of her heart beating in her chest. Longing spreads through her body with a force that shocks her, and her eyes move to the curve of his mouth.

Suddenly an image burns into her thoughts of Jackson's mouth, his lips slightly thinner than Saul's, and she watches as they move around the word, *Don't*.

She jumps to her feet. "I should clear these," she says, sweeping the pizza boxes from the bed. The cardboard is too large for the wastebasket, so she stacks them beside it, keeping her back to Saul. "I'll just wash my hands."

She closes the bathroom door and places her hands on the edge of the sink. The mirror is still misted with condensation and she cannot see the pink shame that's overtaken her face, but she feels it. He's Jackson's brother.

His fucking brother!

She won't let it happen. Whatever it is that she feels for Saul, it's grown out of such a dark place that she's scared the roots are too twisted and fragile. She looks at her face in the mirror. How could she want this? What is wrong with her? She cares about Saul and knows his friendship has helped her survive these past few weeks—but it needs to end there.

Running the tap, she washes the pizza grease from her fingers, then dries her hands carefully. When she leaves the bathroom, Saul is placing his empty beer can in the wastebasket. He tugs his room key from his back pocket, saying, "I'm gonna head off. Been a long day."

Eva feels the burn of disappointment as Saul moves toward the door. When he pulls it open, cool, fume-tinged air breezes into the room, and she watches the beaming headlights from passing cars outside.

Saul gives her a light smile and says, "Catch you tomorrow." He looks at her for a moment and something like resignation settles over his face. "Sleep well, Eva." Then he turns to leave.

She closes her eyes and swallows. "Don't go."

The words, barely whispered to the room, are followed by silence. Then she hears, or just senses, the movement of air as Saul turns back to face her. "What did you say?"

"Don't go."

When she opens her eyes, she sees that Saul is poised in the doorway, his fingers still curled around the handle.

Slowly, he steps back into the room and pulls the door gently closed. "Eva?"

Tears are pricking her lower lids. She doesn't know what she's doing, what she's feeling.

Saul crosses the room and stops in front of her. She can smell fresh soap rising from his skin. Slowly he reaches out and lightly places his fingers on her left cheek, almost at her jawline. Warmth pulses from his touch.

"I don't know what this is . . ." she whispers.

His dark gaze holds her steady. "Neither of us does." He leans down and places his lips on hers. Logic and hesitation dissolve in the heat of her desire.

Their hands reach for one another, their tongues sliding into the intimate warmth of each other's mouth.

It's not rushed or greedy or drunken. It is something tender and filled with compassion, something physical to make up for the words they cannot say. In a city motel, they make love, and for that wonderful stretch of time, she is not thinking of Jackson or the past. She is right here in this moment with Saul.

24

Eva wakes from a deep, dreamless sleep. She's in her motel room, alone. She sits up, pushing her hair away from her face. Glancing at the clock, she sees it is eleven in the morning. She has to check this fact. She blinks and looks again, but the numbers remain the same. It amazes her that she's slept for so long.

Propped against the clock is a note. It's been penned on a torn piece of pizza box, a grease smear spreading from the corner. She leans across to read it.

Saul's written it using a ballpoint pen, the nib sinking into the corrugated insides of the cardboard, making his handwriting look comically knobbly.

> *Gone to the hospital. Back about noon. Then on to Wattle-*
> *boon . . . Saul x*

She sinks back down into the bed, the covers sliding against her naked skin. She thinks about how they'd made love, Saul's body rising above hers. She'd pressed her fingers into his back, pulling him close so they were moving in one rhythm. Afterward they'd fallen asleep curled into the warmth of each other.

Rolling onto her side, Eva sees the indentation in the pillow beside her. She presses her palm into the dip where Saul's head had been, thinking, *Jackson used to sleep on the right-hand side, too.*

Guilt kicks her sharply in the gut and her knees draw up to her stomach. Suddenly she is picturing the mornings she'd woken up beside Jackson, seeing the peppering of stubble dusting his chin, his eyelids lightly swollen with sleep. He'd always cast out a heavy arm, drawing her close to him, his skin warm against hers.

"I've slept with your brother," she whispers, her hand smoothing the pillow, as if feeling for Jackson's imprint. *"I'm so sorry,"* she says, tears rising at the back of her throat.

A low wail builds in her chest, the sound clawing its way out of her mouth in a long, desolate vibration. How could she? Eva imagines Jackson's hurt if he could've seen her with Saul.

But then she thinks of Jeanette. Of Kyle. Of all the ways Jackson had betrayed her. Her fingers clench into a fist around the pillow, feeling the cotton strain beneath her grip. In one hard movement, she flings the pillow across the room. It skims the ceiling as it travels, then hits the door with a dull thump that makes the lock rattle.

She sinks back down into the bed, pulling the covers tight to her chin.

"MORNING," SAUL SAYS AS he approaches his father's hospital bed. "How you feelin'?"

"Like I've got the worst hangover of my life and been beaten up on top of that." Dirk tries to push himself up so he's sitting straight. When he's caught his breath, he asks Saul to fetch him some water.

"Manage to eat anything for breakfast?" Saul asks, pouring water into a plastic cup and handing it to him.

"Just some liquidized vitamin muck. I'm not absorbing the

right things, they reckon." He sips at the water. "Thanks for comin' here last night. Hope I didn't mess up any plans."

Saul moves to the window and looks out over the hospital parking lot. He knows he's got to say something. With his back to Dirk, he begins, "I was in Warrington yesterday."

"What were you doin' up there?"

Saul turns, clasping his hands behind his head. "Listen, Dad. Eva's still here."

"In Tasmania?"

He nods. "She knows about Jeanette."

"What?" Dirk barks, jolting forward. His face twists in pain. "How does she know?"

"She bumped into Flyer. He started talking about Jackson. I couldn't shut him up. He mentioned Jeanette's name, so I had to tell Eva."

"Jesus Christ, Saul! What were you doin' with her in the first place? She should be back in England by now!"

"Yeah, well, she's not. She's still in Tasmania and she knows," Saul says, eyes flashing.

"Tell me you didn't go to Warrington to see Jeanette?"

"Eva wanted to meet her."

"And you let her?" Dirk says, his voice coming out in a weak gasp. "Are you a bloody idiot? Now every fuckin' person in Tasmania will know!"

"Jeanette might not tell anyone. Even if she does—so what? Does it even matter?"

"Matter? I've lost my son. Isn't that enough? I don't want his name dragged through the mud, too."

"We should never have kept it from Eva. She had a right to know."

"She's a nice girl, Saul. I liked her. But what good does it do her knowin'? You tell me that."

"Maybe none. But it was never up to us to decide."

Dirk winces, sucking in his breath as he clutches his stomach. "You all right, Dad?"

He nods, but Saul is relieved when a nurse comes by a few minutes later and gives him another dose of pain relief.

When the nurse leaves, Dirk says, "I'm sorry for yellin'. Comin' off the drink, it's tough for a while. Makes me flare up a bit quick."

"Don't worry about it," Saul says with a shrug. Then he stands and grabs his jacket from the back of the chair. "You better get your rest."

Just as he's heading out the door, Dirk says, "I've been thinking a bit about your offer."

"Wattleboon?"

"Yeah." He sniffs. "I can't go on hiding from that place forever, can I?"

"What? So you'll stay?"

"Yeah," he says. "I'll stay."

PULLING UP OUTSIDE THE motel, Saul cuts the engine but doesn't get out. Eva will be waiting in her room, ready to head back to Wattleboon. He left her sleeping this morning. It was hard to pull himself out of bed with her lying there, an arm flung out over the pillow, her eyelids faintly flickering as if she were dreaming.

He knows exactly why he's sitting here in a motel parking lot, listening to the ticking of the engine as it cools. He's scared that he'll knock on that door and Eva will say to him, *It was a mistake.*

The longer he sits here, the longer he can play back the memory of last night: how her skin was so smooth beneath his hands;

how her lips parted as she moaned so he could see the pink tip of her tongue.

He pulls the key from the engine and climbs out of the truck, telling himself to man up. He crosses the parking lot and bounds up the concrete stairway. Reaching her room, he gives a loud rap on the door, then thrusts his hands in his pockets as he waits.

Behind him, a motorbike roars to life, engine revving. The sound always reminds him of when Jackson bought an old bike off a guy he worked with at the boatyard. He loved riding around on that thing in his jeans and battered leather jacket—told Saul he got laid all summer because of it.

Out of nowhere the image of his brother with Eva lunges forward. Saul's whole body tenses as guilt and jealousy vie for space in his head. He can't stand the thought of his brother's hands around Eva's waist, his mouth on hers. Saul has no right to be jealous—Eva was Jackson's wife—but it doesn't stop the images from searing.

He exhales hard, pushing thoughts of Jackson away. He knocks again, louder this time. As he waits, he runs a hand through his hair. Christ, he's like a teenager on a first date. He leans near the door, listening, but he can't hear any movement from inside.

Stepping back, he checks the door number. It's definitely the right room. He glances at his watch. It's noon. Exactly when he said he'd be back from the hospital. He's starting to worry that Eva's left. Perhaps she got cold feet—her head must be all over the place right now. Christ, he hopes he hasn't ruined things by rushing it.

He pulls his phone from his pocket and is about to dial when he hears a voice. "You calling me?"

Eva is standing behind him holding two coffees. She's wearing a simple cream top, her smooth neck wonderfully bare. She looks impossibly fresh-faced, her eyes wide and clear. "Ran out to get these."

"Oh," he says, relief flooding through him.

She holds out his coffee, smiling almost shyly. "How's your dad?"

"They managed to get a bit of food into him. Hopefully he'll start building up his strength again."

"Good. You'll visit again?"

"Yeah. Tomorrow after work."

Eva unlocks the room. "I'll just grab my bag."

He follows her in. The stale motel smell is disguised by the fresh scent of soap and Eva's perfume. He glances at the bed. The covers are thrown back and all he can think about is the way she'd lain beneath him right there, her body arching toward him.

"I think that's everything," Eva says, picking up her overnight bag.

"Here, let me get that."

As he takes it from her, she pauses, looking up at him.

His pulse accelerates. "You okay?"

She nods slowly. "Yes. I think I am."

EVA WATCHES SAUL'S TRUCK pull away in a cloud of red dust. She is smiling as she turns toward the shack, thinking about the light graze of Saul's stubble against her cheek as he kissed her good-bye. It felt good. More than good.

She looks up, taking in the bay. A light breeze ruffles its surface, but it's still calm enough for a free-dive and she thinks she'll take her things in and then check the visibility.

The key to the shack is lodged beneath a flecked pebble and

she unlocks the door and swings her bag from her shoulder as she steps inside.

Then she freezes.

Her skin prickles along the nape of her neck: she has the strangest sensation that someone has been in here.

She lowers her bag to the ground and moves slowly forward. "Hello?"

There is no answer.

She scans the room. Everything appears to be exactly as she left it—yet she knows something is not quite right.

It is the smell, she realizes, halting. The air carries the faint scent of leather and an earthy musk. Jackson's smell.

Her skin turns cool. The room is so strongly laced with his smell that it's as if he has—just this minute—walked through the shack.

She glances toward the shelf where the photo of her and Jackson used to stand. It is still missing.

She takes a few steps forward until she reaches the bedroom door. She curls her fingers around the metal handle and then pushes it open.

The room is empty, the curtains stirring lightly in the breeze.

Of course it is empty, she tries telling herself lightheartedly. On her pillow she sees Jackson's red-checked shirt that she sleeps in. She had left it folded there before going to Warrington, but something about it strikes her as odd. She drifts toward it trying to see what is different about it.

When she gets closer, she sees it's folded just as she left it. She shakes her head briskly, telling herself that this is absurd. These ideas have got to stop.

Just as she turns to leave the room, she finds her hand reaching for the shirt. She plucks it into the air and presses her face into the fabric.

Eva has worn and worn this shirt in the months since Jackson's death, so any trace of his scent left long ago. But now her nose fills with Jackson's smell. It is so thick and heavy, it's as if she is burying her face into his neck.

Her heart drills, blood surging to her head. She drops his shirt to the floor, the material collapsing at her feet with a sigh.

There were so many times when I thought about telling you the truth. What stopped me was always the same thing: fear of losing you. So I'd keep quiet, and the deeper the lies became, the harder it was to reach the truth.

I used to lay small tests for you, gauging your reaction to situations. Once I told you about my colleague Tony, who you'd met a couple of times and liked. He had a gambling problem that he'd been keeping from his wife for years. Eventually she found out, but by then he'd already remortgaged their home to cover up his debts. His wife had thrown him out and he was sleeping on his stepbrother's sofa.

You listened to his story and said, "It's so sad—for both of them."

I asked, "If it were you, would you have taken him back?"

While you considered the question, I felt my heart starting to race as if you were about to deliver a verdict for us.

Eventually you said, "I like Tony, he's a lovely guy, but if I were his wife, then no, I don't think I could take him back."

"What?"

"It's not so much the gambling—it's the fact that he'd been lying to her for so long. She'd never trust him again."

"But she loves him," I said, my voice raised a notch.

You lifted your shoulders. "Maybe that's not always enough."

25

Saul slides wine bottles from the rack and stands them in a cardboard box. When the rack is empty, he goes to the fridge and opens the lower drawer. Beer bottles lie on their sides, glass gleaming like freshly caught fish. He hesitates for a moment, wondering if he could just keep a couple hidden somewhere. He'll miss the after-work beer he cracks open on the deck, letting the day fade behind him.

No, he decides as he loads the beers into the box, he can't leave any alcohol in the house. He grabs the whiskey and rum from the cupboard above the cutlery drawer, and then leaves with the box held to his chest.

Saul follows the bay toward Eva's shack. It's a Saturday morning and he sees her from a distance sitting on the edge of the deck, her head bent as if she's looking at something in her hands. He's come to think of it as her shack. He knows there's going to be a time when Joe is back from Darwin, or maybe Eva will decide to leave before that even happens. They haven't talked about it—it's almost been a week since they spent the night together in the motel and everything feels tentative, as though they are feeling their way in the dark.

All week Saul's found himself checking his watch at the end

of each day, eager to get out of the lab and back to Eva. The evenings when he's home early enough, they go free-diving together in the bay. Now that she's no longer fighting against the water or trying to force her breathing, he's starting to see a graceful style emerging in her dives. What he loves the most about diving with her is that out in the bay, with the sea on their skin, it feels as though nothing else exists or matters. It's just them.

When he gets closer he can see that Eva is fiddling with the strap of a snorkel mask. She wears a sweater, but her legs are bare and nut brown. She looks up, squinting against the sun. And then she smiles, her lips parting, her teeth white against her tanned face.

That smile. He feels as if it's pouring right inside him like sunlight, heating some central part of himself. There is something strong between them, he can feel it. And the truth is it terrifies him because, what happens from here?

A thought of his, a feeling, is suddenly illuminated, clear and bright. His breath shortens as he understands: he is in love with Eva.

Saul stops in front of her.

She's still looking at him, her smile crinkling into mild bemusement.

He struggles to come up with a single thing to say. All he is thinking is: *I'm in love with you. I'm in love with you.*

She glances at the box in his arms, which prompts him to remember what he came over for. "I've cleared the house of alcohol. For Dad," he adds.

She peers into the box and he sees the smooth skin of the back of her neck. "You're going to trust me with all that?"

He should make a quick retort, but his mind is blank. He places the box down and then sits beside her on the edge of the deck. He is so close to Eva that he can feel the heat of her body in the space between them.

He picks up the snorkel mask and turns it through his hands to give them something to do. "Your mask strap okay?"

"The clasp got jammed, but I've loosened it now."

He nods.

"You still on for hiking up to Eagle Cape?" Eva asks.

"Yeah." They'd planned to walk up to the top of the cape, which gives views right out over the Tasman Peninsular. "If we hike from here, it'll be a couple of hours to the top. You okay with that?"

"Definitely. We've got all afternoon." Eva smoothes her hair back from her face and he can see the sun freckles across her forehead and a tiny scar above her eyebrow.

He cannot stop leaning forward and pressing his lips to hers. She tastes sweet and welcoming and he feels her body respond to his.

Suddenly Saul jerks back.

On the deck behind Eva he's caught sight of a checked shirt belonging to Jackson. It's hanging over the back of a chair, the square angle of the wood filling it out as if Jackson is standing there, broad-shouldered, watching them. Saul remembers the shirt from years ago. Jackson wore nothing else for a whole summer, always having the sleeves pushed up, the collar open.

"Saul?"

When he doesn't answer, Eva twists around, following his gaze. "Oh."

"Sorry . . . I just . . . it took me by surprise." Absurdly, he finds himself taking a step away, putting distance between him and Eva. Looking at the shirt, he could almost believe that Jackson was here minutes ago.

A cloying jealousy sticks in his throat. He rubs the back of his head, saying, "You . . . wear it?"

Eva hesitates, her brow dipping at the question. "I sleep in it sometimes."

Saul swallows hard, trying to push aside the image of Eva's naked body wrapped in Jackson's shirt. What he wants to ask is: *Why, after everything he's done to you, do you still want to feel as if he's next to you?*

But he doesn't ask, because he's not sure he's ready to hear her answer.

AN HOUR LATER, EVA follows Saul up a dirt path that ascends through a forest of gum trees, slices of sunlight slanting through the canopy of leaves. The air is damp and earthy, and sweat builds at the waist of her shorts and across her brow.

Ahead she watches the hard muscles in Saul's calves as he strides on. He keeps his eyes on the ground watching for tiger snakes, which he's told her often doze on the warm path at this time of the year. It's one of the few things they've said to each other so far on the walk.

Eva doesn't want to feel culpable or embarrassed for sleeping in Jackson's shirt. She's barely able to understand it herself; all she knows is that she'd once loved Jackson deeply and she can't just wash away everything she felt.

When she'd found the shirt on her pillow almost a week ago, thick with Jackson's smell, she sat on the bedroom floor with the material pressed into her face, sobbing until the sky fell dark. She knew it was guilt that was causing her mind to play such a powerful trick on her senses, but the experience still left her feeling flayed.

She needs to move cautiously with Saul, almost an inverse pattern of her relationship with Jackson. She has lost confidence in herself and her own judgments and worries whether—just as her mind conjured up the scent of Jackson—her heart is misguiding her, too? She can't tell whether she's falling in love with

Saul, or falling in love with the version of Jackson she is mourning. She shakes her head and picks up her pace, trying to close the distance between them.

It's another half hour before the path begins to level out and they reach the top of the cape. Saul leads them to a clearing in the trees where she can see the sunstruck ocean glinting. The fresh breeze moves over her skin and she closes her eyes and sighs.

Saul slides off his pack and takes out a bottle of water, which he passes to Eva. It's slightly warm, but she drinks from it thirstily, wiping her mouth with the back of her hand.

Behind Eva a fallen log makes the perfect seat and she lowers herself down, the muscles in her legs relaxing. Saul sits beside her, saying, "This spot used to be a lookout point for whalers. They had a station up here so they could see when the whales were coming in and alert the men."

Looking out over the open ocean, she feels the timelessness of the place as if it's been built on ancient bones. "It's so peaceful up here."

"That's what my mum used to say. She'd hike out here when she needed the space to write. When Jackson and I were young, we'd come with her sometimes and sit on a blanket and draw while Mum wrote."

She glances at him and sees that his expression has turned distant. Suddenly she realizes: "This is the place, isn't it?" She remembers Jackson telling her that their mother was writing in her favorite spot when the bush fire happened.

"Yes."

On the hike up she'd noticed that some of the trees were much smaller than the others lower down; young trees that would have grown since the fire. "Is it strange for you being out here?"

He thinks for a moment. "I didn't come for a long time after the fire. Dad never wanted to go back to Wattleboon, so I felt like it'd be wrong somehow if I did." He crosses his arms, tucking his hands lightly beneath his armpits. "But as I got older, I thought it was sad that none of us ever came here. It's where Mum's ashes are scattered. She loved it here."

Eva looks out to sea, where a sailing boat is just visible in the distance. "Jackson used to have nightmares about this place."

Saul turns, surprised. "Did he?"

"He'd wake up coughing. The nightmares were about the bush fire. He was out in the woods trying to reach your mum. Trying to save her."

"I had no idea. We never spoke about the fire. None of us."

"Why not?"

Saul seems to think about this before he says, "I guess some things are just too hard."

THEY FALL INTO STEP, descending through the cool shade of the fir trees, the breeze from the sea at their shoulders. Saul can't pinpoint why he's started talking about the fire; perhaps it's because being with Eva invites an intimacy that he hasn't felt with anyone else. "I was thirteen at the time. Jackson was fifteen. We'd been on Wattleboon all summer and it was our last weekend in the shack before school started up again."

Eva walks at his side, their pace slower than on the climb up. The path is covered in a layer of pine needles and there's almost no sound to their footsteps. "Dad and I had driven to the other side of the island to look at a boat trailer. I'd just gone for the ride because the guy selling it owned some terrapins—apparently I thought terrapins were the height of cool at thirteen."

He catches Eva's smile and it gives him the confidence to go on.

"We were driving back when we saw the smoke. There was this huge, dark cloud that rose into the sky." Because of the position of the sun behind it, the smoke looked backlit, hazy and magical. He feels guilty now as he remembered his excitement: bush fires always signaled drama and exhilaration and he'd been eager to know what was ablaze.

Eva asks, "What caused it?"

"We still don't know. It'd been a dry summer and the bush was like tinder. Could've been anything—a campfire, kids messing around. Sometimes all it takes is for a piece of broken glass to heat up enough to get some dry leaves smoldering."

The path narrows so that they have to walk one at a time. He goes first, and somehow telling the story without looking at Eva is easier.

"Dad dropped me off at the shack and said to make sure everyone stayed there while he went to find out what was going on. But when I went inside, Mum and Jackson weren't home."

He tells Eva how he walked along the bay to Jeanette's shack and found Jackson inside, lounging on her sofa playing Super Mario Kart. It had annoyed him seeing his brother there: Jeanette was Saul's friend and Jackson didn't even like her—but she had a Nintendo and he didn't.

"Seen the fire?" Saul asked.

"Yeah." Jackson had shrugged without taking his eyes off the screen.

Jeanette stepped out onto the deck and looked up at the smoke. "Do you think it'll come this far?"

"Course it won't," Jackson said. "Firemen will be all over it by now."

"Dad said we've gotta wait back at the shack," Saul told his brother.

Jackson didn't move till he'd finished his game. Then he chucked the handset down and said, "Let's go."

They were just getting back to their place when Dirk swung

into the drive. His face was strained and he kept looking up at the sky. "Where's your mother?"

"Dunno," Jackson had said. "Isn't she here?"

"Maybe she's writing?" Saul had suggested.

He knew it was the wrong answer from the way his father's features twisted into a dark expression he'd never seen before. "Get in the car!"

But Saul didn't move because suddenly it had started to snow. He gazed up at the pale flakes that turned and danced with the warm breeze.

A flake the size of his thumbnail landed so lightly on the back of his hand that he couldn't even feel it. He pressed his forefinger to it and the flake disintegrated against his skin, leaving a dark gray smear.

Then he'd felt a sharp yank on his arm as his father started dragging him toward the car.

There was a four-wheel-drive route that took you halfway up the track to Eagle Cape, or you could go on foot through the bush. Dirk knocked the car into its lowest gear, the engine straining as they roared along the pitted track. Overhanging branches thwacked against the sides of the car and Saul and Jackson were thrown around so much in the back that their heads smacked against the roof. They tried bracing themselves each time they saw a pothole, but soon they couldn't even see them because the air was so dense with smoke. It poured in through the air vents and door seals and Saul ducked his head into his T-shirt to stop himself from coughing.

Dirk had glanced back at his sons, his eyes searching their faces. At the time, Saul had wondered what his father was looking for. But now he knew. Dirk was making a decision: *Do I risk my sons' lives to try and save my wife's?*

A moment later, Dirk braked hard and then clunked the car into reverse. His face was a gray mask as he twisted around in his seat to reverse back down the smoke-filled track.

The decision to turn back had haunted him for the rest of his life. The bush burned to the ground. The firemen found their mother's body three hundred feet away from the lookout point where she went to write. She'd been trying to run.

When Saul finishes speaking, he looks at Eva. They are no longer walking and have come to a standstill on the narrow path, facing each other. He'd never spoken about the fire before and it felt good to have shared it with her.

"The fire—that's why your dad hasn't come back to Wattleboon?"

"Yeah. He always said it was too hard—too many memories. But hiding from the past, that's not done him any good. It hasn't done any of us any good."

"Tomorrow you're bringing him back to your place?"

Saul nods. "That's the plan. Although I'm half expecting him to change his mind."

"Maybe it'll be good for him to be here."

"I hope so."

She steps forward and puts her arms around him. Her body is warm and slight and the muscles in his chest contract.

"Eva," he says quietly, pulling back a little. He doesn't want to say this—he wishes everything were simpler and he didn't have to. "I was thinking, if Dad does stay, I'm not sure whether we should tell him . . . you know, about . . . well, us." With the toe of his boot he nudges at the pine needles on the ground. "I want you to know that it's not because I'm in any way ashamed of what's happening. I mean that. It's just, I think right now it might be difficult for Dad to understand."

She nods slowly. "I was thinking the same thing."

They look at each other for a long moment, and then they continue on.

26

Saul parks the truck in front of his house. He glances at his father, who sits in the passenger seat. It's been fifteen years since Dirk last stepped foot on Wattleboon.

Saul climbs out of the truck and opens the door for his father, helping him down.

"The air," Dirk says, his eyes wide. "I remember it exactly."

Saul breathes in the faint peppermint of the gums, the tang of brine, the rich earthy smell of the soil.

Dirk stands very still. "This is right where I parked my old Ford when I brought Lynn and you boys here for the first time. There wasn't a proper track then, just a steep dirt path that I had to put the car in first gear to get up."

"It's changed a lot," Saul agrees. He's graveled and widened the track, and cleared some of the trees to make more of the view. There's new fencing, the old tree stumps have been dug out, and a new water unit has gone in.

Dirk starts moving, ambling forward with small steps as he circles the house. He runs a hand along the woodwork, and Saul sees him checking the sealed knots and smooth joins. Dirk makes a fist of his hand and taps his knuckles against the wood. "Good, strong Huon pine," he says.

When Dirk reaches the front of the house, he stops. "The view." His face breaks into a smile as he looks toward the sweep of the bay. "This was the view that made me buy the plot of land all those years ago. Your mother and I used to love watching you boys running down to the bay together."

Saul smiles. "Here, I want to show you something else."

They move toward the edge of the garden, Dirk struggling on the uneven ground.

"You okay?" Saul asks. "We can do this later."

Dirk waves a hand through the air. "I've been sitting on my arse all week in the hospital. Being up and about in the fresh air—that's the best medicine I know."

They get a little way through the trees when Saul stops, pointing ahead of them.

Dirk halts, blinking. His hands rise to the collar of his shirt. "My God! Our shack!"

Seeing the surprise on Dirk's face, Saul smiles.

"I can't believe it. But . . . how?"

"I dismantled it. Moved it here."

Dirk shakes his head. "I remember building it, erecting the timber structure, hammering down each plank of wood, laying the roof on a hot, windless day. And you've re-pieced it all." He turns to look at Saul. "Why?"

Saul knows life moves on and history is history, but he wanted to keep a piece of their family, show that it meant something to him. He tells his father, "It wouldn't have been right to knock it down. Plus, if you wanted to come and stay again sometime, you may fancy your own space."

Dirk places a large hand on his shoulder. "Thank you," he says with meaning.

THREE DAYS LATER EVA stands in the bedroom holding a large glass of red wine and wondering what to wear. Saul has invited her over for dinner with Dirk and, stupidly, her stomach churns with nerves.

After her disastrous first meeting with Dirk, she has no idea how this will go. She wonders if he will apologize, or whether he still resents her for coming out to Tasmania. Dirk is the one person whom Jackson spoke to about his life in England, the only one who knew Eva existed. He must have some answers. As she thinks about the evening ahead, she realizes she's both desperate to hear, and afraid to hear, what Dirk has to say.

Eva takes a sip of wine thinking it's strange that when she was writing to him from England she believed they had a rapport, yet in person that closeness didn't exist.

A thought spears her: what if Dirk never got her letters? He hadn't wanted Eva to marry Jackson, so why would he be writing to her? Her fingers tighten around her wineglass as she realizes that the letters were probably just another layer to Jackson's deception. It would explain why Jackson had always offered to send the letters from the mail room at work, and why she'd found two of them unsent in his bedside drawer.

It would also mean that Jackson had forged Dirk's return letters. Bile rises in her throat at the thought of all this would entail: perfecting fake handwriting, buying airmail stationery, leaving the letters out for Eva to read. The lengths he'd gone to in order to deceive her were astounding.

Anger pulses through her veins. How dare he! How dare he do this to her! Humiliate her. Tear her memories apart. Tell her he loved her over and over . . .

Glass explodes into the room.

Her hand and chest are covered in red liquid. Everywhere there are fragments of glass.

Her hand, still outstretched, is now empty of the wineglass she'd been holding. Dark red liquid drips from her fingers. She draws her hand level with her face and inspects it. There is not a single cut or nick.

The wine has sprayed over her clothes and puddles on the floor. For a moment, she just stands there, blinking at the mess.

Eventually she propels herself into action; she fetches a dustpan and brush and sweeps up the broken fragments, which slop and drift on the spill of wine. Then she returns with a wad of tissues and crouches to mop up the rest of the liquid.

Eva notices that a slash of red wine has spilled right over the inscription of Jackson's name in the floorboard. She pauses as an image slips into her thoughts: Jeanette kneeling here as a teenager, her brow creased in concentration as she carves Jackson's name into the wood. She pictures the penknife gripped in her pale hands. She would have bent low, carving the letters one after the other, blowing away the fresh shavings, her lips close to his name. Saul had told her that Jeanette had had a crush on Jackson since they were kids, and that the connection was still there when they met up years later.

But Eva had been in Jackson's life for just two short years. Two years that were built on a bed of lies. What claim did Eva ever really have?

She mops up the wine, but it's already seeped deep into the inscription, staining Jackson's name blood-red.

"DAD, YOU REMEMBER EVA," Saul says.

Dirk pulls himself out of his chair. He smiles and stretches out his hand. "Good to see ya, Eva."

"You, too."

There is a beat of silence.

"So. How are you feeling?" Eva asks.

"Strong as an ox." Dirk glances toward the bay, where a brilliant red sun is disappearing into the west, fringing the sky with pink clouds. "Good place to recuperate."

"It is," she agrees.

Saul asks, "Can I get you a drink, Eva?"

"Please. Water would be great."

Once Saul's left the room, Dirk turns to Eva. "I just wanted to apologize—I wasn't on my finest form when we last met."

"It's not a problem."

He clears his throat. "Neither of us probably want to get into everything that's gone on, so all I'll say is—I'm sorry that you've had such a rough time of things."

"Thank you." She doesn't want to push Dirk to talk, not when she's just arrived, but there are things she needs to know. For now, though, she lets him change the subject.

"It's great being back on Wattleboon after so long," he says.

"Saul tells me you used to have a shack here?"

"That's right. Built the place over twenty years ago. Such a surprise to see it still standing."

She tilts her head. "How do you mean?"

"Saul's not told you about his project?"

"No?"

"The old shack used to stand right here where the house is. Saul dismantled the whole thing and rebuilt it at the edge of the garden. I'm calling it my holiday home! Isn't that right?" Dirk says as Saul walks in carrying a glass of water for Eva.

She turns toward him. "Did you? Rebuild the shack?"

"Thought it'd be a shame to get rid of it."

She thinks of Jackson's talk of rebuilding the shack. Was that actually Saul's dream he'd borrowed? "How long have you been planning it for?"

"Been thinking about it for years. Just haven't had the time until now."

She swallows. "Can I see it?"

"Sure," Saul says. "It's just off to the left of the garden, beyond the bushes."

A minute later Eva is standing in front of a rustic shack with a tin roof. She steps forward and places a hand on the aged wood, feeling the texture and grain against her skin. *So this was the old shack.*

She'd loved listening to Jackson's plans to come back out here one day and make it good for his father. But it had been a shallow promise, she realizes, because Jackson never intended on coming back to Tasmania.

It had been Saul's dream. Saul who had quietly gotten on with it. Saul who had brought his father back to Wattleboon after all these years.

THE CANDLES AND MOSQUITO flares are lit and the sound of crickets fills the air. Saul sets down a large oven dish.

"What we got?" Dirk asks.

"Flathead fillets with rice. No fat, no spices, easy to digest. You should be fine with it." Saul removes the foil covering and the smell of freshly steamed fish rises into the dusk.

Eva passes plates and cutlery and they serve themselves with a big metal ladle, the handle clinking against the china dish.

The fish tastes incredible, just lightly seasoned with pepper and lemon. Dirk eats slowly, working the food over in his mouth before swallowing. He and Saul talk about their day, and as Eva listens, a sharp feeling of guilt needles its way beneath her skin. What would Jackson think if he could see them all here: his wife; his brother; his father? And what if he could see her hand hidden beneath the table, held by Saul's? Her loyalties sway and shift and it makes her feel unsteady.

Later, when the plates have been cleared, Saul brings out a colander full of plump strawberries and blueberries from the berry farm at the end of the road. Eva picks at them absently, her gaze drifting over to the dark garden.

A movement at the edge of her vision makes her blink and refocus. She stares toward the bush, where she senses the shadow of something—or someone. Her skin prickles from the nape of her neck to her fingertips.

Saul and Dirk are still talking, neither of them seeming to notice anything. Her eyes strain against the darkness; she can't see what it is, just something darker than the charcoal shade of the bush.

She feels her fingers loosening, letting go of Saul's hand. Her mouth turns dry and it is difficult to swallow. She needs to get up and walk over there, but she knows Saul and Dirk will think it odd. She tells herself to relax. No one is there—it's just the shadows of the trees, or an animal. But she cannot explain the strange chill that skitters down her spine.

Beneath the table her knee twitches with the urge to go over, to be sure. Without deciding to, she finds herself rising to her feet, crossing the deck and climbing down the steps into the garden.

Away from the candles, the darkness feels complete and she narrows her eyes. The shape is still there and she edges closer.

"Eva . . ."

She jolts back, her heart pounding at the familiar timbre of the voice. She's unsure whether it came from in front of her, or behind.

"Eva?"

She turns, realizing it is Saul. He has half risen from his seat and is looking at her from the deck. "Everything okay?"

She glances back to the tree line, desperately searching out the shadow—but it has vanished. She shakes her head, unsure whether there was anything there, or whether it was her imagination taunting her.

Her hands are trembling as she returns to the deck. "Wallaby. Thought I saw a wallaby."

Dirk seems to accept this and tells her there's plenty of them at this time of night, but Saul's gaze lingers on her.

Eva slides back into her seat, her breath short. She pours herself a large glass of water, and as she lifts the glass to her mouth, the candlelight plays over her forearm, showing the trail of goose bumps lining her skin.

27

As Saul and Dirk continue to talk, Eva slips her hands beneath her thighs, sitting on them to stop the trembling. She concentrates on slowing her breathing, trying to shake the eerie feeling that Jackson is there, watching them.

Guilt. That's what is causing her mind to play tricks on her. She feels guilty about her growing feelings for Saul, as if by being with him—allowing herself some happiness—she is betraying Jackson. Tension builds in her temples and she can feel a tightness spreading across her forehead, reaching down into her eye sockets.

"Eva?"

Dirk is saying something to her now and she turns to face him, shaking her head. "Sorry?"

"I was asking whether you were missing your work. You're a midwife, aren't you?"

"Yes." She shifts, drawing her hands onto her lap. "I do miss it. A lot," she says, realizing just how true that is. "But I needed a break."

"Did you always want to be a midwife?"

"No, not really. I trained to be a paramedic to begin with, but it never felt quite right."

"How d'you mean?" Saul asks, beside her.

"As a paramedic you're thrown into people's lives at a point of crisis. You deliver them to hospital—and that's it." The breeze stirs her hair and she smoothes it behind her ears. "I loved parts of the job—like having to think on my feet and working under pressure—but I found myself wanting to know more about the patients. Find out what happened to them. I remember I was working this one night shift in Poplar when we got a call out for a woman in labor. When we got there she was already in the final stages. I was just a trainee at the time but the paramedic I was with knew the woman wouldn't make it to hospital. We had to deliver the baby right there."

She remembers the rush she'd felt knowing she was going to help bring a baby into the world. "I didn't even do much. The midwife arrived a few minutes after us and took control. But I'd never seen a baby delivered before and it was just so incredible. Such an amazing experience. Afterward, I remember seeing this woman holding her new baby—Ziad, she called him—and I just thought, 'This is what I want to do.'"

That's the story she's always told people, but she wonders now if there's another layer to it. Perhaps it wasn't just a single defining moment; rather the desire to be a midwife had always been within her. Eva's sister had died at birth because of a complication with her delivery that could've been avoided. Eva had seen how her sister's death had ripped apart her mother's world. Maybe, in some small way, being a midwife was about trying to fix what had happened.

She pushes the thought aside, knowing she's becoming too introspective tonight.

Dirk says, "Jackson told me you were a fantastic midwife."

Her breathing shallows at the mention of his name. "Did he?"

"He said women were always asking for you to deliver their babies."

Questions about Jackson's past spin around and around in her mind, like a Ferris wheel she can't stop. There are things she needs to ask Dirk. She knows that now isn't the right time, not with Saul beside her, but she cannot stop herself. "Did Jackson talk to you much about his life in London?"

"He'd call every few weeks or so. I guess he'd tell me the bits he wanted me to hear. I knew all about his job and what he thought of the city. But there were gaps." Dirk leans back in his chair and folds his hands in his lap. "Like I said, I knew about you from the start—that he'd met someone. We spoke on the phone, didn't we?"

She nods. It was before they were engaged. She had picked up the phone while Jackson was in the shower. It'd been a brief chat as Eva was conscious she had answered a long-distance call.

"But he never told me he'd proposed. I only knew he'd married you a few weeks after it'd happened." He places his hands flat on the edge of the table and looks at her. "I'd have stopped him if I'd known. It wasn't fair to you, Eva."

"I wrote to you," she says. "I wrote letters every couple of months."

She sees Dirk's eyebrows lift.

"Jackson never sent any of them, did he?"

"No. He didn't."

She had expected this answer, yet her cheeks still burn with humiliation at how wholly she'd been deceived.

A moth flies too close to the flame, singeing its wing. It spirals downward in a staggered dance of death, landing in a pool of melted wax.

She feels a tightness in her chest as emotions she's tried to keep contained are beginning to push out. She hears Saul shifting, the brush of fabric against the chair as he leans back. She knows she should end this conversation, but she can't stop herself. "Why did he marry me?"

Dirk exhales. "He told me he hadn't planned it—the proposal—it just happened. And then he realized he didn't want to undo it."

She's thinking back to the hailstorm on Clapham Common, where they'd sheltered beneath a row of trees as tiny icy spheres bounced against their shins. They'd clung to each other, and pressed into the warmth of Jackson's body, Eva had forgotten about the cold, the sting of hailstones, the roar of wind in the sky. Because there was only Jackson.

That's when he'd said to her, "I want to spend the rest of my life with you." She'd looked up at him and said, "I want that, too." And then he'd asked her to marry him. There was no ring and he didn't get down on one knee, as he didn't want to let go of her, even for a moment, and she'd said, "Yes. Yes a thousand times."

Wasn't that real? How do I know! How can I ever be sure about any of it? Tears begin to fill her eyes and she bites hard on the inside of her cheek, desperate not to cry.

"I know he hurt you," Dirk is saying. "It was wrong of him to marry you. Christ knows why he didn't get a divorce first, get everything square. But then men do foolish things when they're in love."

She is aware of Saul sitting near her shoulder, his presence like a heat in the darkness.

Dirk looks directly at her as he continues, "And he did love you, Eva. That's why he took the risk of marrying you. Because you were everything he wanted."

Eva stays very still. Her pulse ticks in her throat.

"There were lies. Lots of them. But that part is the truth. He loved you."

She has needed to hear this for so long. It's as though something tight and knotted inside of her loosens. Despite everything, he had loved her. It counted for so much.

There is a sudden scraping of metal against wood. Saul pushes back his chair. The flames of the candles jump as he stands. He says something about a drink, and then heavy footsteps disappear inside the house.

EVA REGRETS ASKING THOSE questions in front of Saul. But having Dirk here to talk to makes her marriage feel real and not just a shadow of something that she'd once believed in.

A mosquito buzzes near her ear and she brushes at the air. She pulls her wrap from the back of her chair and drapes it on her shoulders.

"It's hard for Saul," Dirk says. "Hard to lose someone you love when you're on bad terms."

"I know about their feud."

"Bloody pigheaded, the pair of them. Broke my heart, them falling out. They were thick as thieves once. I think Saul forgets all that now. But I don't. You should see the pictures I've got, wonderful ones of them fishing down the jetty, building dens, surfing. They did everything together."

"I'd love to see them sometime," Eva says.

"Yeah? Well, I'll dig them out for you, then. Be nice to show someone." Dirk slips a bottle of painkillers from his shirt pocket and snaps two pills onto his palm. He swallows them with a swig of water. Then he pushes his glass aside and places his elbows on the table.

"I know Jackson messed up. He treated you and Saul terribly. But don't go thinking too badly of him. He was a good lad at heart. He loved his brother, too. He really did. Saul cut himself off completely, said he didn't even want to hear Jackson's name. But Jackson, he wanted to know everything he could about Saul. What he was doin', where he was travelin', whether he was happy. Jackson may not have apologized, but he knew his mistake."

The crickets singing in the bush, a loud orchestra of them, suddenly stop as if the conductor has asked for a pause. The silence is surprising. Eva tilts her head a little to check it's not her ears. A moment later, they start back up and Eva wonders what made them stop.

He continues. "Saul, he doesn't like me talkin' about Jackson. But I'm getting old, Eva. I realized that in hospital. I don't want Saul to be bitter about the past, not like I've been. It won't do him any good. I think it'd help him if he could forgive Jackson for his mistakes."

"They're not mine to forgive."

They both turn. Saul is standing in the doorway. The light is behind him and Eva cannot make out the expression on his face.

"It's not up to me to forgive him for lying to Eva. Or to forgive him for walking out on Kyle. What happened between me and him—that's just one event. Maybe I could let go of that. Maybe I already have. But just because he's dead, I'm not going to shine a golden light on his memory."

Dirk shakes his head. "Come on, son. He was a good boy at—"

"Was he? Sorry if it upsets you hearing this, Dad—and you, too, Eva—but Jackson was a cheat. He lied to us all. He let everyone down. How can anyone walk out on their own child and not look back?"

"There's more to it than that," Dirk says in a low voice. "You don't know all the facts."

"So tell me." Saul steps forward, triggering the deck floodlight, and Eva can see his face is rigid. "You're the one who suddenly wants to break down the silence, talk about our feelings, when our whole lives you've barely mentioned our mother's name. You want to talk about that now, too?" he says, his voice rising.

Dirk swallows. "You're right. I haven't been able to speak about her. Because saying her name out loud leaves a hole in me. I thought it was better to try and forget. But it didn't work, did it? All those nights you had to pick me up off the floor are proof of that."

Dirk shifts in his chair, wincing a little. His voice is softer as he says, "I'm sorry. For all of it. And maybe it's too late to teach you any different, but I don't want that for you, Saul. Coming back out to Wattleboon has made me see that. You need to face your demons, not let them reduce you into something you're not. You want to know about your brother, how he could leave Kyle? Just walk away?"

"Yes."

Dirk pauses. Then, "He found out Jeanette was lying to him. Always had been. Kyle wasn't his. There was some other bloke from Taroona that she was messing around with at the beginning. He's the father—not Jackson." Dirk looks directly at Saul as he says, "That's why he left."

"Why didn't you say anything before?"

"Jackson asked me not to. He didn't want people to know Kyle wasn't his son. He loved him." Dirk sighs. "But I don't suppose what Jackson wants matters much now."

SAUL CROSSES THE DECK, his bare feet padding lightly over the wood. He feels Dirk and Eva's gazes moving with him as he climbs down the steps into the moonlit garden.

He feels the dewy grass beneath his soles, then the hard coolness of the stone steps descending toward the bay, and finally the welcome give of sand as he reaches the beach.

Saul yanks off his T-shirt and unbuckles his jeans. He throws his clothes onto the sand and runs straight into the bay, water slapping at his shins. He makes a shallow dive and the cold grips him tight, squeezing at his muscles. He swims hard, pushing air from his mouth.

He stops in the middle of the bay, where the water drops away so steeply that the seabed must be a hundred feet below him. He takes a long breath, his ribs rising beneath his skin as his body fills with oxygen, and dives down.

Black water surrounds him like night. He feels as if he's diving deep into the soul of the ocean. He equalizes as he goes, thought fading as the sea swallows him.

Deeper and deeper, kicking through ancient places where fish hover, gills pumping, fins flicking; past ledges where abalone lie still and silent, their flesh pulsating with the current; beyond the squid that drift like specters, transparent tentacles brushing his skin.

He stops kicking and opens his eyes. Above there is a faint silver light—the moon beckoning—and he kicks toward it.

At the surface he lies on his back with his arms spread wide, staring at the sky brimming with stars. He knows he shouldn't have left his father and Eva like that, but he couldn't listen to any more. Whenever he's near Eva—whenever he so much as thinks of her—his heart fills with a strength of emotion that is new to him.

It's torn him up these past few weeks seeing how badly Jackson's hurt Eva. Part of him hates his brother for it. But tonight he sees that despite it all, Eva still loves Jackson. Perhaps will always love Jackson.

And as selfish as this thought is, Saul can't help wondering what this means for them.

EVA LEAVES DIRK AT the house and walks along the bay's edge, damp sand clinging to the soles of her feet. She tastes salinity in the air and something earthy from the bush.

Ahead, a pile of clothes is strewn in the sand. She pauses, then turns to the water, scanning the inky surface for Saul. After a moment, she can glimpse movement, moonlight glancing off an arm or a leg. She sits down beside Saul's clothes and waits.

She listens to the tumbling slap as small waves hit the beach, followed by the lighter, liquid sound as the water is drawn back, shifting sand and shells as it moves.

Now she must readjust her picture of Jackson yet again to fit the new information she's just learned. It was Jeanette's deception that caused him to leave Tasmania. It helps Eva to at least begin to understand why Jackson boarded that plane wanting a new life, a fresh start.

She glances up and sees Saul beginning to swim back toward the shore. She reaches over and picks up his jeans from the beach, sand sprinkling onto her lap as she smoothes out the legs. Then she folds them neatly and lays them down. She shakes out his T-shirt and folds it into quarters and places it on top of his jeans.

She presses her palms flat against it, as if she can feel his heartbeat through it. Their relationship is growing tentatively in Jackson's shadow. It is something fragile and new, yet there's no question they have a connection that draws them powerfully together.

But then there is Jackson, too, she thinks, removing her hand. He loved her, Dirk had said. He left his home, his whole life behind, and took the greatest risk to marry her.

She doesn't know what she feels, which is why, when Saul finally wades through the shallows, he will find the beach empty, Eva gone.

Our favorite bar in London was called the Olswin. It was crammed full of reclaimed furniture and retro items that you could buy. We'd often go there on Sunday afternoons, and sit with our drinks picking out all the cool pieces of furniture we'd like for the home we'd one day own.

You said your dream home wasn't big, but that it had a garden with a beautiful stretch of springy lawn. I liked to imagine you lying on a picnic blanket on that lawn, reading with the sun on your face.

One afternoon in the Olswin, we saw an old croquet set for sale. It was in an oak box painted with the words JAQUES CROQUET LONDON. I loved the rusted hinges of the box, and the beautifully carved mallets with their edges worn smooth. "Let's buy it!"

"A croquet set?" you said.

"For your lawn."

You told me I was crazy, that it'd just take up space in our apartment. But I could see the pleasure in your eyes when I went to the cash register.

It was ridiculous, of course. It was hugely overpriced, neither of us had any real desire to play croquet, and I had to lug the thing on my shoulder across London. When we got home, you kissed me on the mouth, your lips tasting faintly of pear cider. "My handsome dreamer."

Sadly you were right: our future was always just a dream.

28

Eva sits on the edge of the deck pressing the heels of her hands into the cool wood, feeling the prickling of pins and needles building in her palms. Her bare legs dangle toward the damp sand, heels knocking in an impatient rhythm against the wood. A weak sun has just risen above the water, no warmth yet to its rays.

Her mind is abuzz with thoughts, each like flies circling over the carcass of last night. They land on Dirk's words: *He did love you, Eva. That's why he took the risk of marrying you.* Her heart had surged at that, relief and happiness flooding into her chest. Jackson had loved her—that at least was real.

But then she'd glanced toward Saul and seen the pain shadowing his expression as he rose from the table. It's as if she's caught between two tides dragging her in opposing directions and is unsure which way to swim.

She takes her phone from her pocket and dials Callie's number.

"Cal, it's me. Is it too early? Did I wake you?"

"Course not. I was going to call you actually."

They haven't spoken in some time, and hearing Callie's voice now, Eva is reminded of how much she's missed her. "Sorry it's been a while. Things have been . . . complicated."

"Are you okay? What's happening?"

"Can I visit?" Eva says in a rush. "I just . . . I think I need to get away from here for a few days. Clear my head."

There's silence. Then Callie sighs. "I'm sorry, but I'm leaving. The show's fallen through."

"What?"

"An investor pulled out. There's no more money. Everything's been shelved."

"Oh, Cal . . . For how long?"

"Indefinitely."

"I can't believe it. Can they do this to you?"

"Seems so."

"But what will you do now? When are you leaving?"

"I have to be out of the apartment in two days. So I'm going back to London."

"Oh," Eva says, disappointment lurching through her.

"But," Callie says, "I was hoping to come and see you on my way home."

"In Tasmania?

"Yes. If that's okay?"

"Okay? I'd *love* you to!"

There is a pause. "What's going on out there?"

Eva looks toward the empty bay. There's too much to say right now—she wouldn't even know where to begin. "Let's talk when you're here."

IN THE LAB, EVERYTHING seems to be against Saul; he finds the refrigerator broken, all his samples from his last field trip lost. Then he makes a mistake entering some recent results, which skews his entire charts. He is terse with a junior member of the team and has to apologize to her later, which she accepts warily.

He's desperate to see Eva, and by the time he gets the ferry back to the island, it's dark. He first checks on his father, who dozes in front of the television with his mouth ajar. Then Saul walks along the bay to the shack.

He finds Eva washing up, her sleeves pushed up, her hands covered in soapsuds. The shack smells of pasta and olive oil, underpinned with a sweeter smell, something he associates with Eva's hair.

"Hi," she says, glancing over her shoulder. "I put a few of your beers in the fridge, if you want one?" Her tone is studiously light.

Eva declines a beer for herself, so Saul takes just one out, twists off the lid, and leans against the kitchen counter while Eva finishes the washing up.

The skin on her forearms is lightly tanned and the sharpness of her elbows is faintly appealing. He watches her sponge a plate and then flick on the tap, rinsing the detergent from the glossy white surface. The pump drums as it draws water from the tank. She sets the plate on the draining board, a crust of food still caught on the underside of the plate. She wipes her hands with a tea towel, missing a patch of foam on her wrist. Saul wants to reach out and slide it from her skin with his thumb.

She turns. "Last night . . ."

"I'm sorry I left like that. I needed to clear my head." He'd needed to wash away Eva's expression of relief when she learned why Jackson had left Jeanette. "You came down to the shore last night when I was swimming."

Her gaze flits past him.

"You folded my clothes."

"Yes," she says, pushing her hair back from her face, revealing the smooth curve of her forehead.

"Were you waiting for me?"

"I suppose I was."

"But you changed your mind?"

Eva pulls her gaze to his. Her eyes are large and watchful. "Can we sit down?"

He follows Eva to the sofa and they sit. She perches forward, drawing her thumb along the hem of her dress, as if counting each of the stitches. She doesn't say anything for a long time and he wonders whether she is waiting for him to speak.

Then she takes a deep breath. "Over the past few weeks I'd begun to hate Jackson. I hated him for lying to me, for marrying Jeanette, for leaving Kyle. I never thought that the man I married would be capable of any of those things."

Saul listens hard, his pulse ticking.

"Then, hearing Dirk talk about him last night, it reminded me how much we were in love. And we were, Saul. It was real. I let myself forget that."

"That's enough, is it? That he loved you? Jackson lied about—"

"Everything? Yes, I know, Saul. I know!" Her hands curl into fists. "And I'll never understand why. I've got so, so many questions. They've been driving me crazy." She stands and crosses the shack. "I lose hours of the day imagining conversations with Jackson where I get to ask him: Why didn't you divorce Jeanette? How did you forge the paperwork? Did you make a conscious decision to lie to me? Did you miss Kyle? Did you ever think about coming clean?" Eva stops by the sink. He sees her chest rising and falling. "I can't keep going over and over them. It's not doing me any good. The thing is, Saul," she says, her eyes locked on his, "I'll never know the truth behind his decisions. But last night Dirk reminded me that instead of fixating on questions—or hating Jackson—I have got to focus on the one thing I do know. He loved me. That much was real."

Saul hears his own voice, low and filled with tension. "What does that mean for us?"

THE AIR IN THE shack feels too warm; there is a dense weight to it. Eva crosses the room and steps out onto the deck, facing the dusky horizon. She is aware of her own breathing and tries to inhale and exhale more slowly.

She hears the creak of wood as Saul moves onto the deck behind her. She feels him reaching out, encircling her around the waist. Her body sighs into the space between his arms.

"What if . . ." she begins, then stops, not quite sure how to frame the thought. "I can't tell whether this—you and me—has happened for the wrong reasons."

"What reasons?" he whispers, his lips close to her ear.

"Grief? Loneliness? Anger? What if you just remind me of Jackson?"

"Eva—"

She turns in his arms to face him. "I was so hurt, so furious with Jackson. What if I'm with you to punish him in some way?"

"That's ridiculous," he says, sadness pinching his features.

"Is it?" Everything that is drawing Eva toward Saul is also what is pushing her away, like a magnetic force that is shifting its field. She steps back. "Maybe we're both just kidding ourselves. We're near enough living as castaways here. But what if we were in Hobart, or London? What if we were to tell people—your dad, my mum, Jackson's friends? Would it still work?"

"We could make it work."

"Yet you didn't even want your dad to know."

Saul looks over his shoulder, out toward the bay.

"I just want us to be honest with each other. With ourselves.

If Jackson had been a wonderful brother to you and a faithful husband to me, would we have needed this?"

"I can't answer that."

"And neither can I." She hugs her arms to her chest. "That's why I need a bit of time. Just to work things out."

When Saul says nothing, Eva continues. "Callie called earlier. Her show's been canceled. She's going to come here for a few nights before flying back to England." Eva looks at her hands. "You've got your dad here and I'll be with Callie. I think maybe we should have some time to ourselves . . . see how we feel in a few days." She pauses, waiting. There's a part of Eva that wants Saul to say no, he doesn't want time apart. Doesn't need to think. He knows what he feels and what he wants. And it's her.

She watches as he draws a thick hand over his face, his expression unreadable. He nods as he says, "Okay, if that's what you need."

29

Eva wraps her arms around Callie, breathing in the soft tones of her perfume as they greet each other at the edge of the Wattleboon dock. Neither of them speaks; they just hold each other, and a silent apology passes between them forgiving the strained weeks since they were last together.

Eventually Eva steps back, keeping hold of Callie's fingers. "Fancy grabbing a coffee and sitting on the dock?" There's so much to say, she doesn't want to get in the car and drive back to the shack. She wants to talk to Callie now.

"I'd like that."

The coffee machine at the ferry booth is broken and the only items on sale are unappetizing packs of sandwiches, and ice creams. They buy two cones and peel off the wrappers as they stroll along the stubby concrete dock.

Glancing up at the overcast sky, Callie says, "Hardly ice-cream weather, is it?"

"It's been cold here the last few days. Autumn's coming."

They sit at the edge of the dock, their legs dangling over the side. The water smells different from the bay, a heavier scent of brine and engine oil. They look out over the water to the tumbling hills of Wattleboon. "God, it's beautiful here," Callie says. "And so quiet. You forget."

Eva nods. "So tell me about the show. How are you feeling? I'm sorry I didn't know all this was going on."

Callie waves a hand through the air. "I'm not sure I even care that much. It was a crap show. I've no idea how it got commissioned." She licks the sides of her ice cream. "Actually, Michael e-mailed yesterday. You know, BBC Michael? With the lisp."

"Oh, yeah."

"He says there's a historical series starting next month and they're looking for a producer."

"You're interested?"

"Very. It's mostly a studio shoot, so I'd be in London." She straightens her legs in front of her, looking toward her toes. "I've been thinking a lot about what you said, Eva. About me running away from things." She pauses. "From intimacy."

"Listen, I should never—"

"No, I needed to hear it. And it's true." She sighs. "I'm thirty. My longest relationship lasted eight months. It's pathetic."

Eva goes to say something, but Callie hasn't finished.

"So I want to spend some time in one place for a while. Slow down a little. Give things a chance."

"With David?"

"What, the eternal bachelor?" she says with a raised eyebrow. "No, not David. Just life in general. I'm always flying from one contract to the next, doing it for my career or pocket—but not for *me*. It'll be good to slow down. I'm excited about it."

Eva looks at Callie and smiles. "Then I'm pleased. I'm really pleased."

Callie tilts her head back, shaking her hair loose. "Anyway, what's going on with you? You met Jeanette. How was that? Tell me everything. How's Saul? How are you?"

Eva watches a shoal of small fish move below their feet. She snaps off the end of her ice-cream cone, then crumbles it between her fingers and scatters it into the water. The fish dart for the surface, grabbing tiny flecks and disappearing with them. "Saul and I . . . we've been seeing quite a bit of each other."

Callie lowers her ice cream. "Oh . . ."

Eva begins to talk, telling Callie everything: about the weeks following the miscarriage when Saul had visited each day and helped coax her out of her misery; about the beautiful moments they've spent free-diving together in the bay; about the unexpected trip to hospital to see Dirk —and the even more unexpected night at the motel. She talks about the tentative relationship that's been growing since, but her voice darkens as she tells Callie how every glimpse of happiness with Saul is punctured by guilt. She tells her about her decision to take some space from Saul so that she can think. When Eva finishes, she exhales with the relief of saying it all aloud.

"Are you in love with Saul?"

Callie's always had a way of asking the hardest questions in the most direct way. "I honestly don't know. I love being with him, but . . ."

"But what?" Callie says.

Eva glances down at the water. "But there's Jackson. There will always be Jackson."

Callie doesn't say anything.

"Do you think all this—Saul and me—that it's a mistake?"

Callie lifts her shoulders into a shrug.

In her work Eva's seen all sorts of irregular relationship dynamics. She's helped deliver a baby with the woman's husband and ex-husband in the room; she's seen a surrogate who has fallen in love with the father; she's seen a twenty-two-year-old woman give birth to her stepbrother's child. She tries not to judge and instead treat the people as individuals, not situations. But it is harder with herself. When she thinks of Saul, she sees the flash of a headline: "He's Jackson's Brother." She wishes they could extract themselves from their pasts and meet again—see how they feel without carrying the weight of everything that's come before.

"I can't tell what I feel anymore." She shakes her head. "Maybe I just need to get out of this place."

They are both quiet for a moment, the words drifting between them. Then Callie gently says, "I wanted to talk to you about that. About coming home." She wipes her hands together and sets them on her lap. "I was thinking that maybe—if you wanted—we could go back together. I've got the spare room in my apartment. You'd be welcome to it."

"It's a lovely offer, Cal. A tempting offer. It would be wonderful living with you. But I . . . I just don't know." Eva runs a fingertip over her lips. "There's so much here that still feels . . . unfinished."

Callie nods. "I'm not trying to sway you, but maybe getting back to London, to your career, would be a good thing."

Eva glances at her sideways, wondering if what she actually means is, *It'll be a good thing to leave Saul.*

"You don't have to make a decision right now. I'm flying out on Friday. If you want to come, there are still seats left. We could go home together. But if you decide you need to be here awhile longer," Callie says, looking at her steadily, "then that's okay, too."

AT DIRK'S PLACE SAUL finds a parking spot behind a rusting Honda with a loose bumper. The morning has turned overcast and the flat, gray sky hangs low over the street. After Wattleboon, the strip of houses seems packed too tightly, a jigsaw of concrete and brick.

Dirk was the one to suggest heading back home. He'd already been on Wattleboon ten days and told Saul it was time he got on with things.

Dirk twists around in his seat to face Saul. "I just wanna say, thanks for putting me up like that. It meant a lot."

"It was good having you there," Saul says with meaning. There is a pause, and then he asks, "What was it like when you went up to Warrington to see Jackson? Did he seem happy?" There is something niggling at Saul that makes him need to know this. He never once asked Dirk about Jackson's life in Warrington, didn't even want to hear his name. But now he needs to fill in those gaps, try to understand what was going on in his brother's world.

"Truth is," Dirk says, "both times I was up there, I came back worried. Jackson wasn't himself. He seemed jaded, like life had worn him down. You know what Jackson was like, always had a story or a joke for you. But not up there. That place shrunk him."

"Do you think he knew Kyle wasn't his?"

"I reckon he had his doubts pretty early on. But he'd already bonded with the boy. Jeanette finally told him the truth about Kyle a month before Jackson left for England."

Saul pulls his head back, surprised. "I thought he left as soon as he found out."

"Nah. Tried to make a go of it, I reckon. Or Jeanette was tightening the screws. When he finally left, he came here without anything. Just brought his passport. Didn't even have a bag with him. I gave him a few of your old clothes to tide him over."

"Why didn't he pack?"

"Didn't want Jeanette to know he was leaving—or that he was going to England. Made me promise not to tell anyone."

This strikes Saul as odd. He remembers Jeanette saying she

had no idea Jackson was even in England until she heard the news that he'd died. Why would it have mattered if she'd known where Jackson was?

The more information Saul has, the less everything seems to make sense. Eva said she felt as though she was going mad with all the unanswered questions and needed to let them go. But Saul isn't ready to.

"The thing I still don't understand," he says, "is why Jackson didn't divorce Jeanette before marrying Eva."

"I know, I know," Dirk says, blowing air from his cheeks. "I told him he was crazy. He could've ended up in jail, for Christ's sake! But he said he wanted to be with Eva—and there was no way Jeanette would sign the divorce papers."

"She'd have had to eventually."

"I suppose so. But she'd have made trouble, I'm sure of it. She's an odd girl. I dunno what you and Jackson ever saw in her, I really don't." Dirk draws a hand from his pocket and scratches the back of his head. "Anyway, what's done is done. Don't suppose any of it matters much now he's dead."

Saul feels the power and finality of that word in his chest. His brother is dead—and they'd never made peace. He feels a deep wrenching inside him, as if something he's tried to bury is scratching for the surface.

"I wish I'd spoken to him," Saul says suddenly. "I shouldn't have let our fight go on for so long. It was my pride that was hurt, that was all. Pride."

"Ah, Saul," Dirk says, clicking his tongue against the roof of his mouth. "I didn't take sides at the time because you're both my sons, but Jackson—he was the one who behaved badly. He should've apologized, but for whatever pigheaded reason, he didn't. What's done is done."

Dirk looks at Saul closely. "Just promise me you won't go

spending all your time wishin' it were different. I wasted too much of my life pondering what-ifs. What if your mother hadn't gone up Eagle Cape that day? What if I'd come home the moment I saw the smoke? What if I'd left you boys with a neighbor and then driven right through the fire and pulled her from the woods myself? If ifs were riffs, I'd have written a bloody symphony! We could waste a lifetime wishing. We've got what we've got, haven't we? And I'm gonna be grateful for that."

SAUL DRIVES TO THE lab, unsettled by his conversation with Dirk. When he arrives he makes himself a coffee, has a brief chat with his supervisor about a field trip later in the week, and then goes to his desk. He switches on the computer but doesn't get to work right away. Dirk had given him a photo album to lend to Eva, and Saul lays it on his desk now, and opens it.

The thick card pages are browned at the edges, globs of glue loosening beneath the cellophane. In the warm hum of the lab, he looks through pictures of himself and Jackson from their early teens onward. He turns a few pages, passing images of them both with skinny legs poking out of salt-stained shorts.

There is a photo of Jackson on a beach holding up two Aussie salmon by their tails. Saul remembers taking the picture: they'd been fishing just off the sandbank at East Way. They had cooked up the fish in a chowder and had eaten bowls of it in the back of their friend's van as the sky grew dark.

On the next page there is a picture he hasn't seen for years. It was taken during a summer on Wattleboon at the tall lichen-stained rocks off Gregg's Bluff. In the shot they are both launching themselves from a rock that must've been a good forty feet high. The photo captures them a split second after they've jumped. Jackson's hair—long then—is blown back from his face, his board shorts flattened to his thighs. Saul's mouth and eyes are wide open, his arms thrown skyward, legs kicking out as if running through the air. The sun is on their faces, making their tanned skin glow golden.

They used to spend hours up at the cliffs, doing dives and backflips, daring each other to go bigger and higher. He'd allowed himself to forget how close they'd once been, but now it comes charging back to him.

The wrenching feeling inside him twists again and he feels his throat closing. He swallows hard, but he can feel a burning sensation rising through him, filling his tear ducts. Saul might've called his brother a cheat—but that wasn't all Jackson was. He was the brother who hauled Saul back up the rocks when he was too tired to pull himself out of the surging swell; he was the brother who punched the air with both fists when Saul caught his first barrel; he was the brother who put iodine on Saul's back when he got scraped along the reef in a bad dive.

He loved his brother. Misses him.

He squeezes his thumb and forefinger into the corners of his eyes and gulps in air as his shoulders quake.

Footsteps sound down the corridor outside and Saul pushes his chair back, wiping his face and standing. The photo album falls to the floor with a slap and he turns from it, pacing to the far side of the lab. He shakes out his shoulders and steadies his breathing until he gets himself together. The footsteps pass his lab and continue on.

He pushes open a window to get some air flowing through the place. Once he's gathered himself, he bends down and grabs the album. It's open on a page showing a photo of him and Jeanette. It must've been taken in the few months they were together. He has his arm around her waist and he's looking toward her, smiling. She's wearing her hair loose, a red wave of it, and is looking directly into the camera, a slight smirk playing over her lips. He remembers being smitten by those lips, by the way she shook her hair loose from a ponytail, by the swing of her hips as she moved.

But thinking of the woman she is now, he doesn't feel any of that desire: he sees someone damaged, controlling, who lied to Jackson about Kyle to stop him from leaving.

There's a thought swimming in his head, something to do with Jeanette and Jackson, which he can't quite reach. It's as if he's trying to read it underwater, so the message is blurred, not clear enough to make out.

He keeps returning to the fact that Jackson didn't want Jeanette to know he was in England. Did he think she'd follow him?

A light sweat crawls over his brow. More questions are pushing forward, nagging at him. Why didn't Jackson file for divorce when he decided he wanted to marry Eva? He'd certainly have had grounds to, if a paternity test proved Kyle wasn't his. And why did he leave without any belongings, as if he were desperate to be free of her?

It's clear that Jackson had been running away from Jeanette, but what Saul can't work out is, *Why?*

I don't know whether you've ever done anything you regret, Eva. I can't imagine it. I don't mean those small regrets like something you wish you hadn't said; I mean the ones that keep you awake at night when the rest of the world sleeps. The type that makes you question the very essence of who you are and what you are capable of.

I have lots of regrets. They stem like twisted branches from the roots of a decision I made back when I was fifteen years old.What happened that day isn't a story I need to just tell you, Eva. I've said it a thousand times over in my head, but I was never brave enough to say it aloud.

That's the thing about me: I've always been a coward.

30

Saul finds Eva standing on a chair, trying to balance a radio on top of the bookshelf. She's wearing a teal cotton dress that tapers in at the waist, and her feet are bare. "All right up there?"

She turns, surprised. "Saul."

They haven't seen each other since Callie arrived a few days ago, Saul forcing himself to keep his distance.

The radio signal fizzes and then, with a final tilt of the antenna, music blares on. "Aha!" Eva adjusts the volume, then jumps down from the chair and stands facing him.

Her short hair looks salt-thickened and wavy around her face and her cheeks are lightly flushed. "You look well," Saul says.

"Thank you." She glances at her hands, and then up at him. "It's good to see you," she says with meaning.

A pause unfolds between them. Saul's gaze moves to Eva's mouth, studying the bow of her top lip. He experiences the strongest urge to kiss her. Every reason they'd discussed for needing some space from each other deserts him, and all he can think is how much he wants her.

"Where's Callie?" he asks quietly.

"Here."

He looks up and sees her standing in the entrance to the back bedroom with wet hair and a towel in her hand. She is glancing between him and Eva, a look of interest on her face.

He takes a small step back from Eva, saying, "Good to have you on Wattleboon again, Callie."

"It's lovely to be here—if a little unexpected."

"Sorry to hear about the show."

"Oh, it's fine. I think the world can survive without yet another celebrity chef program. Anyway, how are you? What's going on in the world of cephalopods?"

"No giant squid reports this week, but I remain hopeful." He smiles. "So how long are you here for?"

"Three more nights. I'm flying back to London on Friday."

He notices Callie glancing toward Eva as she says this.

Callie hangs the towel over the back of a chair and says, "I'm going to grab that wine for dinner before the store closes."

"Oh. Okay," Eva says. "Do you want to take the car?"

"I'll walk. I fancy the fresh air. Catch you both later."

Saul stands aside as Callie slips past him onto the deck and then disappears.

Then they're alone.

Eva turns to Saul. "Drink? Tea? Beer?"

"I'd love a beer. Can't stay long, though—I've got work stuff to sort out. I just came to drop this off," he says, handing her a photo album. "Dad said you might want to have a look at it."

"Kind of him to remember."

He wonders if she's eager to see photos of Jackson, but she doesn't open the album right away. Instead, she places it on the coffee table and then fetches him a beer, getting one for herself, too. They take the bottles to the sofa and sit together; the way the cushions sag in the middle means their legs roll slightly inward and their knees touch. It would be easy for either one of them to adjust their positions to avoid this, but they don't.

Saul is acutely aware of the heat passing between them where their skin meets. He glances down at her knees, as if he might actually find them glowing with heat. There is something oddly desirable about the curve of her knees, the way the skin there is slightly more tanned than the rest of her legs. Has he found knees sexy before?

A song on the radio ends and the news comes on. He tries to tune in to drag his thoughts away from Eva. There's a report about changes in state welfare, but all he is thinking about is how much he wants to run his fingers over her knee, trace the skin as it softens and pales toward her thigh.

"You took your dad back to his place?"

"Yeah," he says, shifting his legs and sitting up straighter.

"How was he?"

Saul takes a gulp of beer to moisten his throat. "He said he was fine—that he was ready to go back—but I dunno, I just felt bad leaving him there on his own."

"Has he got friends nearby?"

"Yeah, but they're all drinking buddies. Friends he sees down the pub. He can't go there now. Not if he's serious about staying dry."

She nods thoughtfully. "How did he find being on Wattle-boon?"

"Okay, I think. He liked being by the water again. He's a fisher-man who's somehow ended up living inland." He shrugs. "I guess life has a way of taking you on a course you weren't expecting—and then you look up wondering how the hell you got there."

She laughs, a slightly sad note to it. "I know how that feels."

Eva finishes her beer, then crosses the room to the fridge. She glances back at him asking, "Another beer, Jackson?"

She freezes at her mistake, her mouth still open around his name.

Saul stares as heat rises to her cheeks. She wishes she could retract that one word—*Jackson*—swallow it down. But it is too late. They both heard it.

The name resonates between them as though a bell has just tolled.

"I'M SORRY," EVA SAYS, mortified by her mistake.

"Don't be," Saul says with a weak smile. "I won't have another, though—gotta head off in a minute."

She doesn't want him to leave. Not like this. She's missed his company these past few days. There's so much she wants to talk about: how his project at work is going; the dive she made when she had two boxy little cowfish eyeballing her; how he's feeling about his dad. "Have you got work to do?"

He nods. "I'm off up the east coast first thing. I've got some gear to sort out."

"Field trip?"

"Yeah. They want me to look into a test site up there for more squid tagging."

"How long are you going for?"

"Couple of nights. I'm drivin' up early with my lab partner. Should be back Thursday night."

"Right," she says, trying to busy herself with putting the empty beer bottles in the recycling bin. She knows she has to tell him what's going on, what she and Callie have been discussing.

Drawing a deep breath, she turns to face him. "Listen, Saul. I need to talk to you."

He must see something in her expression because his eyes widen. "You're going to leave with Callie, aren't you?"

She swallows. "I'm thinking about it, yes." The words hang in the shack like mist, chilling any remaining warmth.

An ad trills on the radio, a jingle about booking driving lessons with "License to Wheel."

Saul gets to his feet and moves toward the doorway, rubbing a hand over his brow.

"Saul?"

"What do you want me to say, Eva? I don't want you to go back to England, you know that." His tone is level, there is no animosity there. "But it's not my decision."

"I know. I know. I just . . . I'm not sure what to do." She sighs, running out of steam. Eva is a decisive person, someone who's always steered her own course in life rather than letting life lead her; at least, that's who she used to be. Now she isn't sure who she is— or what she wants. She's lost confidence in her own judgment, a voice in her head constantly taunting her: *Look how monumentally wrong you got it with Jackson.*

She's talking herself in circles about whether to leave with Callie: she's already been here longer than she had planned; her mother is desperate to have her home; she needs to get back to work.

Yet she also feels an inexplicable desire to stay: to wake up on the beach for a little while longer, knowing the day is hers to do with as she pleases. She feels connected to Wattleboon as if part of her has taken root here. To go now would be to leave something—she isn't sure what—unfinished.

"Eva," he says, causing her to look up.

His expression is deadly serious.

"I understand how hard all this must be on you. I'm Jackson's brother and maybe you feel guilty because of that. I know I do. But there is something between us. I can feel it and I don't want to give up on that. If you leave with Callie, then we'll never know. You won't have given us a chance." He stares at her, unblinking. "After what happened before, I promised myself I'd always be honest with you. So this is me being honest with you right now: I'm in love with you."

Heat rises to the surface of her skin. She can hear the drumming of her heart. *He is in love with me.* Her head fills with images of Jackson telling her he loves her: on a packed bus with a wet umbrella gripped between his knees; over lunch at her mother's when he was carving the beef; in bed as he kissed her bare ankle.

Eva is hesitating, not sure what to say.

Saul watches her closely.

"I . . ." She cannot seem to find any words. Her lips open and then close again, a fish without water. "I see."

Saul's gaze falls away to the ground. He runs a hand back through his hair and exhales hard, as if pushing something sharp out of his chest. "I get back Thursday night. I guess you'll tell me then if you're leaving."

"Okay," she manages—and then he's gone.

THE FOLLOWING AFTERNOON, CALLIE pulls out the grill tray with a clatter and drops the toast onto two plates. Toast has always been her and Eva's comfort food, and she thinks Eva could use some comfort right now. "Jam or peanut butter?"

"Please," Eva answers distractedly. She is looking through the photo album Saul delivered, her lips pressed together as she absorbs each picture.

Callie fetches the jam and gives the lid a fierce twist to remove it. As she smears black currant into the edges of the toast, she wonders about Saul and Eva. She'd seen the way they looked at each other yesterday before they realized she was in the doorway. Eva told her what Saul had said afterward—that he's in love with her—but what Callie can't get to the root of is what Eva feels for him.

Callie likes Saul; she thinks he's a man of great value, and in truth, she wishes it was Saul whom Eva had met two years ago, not Jackson. But she can't help thinking it'd be cleaner if Eva returned to London and let go of Wattleboon. And of Saul.

She slices the toast into triangles and then carries both plates to the sofa, where mugs of tea wait. "Any good pictures?"

"Thanks," Eva says, taking her toast. "A few. Look at this." She holds up the album with one hand and lifts her toast to her mouth with the other.

Callie sees a picture of the brothers as teenagers in scruffy jeans with bare chests and skateboards. "The Kurt Cobain phase," Callie says, looking at their shoulder-length hair and sullen faces.

Eva flips through a few pages to some shots where the brothers are older, in their twenties: Jackson making the peace sign in the middle of a crowd; the two of them doing a backflip from the side of a boat, ribs protruding as they arch.

Callie reaches for her tea, and as she does so, something on the next page catches her attention. She pauses, leaning closer to the album. "How strange."

Eva glances at her. "What?"

Callie's concentrating on a photo of a woman with her waist encircled by Saul's arm. "I'm sure I recognize her."

She angles the album toward her, light bouncing off the image. Saul must have been in his midtwenties when the photo was taken—there are fewer lines on his brow and his hair is cut shorter. Then her gaze returns to the woman. "I'm just trying to think where I know her from . . . Maybe I've worked with her," she says, her fingertips lightly drumming her thigh. "Yes, that's it. She's a client of Jackson's."

"She can't be . . ."

"I'm certain," Callie says, confident now. "I met her at Vernadors. They were having a client dinner. That was when I ate those bad mussels—I told you about it." Callie remembers the woman's fox-red hair, which she wore loose over her shoulders. "It's definitely the same woman."

"It can't be," Eva repeats so sharply that Callie looks up. "The woman in this photo is Jeanette."

EVA WAITS, HER PULSE ticking in her throat as Callie stares at the photo again.

When Callie finally lifts her gaze and speaks, her words come out carefully and precisely, as if she knows they are lighting a fuse. "I'm certain, Eva. I've met this woman."

All the blood seems to drain from Eva's head and she feels as if the sofa is giving way beneath her. "No . . ."

"I'm sorry. I'm so sorry. That's who Jackson was having dinner with."

"Then . . . Jeanette was in England. But she said she'd never been . . . She told me she didn't even know that's where Jackson was."

Callie opens her palms. "She must've been lying."

Eva presses her fingertips to her mouth, her thoughts scattering. If Jeanette and Jackson had been seeing each other in London, were they still in a relationship? Had Jeanette known about Eva all along? Her voice is breathless as she asks, "You saw them together? Just the two of them?"

"They were sitting in the far corner of the restaurant, near the piano. But honestly, Eva, I didn't think that anything odd was going on. They were just sitting there, having a meal."

"And he saw you? You spoke to Jackson?"

She nods. "When I arrived I just waved hello as we were being seated across the room. But I went over later. Jackson introduced her. Said she was a client. I don't think he gave her name."

"How was he acting?" Eva asks, her hands running back and forth along the neckline of her top. "Did he seem nervous?"

Callie looks up toward the ceiling concentrating. "I can't remember. I don't think so. Maybe . . . I can't really say. Shit, I'm sorry."

"What about her? Did she say anything?"

"She didn't speak. She seemed a bit cold, I suppose. She just sat back, looking at me."

"When was this?"

"It was our wrap party, so that must've been the end of November." She thinks for a moment, running a knuckle over her lips. "That's right—it was David's birthday the following day. So it was November twenty-seventh."

Eva remembers the night now. It was a few days before they left for their trip to Dorset. She'd been in bed when Jackson got in. As he undressed he'd mentioned bumping into Callie at Vernadors. Eva hadn't even asked how his client dinner went, just said, "How is she?" They talked for a minute or so and then he'd slipped into bed, pressing his body against hers, and they'd fallen asleep, waking in the morning still in each other's arms.

"What are you thinking?" Callie asks.

"I don't know. I don't know," Eva says, getting up and pacing across the shack. "Maybe they were still together." Just saying these words makes the muscles in her throat constrict. She had believed that Jackson loved her, just like Dirk said. But maybe Dirk was wrong.

"Do you think Jeanette knew about you all along?"

Eva is about to say no, but then she hesitates. She is thinking about Jeanette's reaction when Eva turned up in Warrington.

Her thoughts are whirring back through every detail of that meeting. Now it strikes her as odd that Jeanette had asked so few questions. Surely she'd have wanted to know why Jackson had married Eva, how long they'd been together, whether he talked about his life in Tasmania. She remembers how quick Jeanette was to tell Eva that she was his first wife, the woman Jackson loved, as if she'd been waiting for the chance to prove herself.

Eva's throat feels dry. She goes to the sink, fills a glass with water, and swallows it back too quickly, making her cough.

"Eva? Are you okay?"

She shakes her head. "I don't understand what any of this means. Why was Jeanette in London? Were they still together?"

Eva had wanted to let go of all her questions about Jackson and focus on the one thing she did know: that Jackson had loved her. But hearing this is like ripping open stitches to find an infection beneath the skin.

"You know how we can find out, don't you?"

Yes, Eva thinks. *I do.*

SAUL STAKES OUT HIS tent by head lamp, forcing a peg down into the hard earth with his heel.

"We're in business," Tom, his lab partner, calls as he stokes the fire with a branch. They've decided to camp out since the nearest motel is about thirty kilometers south. Plus, this way, they're right by the water, ready to start again in the morning.

When Tom's cell phone rings, he yanks it from his pocket and his whole face stretches into a grin as he says, "Hey, Tina! How's it goin'?" He walks off a little way to speak to his girlfriend in private.

Saul is shattered. He was up at five to get the first ferry off

Wattleboon, and then he had to swing by the lab and pick up the final pieces of equipment before gunning it up the east coast. They were on the water by midday and made three dives in different spots. Their supervisor will be pleased because they found exactly what they came for: rows and rows of southern calamari eggs nestled into the sea grass beds. They logged the GPS coordinates and still had time to hook themselves a couple of flatties for dinner. The fish are gutted and wrapped in foil, ready to throw on the fire with a pan of noodles. Perfect camping food, Saul thinks. Quick and easy.

He grinds in the final peg, annoyed that he forgot his pack with all his gear and sleeping bag. He can picture exactly where he left it—right by the door, so he actually walked past it on his way out.

Saul does up the fly sheet and then goes back for the pot. As he's walking, a light in his peripheral vision catches his attention.

He is turning toward it, his legs bending into a run before his mind has actually connected with what's happening. A spark from their campfire has ignited the saltbush beside it, the dry leaves starting to burn. He acts on instinct, stamping down on the flames. They lick at his ankle and every time he lifts a foot, they seem to come back higher. "Christ," he says as he feels the heat against his skin. He eventually manages to suffocate the flames and soon all that's left is a patch of charred earth.

He pokes a stick at the campfire, shifting the wood around to keep the heat more central, then bends down to inspect the singed hair above his ankle. *God, the smell!* Lifting up his foot, he sees that the sole of his right shoe has blackened from the heat. As he's feeling the place where the rubber has melted and thinned, something from his memory is pushing forward, trying to surface.

He's thinking about the day of the bush fire, when smoke billowed into the sky. He'd found Jackson at Jeanette's shack, coolly disinterested in the drama outside. Studiously cool? Then he thinks of the nightmares Jackson still had as a grown man, the ones Eva mentioned where he'd search the blazing bush for his mother and wake coughing and choking.

Saul looks into the glowing red pit of the campfire. His skin grows hot as he begins to see what has been there all along.

31

The knot in Eva's stomach tightens as they pass the sign for War-rington. In a matter of minutes they'll be at Jeanette's house. Her throat burns with all the things she wants to say —and this time she will not be leaving without answers.

"Try him again," Callie says, who is at the wheel. They have been taking turns driving. They left Wattleboon yesterday after-noon, only pulling in at a motel when dusk fell and the wallabies and possums emerged, bright eyes glinting in their headlights.

Eva dials Saul's number, then lifts the phone to her ear. She is eager for the reassurance of his voice, but instead the call goes straight to voicemail for the third time this morning. She ends the call without leaving a message.

"Still no answer?"

Eva shakes her head. "He's avoiding me."

"He's probably out on the boat without reception."

"Maybe," she says, without conviction. She knows how hard it must have been for Saul to open up to her and tell her how he felt—and all she'd said in return was *I see.* The last thing she wants is to hurt him, but love feels like dangerous territory right now. Everything she believed in was shattered by Jackson and she's just not sure she's strong enough to take that risk again.

When Eva looks up, she recognizes the line of poplar trees and the stock grid ahead. "It's the next house on the right."

They turn into the gravel driveway and find two vehicles parked outside the house. "That's like Saul's truck, isn't it?" Callie says, pulling up beside it.

Eva studies the faded blue paintwork and the rusted bull bar on the front. She twists around to peer through the truck windows; inside there's just a road map on the passenger seat and a carton of iced coffee in the cup holder. She glances in the back cab, where two fishing rods lie across the shelf. Plenty of Tasmanian's drive blue trucks—and most of them probably own fishing rods, too—but what makes Eva's mouth turn dry is the sight of masking tape wrapped around the base of the second rod. She recognizes it because she has fished with it.

"Saul's here."

SAUL HAD WOKEN AT dawn knowing instinctively what he must do. He'd packed up the tent, dusting off ants clinging to the ground sheet, then shaken his lab partner awake, explaining why he had to shoot through. He'd driven for five hours straight—and now he's here, walking down the hallway of Jeanette's house.

He follows her into the living room, stepping over the vacuum that's plugged into the wall. On the coffee table the browning skin of a banana lies beside an empty mug. "Where's Kyle?"

"Mum has him Thursdays. Gives me a chance to get stuff done." Jeanette indicates for him to sit. "Push that aside," she says, nodding toward a sewing box and a purple coat strewn on the sofa. He places them on the armrest, then lowers himself down.

Jeanette sits on the adjacent sofa, arms folded. She is wearing a loose V-neck sweater over leggings and her hair is piled on top of her head. "Twice in a month. You're starting to make me feel very popular."

He's not in the mood for small talk. His palms are damp and he wipes them against his jeans. He looks at Jeanette closely as he says, "I know Jackson wasn't Kyle's father."

She arches an eyebrow. "Do you, now?"

"Let's not mess around here, Jeanette. Jackson told Dad."

"I thought Dirk must've known. He never visited Kyle after Jackson left."

"Why did you tell Jackson the baby was his? So he'd marry you?"

"I wasn't trying to trap him, if that's what you think. When I found out I was pregnant, I honestly wasn't sure who the father was. I hoped—I wanted to believe— it was Jackson." She looks down at her lap, where her hands are loosely clasped, her nails bitten to the fingertips. "I loved Jackson. I didn't want to lose him."

He could tell her that that's not love, or that she cheated not only Jackson, but Kyle and Kyle's real father, too. Instead, he says, "Tell me about the bush fire, Jeanette."

Her head jerks up. "What do you mean?"

"I know you and Jackson were there. I want to know what happened." He holds her gaze, wondering if she'll see through his bluff. He doesn't *know* they were there, he only *suspects* it. Last night he'd lain awake in his tent as one theory rolled into another—and now he needs Jeanette to provide the facts.

He lays down his next card, speaking slowly to give his voice a quiet authority. "I've been going through some of Jackson's things and I came across an old diary of his."

Jeanette is listening closely; her fingers slide to her wedding band and she twists it around and around. "What exactly do you think you know, Saul?"

"He wrote about what happened that day. The bush fire. I know the diary only tells Jackson's version of events." He continues pinning Jeanette with his eyes. "So now I'd like to hear yours."

Her eyes close and that's when Saul knows he's got her.

She exhales, her shoulders rounding as the air leaves her. "I just happened to be with him. That's all."

He nods at her to continue, trying to keep his expression neutral and not give away the fact that his heart is thundering.

"We were in the woods—up near the cape. We used to go there sometimes for a smoke. That day wasn't anything different. We hung out for a bit, smoked a couple of cigarettes, then left." Her gaze drifts beyond Saul, out toward the garden. "Only, as we were going, I saw a curl of smoke coming from the ground. Jackson hadn't stubbed out his cigarette properly and the leaves were smoldering, starting to flame. He ran back and tried to put it out—but it caught so quickly."

She looks back at Saul, imploring. "There was nothing we could do. We didn't have any water, not even a blanket or a jacket to smother it with. Nothing. The flames were too big to stamp out. So we ran. We had to."

Saul tastes something acidic at the back of his throat. He wants to open a window, let fresh air into the room, but he can't move.

"We went back to my shack," Jeanette is saying breathlessly, "and I grabbed the phone to call the fire department. But Jackson stopped me. He said, 'Let someone else make the call. We'll be in the shit if our folks find out.'"

The blood drains from Saul's body and his lips feel numb as he says, "You let it burn?"

Jeanette hugs her arms tightly to her chest. "I was thirteen. Jackson was fifteen. I looked up to him—cared about him, even then. So I did what he told me." She swallows, her eyes filling with tears. "Don't think I don't regret that. I do, Saul. And so did Jackson. We didn't know your mum was there, I promise you! We hadn't seen anyone around."

Saul feels his hands trembling with shock. It was Jackson. He started the bush fire that killed their mother.

He realizes that some part of him, deep in his subconscious, had always suspected it. He knew Jackson used to go up to those woods to smoke; he'd seen the look in Jackson's eyes whenever the fire was mentioned; he'd watched his brother indulge their father's drinking, always sharing a bottle of whiskey with Dirk so he wouldn't be drinking alone. Maybe Saul hadn't wanted to delve deeper into his suspicions, because otherwise he'd have had to face the fact that Jackson was responsible for their mother's death.

Now the blood comes bellowing back into his head and he hears the surge of his pulse in his ears. His muscles twinge and his hands clench into fists. He wants to roar. He wants to pick up the coffee table and launch it through the window. He wants to rip the pictures from the walls. He lurches to his feet and crosses the room, pressing closed fists into the wall.

"You don't know what the fire did to him," Jeanette says to his back. "It wrecked him. He kept it from everyone and the lie became this . . . this poison slowly leaking inside him." She pauses. "Don't hate him for what he did—he already hated himself."

Saul breathes in deeply, filling his chest with air. He faces her. "You were the only person who knew?"

"Yes."

"And you kept his secret all this time?"

"I never told a single person."

Everything is beginning to come together—all the fragments of Jackson's lies that have confused Saul for months are drawing toward a central point. He is trying to fit the pieces together, order them into something coherent.

A loud rapping at the door interrupts his thoughts, and he watches as Jeanette rises and leaves the room.

When she's gone he hangs his head forward and exhales. For years Jackson had had to live with the knowledge of what he'd done. A shared secret is a forceful connection. But a toxic one, too. Saul squeezes his temples, thinking what power that must've given Jeanette.

Out in the hallway, he hears Jeanette's voice, the pitch of it rising sharply.

Then he hears a second person speaking, and suddenly he is crossing the living room and rushing down the hallway.

EVA'S PULSE RACES AS she waits on Jeanette's doorstep, Callie at her shoulder. Questions fly through her thoughts: *Why is Saul here? Does he already know Jeanette had been in England? Is he lying to me, too?*

When the door opens, Jeanette's features stretch into surprise. She keeps her fingers gripped around the door handle as she says, "What are you doing here?"

"I want to talk to you."

Jeanette shakes her head sharply. "Leave. Just leave!"

She moves as if she's going to close the door, but Eva steps forward and presses the flat of her hand against it. "No."

There are footsteps behind Jeanette, and Saul appears, his face flushed. "Eva?"

It is hard to even look at him because with every cell of her body she is begging: *Please don't be lying to me!* She fights to keep her voice level as she says, "I thought you were on a research trip."

"I was. I left early . . ."

She shakes her head. "Don't lie to me, Saul."

"I'm not," he says, holding her gaze so levelly, it's as if he's willing her to trust him. He speaks slowly, explaining, "I came here because I needed to find—"

"Get out!" Jeanette's voice cuts across them. "All of you. Get out of my house!"

But Eva doesn't move. She glares at Jeanette. "What were you doing in London with Jackson?"

"I've never been to London," she answers, without missing so much as a beat.

For an awful moment, Eva thinks Callie has made a mistake. It was a different woman she saw with Jackson that night.

But then Callie is stepping forward with her brightest smile, saying, "Don't you remember me? We've met before. When you were having dinner with Jackson. In London."

Jeanette's eyes widen with recognition.

Then Saul is turning toward Jeanette. His voice is a blade edge, sharp and unforgiving. "What?"

THE FOUR OF THEM stand in the living room. The saccharine smell of the rotting banana skin fills the room. Eva faces Jeanette and says, "When I came here before, you knew who I was, didn't you?"

Jeanette nods.

"How did you find out about me? Did Jackson tell you?"

"He didn't tell me anything."

"So . . . how?"

"A friend of mine from Hobart was over in the UK. He bumped into Jackson at a jazz festival. You were with him."

Eva remembers. It was the same day that the photo of them had been taken in their 1920s outfits, Jackson touching the brow of his hat and grinning, the sun flare caught in their eyes. An hour or so later they'd been at the bar when a man with a blond goatee had slapped Jackson hard between the shoulders, saying, "Jackson Bowe! What the fuck are you doing here?" Jackson's face had flushed red—Eva assumed from surprise. But now that she thinks back, when Jackson made the introductions he hadn't called her his wife, just used her name.

Jeanette explains, "My friend told me he'd seen Jackson. He thought I already knew he was in London. He mentioned the name of the company Jackson was working for, so I looked it up. Found out where his office was. Mum agreed to look after Kyle for a couple of weeks, so I flew over."

Saul asks, "Why go? You were separated."

"I still loved him," Jeanette says simply. "I never wanted him to leave. I thought by going there, showing how serious I was . . . perhaps he'd give us another chance. But what I hadn't counted on," she says, turning to Eva, "was you."

Silence gathers in the room.

"I waited for Jackson outside his office. It was a nice place, off Soho. You know. When he came out, I barely recognized him." She smiles weakly. "He looked so smart in his shirt and tie, his hair cut short. So successful. There was a moment when I honestly thought about turning around, leaving. It was obvious he was happy, that he'd made a new start for himself—and I was pleased for him."

There is a pause, and Eva realizes she is holding her breath, waiting.

"But then," Jeanette continues, "I noticed his wedding ring. I knew it wasn't the band I'd given him. He'd left that here. And that's when I realized what he'd done."

The room is still. No one moves.

"When Jackson noticed me, the color drained from his face as if he'd seen a ghost. It's ironic, really, as that's how I felt—like a specter that'd been invisible to him for months. We went to a pub far away from his office, somewhere dingy and quiet, where he wouldn't see anyone he knew." She shakes her head. "He tried to slip his wedding ring off as we were walking there, but it was too late for that. I'd already seen it. 'Who is she?' I asked. Eventually the truth came out; he told me about you, how you'd been living together for a few months and had gotten married in February."

"Why didn't you tell me when I came here before?"

Jeanette looks at Eva closely, sadness filling her eyes. "It was humiliating. I'd gone to England to get him back. But he didn't want me."

Callie says, "If that's true, why were you having dinner with him?"

Jeanette turns toward Callie, stiffening. "We had things to talk about."

"I'll bet you did," Callie says, "because if I discovered my husband had married someone else, I'd have a thing or two to say about it. To the police, perhaps. To his new wife, certainly."

Jeanette glares at her.

"What I've been wondering"—Callie goes on, undeterred—"is why Jackson didn't divorce you before marrying Eva?"

From the corner of the room Saul says, "It's because you threatened him, isn't it? If Jackson tried divorcing you, you would've told everyone about the bush fire."

Jeanette faces him, her eyes narrowed.

"I don't follow," Eva says.

Anguish creases Saul's face as he explains how Jackson caused the bush fire. "After you talked about Jackson's nightmares about the fire, something started niggling at me. That's why I came here, Eva," he says, and she hears the earnestness in his voice. "I needed to know the truth."

Eva's legs are trembling. She needs to sit. She crosses to the sofa, where a sewing box and purple coat are balanced on the armrest. She lowers herself down, trying to absorb everything he's saying. *Jackson started the bush fire that killed his mother. Jeanette knew. Has always known.* She runs a hand over her face. Her skin feels greasy from too many hours in the car.

Saul addresses Jeanette. "When Jackson found out Kyle wasn't his, he wanted to leave you. But you threatened to tell people about the bush fire, didn't you?"

Jeanette says nothing.

"That's why Jackson eventually left for England and didn't tell you where he was going. Why he couldn't risk getting a divorce."

"No!" Jeanette says.

Eva doesn't trust her. There is something Jeanette's not telling them. "How many times did you see Jackson when you were in England?"

"I don't know. A few."

"When?"

"The day after I arrived, I went to his office. I've already said that."

"When else?"

"Then we met up for dinner a couple of days later."

"That's twice. A few is more than twice."

"Okay, twice then."

Jeanette is lying. Eva can see it from the color that's risen up her neck. "Earlier you told us you were in England for a couple of weeks."

"Thereabouts."

"When you had dinner with Jackson—the night Callie saw you both—it was a Monday. That's right, isn't it, Callie?"

"Yes. Monday, November twenty-seventh."

"And Jackson died on December first. Four days after you had dinner with him."

"So?" Jeanette says.

"So it means you were probably still there, in England, when he died. Weren't you?"

She shakes her head, saying, "I don't know."

Eva lifts her hands to her head, and as she does, her elbow connects with the wooden sewing box balanced on the armrest. She makes a grab for it but isn't quick enough, and it lands on the thin carpet with a thud. Buttons and needles scatter and spin across the floor, and the coat that was beneath it slides free, pooling at her feet.

Eva stares at the dark purple material of the coat, a trail of goose bumps traveling down her spine.

Bending forward, she lifts the coat from the floor and holds it in front of her so it hangs to its full length. Her fingers trail along the heavy woolen sleeve toward the shoulders, then over the collar. She stops at the hood. It is fur-trimmed, just as she knew it would be. "My God . . ." she gasps, making the connection.

Eva has seen this coat before. She remembers how the wind had flattened it against the woman's back, the fur-trimmed hood pulled tight to her face. "I saw you."

Jeanette looks up, her jaw rigid.

"On the beach, in Dorset. We were walking in opposite directions. I was going toward the rocks—and you were leaving." She swallows, and the truth surges forward. "You were there the morning Jackson died."

Looking back on that last morning, I wish I'd done everything differently. I wish I'd stayed in bed with you, switched off the dark thoughts turning through my mind, and just lain there, breathing you in.

But I didn't.

I pulled on my winter clothes, planted a kiss on your shoulder, then picked up my fishing gear and left. Had I known then that it would be the last time I'd kiss you, I would've taken my time, memorizing the feel of your body beneath my hands and the taste of your skin against my lips.

I strode along the desolate, windstormed beach and over the outcrop of rocks. When I reached the very end, I threaded a lure onto the line and then cast out.

I hoped that fishing would center me, give me space to work out my next move. I wanted to believe there was a solution, a way out from all of this. I was racking my brains trying to think what I could do. I wanted to protect what we had more than anything.

When my phone rang, I answered thinking it would be you. I was picturing you still in bed, imagining your beautiful body curled beneath the duvet.

Only it wasn't you, Eva.

It was her.

And that's when I knew it was over.

32

"I loved him," Jeanette says as she stands in the doorway of the living room, her face pale. She grips the doorframe with one hand, and the other is clutched against the neckline of her sweater.

Eva sits very still, her chin raised, her eyes on Jeanette. Beyond her Saul and Callie stand silently. "Just tell me what happened the morning he died."

Jeanette sucks in her breath. "I followed you both to Dorset. I rang Jackson and told him where I was—that I wanted to talk." She pauses. "I met him on the rocks where he was fishing. The weather was awful—the wind was up and waves were smashing right into the rocks. When I reached him, we had to shout to be heard over the wind. I told him I wanted him to come back to Tasmania with me. I could forgive him for coming to England and meeting you, if he could forgive my mistakes, too."

Jeanette's hand drops from the doorframe and she hugs her arms around herself. She shakes her head sadly as she says, "But Jackson said no. Told me I was crazy if I thought he'd want that." Her gaze turns distant and Eva knows she is standing back on that jetty, the hood of her coat pulled tight around her, the waves agitated and shifting around them.

"I didn't want to threaten him," she says to the room, her

voice barely more than a whisper. "But he wouldn't listen. He kept saying things—cruel things he couldn't mean. So I . . . I said if he didn't come back to Tasmania, I'd go to the police. Tell them what he'd done. Tell them about the fire. Tell them he'd committed bigamy, forged documents, faked an entire life."

Jeanette looks up, her hands opening. "But I would never have done that. I loved him too much. They were just words to make an impact. Make him think." She pauses, rubbing her forehead. "He started yelling, calling me a bitch. He grabbed my arm and began marching me down the rocks. Said I should go home to Kyle. Be a mother."

Her expression twists into something harder. "I hated him for saying that. I am a good mother to Kyle. I love my boy. It was Jackson who walked out, left us. I yanked my arm free and pushed him away. And then . . ." She shakes her head. "I don't know what happened . . . he just seemed to slip. The rocks were wet. I saw him staggering backward and he tripped over the tackle box. It all happened so fast. One moment we were standing right there on the rocks . . . and the next he was falling, disappearing into the sea."

Jeanette's fingers find her wedding ring and she twists it. "I tried to reach out but there was so much water everywhere . . . and he didn't come up. I was shouting, calling out to him. When I finally saw him, he was so far away. The current was dragging him and I ran down the rocks and along the beach, trying to keep sight of him. A couple were moving toward the shoreline, pointing. They'd seen him, too. By the time I reached them, the man was already on the phone to the coast guard. His wife was saying they'd seen him fishing earlier and had worried he might get swept in.

"I realized then that they hadn't seen me with him. They must've passed the rocks before I got there . . . So I just agreed with them—said a wave knocked him in. I knew how it'd sound if I admitted we'd been arguing . . . that I'd pushed him. I didn't mean for any of it to happen. I would never, ever have done anything to hurt him. I loved him.

"I stayed on the shoreline, trying to keep sight of Jackson. But the water was moving so fast and . . . we lost him. Other walkers started arriving. Someone had binoculars. Everyone was scanning the water, trying to locate him. But I knew it was too late. I could feel it. He could've hit his head as he fell. He might not have been conscious. And the sea was so cold . . . no one could survive for long out there.

"I was on the shore for ten, maybe fifteen minutes. By then, there were about a dozen people. I knew the coast guard was on their way and they'd take control of everything, so I slipped out of the crowd. If I stayed, questions would be asked. They'd have found out I was from Tasmania and make the connection, start looking into things. I didn't want that. There was nothing I could do for him . . . I had to leave . . . I had Kyle to think about." Her voice breaks as she says, "There was no choice."

THE AIR SEEMS TO have been sucked out of the room, only the echoes of Jeanette's words remaining.

Eva has spent hours imagining Jackson's final moments, wondering what had caused him to lose his concentration and not see the wave coming that knocked him down. But now she is adding Jeanette to that picture, placing her on the rocks in front of Jackson. She can see the anger blazing between them; the way Jackson reaches out and grabs Jeanette's arm; the force as Jeanette yanks herself free, then pushes him away. Eva pictures him stumbling backward, his heel connecting with the tackle box, his arms flailing as he goes over.

Eva stares at the coat still in her hands. She has a vague memory of seeing it hanging in Jeanette's wardrobe when she went searching the house, but she'd only glanced over it then, not linking it to the woman she saw leaving the beach. Now she remembers the rich, dark purple color, the generous fur-trimmed hood that was pulled around the woman's face as she hurried along the shoreline, the wind pushing her forward. Eva had thought she'd been cold, rushing to get home, when, in fact, she was hurrying away from an incident that would change all of their lives.

If Jeanette hadn't followed them to Dorset, Jackson would still be alive. If she hadn't pushed him on the rocks, he'd still be alive. If the tackle box hadn't been behind him . . . If the waves and current hadn't been so fierce . . .

Her mind whirls and tips. Her scalp is too hot. She needs air. She lets go of the coat and rises unsteadily to her feet, Callie and Saul's gazes moving with her as she crosses the room.

Jeanette stands in the doorway, her face white. "I never meant for it to happen. I loved him."

As Eva passes her, she reaches out and grips Jeanette's left hand, looking at her gold wedding band. "You don't deserve to be wearing that."

Then she lets go, and Jeanette's arm drops in the space between them.

Leaving the room, Eva moves along the hallway where she'd once tiptoed around, stealing through doorways in search of Jackson. For months she'd been living with the feeling that something about Jackson's death was being concealed. As she steps out into daylight, her body trembles with adrenaline and the relief of finally knowing the truth.

33

The journey back to Wattleboon Island takes six hours and it's dark by the time they pull up in the lane behind the shack. Stepping from the car, Callie arches her back to loosen the tension knotted around her shoulder blades. She can feel a headache stirring, sharp needles behind her eyes.

Eva fetches her bag, then pushes the passenger door shut. The inside vehicle light goes out, and for a moment, Callie and Eva both stand in the darkness listening to the bay stirring ahead of them.

Eva's barely spoken a word the entire journey, just gazed out of the window, her arms hugged tight to her middle. Callie tried talking to her, gently asking how she was feeling, but she'd shrugged off any answer.

Now, in the darkness beneath the trees, Eva speaks. "I've decided. I'm going back to England with you."

"You are? Tomorrow?"

"If there are still seats available."

"I'm sure there will be. I'll call the airline to book." Callie touches her brow. "Right. Wow. And what, you'll go back to London? Take my spare room?"

"If that's okay?"

"Of course." Callie's thoughts race ahead, thinking how she

will look after Eva and help her start a new life, one where Tasmania is only a dot on a map on the other side of the world.

Yet she also feels herself hesitating because, despite how much she'd love Eva to come home, she wants something else for her, too. "What about Saul?"

"I'll go over and tell him."

"That's it?"

Eva's gaze drifts over the dark bay. "That's it."

Callie might have had her reservations about Eva's relationship with Saul, but since returning to Wattleboon, she's beginning to understand how deeply he cares about her. At Jeanette's his eyes barely left Eva, and in the driveway outside he'd caught up with Callie, saying, "Please, don't let her drive." Up until now she'd felt it'd be cleaner if Eva walked away, as it all seemed too hard, too complicated. But then, isn't anything worth having always hard? "I'm not sure this is the right decision."

"What?" Eva says, turning to face her. "I thought you wanted me to go with you."

"I do. I really do. But only if it's the right thing for *you.*"

A wallaby or a possum shifts somewhere in the bush and a bird comes flying out, dipping low over Callie's head. She feels the breeze from its wings reach her neck and she shivers.

Eva looks back at the black depths of the bush. Her voice is low as she says, "I've already stayed too long."

Callie allows a pause. "Why have you?"

"I was looking for answers."

"I don't think that was the only reason."

Eva says nothing and Callie can't read her expression in the dark.

"I just don't want you to leave because it's the easiest route— or because you're afraid of what staying might mean." Callie pauses. "We haven't even talked about what went on at Jeanette's."

Eva remains silent.

"Please, just tell me what you're feeling. I want to help."

"I feel like I'm being torn in two!" Eva says with a sudden force, like a door blown open by a sharp gust, before quickly slamming shut again.

After a few moments, she says more softly, "I'm shattered, okay? I just want to get on with packing up the shack. I know you're trying to help by making sure I've thought this through, but I have. I've been sitting in the car for hours and hours thinking about it. I'm going home and you won't change my mind."

There's not much Callie can say to that, so when Eva picks up her bag and walks toward the shack, she lets her.

IT IS EASIER TO do it without thinking, to keep moving and not pause. Eva piles her clothes into her case, only lingering a moment on Jackson's checked shirt, her fingers caught in the tired and worn material. She still hasn't recovered the photo of them at the jazz festival and wonders if it'll turn up. She collects her shampoo, conditioner, soap, and face wash from the shower and zips them into her toiletries bag. She puts a few things aside for hand luggage: book, toothbrush, change of underwear, iPod, and headphones.

Next, she works through the shack emptying the fridge, sweeping out sand, wiping over surfaces with a damp cloth. She wants to keep up this motion—needs it in case she starts questioning her decision. But the plane seat is booked now. Callie made the call and Eva handed over her credit card.

She eats a slice of bread and a hunk of cheese while standing against the kitchen side. Then she pulls on a sweater and gathers the wetsuit, mask, and fins that Saul lent her. She leans in through Callie's door. "I'm going to take this stuff back."

Callie, who's rolling a pile of dresses into her suitcase, looks up. She smiles at Eva, her face stained with regret. "Hope it goes okay."

Outside, the air is cool, the sky clear and moonlit. Eva kicks off her sandals, wanting to feel the bay beneath her feet for a final time. She wanders close to the shoreline, where the sand is smooth and damp now that it's low tide. It clings to her soles and she digs her toes into it as she moves.

The natural beauty of this island has settled deep within her; the salt has been on her skin, her lungs are filled with its air, the bay has carried her weight. She's never experienced a connection to a place the way she has here and she feels the wrench of forcing herself free from it.

Eva pauses for a moment, tipping her head back to look at the night sky. She would love to free-dive one last time, kick deep beneath the layers of the ocean and simply hover among the fish, hear the fizz and whispers of the water. But she has run out of time. They are leaving first thing in the morning.

Instead she drops the wetsuit, mask, and fins on the shoreline and rolls up her jeans and wades into the bay. Cool water wraps around her ankles, sand shifting beneath her soles. Eva stirs the shallows with her toes. Moonlight catches on the ripples, painting them silver—the bay's final attempt to seduce her.

Glancing up, she sees Saul's house, the lights on. She thinks she catches his shape moving past the window. She doesn't want to have to tell him she's leaving, or have to look into his eyes knowing it is the last time she'll see him.

But leaving is the only decision. She can't stay because out here, surrounded by Jackson's past, she feels herself slowly coming undone. Earlier, when she turned up at Jeanette's and saw Saul's truck parked outside, her gut reaction had been distrust. Maybe she would always see Saul as an extension of Jackson's mistakes. And that wouldn't be fair. Saul was worth more than that. Far more.

FROM THE LIVING ROOM, Saul can see the warm orange glow of light from Eva's shack. She's been back for an hour now but still hasn't come to see him. He's restless, unable to settle, fearing that she's going to leave Tasmania.

He fetches a beer and drinks it, pacing around the house. His thoughts churn between Eva and Jackson and Jeanette. He stops by the window, looking through his reflection into the night as he thinks about everything Jeanette said. The guilt Jackson lived with over the bush fire must've been immense. The single decision not to phone the fire department shaped who he was to be ever after. Jackson must've seen the wreckage caused by that decision—their mother's death, their father's unraveling—and he would have blamed himself for it all.

Saul runs a hand over his jaw, trying to picture the morning Jackson died. His brother was fishing from the rocks when Jeanette came to him, threatening to destroy the only real piece of happiness he'd found. She had the power to break up his marriage, rip apart his family, and put Jackson in jail.

As Jackson stared into her eyes—the woman who had led him to believe Kyle was his son—he must've known she was about to ruin him. Saul imagines his brother's anguish in those last few moments of his life and his heart caves with sympathy.

EVA REMAINS IN THE shallows, feeling her feet sinking deeper into the seabed, the cold numbing the small bones in her toes.

She recalls the bellowing fury of the waves that morning, smashing into the rocks in booming white explosions. She thinks of the current rolling and dragging Jackson, waves drawing back and sucking him under. And all the while Jeanette pacing the shoreline, desperate not to lose sight of her husband.

Of Eva's husband.

Tears arrive, a warm stream spilling over her cheeks. She leans forward, burying her face in her hands as she weeps. Her shortened breath is warm against her palms; her shoulders quake. She wants to feel his arms around her one more time, to press her face against his neck and be held. She can't bear that it is over.

She has no idea how long she stands there in the bay, but a movement on the shore breaks the rhythm of her sobs. There is a faint brush of fabric, the light sound of sand shifting beneath a shoe. She freezes, a cool shiver weaving down her spine as she realizes she's not alone.

She knows Callie is in the shack and she thought she'd just seen Saul at his window. She removes her hands from her damp face, slowly looking up.

The dark shadow of a person stands on the shoreline, watching her. Then the person begins to turn, moving away from the water's edge. There is something about the motion that is familiar.

She takes a step forward, her throat tightening. "Saul?"

The person pauses, his back to Eva.

Beneath her toes the seabed is sinking away. She thinks of the crabs stalking the shallows, black eyes searching. "Saul?" she says again.

And then, very slowly, the person turns.

She no longer hears the lapping of water against the shore, or the chorus of crickets in the bush. Every muscle in Eva's body contracts and the force seems to push her outside herself, so she is hovering with the burning stars.

I want——so desperately——to make this better in any way I can.

I used to be the one who could soothe you. I would wrap my arms around you and whisper into your hair that everything would be okay, or squeeze your hand twice within mine, telling you: I've got you.

I want to do that now. I want to touch you, hold you, feel the warmth of your skin, breathe in the smell of your neck, trace the clavicle of your throat.

There is so much I need to tell you that would help you understand. I've been trying——moving the words around in the safe space of my thoughts. But it is no longer enough.

I need you to hear the truth.

I need to tell it.

"Eva," I begin.

34

In the moonlight, Eva stares into a face that is so familiar, yet startlingly different. She doesn't recognize the shaven head or the thick beard that hides his mouth. He wears dark trousers and a big jacket that overwhelms him so she can't see his shape beneath it, can't be sure.

But then he says her name—and it is his voice.

She steps backward, splashing into the shallows, her hands clasped to her mouth. The bay is around her ankles, the stars spinning in the sky. She needs to hold onto something, but there is only water and night.

"Eva," he says again, that single word charged with emotion.

She stumbles back, but the seabed seems to slide out from beneath her and she falls, reaching out with her hands—but they slip through the water and her body follows. The bay closes around her, salt water shooting up her nostrils, filling her mouth.

She struggles to her feet, gasping, choking. Her clothes cling to her skin, weighing her down as if they're pulling her back under. She staggers toward the shoreline—but he is rushing forward, toward her.

"No! No!"

He stops.

She stands up panting in the shallows, salt stinging her eyes.

"It's me, Eva," he is saying, but her hands are rising to her ears, covering them to block out what can't be real.

She whispers to herself, "This isn't real. It's just in my mind . . ."

He takes a step forward until he is at the edge of the shoreline. The breeze carries his smell to her. The same earthy scent that had filled the shack and clung to the fabric of his checked shirt.

Jackson.

EVA'S HEAD IS FILLED with a rushing sound as if the sea is raging through her. She presses her fingers to her mouth, tries to speak, but no words come out. Everything seems to swirl and spin around her, the bay tilting behind her, the dark tree line ahead wavering. She tells herself to breathe. Breathe.

"I need to explain," Jackson is saying. "There's a lot . . . I don't even know how to begin. I've imagined telling you this—telling you everything—for so long and now—fuck—I can't think straight!" His hands move as he speaks—opening in front of him, touching the back of his head, scratching his jaw—the quick gestures dizzying her further. "I've been going through everything, explaining. Explaining it all. But now I'm here . . . saying it aloud, I don't know . . . I can't get the words . . ." He pauses, rolls back his shoulders, and takes a deep breath.

Eva hears the air being drawn into his lungs. Jackson is here. Breathing. On this beach. It is impossible. Yet he is here.

She looks down. She is still standing ankle-deep in the bay, her clothes are soaked, the sea dripping from her skin. Dark water moves around her feet but she does not feel the cold. She does not feel anything other than a looming, vertiginous sense of unreality.

Jackson steps forward again so he is now standing in the shallows right in front of her, no more than a couple of feet away. She is looking at his boots; they are heavy and dark, like workman's boots. Her husband liked leather shoes that were well fitted and light to walk in.

"Eva?"

She lifts her head so her gaze meets his and she feels the familiarity of the angle her head has to adjust to. She is not mad. This is real. Real. A strangled gasp escapes her and she clamps a wet hand to her mouth.

"I'm sorry . . . I'm so sorry, Eva. I didn't drown that day. I thought I was going to . . . I really believed I would die." Jackson shifts his weight from foot to foot. "The waves—they kept knocking me down . . . I got dragged right into the next bay." There is a tremor to his voice and he snatches breaths as if he is not getting enough air. "I seized up with the cold—could barely swim. I got dragged as far as the harbor entrance." He pauses. "That's where I managed to scramble out."

Eva feels as if the words are just skimming over her, not sinking in. Because all she is thinking is, *You're dead. You're supposed to be dead.*

"I was so cold." Then he shakes his head, saying, "No, cold's not even the word for it. I've never felt anything like it. Maybe I was hypothermic. I couldn't think straight. I crawled up the beach toward those boats—y'know, all the Lasers and rowing boats lined up on the sand?"

She stares. Water drips from her wet hair down her face. She feels salt stinging her eyes.

"I pulled off a tarp to wrap around me and beneath it there was an oilskin. I put it on and got in the boat to keep out the wind. I was exhausted, freezing. Maybe I passed out, I don't know. Next thing, it was dusk. I saw the lifeboat and helicopter. I remember thinkin', 'A boat must've got into trouble.'" He swallows. "Then I realized that they were searching for me."

He looks down, shaking his head. "I'm sorry. I should've gone then, told someone I was okay. That's what I should've done."

In the darkness she stares at him, unblinking. "Only you didn't."

SAUL IS MOVING ALONG the beach toward the shack when he hears people talking. He slows, scanning the bay for Eva.

She is standing in the shallows, her arms hanging at her sides. The pale light of the moon illuminates her wet, glistening clothes. *What?* Saul thinks.

Then the second person comes into focus and his mind stalls as if it's changed gear too quickly. It is Jackson—a ragged, older Jackson, with a heavy beard and worn clothing. Saul can't believe what he's seeing. "My God . . ."

Jackson talks quickly, saying something about a powerful current, a harbor entrance, a fishing jacket, but Saul does not follow the thread as he is turning away and looking again toward Eva. In the moonlight her skin looks bleached and she is shaking. He wades into the bay and places his hand on her back. Her cardigan is soaked and he feels her shivering. "Eva? Are you okay?" he asks, unable to register his brother's presence.

She doesn't answer.

"Here, come out of the water."

He keeps a light pressure on her back and she slowly drifts with him, their feet splashing through the shallows.

Once they're on the shore, Saul faces his brother. He is here. Alive. Standing in front of them. Saul wants to both hug him and punch him. "What the hell is going on?"

"I fucked up . . . I've totally fucked up! I don't know how to make this right." His voice is so strained it sounds as though it is tearing.

They can't be out here—he needs to get Eva somewhere warm. "My house," is all he says.

No one talks as they move along the shoreline. Every now and then Saul glances over his shoulder to check Jackson hasn't disappeared. He tries centering himself by listening to the nighttime sounds and the stir of the tide.

When they reach the house, he leads Eva to the bedroom and hands her a towel while he searches for dry clothes for her to wear. He works on autopilot, not ready to think about the person pacing in his living room.

He pulls out a long-sleeved T-shirt, a thick sweater, and a pair of wool socks. When he turns back to Eva, he finds her still holding the towel, not moving. Her clothes are sopping and her wet hair is pasted to her face. Her entire body trembles, shivering water droplets to the floor. "Eva," he says gently, "we need to get you into something dry."

Her wide gaze doesn't leave the doorway. She is watching for Jackson.

He takes the towel from her hands and carefully dries her hair with it. When that is done, he says, "I'm going to undress you." As swiftly as he can, he unbuttons her wet cardigan and removes her jeans and underwear. Her skin is pale and covered in goose bumps.

He helps her on with the dry clothes. The T-shirt and sweater hang to the middle of her thighs. He finds her a pair of cotton boxers that serve as shorts, then slides the socks onto her damp feet.

"You warm enough?"

She nods.

In the next room Jackson is circling the coffee table, his wet boots leaving a ring of water across the floor. He stops when he sees Eva, pain marking his face.

Saul takes a blanket from the arm of the sofa and wraps it around Eva's shoulders. He asks if she wants to sit, but she remains standing, her hands buried in the long sleeves of his sweater.

Saul lights the fire, the sawdust scent of kindling filling the room. Then he fetches a bottle of whiskey and pours three glasses. He passes one to Jackson, who takes it in dirt-stained hands. Eva stands in front of the fire, which is just starting to take, while he slips into the kitchen for a moment to call Callie.

Saul says nothing about Jackson to her, just briefly explains that Eva is with him and she's going to stay for a while.

"Listen, Saul," Callie says, her voice unusually gentle. "Tell her to stay as long as she needs, but just remind her we've got to leave tomorrow morning by seven." She adds, "I'm sorry, Saul. I really am."

Saul reaches a hand to the kitchen counter as a new pain hits him square in the chest: Eva's decided to leave.

ALL THIS TIME IT'S as though Eva's been holding her breath, waiting. Her gaze doesn't stray from Jackson. He looks so much older than she remembers, as if he's aged years in the months she hasn't seen him. His face is gaunt, the lower half covered by a thick, dark beard, and his eyes have sunk deep into his face. His hair has been badly shaven, some patches taken too close to his scalp, and he's thin. Too thin. He's wearing clothes she's never seen before: army-green combat trousers with a tear in the knee and a heavy canvas jacket.

His fingernails are black with dirt and his hand trembles as he lifts the whiskey glass to his mouth. *Dirk,* she thinks. *He looks like Dirk.*

Then her gaze travels to his left hand. His third finger. "Where's your wedding ring?" It's the first question she has asked him.

He lifts his hand toward his face, turning it slowly as if it's the first time he's seen it. "I . . . I had to take it off."

"Where is it?"

His eyes close for a moment.

Eva remembers leaning over Jackson in bed and lightly pressing her lips against his eyelids, finding something tender and vulnerable about the delicate skin there.

"I sold it."

Her breath snags.

"I had to. I had nothing, Eva."

"Did you sell your other wedding ring, too?"

The question cuts through the room. A taut silence holds each of them still.

"I've met her," Eva tells Jackson. "Jeanette told me everything: about your marriage. Kyle. The bush fire."

Jackson blinks rapidly, his gaze shifting to Saul, who reenters the room.

"Jeanette thinks she killed you," Eva says.

"We were arguing and she pushed me. I staggered, tripped. It was an accident."

"You let us think you'd drowned."

He scratches roughly at the corner of his mouth, a new gesture she doesn't recognize. "I had no choice. Jeanette was threatening to go to the police. I knew I'd lose you, Eva. End up in jail. I never wanted you to find out about my past. I thought it'd be better if you believed I was dead."

"How?" she says, the word a whisper of disbelief.

"I don't know," he says, shaking his head. "It was a terrible decision. But once I'd made it . . . it was too late. There was no going back."

"What did you do afterward?" Saul asks.

"I left the beach once it was dark. Jumped a train back to London. I went to the apartment—"

"What?" she says, stunned. "You went to our place?"

"My clothes were soaked. The only dry thing I was wearing was the oilskin from the boat. And I needed some money."

Eva tries to make sense of this: he had been in their apartment, collected money. Had he put some money aside? Eva had been through his things and sorted out the clothes in his wardrobe, but hadn't noticed anything was missing. She remembers how dazed she'd felt in her first weeks as a widow. The loneliness had been so overwhelming that she'd thrown open the windows and switched on all the lights and the television just for company.

A memory from that day flashes into her thoughts. She'd gone to fill the kettle, but had frozen at the sight of a tea bag lying in the sink. At the time it had felt out of place and now she realizes why: before they drove to her mother's for the weekend, Eva had cleaned the kitchen, emptied the dishes from the draining board, and scoured the sink.

She lifts her gaze to meet Jackson's. "Did you make tea at the apartment?"

He blinks. "I was freezing. I needed to warm up."

She pictures the dark tea stain in the basin that wouldn't scrub off. "You left a tea bag in the sink."

His eyes widen as if surprised by his mistake.

Her voice is low and edged with steel as she says, "When the coast guard called off the search, I wouldn't accept that you'd drowned. I couldn't give up. So I went to the quay and begged a fisherman to take me out in his boat. It was rough on the water. Freezing. I got a flashlight and scanned the sea looking for you. I was out there in the dead of night searching for you—while you, *you,* were warm and safe drinking tea!"

"Eva—" he says, stepping forward, his hands reaching for her.

She shoves him away with a hard push, feeling his ribs beneath her hands. For a moment, she is Jeanette standing on that jetty filled with rage, watching as he staggers backward. She wishes he would fall. Disappear for good.

Jackson looks shocked by the force. "Please! I wasn't thinking straight! I thought it was the best decision for everyone."

"No," she says, with a deadly cold tone. "It was the best decision for *you.*"

"WHERE HAVE YOU BEEN all this time?" Saul asks Jackson. "It's been months."

"I stayed in the UK. Manchester. That's where I ended up."

Manchester, Eva thinks, trying to picture Jackson there. It's a city they'd never visited together, a huge sprawling place where he could lose himself in the crowds.

"I found a hostel, picked up some cash work on a building site, tried to get my head straight."

"And then you decided to come back to Tas?" Saul asks.

"No. Not at first. I didn't know where to go . . . All I knew is I didn't want to leave the UK." He looks over to where she stands in front of the fire, the thick heat drying her hair and easing the chill from her bones. "I wanted to be in the same place as you. Not seeing you . . . it was torture. I couldn't bear it." His head shakes slowly from side to side. "I rang the apartment once—just to hear your voice. But it wasn't you who answered. It was a new tenant. She said you'd moved out. I had no idea where you'd gone, if you were okay. So I wrote to your mother."

"You wrote to my mother?"

He nods. "I made out I was a friend of yours from college."

"Sarah," she says. "You wrote saying your name was Sarah."

"That's right."

"My God . . ." she whispers as she starts to see the things she'd missed.

"When I heard you were in Tas," he says, running a hand over his forehead, "I knew it was all gonna unravel. But I couldn't stop it. There was nothing I could do."

"How did you get here?" Saul asks.

"I flew. A guy on the building site had a friend who knew how to get hold of a passport."

"And when you arrived here, then what?" Saul asks. "Where did you go? Where are you getting—"

"It doesn't matter!" Eva shouts, her hands slicing through the air in front of her, the blanket slipping from her shoulders. "I don't care where you've been, or how you got here. I don't care about any of that. I just need to know, *why?* I need you to tell me, Jackson"—her voice catches on his name—"why you've done this to me?"

He stares at her, his bloodshot eyes hooded with sorrow. His lips move over his teeth as if feeling for the words he can offer her. She sees him look up to the ceiling and swallow hard. He draws a breath as if to speak, but then his face crumples. His head drops forward, shoulders rounding, as a wretched sob rocks through his body.

35

"I need some air," Eva says, her eyes anywhere but on Jackson.

There is something about the set of her jaw that tells Saul not to follow as she goes out onto the deck. The floodlight trips on and he watches through the glass doors as she leans against the railing, staring out into darkness. He cannot imagine what this is doing to her.

He glances at Jackson, who is rubbing his eyes with the heel of his hand. Saul feels anger thicken in his throat. "The bush fire," he says as levelly as he can manage. "Jeanette told us. Said it was your cigarette that started it. That true?"

Slowly, Jackson looks up and nods.

"You never called the fire department," Saul says, tightness spreading across his chest. "You let it burn."

"I was scared. Scared of getting in trouble. How fucking ridiculous, I know!" He looks directly at Saul. "That's who I am. Someone selfish enough to let it burn." His face twists, teeth clamped together. "When I think of Mum . . ."

A log crackles and then falls in the wood-burning stove, sending sparks flying upward. Saul turns to watch.

"I've been up there, to Eagle Cape," Jackson says a few moments later. "First time since we scattered Mum's ashes. I've been sleeping out that way—there's an old fishing hut tucked back from the shoreline that no one ever visits."

Saul keeps watching the red and orange flames dance, thinking how easy it would be to hide out on Wattleboon; all the wild space empty of people.

"I sat at the lookout—you know, where she used to go to write—and I just watched the sun rising out of the sea, remembering all those times she brought us there. All those stories she used to tell about the whales, how they'd sing to warn each other when the whalers were coming."

Saul remembers. He used to love her stories of the ocean—about fish that danced, dolphins that talked, shells closed tight around secrets.

"I see her, Saul. Mum. I see her face all the time. Even now."

Saul turns and looks at Jackson. Guilt haunts his brother's features and his hands are locked together in front of his mouth.

"There were so many times I thought about telling you and Dad."

"Why didn't you?"

"You saw what her death did to Dad. She was his whole world. He fell to pieces. I just . . . couldn't bear him knowing it was because of me. Then—the more time that passed, the harder it seemed to say anything."

Saul feels the heat of the wood-burning stove against the backs of his legs, drying the bottoms of his jeans. "So you pretended it never happened. Kept quiet."

"Isn't that how we did things in our family? No one ever talked about anything," Jackson says, his voice lifting. "There was this fucking cloud of silence above everything: Mum's death, Dad losing the business, his drinking. We didn't talk about *anything*."

"So let's start now, because there's a hell of a lot I wanna know."

Jackson lowers himself down onto a wooden chair. "Then ask."

"The night of my birthday," Saul says, digging his hands deep into his pockets. "Why did you go after Jeanette?"

Out of all the reams of questions that are filling his head, he's surprised that this is the one he picks first. But then, perhaps that night was the trigger for everything that followed. Or was the trigger fifteen years earlier, the cigarette shared in the woods? There are so many possible starts, but they all lead to the same place: right here, on this night, with his brother and the woman they both love.

Jackson leans back, the wooden bones of the chair creaking beneath him. "Because she was yours."

Saul blinks, surprised.

"I turned up late to your barbecue. I was already drunk, d'you remember? Told you I'd been drinking with my boss. But that wasn't it. I just needed a few drinks before I could face the party."

"Why?"

"Seeing you surrounded by all your friends—seeing this incredible life you'd made—it was tough for me. I knew I could never have that. I didn't deserve it."

Despair radiates from Jackson like a second heat in the room. He rubs a hand over his mouth and continues: "When I saw Jeanette again on your birthday, we talked about the fire. She'd been there that day; she'd lived with her own regrets. It was a relief to finally speak to someone who understood." He shrugs. "I told myself you had everything, so why couldn't I have her? Maybe I needed to prove to you—to myself—I was as good as you."

"Did you love her?"

Jackson places his hands on his thighs. "In the beginning, when we were dating, it was pretty intense. I thought maybe it was love, but looking back, I think we were just connected by the fire. We only had each other to talk to. That made us feel close, I guess. So no, it wasn't love. I never loved Jeanette."

Saul sees now the hollowness of Jackson's victory. "You never even apologized."

"Because I didn't feel sorry. I felt like I *deserved* Jeanette. That's the truth. You saw us together in the club, but you didn't confront me—you just walked away. Didn't even fight for her. Didn't fight for nothing. How much could she've meant to you?"

Perhaps it suited Saul to walk away. His and Jackson's relationship had been fraying for years. Maybe Jeanette was the excuse Saul had needed to leave his brother behind. "But you didn't only take Jeanette, did you? You took my whole past. Fed it to Eva as your own."

"It wasn't like that. I never planned to. It just happened."

"How?"

Jackson glances out toward the deck and Saul follows his gaze. The floodlight has gone out and in the darkness Eva is a charcoal silhouette. "When I met her I just felt . . . I don't know how to explain it. I suppose the word is *hopeful*. I felt hopeful about life again."

Saul keeps his breath steady, wanting to hear the rest.

"I never set out to lie to her, I really didn't. When I got on the plane I was wearing an old college sweatshirt of yours that Dad loaned me—and Eva asked me what I'd studied." Jackson continues staring at Eva outside. "I feel like there are these moments . . . these hinges in my life, when all this possibility hangs on what I'm gonna do next—only I do the wrong thing."

He turns back to Saul. "I told Eva I'd studied marine biology. Just like you. And those words—they sounded so good spoken aloud that I kept on lying. I never set out to mislead Eva. To mislead anyone. I just wanted to start again, Saul. I wanted to be a better person than the one I was here."

OUTSIDE, THE WIND HAS dropped and the night feels still and cool. Eva stands on the deck drawing the briny air deep into her lungs.

Looking up at the sky, she sees that the moon is almost full tonight, its glow stealing the brilliance of the stars. She's just able to make out the wide band of lighter sky that is the Milky Way and she focuses on it, remembering the time Jackson told her there are 200 billion stars within its galaxy. It had been their wedding night and they'd been sitting in the lantern room at the top of the lighthouse watching the sky together, and Eva had felt the excitement of their future laid before them in the stars.

Behind her the glass doors slide open and someone steps out onto the deck. The floodlight is triggered and she closes her eyes against the sudden flare. Footsteps move toward her, coming to a stop at her side.

After a moment, she hears Jackson's voice: "You're so beautiful."

The words are all wrong. They make her skin itch. When there is so much else to say, how can he think that's what she wants to hear? She turns to look at him, trying to find something recognizable in the man she once loved. She had adored his smile; it was wide and open, showing the full stretch of his teeth, and his eyes would dance with light. But now his beard shadows so much of his face she feels as though she's only seeing part of him. "I don't know you."

Anguish flickers in his eyes. "Please, Eva, don't say that! You're the only person who really did. You made me feel more like myself than anyone else. You looked at me like I was worth loving."

"There were so many lies. How do I know what was real?"

"I loved you. I still love you. That's what's real."

She shakes her head and turns back toward the bay. "It's not enough."

Jackson stands silently beside her, his hands spread on the wooden railing. Despite everything, she wants him to reach out and place his hand over hers. Wants to feel the warmth of his fingers. Wants him to hold her and tell her it's going to be okay.

"I'll never have enough words to explain, but I want to try." He smoothes his hands over the railing as he talks. "Before I came to England . . . before I met you . . . I was a mess. I'd wrecked everything: my family, my relationship with Saul, my marriage." He pauses. "I'd lost myself, Eva. I no longer knew who I was."

"So you became someone else."

"Yes, because when you came into my world, you gave me a reason to change. I felt I could be someone different, someone better, because I started seeing myself through your eyes."

"But that person didn't exist."

"That's the thing, Eva. He did. I know the details were borrowed—I didn't do a degree, I didn't work on dive boats or travel to South America—but the rest, that was real. That was *me*. You fell in love with *me*."

She closes her eyes. Her head throbs. How will she ever know, how can she ever unknot the lies from the truth? He'd hidden so much of himself beneath layers of lies and deceit that she'd only ever known part of him.

His voice is low, contemplative. "So many nights I'd lie awake beside you and wonder, if I'd told you the truth from the start, would you still have fallen in love with me? A married bartender from Tasmania who'd committed manslaughter. Would you have? Because I was never sure."

"You didn't give me a chance."

"You're right, because once I started lying, I couldn't go back," he tells her, his voice heavy with emotion. "I knew I'd lose you, so I just . . . kept going."

The floodlight goes out and the deck falls into darkness. Eva stands completely still, blood beating in her ears. She sees how Jackson's lies outgrew him, became something larger than him. Yet even though he knew the unsustainability of his situation, he'd kept pushing forward, creating more lies. "You should never have asked me to marry you."

"I don't regret it. It's one of the only things I don't regret. Forging paperwork and keeping secrets from you, that wasn't how I wanted to do things. But I did want to be your husband. More than anything, that's what I wanted from life."

"Yet then you let me believe you were dead," she says coolly.

At that, his head drops down. "When Jeanette turned up in London, standing there right outside my office, I knew it was over."

He grips the railing harder, saying, "I couldn't go back to Tasmania like she wanted. But if I stayed, then she'd go to the police, tell you what I'd done. I couldn't let that happen. I wasn't worried about jail—I'd survive that. What I couldn't bear was for you—for Saul, for Dad—to know who I really was. What I'd done. I felt like if you were to stop believing in me, Eva, then I'd stop believing in myself, too. I couldn't let Jeanette drag me back to who I was before . . . I couldn't. So I chose to disappear."

In the darkness she can feel him looking at her.

"But it was a mistake. It was the biggest mistake of my life to walk away from the beach that day and let you think I was dead. Because what I've discovered, Eva, is that life without you isn't worth living."

"That's what I said," she tells him. "That's exactly what I said at your memorial."

THEY REMAIN ON THE deck, listening to the murmuring bay. It sounds mournful tonight, a low pulsing of waves falling onto the beach and being dragged back again.

Eva's voice is quiet as she says, "I was pregnant with your child."

"What?" Jackson says, with a start.

"I was here, on Wattleboon, when I found out. I'd come to meet Saul . . . but I fainted. He took me to the medical center. I did a pregnancy test and it was positive."

She hears the scrape of Jackson's beard as he rubs a hand over his mouth. "I can't believe it. Are you . . ." he says, eyes traveling down to her stomach.

"No. No, I'm not. I miscarried at twelve weeks."

"Jesus Christ, Eva. What happened? Were you okay?"

"I was with Callie and Saul. They looked after me. But no, I wasn't okay. To lose a baby . . . it is . . ." She breaks off, thinking of the hollow ache that filled her womb. But she can't get lost in those memories. Not tonight.

"I wish I'd known. Wish I'd been there for you . . ." Jackson reaches out and places his hand over Eva's. She doesn't move. She feels the cool pressure of his fingers and the hardness of the wooden railing beneath her palm.

"Was it my fault . . . the miscarriage? Was it stress that made you lose the baby?"

There is no answer to that question, so she remains silent.

"I'm so sorry," he says slowly. "You would've been an incredible mother. Having a baby with you, that is everything I could've wanted from my life. Everything. But I didn't deserve that gift." He takes a deep breath and squeezes her hand. "But you did, Eva. You did. I'm so sorry. I'm truly sorry for everything I've done to you."

The waver of his voice draws an instinctive emotional response from Eva. She feels herself wanting to pull him to her, run her hand over the back of his neck, for them to comfort each other. She thinks of the way they used to lie together, his head on her stomach, her fingers buried in his hair.

Her memories of Jackson are tangled together, the beautiful moments knotted so tightly to the awful lies that neither thread can be undone.

36

Saul turns away from the window; he doesn't want to see Eva and Jackson standing together on the deck, hands joined. He crouches down in front of the log burner and watches the flames leap and dance, his cheeks and lips beginning to tingle from the heat. He listens to the soft whir of air and smoke being drawn from the flue.

As boys, he and Jackson used to stand in front of the wood-burning stove in the shack and spit on its cast-iron lid. Their saliva would become molten balls that sizzled and bounced, and they'd watch to see whose would last the longest before transforming into steam. Saul remembers the kick of satisfaction he'd feel if the winning spitball was his. Even over the smallest things, there had always been an element of competition between them.

But there will be no winner in this.

Behind him the glass doors slide open and he turns, expectant. Jackson tramps inside, bringing with him the cold, pine scent of the garden.

"How is she?"

Jackson crosses the room and sinks down onto the sofa. He leans forward, locking his arms over his head. "She was pregnant."

Saul waits.

"I can't believe it. We could've had a baby together. Been a family."

"How?"

Jackson drops his arms and looks up. Just for a moment, Saul catches his surprise at the question, before his face clouds as he says, "I don't know." It reminds Saul of his brother's formidable capacity for fantasy.

"You were with her when she miscarried," Jackson says.

He nods. "And Callie."

"Eva said you arranged for her to stay in the shack. Said you came around every day, brought meals for her."

Saul nods, remembering how broken Eva was in those early days, unable to even leave her room. He had no idea how to find words for a loss he could never experience, so instead, he'd talked with her about the small goings-on of his days: the fish he saw on each dive, the project he was working on in the lab, the rhythms of the bay.

He glances out over the deck, where he sees Eva still leaning on the railing, watching the bay. She wears his sweater still and the sleeves fall down beyond her hands. Jackson must follow his gaze because when Saul turns back to the room, Jackson is staring at him. "You must've spent a lot of time with Eva."

"Some."

"I've seen you free-diving together."

Saul feels the heat of the wood-burning stove at his back and steps slightly away.

"And I've seen you on the deck."

There's an edge to Jackson's tone and Saul feels himself rise to it. "So you've been lurking around, watching her?"

"I wanted to know she was okay."

"Magnanimous."

Jackson's lip curls. "So what, are you two . . . ?"

"I care about her."

Jackson exhales loudly, as though the air has been forced out of him. He gets to his feet and paces to the corner of the room, saying, "I've had to see you with your arms around her. Kissing her. Holding her." He stops, sniffs hard. "Is she, what, in love with you?"

"I don't know. I don't know what she feels."

Jackson turns toward the glass doors, watching Eva. "She's everything to me. I know I've hurt her. I know I've let her down, but she's *my* wife, Saul."

"No," Saul says firmly. "She *was* your wife. You let her believe you were dead."

Jackson swings around to face Saul. "I had no choice!"

"How many times have you consoled yourself with those words? Is that what you told yourself when you ran from the bush fire? Because it's bullshit, Jackson! There's always a choice."

"Is it payback?" Jackson says, his eyes narrowing. "Is that it? For Jeanette? I fucked your girl, so you wanna fuck—"

Saul lunges forward, covering the room in two paces. He seizes Jackson by the throat, slamming him up against the wall. The back of Jackson's head hits a framed picture and the glass shatters, fine shards raining over them both. Tiny needles of it are caught in Saul's arm hair but he keeps his grip strong.

"It's no fucking payback!" Saul shouts. "I love her!" The picture frame creaks and strains against the back of Jackson's head. Their faces are inches apart and Saul can feel the stale heat of Jackson's breath. All the anger and swallowed rage burns in this space between them.

"Fuck you!" Jackson shouts, his voice strangled by Saul's grip.

Saul feels the tendons in Jackson's neck pulsate beneath his fingers. "You almost destroyed her! I don't care what your reasons were, or why you're back, but you don't deserve her."

"And you do?"

Saul raises his free hand, his fingers curling into a fist. The veins in his forearm stand proud as his fist hovers level with Jackson's face.

"Hit me!" Jackson spits through gritted teeth, his eyes blazing with fury. "Do it!"

Saul understands that every frustration, every bad decision, every regret of Jackson's is right here hovering over Jackson. His brother wants the pain of a fist in his face—he needs to feel as though he's being punished, feel the guilt being beaten from him. It's the same look he's seen on their father's face when he has a bottle in his hand.

"Come on!" Jackson yells. "You hate me, so just do it! I started the fire. I ruined our family! Fuckin' do it!"

The rage contorting Jackson's face begins to weaken. Saul's hand is still gripped on Jackson's throat and he feels the sob move beneath his fingers, hears Jackson's voice crack as he cries, "I killed her! I killed Mum!"

Saul's fist drops and he pulls Jackson toward him, clasping him in his arms, splinters of glass pressing between them. He feels the heat of his brother's body, the sweat from the back of Jackson's neck in the crook of his arm. Jackson's chest shudders as he gulps in air.

EVA IS ROOTED TO the spot. The heat from the stove thickens the air.

She was drawn inside by the yelling and saw Saul's hands at Jackson's throat. She'd watched, unable to move.

And now their arms are grasped around each other. She smells the tang of sweat, whiskey, fear. They cling to each other as though the ground is sinking and it is just the two of them left.

She thinks of all the photos she's seen of them growing up: dive-bombing from the rocks; standing shoulder to shoulder holding a glistening fish by its tail; grinning with skateboards tucked under tanned arms.

For the past four years they haven't spoken to one another, letting silence and anger fill the space between them. But now she sees that beneath that, all their history is still there.

Saul will always love Jackson.

As she looks at Jackson's anguished face, she wonders, *Will I?*

Watching the brothers together, she can pinpoint their similarities more closely: how they both stand with their feet planted wide; the similar length of their backs broadening into their shoulders; how emotion can deepen their expressions in an instant.

The only two men she's ever really loved, right here.

But which love was real? Had she fallen in love with Jackson because he was borrowing the details of Saul's life, or had she fallen for Saul because he was an extension of Jackson?

Over the past few months she's come to understand that her marriage to Jackson never had solid foundations. He had a magician's talent for distracting her, diverting her attention away from the gaps in his past, and with sleight of hand, he created a present that was so vivid and full, she hadn't noticed it was all just a performance.

With Saul, it was different. Their relationship had grown tentatively. They had found each other when Eva was at her lowest, yet he'd still seen something to love in her. And wasn't every reservation she had about her relationship with Saul really about Jackson?

Saul is solid, grounded, honest; whereas Jackson is passionate and spontaneous, as ungraspable as air.

But does she need air to breathe?

Saul and Jackson step away, glass crunching beneath their feet. And then they are turning, suddenly noticing her in the doorway.

"Eva," they say at the same time, their voices an echo of each other.

Now she sees the wall behind them where the photo of Saul at Machu Picchu hangs at an angle, its glass frame shattered.

She can feel the heat of the log burner as if it's roaring inside her. They are both looking at her expectantly, as if they are waiting for an answer only she may have.

But all Eva is thinking is: *What now?*

37

Time crawls forward. The fire is stoked. Coffee is brewed and drunk. The clock on the bookcase chimes at 2 A.M. and then again at three. A pack of cookies lies on the table unopened.

Eva now sits in the corner of the sofa, her bare knees hugged to her chest. A deep tiredness fills her, dragging down her eyelids, making her breathing shallow, her limbs heavy. It feels as if the three of them are pressed together in the depths of the night, cocooned with this dark, shared knowledge.

The glow from the lamps paints the room in a soft orange light. Saul looks contemplative as he leans against the door with his hands pressed in a prayer, the tips of his fingers resting against his mouth. Every now and then his gaze roams to Jackson, who sits quietly on the wooden rocking chair picking at a thread in the fraying knee of his trousers. It's as if all his nervous energy has fled and now he's exhausted.

Eva thinks of all the lost hours she'd spent imagining Jackson returning to her; when she lay in bed alone at night listening to the empty silence; when she padded along the bay retreading the paths of his childhood; when, in any moment of the day, she was caught off guard by the overwhelming need to be held by him.

Because there was no body, a feather of hope had always

floated inside her, lightly brushing her longing that Jackson would one day walk back into her life.

I wished for this. I wished he wasn't dead. That he'd come back to me. And now he has.

Into the quiet she casts a question at Jackson. "After everything you did to disappear, everything you put us all through, why come back to Wattleboon?"

He looks up, his gaze filling with both tenderness and remorse as it falls on her. He draws his hands along the wooden arms of the chair and says, "I needed to see you were okay. I wanted to be near you. I never planned to show myself. But then tonight I heard you talking to Callie about visiting Jeanette . . ."

Her back stiffens against the sofa. He was there? Standing in the shadows, listening? How many other times had he been nearby? How often had she doubted herself, questioned her sanity, thinking she was sensing things that weren't real? "How long have you been in Tasmania?" she asks, her mind sliding from one thought to the next.

"A month."

She blinks. "Have you been in the shack?"

He looks at her, then down to the floor as he nods.

She knows then that she didn't imagine it—his scent. She pictures Jackson walking through the shack, trailing a hand over her belongings. He'd have gone into her bedroom and seen his old checked shirt on her pillow. She can see him putting it on, buttoning it up over his chest, feeling the familiar fit of the cotton against his skin, and remembering what it was to feel like himself once more.

"I thought I was going mad," she tells him, shaking her head. "I knew you'd been in there—the air smelled of you. But I kept telling myself that I was imagining it."

"Eva—"

"And you took our photo, didn't you? The one of us at the jazz festival."

"I'm sorry."

She closes her eyes and sighs. Already those two words have lost their impact.

"Why tonight, Jackson?" Saul asks from his position by the door. Eva cannot tell if he's standing there ready to leave, or because he wants to make sure Jackson stays. "Why show yourself tonight?"

"I hadn't meant to. I heard Eva crying." He shifts his gaze to her. "You waded out into the bay. I was worried about you. I came closer to make sure you were okay . . . and you saw me."

"No," she counters, shaking her head. "You wanted to be seen. If you'd heard me talking to Callie, then you'd have known I was leaving, too. The temptation was too great, wasn't it? You got close enough so I'd see you—take the decision out of your hands."

"No . . ." he says, but she can see he's losing conviction in his own theory. "You were sobbing. I hated seeing how much I'd hurt you. I wanted to comfort you. I'm your . . ." He grinds to a halt.

"Husband?" Eva finishes. She looks closely at Jackson, trying to find traces of the man she'd married, the man she'd promised her future to.

But he is no longer her husband. In truth, he never really was.

A TAP ON THE window makes Saul turn. A large tiger moth has hit the glass and is trying to beat its way through to the light.

"So what now?" Saul says, turning back to the room and pushing his hands into his pockets. "What do you want? Are you gonna go to the police? Tell Jeanette?" He wonders if she's owed that honesty, or whether it'll be worse hearing the great lengths Jackson went to in order to excavate her from his life.

"I . . . I don't know," Jackson says, his fingers kneading at his forehead. "I can't decide what to do."

It was so like Jackson: reactive, impulsive, thinking only of the moment and not the potential consequences of his actions.

"What about Dad?" Saul asks.

Jackson stares at Saul. "How is he?"

"He's doing okay," Saul says more gently. "Given up the drinking."

"Yeah? That's really good to hear."

"If it lasts, it is."

"I saw him. Here. Saw you all having dinner together out on the deck."

From the sofa, Eva glances up sharply.

Saul sees her surprise and remembers how, the evening Jackson is talking of, Eva had suddenly risen from the table and drifted down to the garden's edge, her face washed pale. Now he wonders whether she had sensed Jackson watching them all from a distance.

"When I saw Dad, he didn't look too good," Jackson says. "He's ill, isn't he?"

"Pancreatitis. Like before."

"Is it serious?"

Saul nods.

"You reckon he'll stay off the drink?"

"He says he wants to. But who knows. If he doesn't, it could end him."

Jackson is silent for some time. Then he says, "He couldn't cope with . . . this. Could he?"

Saul's been asking himself the same question. It's not only the deception that Jackson is alive that Dirk would have to deal with, but also the truth about the bush fire, which would unearth all the pain of losing his wife. Saul worries that he's too fragile, that it'll send him straight back to the bottle. Eventually he answers, "No, I don't think he could."

He sees Jackson swallow as he absorbs what this means.

As Saul stands at the edge of the living room looking at his brother, he feels a decision beginning to form. He can't control what Jackson does next, or what Eva wants, but he does know his own mind. Sweat builds at his temples and across his brow as he realizes what he's about to say.

"I don't want to lie to Dad, live a split life where I'm in contact with you but keeping it from him. It wouldn't work."

Jackson remains very still, so Saul forces himself to go on. "What happened the day of the bush fire was an accident. You were just a kid who made a mistake. I wish you'd told me what happened, trusted me with the truth, but what's done is done." He pauses, letting his eyes meet his brother's as he says, "I forgive you for it."

Emotion stains Jackson's face as he battles against the tears that are welling in his eyes.

There is more to say and Saul holds Jackson's gaze steady as he talks. "But I need to ask you to forgive me, too. You're my brother and I love you, but I can't have you in my life. Not now, Jackson. Not ever."

Jackson's expression is stretched thin with pain as he nods. "I understand."

After a moment, he rises from his chair so that he is standing eye level with Saul. He reaches out his hand.

Saul looks at it for a moment, then clasps it.

They do not hug, or hold each other, but instead shake hands: it is a gesture of agreement, of forgiveness, of good-bye.

EVA WATCHES AS SAUL slips out onto the deck, pulling the sliding glass doors behind him. A fresh drift of sea air reaches her and then disperses in the dry heat of the room. She has the fleeting sensation that she is trapped here with Jackson, sealed indoors.

Jackson's face is filled with anguish as he watches his brother go.

"Oh, Jackson." Eva sighs, feeling worn down, exhausted. She wonders if she can walk away from him, too, abandon the man she'd loved. "What is it you want?"

His gaze is heartbreakingly sad and he holds her in it as he says, "To go back."

She closes her own eyes. "We can't."

"I could come clean, go to the police, tell them what I've done."

"And go to jail? Ruin your dad? You lied to everyone, Jackson." She thinks of the memorial service and all the people who'd come, telling her what a good man Jackson was. Who would he have left to go back to?

"Or we could go somewhere, you and me. Start fresh." The words sound hollow and she sees he doesn't believe them himself.

She gets to her feet and moves toward Saul's bookcase, letting her eyes trail the titles. Her gaze rests on *The Sea Around Us,* the book Jackson had once told her inspired his decision to be a marine biologist. A lie. So many lies.

When she turns back to Jackson, she says, "You told me that we'd visit Tasmania together in the autumn."

His eyes brighten. "I'd always wanted to bring you here."

"But you couldn't have," she says, a fist of anger clenching tight in her stomach. "You'd have had to make up an excuse about why we couldn't come. What would you've said, Jackson?"

"I . . . I don't—"

"That your dad was ill, or the flights were too expensive, or work wouldn't let you go?" All the lies he'd told begin circling in her thoughts; the letters from Dirk he'd forged; the stories about traveling; his fake career as a marine biologist; the wedding day he'd had before; Jeanette's arrival in London; the final moments fishing on the rocks. "I was so pathetically trusting, lying to me must have been easy."

"I *hated* lying to you!" Jackson shouts, his face flushed, his eyes glassy. "It tore me up. I wanted it to be true so much that I couldn't bear it."

If that were true, she cannot begin to imagine the stress Jackson must've been under keeping all those lies spinning. He would've been constantly on edge, needing to remember each of the intricate mistruths that he'd woven together.

She pictures him on the morning he disappeared, sheltering beneath a tarpaulin in a boat. As his body shuddered with cold and shock, his thoughts must have been pared right back to the desire to survive. Perhaps he'd felt so exhausted by it all that he just wanted to begin again, have a clean slate. He must've known that it wasn't just Jeanette's arrival in the UK that pushed him into a corner: his lies had already boxed him in a long time ago.

"You were always going to run," she says, straightening as re-alization dawns. "That's why you allowed your lies to get bigger, more complicated. You were in so deep that you knew one day your only choice would be to leave."

She wants him to refute this statement and tell her that he saw his future with her, but Jackson gives the lightest of nods.

Something within her collapses, like a tent sighing to the

ground. "My God," she whispers, putting a hand to her mouth. "You knew one day all the lies would catch up with you. That's why you put money aside, wasn't it?"

He looks at her, tears spilling onto his cheeks.

"You were *always* going to run," she repeats, the truth spooling out before her. "You've done it before. You ran from the bush fire, you ran from Jeanette and Kyle, and you ran from me."

Her heart breaks—for him, for herself—as she says, "And you're still running now."

SAUL SITS ON THE deck watching the pearl-gray glow of daylight emerging at the edge of the horizon. He feels drained. He doesn't want to think about what's happening inside the walls of his home so he keeps his gaze steady on the bay.

Sometime later the sliding doors open and Eva steps out. The floodlight flares on, but she reaches for the wall and flicks it off, a fading darkness settling over the deck once more. She pulls up a chair beside his and looks out over the bay. They sit in silence listening to the murmur of the water and the first notes of birdsong rising from the bush.

Despite everything that's happened in the last twenty-four hours, sitting here beside Eva, Saul feels almost peaceful. When she first arrived on Wattleboon, it was as though she had opened a window inside him and shown him an entirely new view of the world. Now he cannot imagine his life without her in it.

"Callie said you've decided to leave tomorrow."

"Yes."

"You were on your way over here to tell me."

She nods.

He shifts his chair so he's directly facing her. She still wears his sweater, the sleeves bunched at her wrists. Her hair has dried in soft waves around her face and he thinks she looks young, tired. He leans across and takes both her hands. They are warm and small within his.

"Eva, I'm so sorry for everything you've been through. I truly am." He plans to tell her that she is strong and brave and will cope with whatever decision she makes, and that there is no pressure from him. But when he opens his mouth, instead he says, "Earlier Jackson told me I never fight for anything—and he is right. So this is me fighting: I don't want you to leave, Eva."

He holds her hands tighter within his. "This place has come alive since you've been here. It feels like home to me now, not because it's tied to my past—but because I can see a future here. If none of this had happened—if you hadn't married my brother, if Jackson hadn't chosen to disappear, if he wasn't sitting inside right now—then you'd just be an English girl that came to Tas. And when everything is stripped away and I think of it like that, suddenly it's simple: I'm in love with you."

He thinks of the weeks she's been here and it's not the difficult times that he remembers, it's the sound of her laughter at the squid ink on Callie's shins; it's the beautiful moment they hung suspended underwater watching a sea dragon; it's the way sunlight glances off her face, lighting the amber flecks of her eyes. They made those moments, the two of them. And if they managed to find happiness among all the turbulence, then he knows they can find it again.

Tears gather on Eva's lower lids. She presses her lips together and does not speak.

"I don't have any answers about what happens next," Saul says, "or how we can make this work. All I know, all I can tell you, is that I'll do my best to make you happy. Always. So please, Eva. Stay."

38

Eva leaves the house, her footsteps moving in rhythm with his. Outside the sky has lightened, a pale oyster dawn yawning. It won't be long until sunrise. They've talked through the night and Eva feels as though she has no more words left in her, no more energy to listen. But oddly, she no longer feels afraid.

What she feels is a strange sense of calm. It reminds her of the long, stressful nights on the labor ward, when the more pressure she was under, the more lucid her thoughts became, giving her the composure to take control of whatever situation she was faced with.

They move through the damp garden, a chorus of birds singing their greetings. Soon the sun will lift out of the sea and a new day will begin.

The stone steps are cool against her bare soles as they climb down to the bay. In the predawn light she feels as if they don't really exist, that they are drifting somewhere transient, caught between night and day.

They walk side by side along the empty beach, moving in a dreamlike state, the sand absorbing the noise of their footsteps, the lapping of the water almost in beat with their breath. Neither of them speaks.

They are halfway along the bay when Eva notices a dark shape on the shore. At first she thinks it is a pile of kelp, but as they draw nearer she realizes it's her wetsuit and fins that she left here last night. It already seems a lifetime ago that she was standing here, swilling the shallows with her feet.

She gazes out over the bay. The water is a soft mauve, glassy and still. Without a word, she slips off her clothes. She feels his eyes on her body but she does not mind that he sees her. She shivers as she pulls on the wetsuit, the cool neoprene damp with dew.

Then she turns and faces Jackson. She takes his hand and feels the warmth of his fingers closing around hers.

"What will you do now?"

He smiles at her bravely. "Go somewhere else. Start again."

She knows that he will. Jackson will be able to build a new life—a good life. She believes that. She has to.

Eva doesn't hate him for what he's done. She knows it was a child's lie that spawned a chain of events he couldn't break out of. She holds his hand tight in her own as she says just one word. They both know it is the only word there can be.

"Good-bye."

Then her fingers slide free of his.

Eva wades into the sea, the water slipping over her feet, around her legs, circling her waist. She pulls on the mask and fins, then falls forward letting the bay carry her. She swims out with clean, smooth strokes, slicing through the water until she is in the middle of the bay.

She floats with her arms outstretched at her side, her face gazing down into the sea. The cold chills her cheeks and she tastes salt on her lips. Her breathing begins to settle and her heart rate slows.

Only then does she draw a deep, full breath, filling her lungs with crisp air. She dives down and the world closes behind her. She descends through layers of cool blue as if the sea is melting around her. She slides downward, arms pressed to her thighs, her legs working as one.

As she moves deeper underwater she sees there is so much beneath the surface that she hasn't noticed before; tiny flecks of plankton that spin and dance in the light; intricate patterns on the ribbons of seaweed swaying beneath her; the way the whole sea sparkles with air bubbles so tiny they look like glitter.

When she begins to feel her lungs whispering their desire for air, she stops kicking and, for a moment, she feels as if she's hovering, entirely weightless.

The peaceful motion seems to loosen her thoughts, unknotting them. They are set free and she sees everything with a bright, liquid clarity. She thinks of the babies she has delivered in birthing pools and how they can stay peacefully underwater until they take their first breath and then their whole world changes. She thinks of the early free-dives she made with Saul when she had gone down fighting the ocean—but come up having understood something about it and herself. She thinks of Jackson in the freezing sea, the shadow of his past standing over him, the trace of a decision already being made.

She realizes how much can change with a single breath.

Her lungs call to her now, demanding air—but she holds herself still. She imagines an airplane taking off for England in a few hours' time, her sitting beside Callie, watching the contours of Tasmania shrinking until it is only the size of a thumbprint left behind on her heart.

And then she knows what it is she wants.

Eva looks up and kicks for the surface. As she floats toward the silver skin of the sea, she sees a brilliant red orb glowing above the bay. She knows that when she surfaces, the first rays of sunlight will be breaking, pouring over the sea. She understands that the beach will be empty, Jackson gone. And she hopes that Saul will be standing on his deck, the light of the new day warm on his face as he holds onto the railing, watching for her.

Author's Note

Bruny Island, which lies off the southeastern coast of Tasmania, was the inspiration behind the fictional setting of Wattleboon. Good friends introduced me to the wild landscapes and seascapes of Bruny over two Tasmanian summers. We camped, fished, dived, and hiked, and Bruny nestled so deeply into my heart that by the time I returned to England, I knew I must set my novel there. I chose to apply some artistic license and reimagine the landscape to suit the fiction of *A Single Breath*.

Acknowledgments

This book started out as just a thread of an idea. That thread was slowly woven into a story, onto a page, and finally into this book you're now holding. There are many people I have to thank for that.

Firstly, a huge thanks to Becky and Hugo Jones, great friends and fellow adventurers, who introduced me to the rugged beauty of Tasmania, and showed me how to catch a squid, shuck an oyster, and cook a flathead. Know this: James and I will be back!

Secondly, I'd like to thank my wonderful agent, Judith Murray, for her smart counsel and continued support. (I sleep easier knowing you're in my corner!) I also work with a brilliant and enthusiastic team at HarperCollins, and across the pond at Touchstone/Simon & Schuster. In particular, thank you to my insightful editors, Kimberley Young and Sally Kim.

Many people have helped with the research for this novel, including Dr. Gretta Pecl, who has an expansive knowledge in the field of cephalopods; Dr. Oliver Atkinson for his help with medical queries; Hannah Stone for her insights into midwifery; and Emma and Jane Reed-Wilson for talking to me about TV production.

I'm VERY grateful to my network of friends who are kind enough to read my early drafts—and brave enough to share their thoughts. Thank you for helping shape this book.

Thank you to my parents and parents-in-law, who are my cheering squad and editorial advisors. A special thanks to my mother—always my first reader—who somehow manages to leave a message of encouragement on my answering machine just when I'm hitting a wall.

And finally, my husband, James. I'm dedicating this book to him because he's the one I talk to in the kitchen about plot problems and misbehaving characters; he's the one who traipses around the world with me on quests for inspiration and setting details; he's the one who surfaces from a free-dive and lets me question him about what he saw. He's the one who hugs me when I'm struggling; the one who laughs with me when I'm celebrating; the one who anchors me when I'm adrift. He's the one.

A Single Breath

When Eva's husband, Jackson, dies in a fishing accident after less than ten months of marriage, she travels to his native Tasmania, hoping to find comfort and closure by visiting his estranged family. What she discovers, however, is that her husband was not the man she thought he was. As she struggles to come to terms with Jackson's deception, she finds herself more and more drawn to his brother, Saul, who offers her intimacy, passion, and a window into her husband's past. When a shocking secret about Jackson comes to light, Eva must find a way to rediscover her own truths and forge a new future.

Questions for Discussion

1. Eva suffers greatly in the first half of the novel. She's devastated by Jackson's death and then by the miscarriage of their baby, but she also deals with aching loneliness and feeling like she's lost her identity. Why do you think she repeatedly pushes away her family and Callie to be in Tasmania alone? Do you think it was the right decision for her?

2. When they first meet, Saul is distant toward Eva, yet over time they develop a close relationship. Despite his desire to tell Eva the truth about Jackson, he does not, and Eva only finds out accidentally. How do you think Eva should have found out? What would you have done if you were Saul?

3. As the backstory of Jackson and Eva's relationship emerges, it becomes clear that Eva overlooked a few red flags about her husband: the occasional white lie, his irresponsible spending habits, and the evening she found him crying in the shower.

Do you think Eva was too naïve about Jackson? Would you have questioned any of these incidents?

4. Do you find Jackson at all sympathetic? What do you make of his decision to hide his first marriage from Eva? Do you think his good intentions and genuine love for Eva excuse his behavior in any way?

5. Jackson tells Eva that meeting her gave him the opportunity to start over: "So many nights I'd lie awake beside you and wonder, if I'd told you the truth from the start, would you still have fallen in love with me? A married bartender from Tasmania who'd committed manslaughter" (p. 328). Do you think Eva would have felt the same way about Jackson had she known the truth?

6. Discuss how Jeanette and Jackson's decision to cover up the truth about the bush fire impacts the rest of their lives, shaping their relationship and spawning a series of other lies that spin out of their control. Do you blame one more than the other for the terrible repercussions of this tragic event?

7. Eva is initially ashamed to tell Callie that she might have feelings for Saul: "She can see by Callie's expression that she is thinking the exact same thing as Eva: *But he's Jackson's brother*" (p. 160). Were you ever opposed to Saul and Eva's relationship? Is there a moment in the book that changed your initial opinion?

8. On p. 336, Eva wonders, "Had she fallen in love with Jackson because he was borrowing the details of Saul's life, or had she fallen for Saul because he was an extension of Jackson?" What do you think attracts Eva to Saul? Would she have fallen for Saul if she hadn't known Jackson first?

9. Both Eva's mother and Saul and Jackson's father have endured terrible losses in the past, and their grief has shaped their relationships with their children. Compare and contrast how Eva, Saul, and Jackson cope with the emotional fragility

of their respective parents. Do you think it is justifiable to lie to your loved ones if you believe it will spare them from suffering?

10. Ultimately, Saul forgives Jackson for his mistakes, but he never wants to see him again. What do think about this decision? Do you think Saul and Jackson will ever fully reconcile?

Enhance Your Book Club

1. Lucy Clarke indicates in the Author's Note that Bruny Island was her inspiration behind the fictional setting of Wattleboon. Research Bruny Island with your book club. Does it look the same as you imagined? Why or why not?

2. Eva finds solace in learning how to free-dive. Have each member of your book club discuss their favorite way to destress and unwind. How do these activities make you feel? Why do you think you are drawn to your particular passion?

3. If you enjoyed *A Single Breath*, read Lucy Clarke's previous novel, *Swimming at Night*, for your next book club meeting. Discuss the similarities and differences between the two novels.

4. Learn more about Lucy Clarke at www.lucy-clarke.com or follow her on Twitter @LucyClarkeBooks.

A Conversation with Lucy Clarke

Where did the inspiration for *A Single Breath* come from?
The idea came from two very separate threads. In 2011, I visited Tasmania for the first time and fell in love with its wild beauty and its remote shacks. Later on that year, I heard about a friend-of-a-friend who was leading a double life in order to hide a huge secret from their family. I was intrigued by the idea of the unknowability of those closest to us and thought how devastating it would be to find out the truth only when that person had gone.

These two threads began to weave together, stitching themselves into the beginning of a story.

In the novel, Saul shares his passion for free-diving with Eva. Do you free-dive?
I learned to scuba dive in Tasmania and had a fantastic time swimming alongside sea dragons, draughtboard sharks, and huge rays, but I found the dive tanks and thick winter wetsuits very heavy and restrictive, so I was excited to try free-diving instead. However, it quickly became apparent that I have the lung capacity of an aging hamster, so my free-diving career never really took off! Luckily my husband free-dives and spearfishes and is very patient when answering the barrage of questions I fire off when he returns to shore.

Secrets play a large role in *A Single Breath*. Under what circumstances is keeping a secret necessary?
There is something so irresistible about secrets. The moment I hear someone whisper, "I've got a secret," my ears prick up. I'm sure that many people keep the odd secret in order to protect someone they care about, and most of these will be harmless enough. But then there are those darker secrets, the ones that are tightly wrapped with lies and presented as truth. Those are the dangerous ones—and also the ones that are wonderfully exciting to explore in fiction!

What's next for Jackson, Saul, and Eva? Do you imagine a future for them beyond the ending of the book?
It is not an easy story with easy answers. I think that Eva and Saul have a tricky path ahead of them. They will have to negotiate many issues, such as: Will their friends and families accept their relationship? Will they choose to make their home in Tasmania or England? Will they one day regret not allowing Jackson back into their lives? For my part, I like to believe that Saul and Eva's love for each other is strong and deep enough to survive the challenges that await them.

Jackson tells us that a shack is a bolt-hole, "a place to disappear to when you're craving some space, some wilderness" (p. 73). Do you have a bolt-hole?

Yes, I do! My bolt-hole is actually a beach hut on the south coast of England, where I do much of my writing. I love being near the water when I write, and I also love that feeling of space and quiet: no emails, no phone calls, just the sea and my notebook. Heaven!

According to your author bio, you and your husband spend your winters traveling. How does travel inform and inspire your writing?

There is something about slinging a few belongings into a bag and heading off on a plane, train, or ferry that gives me the most incredible sense of freedom. The break from routine, the stepping out of one's ordinary world and into another, is surely good for the soul. (At least, it feels very good to *my* soul!) What I see, hear, smell, and taste while traveling certainly inspires my writing, but it is also the very fact of being *away* that I find interesting in terms of fiction. I'm intrigued to see how characters behave outside the usual parameters of their daily lives. Routine can be limiting, so I like to explore what happens when a character is taken out of their comfort zone and dislocated from their family and friends. What then?

How was the process of writing *A Single Breath* different—if at all—from writing your debut novel, *Swimming at Night*?

The process was very similar in that both novels started as a simple idea, which I then drafted and redrafted, layering it into a story. The main difference was that I was running a business when I was writing *Swimming at Night*, so it took me much longer to complete the novel. With *A Single Breath*, I was able to enjoy the luxury of being a full-time novelist, so I could completely immerse myself in the story for long stretches of time.

Read on for a look at Lucy Clarke's

Swimming at Night

Available in paperback July 2014 from Touchstone Books

A young woman travels around the globe in search
of answers about her sister's mysterious death in
this "tender and intricate meditation on sister-
hood and family . . . an accomplished debut" (*New
York Times* bestselling author Lisa Unger).

> *People go traveling for two reasons: because they
> are searching for something, or they are running
> from something.*

Katie's world is shattered by the news that her head-
strong and bohemian younger sister, Mia, has been found
dead at the bottom of a cliff in Bali. The authorities say
that Mia jumped—that her death was a suicide.

Although they'd hardly spoken to each other since
Mia suddenly left on an around-the-world trip six
months earlier, Katie refuses to accept that her sister
would have taken her own life. Distraught that they never
made peace, Katie leaves behind her orderly, sheltered
life in London and embarks on a journey to discover the
truth. With only the entries of Mia's travel journal as her
guide, Katie retraces the last few months of her sister's

life and—page by page, country by country—begins to uncover the mystery surrounding her death.

"A great read for fans of smart contemporary women's fiction as well as thriller and mystery readers" (*Library Journal*, starred review), *Swimming at Night* weaves together exotic settings, suspenseful plot twists, and familial bonds in a powerful tale of secrets, loss, and forgiveness.

1

Katie

(London, March)

Katie had been dreaming of the sea. Dark, restless water and sinuous currents drained away as she pushed herself upright on the heels of her hands. Somewhere in the apartment her phone was ringing. She blinked, then rubbed her eyes. The bedside clock read 2:14 a.m.

Mia, she thought immediately, stiffening. Her sister would get the time difference wrong.

She pushed back the covers and slipped out of bed, her nightdress twisted around her waist. The air was frigid and the floorboards were like ice against the soles of her feet. She shivered as she moved through the room, her fingers spread in front of her like sensors. Reaching the door, she groped for the handle. The hinges whined as she pulled it open.

The ringing grew louder as she picked her way along the darkened hall. There was something troubling about the sound in the quiet, sleep-coated hours of the night. *What time would it be in Australia? Midday, perhaps?*

Her stomach stirred uneasily remembering yesterday's terrible fight. Words had been sharpened to injure and their mother's name had been flung down the phone line like a grenade. Afterwards, Katie was so knotted with guilt that she left work an hour early, unable to concentrate. At least now they'd have a chance to talk again and she could tell Mia how sorry she was.

She was only two steps from the phone when she realized it was no longer ringing. She hovered for a moment, a hand pressed to her forehead. Had Mia hung up? Had she dreamed it?

Then the noise came again. Not the phone after all, but the insistent buzz of the apartment intercom.

She sighed, knowing it would be late-night visitors for the traders who lived upstairs. She leaned towards the intercom, holding a finger to the Talk button. "Hello?"

"This is the police."

She froze, sleep burning off like sea mist on a sunny day.

"We'd like to speak to Miss Katie Greene."

Her pulse ticked in her throat. "That's me."

"May we come up?"

She released the front door, thinking, *What? What's happened?* She switched on the light, blinking as the hall was suddenly illuminated. Looking away from the glare, she saw her bare feet, toenails polished pink, and the creased trim of her silk nightdress against her pale thighs. She wanted to fetch a robe, but already the heavy tread of feet sounded up the stairway.

She opened the door and two uniformed police officers stepped into her hall.

"Miss Katie Greene?" asked a female officer. She had graying blonde hair and high color in her cheeks. She stood beside a male officer young enough to be her son, who kept his gaze on the ground.

"Yes."

"Are you alone?"

She nodded.

"Are you the sister of Mia Greene?"

Her hands flew to her mouth. "Yes . . ."

"We are very sorry to tell you that the police in Bali have informed us—"

Oh God, she began to say to herself. *Oh God . . .*

"—that Mia Greene has been found dead. She was discovered at the bottom of a cliff in Umanuk. The police believe she fell—"

"No! NO!" She spun away from them, bile stinging the back of her throat. This couldn't be real. It couldn't be.

"Miss Greene?"

She wouldn't turn. Her gaze found the bulletin board in the hallway where invites, a calendar, and the business card of a caterer were neatly pinned. At the top was a map of the world. The week before Mia left to go traveling, Katie had asked her to plot her route on it. Mia's mouth had curled into a smile at that, yet she indulged Katie's need for schedules and itineraries by marking a loose route that began on the west coast of America and took in Australia, New Zealand, Fiji, Samoa, Vietnam, and Cambodia—an endless summer of trailing coastlines. Katie had been tracking the route from Mia's infrequent bursts of communication, and now the silver drawing pin was stuck in Western Australia.

Staring at the map, she knew something wasn't right. She turned back to the police. "Where was she found?"

"In Umanuk," the female officer repeated. "It's in the southern tip of Bali."

Bali. Bali wasn't on Mia's route. This was a mistake! She wanted to laugh—let the relief explode from her chest. "Mia isn't in Bali. She's in Australia!"

She caught the exchange of glances between the officers. The woman stepped forward; she had light-blue eyes and wore no makeup. "I'm afraid Mia's passport was stamped in Bali four weeks ago." Her voice was gentle, but contained a certainty that chilled Katie. "Miss Greene, would you like to sit down?"

Mia couldn't be dead. She was twenty-four. Her little sister. It was inconceivable. Her thoughts swam. She could hear the water tank downstairs humming. A television was playing somewhere. Outside, a late-night reveler was singing. *Singing!*

"What about Finn?" she asked suddenly.

"Finn?"

"Finn Tyler. They were traveling together."

The female officer opened up her notebook and spent a moment glancing through it. She shook her head. "I'm afraid I don't have any information about him currently. I'm sure the Balinese police will have been in contact with him, though."

"I don't understand any of this," Katie whispered. "Can you . . . I . . . I need to know everything. Tell me everything."

The police officer described the exact time and location at which Mia had been found. She told her that medical assistance had arrived swiftly on the scene, but that Mia was pronounced dead on their arrival. She explained that her body was being held at the Sanglah morgue in Bali. She confirmed that there would be further investigations, but that so far the Balinese police believed it was a tragic accident.

All the while Katie stood completely still.

"Is there someone you would like us to contact on your behalf?"

She thought instantly of their mother. She allowed herself a moment to imagine the comfort of being held in her arms, the soft cashmere of her mother's sweater against her cheek. "No," she told the officer eventually. "I'd like you to leave now. Please."

"Of course. Someone from the Foreign Office will be in touch tomorrow with an update from the Balinese police. I'd also like to visit you again. I've been assigned as your Family Liaison Officer and will be here to answer any questions you have." The woman took a card from her pocket and placed it beside the phone.

Both officers told Katie how sorry they were, and then left.

As the door clicked shut, the strength in Katie's legs dissipated and she sank onto the cold wooden floor. She didn't cry.

She hugged her knees to her chest to contain the trembling that had seized her. Why had Mia been in Bali? Katie didn't know anything about the place. There was a bombing outside a nightclub some years ago, but what else? Clearly there were cliffs, but the only ones she could picture were the grass-covered cliffs of Cornwall that Mia had bounded along as a child, dark hair flying behind her.

She tried to imagine how Mia could have fallen. Was she standing on an overhang and the earth crumbled? Did a sudden gust of wind unbalance her? Was she sitting on the edge and became distracted? It seemed absurdly careless to fall from a cliff. The facts Katie had been given were so few that she couldn't arrange them into any sort of sense. She knew she should call someone. Ed. She would speak to Ed.

It was her third attempt before she managed to dial correctly. She heard the rustle of a duvet, a mumbled, "Hello?" and then silence as he listened. When he spoke again, his voice was level, telling her only, "I'm on my way."

It must have taken no less than ten minutes for him to drive from his apartment in Fulham to hers in Putney, but looking back she wouldn't remember any of that time. She was still sitting on the hallway floor, her skin like gooseflesh, when the intercom buzzed. She stood groggily. The floorboards had marked the backs of her thighs with red slash-like indentations. She pressed the button to let him in.

Katie heard the thundering of his feet as he took the steps two at a time, and then Ed was at her door. She opened it and he stepped forwards, folding her into his arms. "My darling!" he said. "My poor darling!"

She pressed her face into the stiff wool of his jacket, which scratched against her cold cheek. She smelled deodorant. Had he sprayed himself with deodorant before coming over?

"You're freezing. We can't stand here." He led her into the living room and she perched on the edge of the cream leather sofa. *It's like sitting on vanilla ice cream,* Mia had said the morning it was delivered.

Ed removed his jacket and draped it over her shoulders, rubbing her back with smooth circular strokes. Then he went into the kitchen and she heard him open the boiler cupboard and flick on the central heating, which rumbled and strained into life. There was the gush of a tap as he filled the kettle, followed by the opening and closing of drawers, cupboards, and the fridge.

He returned with a cup of tea, but her hands didn't move to take it. "Katie," he said, crouching down so they were eye level. "You are in shock. Try and drink a little. It will help."

He lifted the tea to her lips and she sipped it obediently. She could taste the sweet milky flavor on her tongue and the urge to retch was immediate. She lurched past him to the bathroom with a hand clamped to her mouth. The jacket slipped from her shoulders and fell to the floor with a soft thump.

Bending over the sink, she gagged. Saliva hit the white ceramic basin.

Ed was behind her. "Sorry . . ."

Katie rinsed her hands and splashed water over her face.

"Darling," he said, passing her a blue hand towel. "What happened?"

She buried her face in it and shook her head. He gently peeled the towel away, then unhooked her robe from the back of the bathroom door and guided her arms into the soft cotton. He took her hands in his and rubbed them. "Talk to me."

She repeated the details learned from the police. Her voice sounded jagged and she imagined that if she were to glance up at the bathroom mirror, her skin would be leached of color, her eyes glassy.

As they moved back to the living room, Ed asked the same question to which she wanted the answer: "Why was your sister in Bali?"

"I have no idea."

"Have you spoken to Finn?"

"Not yet. I should call him."

Her hands shook as she dialed Finn's cell. She pressed the phone to her ear and listened as it rang and rang. "He's not answering."

"What about his family? Do you know their number?"

Katie searched in her address book and found it, the Cornish dialing code stirring a faint memory that she wasn't ready to grasp.

Finn was the youngest of four brothers. His mother, Sue, a curt woman who was often harassed, answered, sounding half asleep. "Who is this?"

"Katie Greene."

"Who?"

"Katie Greene." She cleared her throat. "Mia's sister."

"Mia?" Sue repeated. Then immediately: "Finn?"

"There's been an accident—"

"Finn—"

"No. It's Mia." Katie paused and looked at Ed. He nodded for her to go on. "The police have been here. They told me that Mia was in Bali . . . on a cliff somewhere. She fell. They're saying she's dead."

"No . . ."

In the background she could hear Finn's father, a placid man in his sixties who worked for the Forestry Commission. There was a brief volley of exclamations muffled by a hand over the receiver, and then Sue returned to the line. "Does Finn know?"

"I'd imagine so. But he's not answering his cell."

"He lost it a few weeks ago. Hasn't replaced it yet. We've been using e-mail. I've got his address if you want—"

"Why were they in Bali?" Katie interrupted.

"Bali? Finn wasn't."

"But that's where they said Mia was found. Her passport was stamped—"

"Mia went to Bali. Not Finn."

"What?" Katie said, her grip tightening.

"There was an argument. Sorry, I thought you knew."

"When was this?"

"Good month ago, now. Finn spoke to Jack about it. From what I heard they had a falling-out—God knows what about—and Mia changed her ticket."

Katie's thoughts whirled. Mia and Finn's friendship was unshakable. She pictured them as children, Finn with a wig of glistening seaweed draped over his head, Mia bent double with laughter. Theirs was a friendship that was so rare, so solid, that she couldn't imagine what would be terrible enough to cause them to separate.

TEN DAYS LATER, WINTER sun flooded Katie's bedroom. She lay perfectly still, her arms at her sides, eyes shut, bracing herself against a distant threat she couldn't quite recall. She blinked and, before she had a chance to recall why her eyelids felt stiff and salted, grief bowled into her.

Mia.

She curled into herself, tucking her knees to her chest and pressing tight fists to her mouth. She screwed her eyes shut, but disturbing images bled into her thoughts: Mia dropping silently through the air like a stone, the rush of wind lifting her dark hair away from her face, a rasped scream, the crack of her skull against granite.

She reached for Ed, but her fingers met only with the empty curve of where he'd slept. She listened for him and, after a moment, was relieved to tune into the light tapping of a keyboard coming from the living room: he was e-mailing his office. She envied him that—the ability for his world to continue, when hers had stopped.

She knew she must get to the shower. It would be too easy to remain cocooned in the duvet as she had done yesterday, not rising until after lunch, by which time she was drowsy and disorientated. Taking a deep breath, she forced herself from beneath the covers.

Drifting toward the bathroom, she passed Mia's room and found herself pausing vaguely outside the door. They had bought this apartment using the small inheritance they received after their mother's death. Everyone was surprised that they were moving in together, not the least Katie, who had vowed she'd never live with Mia again after their acrimonious teenage years, yet she'd worried that if Mia didn't put her share of the inheritance into something solid, it would slip through her fingers as easily as water. Katie had been the one to organize viewings, deal with estate agents and solicitors, and run through the rain with a broken umbrella to sign the mortgage papers on time.

Wrapping her fingers lightly around the brass door handle, she turned it. A faint trace of jasmine lingered in the cold, stale air. Mia had positioned her bed beneath the tall sash window so she could wake and see sky. A sheepskin coat, which once belonged to their mother, was draped over the foot of the bed. It was an original from the seventies with a wide, unstructured collar, and she remembered Mia wrapping herself in it all winter like a lost flower child.

Beside the bed a pine desk was heaving with junk: an old stereo, unplugged and dusty; three cardboard boxes bulging with CDs; a pair of hiking boots with their laces missing; a mound of paperbacks, well thumbed, beside two pots of pens. The bedroom walls were bare of the photos and paintings that had adorned Mia's previous rooms and she'd made no attempt to decorate; in fact, it was as if she had never intended the move to be permanent.

Katie was the one who'd persuaded her sister to move to London, using words like "opportunity" and "career," when those words had never belonged to Mia. Mia spent her days wandering the parks, or drifting in one of the rent-a-rowing-boats in Battersea Park, as if dreaming she were somewhere else. She'd had five jobs in as many months because she would suddenly decide to get out of the city to go hiking or camping, and take off, just leaving a note pushed under Katie's door and a message on her employer's voicemail. Katie tried searching out job opportunities using her recruitment contacts, but fixing Mia to something was like pinning a ribbon to the wind.

Noticing a pair of mud-flecked running shoes, she remembered the evening Mia announced she was going traveling. Katie had been in the kitchen preparing a risotto, slicing onions with deft, clean strokes. She tossed them into a pan as Mia wandered in, a pair of white earphones dangling over the neckline of her T-shirt, to fill her water bottle at the tap.

"Going running?" Katie had asked, blotting her streaming eyes with the sleeve of her cardigan.

"Yeah."

"How's the hangover?" When she'd gone to shower before work, Katie had found Mia asleep on the bathroom floor wearing a dress of hers borrowed without asking.

"Fine," she replied, keeping her back to Katie. She turned off the tap and wiped her wet hands on her T-shirt, leaving silver beads of moisture.

"What happened to your ankle?"

Mia glanced down at the angry red cut that stretched an inch above her sock line. "Smashed a glass at work."

"Do you need a Band-Aid? I've got some in my room."

"It's fine."

Katie nodded, tossing the onions with a wooden spoon, watching their sharp whiteness soften and become translucent. She turned up the heat.

Mia lingered by the sink for a moment. Eventually she said, "I spoke to Finn earlier."

Katie glanced up; his name was so rarely spoken between them.

"We've decided to go traveling."

The onions started to sizzle, but Katie was no longer stirring. "You're going traveling?"

"Yeah."

"For how long?"

Mia shrugged. "A while. A year, maybe."

"A year!"

"Our tickets are open."

"You've already booked?"

Mia nodded.

"When did you decide this?"

"Today."

"Today?" Katie repeated, incredulous. "You haven't thought it through!"

Mia raised an eyebrow: "Haven't I?"

"I didn't think you had any money."

"I'll manage."

The oil began to crackle and spit. "And what, Finn's just taking a sabbatical? I'm sure the radio station will be thrilled."

"He's handed in his notice."

"But he loved that job . . ."

"Is that right?" Mia said, looking directly at her. The air in the kitchen seemed to contract.

Then Mia picked up her water bottle, pushed her earphones in, and left. The pan started to smoke, so Katie snapped off the stove. She felt a hot flash of anger and took three strides across the kitchen to follow, but then, as she heard the tread of Mia's shoes along the hallway, the turning of the latch, and finally the slam of the door, Katie realized that what she felt most acutely was not anger or even hurt, it was relief. Mia was no longer her responsibility: she was Finn's.

IT WAS MID-AFTERNOON WHEN the phone rang. Ed glanced up from his laptop; Katie shook her head. She had refused to speak to anyone, allowing her voicemail to record friends' messages of condolence that were punctuated with awkward apologies and strained pauses.

The machine clicked on. "Hello. It's Mr. Spire here from the Foreign Office in London."

A nerve in her eyelid flickered. It was Ed who reached for the phone just before the message ended. "This is Katie's fiancé." He looked across to her and said, "Yes, she's with me now." He nodded at her to take the phone.

She held it at arm's length, as if it were a gun she was being asked to put to her head. Mr. Spire had called twice since Mia's death, first to request permission for an autopsy to go ahead, and later to discuss the repatriation of Mia's body. After a moment, Katie pressed her lips together and cleared her throat. Bringing the phone towards her mouth, she said slowly, "This is Katie."

"I hope this is a convenient time to talk?"

"Yes, fine." The dry, musty warmth of the central heating caught at the back of her throat.

"The British Consulate in Bali have been in touch. They have some further news concerning Mia's death."

She closed her eyes. "Go on."

"In cases such as Mia's, a toxicology report is sometimes re-quested as part of the autopsy procedure. I have a copy of it in front of me, which I wanted to talk to you about."

"Right."

"The results indicate that at the time of death, Mia was intox-icated. Her blood alcohol content was 0.13, which means she may have had impaired reflexes and reaction times." He paused. "And there's something else."

She moved into the living room doorway and gripped the wooden frame, anchoring herself.

"The Balinese police have interviewed two witnesses who claim to have seen Mia on the evening of her death." He hesi-tated and she sensed he was struggling with something. "Katie, I'm very sorry, but in their statement, they have said that Mia jumped."

The ground pitched, her stomach dropped away. She hinged

forward from the waist. Footsteps crossed the living room and she felt Ed's hand on her back. She pushed him away, straightening. "You think she . . ." Her voice was strained like elastic set to snap. "You think it was suicide?"

"I am afraid that based on witness statements and the autopsy, the cause of death has been established as suicide."

Katie reached a hand to her forehead.

"I understand this must be incredibly hard—"

"The witnesses, who are they?"

"I have copies of their statements." She heard the creak of a chair and pictured him leaning across a wide desk to reach them. "Yes, here. The witnesses are a 30-year-old couple who were honeymooning in Bali. In their statement, they say that they had taken an evening walk along the lower cliff path in Umanuk and paused at a lookout point—this was close to midnight. A young woman, matching Mia's description, ran past them looking extremely anxious. The male witness asked if she needed help and Mia is said to have responded, 'No.' She then disappeared along what used to be the upper cliff path, which has apparently been disused for several years. Between five and eight minutes later, the witnesses looked up and saw Mia standing very near the cliff's edge. The report says that they were concerned for her safety, but before they were able to act, she jumped."

"My God." Katie began to tremble.

Mr. Spire waited a moment before continuing. "The autopsy suggested that, from the injuries sustained, it is likely that Mia went over the cliff edge facing forwards, which collaborates with the witnesses' reports." He continued to expand on further details, but Katie was no longer listening. Her mind had already drifted to the cliff top.

He's wrong, Mia, isn't he? You didn't jump. I won't believe it. What I said when you called—oh, God, please don't let what I said . . .

"Katie," he was saying, "the arrangements are in place to have

Mia's body repatriated to the UK a week on Wednesday." He required details of the funeral parlor she had selected, and then the call ended.

She felt shooting pains behind her eyes and pressed the arched bones beneath her eyebrows with her thumb and index finger. In the apartment below the baby was wailing.

Ed turned her slowly to face him.

"They are saying it was suicide," she said in a small, strained voice. "But it wasn't."

He placed his hands on her shoulders. "You will get through this, Katie."

But how could he know? She hadn't told him about the terrible argument she'd had with Mia. She hadn't told him of the hateful, shameful things she'd said. She hadn't told him about the anger and hurt that had been festering between them for months. She hadn't told Ed any of this because there are some currents in a relationship between sisters that are so dark and run so deep, it's better for the people swimming on the surface never to know what's beneath.

She turned from Ed and stole to her room, where she lay on the bed with her eyes closed, trying to fix on something good between her and Mia. Her thoughts led her back to the last time she had seen her, as they hugged good-bye at the airport. She recalled the willowy feel of Mia's body, the muscular ridges of her forearms, and the press of her collarbone.

Katie would have held on for longer, treasured every detail, had she known it would be the last time she'd feel her sister in her arms.

About the Author

Lucy Clarke is the author of *Swimming at Night*, which has been published internationally. She spends her winters traveling and her summers at her home on the south coast of England, where she lives with her husband, James.

www.lucy-clarke.com